D1017049

REBEL GIRLS

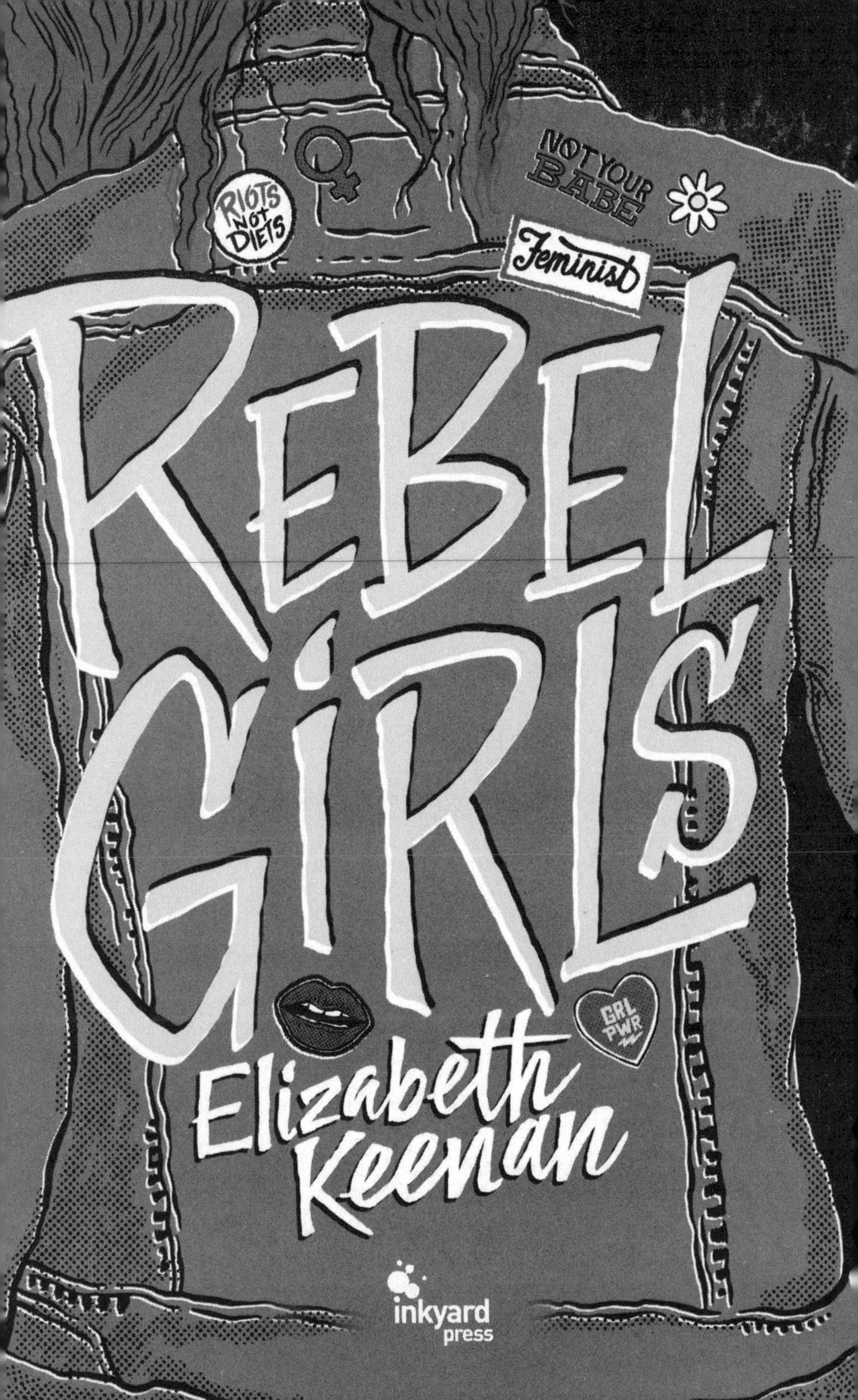

RIOTS NOT DIETS
NOT YOUR BABE
Feminist
REBEL GIRLS
GRL PWR
Elizabeth Keenan
inkyard press

Recycling programs for this product may not exist in your area.

ISBN-13: 978-1-335-18500-6

Rebel Girls

This edition published by arrangement with Harlequin Books S.A.

For questions and comments about the quality of this book, please contact us at CustomerService@Harlequin.com.

InkyardPress.com

Printed in U.S.A.

For my sister, Juli, for reading this book approximately ninety-two times.
I hope, upon finding your name here,
you will have it in you to read it a ninety-third time.

For my amazing husband, Ryan, for all the encouragement and PMA.

And for all the girls reading this, their sisters and their best friends.

1

At my school, the only place with any freedom from the dress code was your backpack. You could put almost anything on it, as long as it didn't contain swear words, advertise a band the guidance counselors had arbitrarily decided wasn't acceptable, or endorse a controversial political message. Last year, my best friend Melissa had tested those limits with a Suicidal Tendencies patch and a Planned Parenthood button. She got sent home for Planned Parenthood, which obviously violated our Catholic school's pro-life policies, but Mrs. Turner, the guidance counselor, also expressed concern to her parents that Melissa might be calling out for help with depression. It wasn't until she brought in a Suicidal Tendencies cassette to prove the band existed that Mrs. Turner dropped the issue.

In order to avoid Melissa's predicament, my assemblage had to negotiate the shoals of being acceptable to authorities while signaling cool, not poseur. It was an almost-impossible task.

I dumped the contents of my jewelry box onto my bed in a heap of one-inch band buttons, costume jewelry, and concert ticket stubs. I looked from the pile to my new backpack and back again, trying to figure out what belonged. My pins and patches needed to say, *I am Athena Graves. I'm cool and mysterious, not just some sophomore nerd who got bumped up into senior-level math and science classes. I have good taste in music, and I am not a phony Holden Caulfield would hate.*

Right now, the bright red backpack said the opposite, silent and mocking and terribly, terribly new, like I'd sat down the night before school started and carefully selected everything, instead of forging an organically coherent collection of awesome buttons. And though I *was* sitting down and picking out buttons the night before school started, I didn't want anyone to know that.

The pile of pins on my bed also felt inadequate for the task of broadcasting a relatively cool persona. I had exactly three acceptable choices: the Clash, classic, and my favorite band; Pixies, loud-soft-awesome; and Duran Duran, an unexpected, somewhat irony-driven choice. Otherwise, the buttons didn't feel right. Prince and Madonna hung out with the B-52s, Depeche Mode, and U2 in the unfortunately middle school pile. Sure, they might have been cool in sixth grade, or even in eighth, but now they made me look like I'd held on to them for too long—or, worse, like I'd raided the free pin bucket at the used record store.

The rest were just so *mainstream*. Nirvana was great last year, but now *everyone* liked them. Ditto with Pearl Jam. Putting a Pearl Jam button on my backpack now would be like wearing a flannel shirt in August here in Louisiana—nothing but evidence of jumping someone else's train. And speaking of jumping someone else's train…the Cure were out, too, because

"Friday I'm in Love" had birthed a whole new generation of black-clad trend followers.

I didn't have anything delightfully obscure or truly cutting-edge because Baton Rouge record shops didn't have such things, and my mail order of cool buttons and patches from the Burning Airlines catalog hadn't shown up yet. The Blur button Melissa had given me had an awesome font, but I didn't actually listen to them, so it would be weird and fake to put it on my backpack. There was nothing worse than someone asking you about your button or patch and having no explanation for why it was there other than "I thought it looked cool." But if you could pull *that* statement off without flinching, you'd definitely be cool—an arbiter of good graphic design instead of musical taste, but cool.

There was no way I was that cool.

My sister, Helen, twirled into our room, a bouncy ball of exuberance dressed in our school uniform. Last year, the gray, black, and red plaid skirt she was wearing had been mine, and would be again in about a week. But our dad had recently started his new job as a corporate attorney after years of working for nonprofits, and he'd forgotten about our back-to-school shopping until the very last Saturday before school started. Unfortunately for Helen, the store that sold our school's uniform was out of tall-girl sizes, so she was borrowing one of my spares until her special order arrived.

On me, the skirt had hit an extra awful spot just below my knee and turned my calves into tree trunks. On Helen, it was the primary ingredient in an instant sexy Catholic schoolgirl formula, evidence of what seven inches of extra height will do for a girl.

She pranced in front of me. "Hey, Athena, how do I look?"

Like jailbait, I wanted to say, and might've said as recently as last week. But I stopped myself with a reminder that it wasn't Helen's fault that she got all the height in our family, and I was stuck at a measly five foot three.

"It's a little…short," I said as diplomatically as possible.

"*You're* a little short," she said, narrowing her eyes at me. She turned back to our full-length mirror and fussed with the white Oxford shirt that completed our uniform, pulling it out so it bunched against the skirt's waistband, creating a giant-shirt-tiny-waist juxtaposition. She struck a pose that mimicked Claudia Schiffer on the cover of the *Vogue* magazine sitting on her bed. The special fall fashion edition seemed to be about 90 percent ads and was so huge it was currently making a significant indentation on Helen's fluffy comforter.

"I didn't mean it as an insult." I shrugged an apology at her reflection. She looked back at me with a quick glance of her wide-set blue eyes, then went back to making serious faces at herself in the mirror. "Last year, half the girls in my homeroom got sent to Sister Catherine's office in the first week for skirts that were too short for the dress code. So you might want to have Dad write a note about your skirt being on order."

She turned to look at me, her face wrinkled up in annoyance. "You're such a goody-good." Her eyes lit up when she saw the band buttons on my bed. "Hey, can I have that Pearl Jam button?"

Her hand hovered in the air, ready to snatch it from the pile.

I eyed her suspiciously. It wasn't that Helen didn't like Pearl Jam—she had a crush on the band's singer, Eddie Vedder, that teetered on obsession—but there was no way she'd wear the pin in public, let alone put it on her backpack. It just wasn't *her.* She was too *organized* for the casually arranged, haphazardly cool collection I was aiming for. She had already labeled her new school binders—all black, red, and white, our school colors—with the titles of her classes, complete with classroom number and teacher's name, in her neat handwriting with a silver paint pen. Even her interest in fashion was methodical, with her magazines, books, and scrapbooks full of clippings carefully lined up on her bookshelf.

"Why do you want it?" I edged the Pearl Jam button closer to my jewelry box.

"You don't like them anymore," she said. "And I do. God, you don't have to be so mean."

I wasn't being mean, just guarded. Helen was always taking things from me when I was done with them, sometimes before. And like the uniform skirt, it usually looked better on her than it did on me. I almost always felt like the prototype version of the Graves sisters' operating system, with everything that was average about me physically turning into something unfairly exquisite with Helen. It wasn't just her height, either—she got the cheekbones of my dreams; a version of my nose without the bump I'd acquired in a fall from a playground balance beam; and straight, wheat-blond hair that defied the Louisiana humidity, unlike my own dirty-blond waves, now dyed a fiery red, which turned frizzy approximately 363 days of the year. Our eyes were the only feature where we were about on an even playing ground, in that they were essentially the same size and shape. In terms of their color, I sometimes thought I'd eked out a small victory in that my eyes were a more interesting blue green to her blue ones.

I handed the pin to her anyway. At the end of the day, that pin deserved to find a home with someone who loved Pearl Jam, and that wasn't me.

"Thanks!" Helen pinned it to her shirt and flipped her hair over her shoulder. It was the least punk rock gesture ever.

"You can't wear it like that at school." I cringed at my rule-following urges. I might *want* to look punk rock and be a riot grrrl, but my instinctive aversion for getting into trouble kept tripping me up. "Violates the dress code."

"I know," she said, shrugging. "I wasn't planning to wear it to school. Or maybe I will. It might be nice to break some rules."

"Oh, really?" I asked. "You? Breaking the rules?" Helen never broke the rules. She might gently massage them into a form more suitable to her tastes, but she never broke them, exactly.

"Oh, come on," she said, facing me with crossed arms. "You know that the dress code is stupid. It's designed to destroy any sense of fashion."

She was right, but I didn't see how pins figured into the equation. And then I noticed the fashion book on Helen's bed was flipped open to a spotlight on Vivienne Westwood and punk fashion of the 1970s. It figured that something I viewed as a carefully cultivated expression of my innermost self would be just another fashion statement to my sister.

"You really think this skirt is too short?" Helen asked, turning back to her reflection. She tugged the skirt down around her thighs, trying to make it reach regulation length.

"Probably, but it's too late to do anything now." I shouldn't have said anything. "And it really doesn't matter, honestly. Half the cheerleaders hem theirs shorter than that anyway."

"Like Leah?" Helen narrowed her eyes. Leah Sullivan was my friend Sean Mitchell's girlfriend, and stereotypically enough, captain of the cheerleading squad to his quarterback. While the rest of the cheerleaders were pretty nice and friendly, Leah was at best distantly cordial to me, and at worst a serious impediment to my commitment to the riot grrrl revolution's feminist message of not trashing other girls.

"Yeah, like Leah." I sighed.

"I'm okay, then," she said. "No way could I look like more of a slut than she does."

"That's a gross word," I said, looking up at Helen to let her know I meant it. "And also, because she's been dating Sean for almost a year, not true. But that's beside the point."

Helen threw herself back on her bed with a more dramatic flair than required.

"I don't understand what he sees in her!" Exasperation strangled her voice.

"Me, neither." I didn't say what I thought Sean saw in her, which was a cute girl who would make out with him on a regular basis. My opinion flunked any kind of feminist test, though I'd often tried—and failed—to find something worthwhile in her personality, for Sean's sake. "But why do you care?"

"I don't," she said, too quick and defensive for me not to notice. "I mean, he's *your* friend, but she's *terrible*. She's..." Helen paused for a second, trying to come up with a concrete reason to dislike Leah, who, as far as I knew, hadn't given much thought to Helen. "She's not nice to Mrs. Estelle. So it's hard not to hate her, just on principle."

"Fair enough." Being rude to Sean's mom, Estelle, was something that Helen and I would never, ever consider doing, especially after how well she'd taken care of us when our parents were getting divorced. I'd never actually seen Leah being rude to her, but it certainly wasn't outside the realm of possibility.

I looked back at my bed with a frown. The pile of buttons just wasn't right. There was nothing to telegraph to the world that I wasn't some weirdo obsessed with music from ten years ago. I'd thought the eighties buttons were hilarious when I bought them, but now that I had them in front of me, they seemed so not cool.

I didn't want my backpack to be a cheesy joke. The collection needed to be perfect, but everything rubbed the wrong way, awkward and staged instead of cool and mysterious.

I scooped the pins back into my jewelry box. Better to say nothing at all on my backpack than to say the wrong thing.

St. Ann's Regional Diocesan Catholic High School spread out as long as its name, low to the ground in beige-painted concrete stucco. Our school was a vaguely brutalist monstrosity, especially compared to some of the other schools in town. Baton Rouge High and St. Ursula's looked like Hollywood sets for the ideal arts school and a snobby wood-paneled private school, respectively.

But St. Ann's was hastily built about ten years ago to deal with the overflow of kids from Baton Rouge's oil-industry-based population boom. The stretched-out single-story building gave the impression that it would soon sink back into the swamp that made most of the campus's forty acres unusable. We no longer had a football field, since it had flooded last spring and was now referred to as a "seasonal pond." This year's home games were going to be at Greenlawn, a public school nearby.

Helen bounced off to find her friends Sara and Jennifer, who were probably as excited to be starting school as she was, but more scared. I looked around for Sean and Melissa, but couldn't find them in the crush of bodies moving toward the glass double doors at the front of the school. With seven hundred students, the everyday task of getting through the front doors was more like a mosh pit at a hardcore show than an orderly exercise in school attendance.

"Athena! Over here!" Melissa was shouting from somewhere near the entrance. Since Melissa was a junior and I was an ambiguously scheduled sophomore, we only had two classes together this year, so the five minutes before morning assembly were crucial in our social life. Otherwise, we'd be stuck with passing notes in physics and calculus or just hanging out at lunch.

Melissa and I first met in orchestra camp the summer after I was in seventh grade. I'd been super into Depeche Mode at the time, and the day I wore one of their band T-shirts, Melissa bounded over and asked me to join her minor-key synth-pop band. Our musical tastes have changed since then, but we were always halfway into the process of starting a band that never truly materialized.

I struggled to spot Melissa's army surplus backpack in the crowd. Finally, there it was, bobbing along in the opposite direction I'd expected. I swam through the sea of plaid toward that backpack. Melissa must have added a patch and a few buttons to it last night—she'd said she was going to at some point—but I was surprised she'd taken the time for backpack arts and crafts the night before school started. I would have expected her to be too busy organizing her binders by each class's estimated output of effort, then bleaching her roots so she could apply a fresh round of hair dye, most likely purple.

The new buttons aligned with my musical tastes more than Melissa's: a large patch with the Clash, a smaller one with Green Day's *Kerplunk!*, and K Records and Bikini Kill buttons. Maybe Melissa had finally switched her allegiance from the Sex Pistols to the Clash, or listened to that Bikini Kill demo cassette I'd sent her over the summer from my mom's house in Eugene, Oregon, after I got super lucky and found a copy in a local record store. But K Records seemed impossible, even if Kurt Cobain had made people slightly more aware of the tiny independent record label with his tattoo of their logo. Melissa had always said that Beat Happening was fey and twee, not to mention musically incompetent. I'd tried to point out that they were fey and twee in a punk rock way, but she wasn't having it. I wondered what had made her change her opinion over the summer. Maybe she'd met a boy.

The backpack was just out of reach. I grabbed for it, before it floated away again in the Great Plaid Sea. Or before the two-minute warning bell rang for morning assembly, whichever came first.

I tugged down on her backpack. "Hey, Mel—"

The wearer of the backpack, a boy who was decidedly *not* Melissa, turned around and smiled at me. He wasn't anyone I had ever seen before. He was tall and muscularly slender, with broad shoulders, almost stereotypically perfect in his proportions. His golden-brown, slightly messy hair flopped into his face. It should have made him look sloppy, but instead it drew attention to his eyes.

Oh, his eyes. Anyone could have brown eyes. Most people, statistically, did. But his eyes were a warm amber, rimmed with dark brown, like deep caramel surrounded by dark chocolate. I ignored the fact that my brain had gone straight to a food simile that reminded me of Rolos—like, I didn't want to *eat* his eyeballs, but I couldn't think of anything else.

"Oh, I'm so sorry!" I squeaked.

How could I have ever mistaken him for Melissa, even in this crowd? I knew there was no way she'd ever admit to liking anything on K Records. At the start of last year, Melissa and I had been the only ones with buttons and patches of the alternative kind, until grunge became popular and suddenly weird was cool and we were almost popular—or at least Melissa was. I was more "the almost-popular girl's nerdy friend." But K Records was a step too far, and I didn't know anyone aside from my summer friends in Eugene who even knew the label existed.

He was cute—far cuter than any of the boys at my school. He had to be a transfer. At least I hoped he was—he couldn't possibly be a freshman. That would be awful, because then I'd probably never see him again. It would be even worse if he was a senior. Then I would never see him, *and* he'd probably consider me beneath his attention.

The boy melted back into the crowd with another smile before I had a chance to ask him. The dread of the first day of school had now entirely disappeared from my thoughts, replaced with something fluttery and disorienting.

2

Melissa yanked me into the girls' bathroom with a totally unnecessary level of force. We hadn't had time to talk this morning—*hello, Cute Boy distraction*—but it wasn't like we hadn't hung out on Saturday to catch up on the events of the summer, which we'd spent half a continent apart.

For me, the summer had involved biking around and looking for cool record stores near my mom's house in Eugene, drinking coffee, practicing cello, and ignoring Helen. Our mom was a classics professor at the University of Oregon, which meant that in theory, she should have had plenty of time to spend with us. And, most summers, she did, even if she often used that time to drive us to Mount St. Helens so we could better understand what volcanic damage looked like, after she spent a day boring us with Pliny the Younger's letter about Pompeii. But this year, she'd needed every second of her summer off from teaching—or so she'd said—to finish the book she was writing about Catullus before she started her new job at New York University in the fall. It was a Big Deal, so Helen and I were mostly left to our own devices.

So I'd decided to use my summer to become a riot grrrl, and not just someone who read about them in *Sassy* magazine. Over the past year, I had amassed a small collection of handmade, photocopied zines like *Riot Grrrl* and *Girl Germs*, all ordered through the mail. I knew what the riot grrrl ideals were. Support girls around you. Don't be jealous of other girls. Avoid competition with them. Being loud and crying in public were valid ways of being a girl. Being a girl didn't mean being weak or bad. Claiming your sexuality, no matter what that meant to you, was a good thing. And the revolution was open to anyone.

That last one felt like a stretch to me because I never felt quite punk enough. And there were other barriers to entry, too. Writing about my life, or music, or whatever in a zine was great in theory, but what if no one wanted to read it?

Besides, photocopies cost money, unless you scammed Kinko's, and again, I wasn't punk enough to get away with that. After working at nonprofits for years, Dad was inclined to give me and Helen money solely for things classified as potentially useful for college applications, like music lessons for me and art classes for Helen. He had balked at Helen's modeling classes, which our grandmother paid for, so I didn't think I could get money for a zine from him—or from Grandma, for that matter, who would die if she knew I wanted money for anything associated with punk rock or feminism. Mom gave us a small allowance during the summer, but I preferred to spend it on new music rather than copies of a zine I thought no one would read.

Before the end of the summer, I'd had exactly one bit of riot grrrl success, which was tracking down Bikini Kill's *Revolution Girl Style Now* demo cassette—the one I'd immediately copied and sent to Melissa. Other than that, I'd chickened out of going to all-ages shows in people's basements at least six times and spent too much time hoping I looked cool enough at the coffee shop for someone to talk with me. In the end, I got so desperate I took knitting lessons, where, weirdly enough, I finally met a group of girls who listened to the same music I did. They told me all about the legendary shows I'd missed out on the summer before, like the International Pop Underground festival, where Bikini Kill played and Bratmobile had their first show. I tried to live vicariously through their stories, but I left Eugene feeling like I had missed my only chance to be a riot grrrl.

Melissa's summer in Baton Rouge had been far more intense. Instead of being a failed riot grrrl like me, she'd been a real activist. In direct violation of our Catholic school's very pro-life policy, she'd volunteered as a clinic defender at the Delta Women's Clinic, the only abortion clinic in town. Operation Rescue, a nationwide anti-abortion group, had selected Baton Rouge for its "Summer of Purpose," a sequel to its huge protest in Kansas the year before.

Baton Rouge made a lot of sense—after Louisiana passed a super restrictive abortion law last year, Governor Roemer had vetoed it. But then the state legislature overrode the veto with a two-thirds majority, and now it was winding its way through the federal courts. Operation Rescue wanted to drum up local support for the abortion ban, and Baton Rouge was an easy target, since it wasn't liberal like New Orleans. Even the local Planned Parenthood didn't do abortions.

About a thousand mostly out-of-town protesters came to the city to try to shut down Delta Women's Clinic the week after July Fourth. In response, pro-choice people like Melissa defended the clinic, helping to keep it open and protect the women who wanted to get abortions. It got a little violent—

nothing major, just some pushing and shoving, but the cops put up a fence between the protesters and the clinic defenders. Lots of people got arrested, and it made national news.

As I'd watched the national news from my mom's couch, Melissa, with her wavy bright purple hair blazing in the July sun, was clearly visible on the inside of the giant chain-link fence, leading girls into the clinic with her arm hooked in theirs. She'd sent me more than a dozen long letters, each in her perfectly stylized handwriting, detailing the month of July.

I didn't know how she'd had time to write, with all that was going on. In one, she told me about the preacher who'd tried to grab her and pray the sin out of her as she covered the license plates of cars entering the parking lot so the protesters couldn't track the women down and harass them later. Another featured a lengthy description of the swarms of television crews who had descended on the clinic after the protester count reached nine hundred. And in still another, she detailed how she'd seen a group of girls from our school drive slowly by, giving her a thumbs-up and waving, but clearly too afraid to get out of their car. She couldn't decide if they were hypocrites or just saner than she was.

When we saw the protests on TV, Helen wanted to head home to get in on the action—but on the opposite side. Last year, she was president of her middle school's pro-life club, and as an incoming freshman, she wanted to impress the powers that be at our high school with some pro-life summer activities. Mom, as liberal and pro-choice as they come, took Helen aside for an afternoon talk about reproductive rights and the long legacy of coat-hanger abortions. It didn't sink in, but, then again, Mom wasn't the best at being human. Her heart-to-heart with Helen was more like a lecture that also included some references to feminist theories of the body, and anyone would have tuned out at that point. After that, Mom ignored Helen's pleas to go home and worked some more on her book.

In any case, I was glad she hadn't let Helen come back. I didn't need a clash between Melissa and Helen about abortion rights. Not again.

But right now, I didn't have time to hang out, talk about abortion rights, or discuss the cute guy I met outside school. I had exactly five minutes between first and second period to get to religion class, and no way was I going to make it, because my next class was all the way on the opposite side of the school. I shuffled impatiently on the checkered bathroom tile and waited for Melissa to reveal whatever it was that she apparently thought was worth nearly tearing my arm off for.

Melissa took a hard pack of Camel Lights from her backpack and smacked it against the heel of her hand three times. The extra time she took unwrapping the box, the careful selection of the cigarette, and the exaggerated first drag all seemed to be part of her plan of taking for-e-ver to tell me. She knew I hated the smell of smoke and thought smoking was a terrible idea, but I'd long since given up on calling her out on it. Her casual slowness made me painfully aware of how the smoke would cling to me, and also manage to waft through the crack below the door frame. Both could incriminate me for a crime I didn't commit.

"I have a present for you," Melissa said, clenching the cigarette between her eggplant-colored lips. She rifled through her backpack and pulled out a small rectangle wrapped in purple foil paper and tied with a silver ribbon that formed curlicues. She handed it to me gently. Melissa was usually more of a casually-tossed-present kind of girl, so this was unusual.

So was the fact that she was giving me a present for no real reason.

"What's this for?" It looked like a credit card. That made no sense. Melissa wouldn't have gotten me a credit card.

"It's in honor of your dad finally letting you leave the house on Friday and Saturday nights." Her smoker's boredom switched to an eager, nodding anticipation. I felt her staring at me, like I should already know what was hidden in the foil. I didn't.

I ripped open the paper. Inside was a perfect fake ID, complete with my own learner's permit photo, the fancy Louisiana seal, the little reflective bit, the lamination, and a believable name—"Allison Moore." The birth date made me nineteen years old as of this past Monday. In Louisiana, that was old enough to get into bars, but not old enough to drink. In other words, I could finally—*finally*—see some good bands.

Melissa looked at me expectantly, her eyebrows raised halfway up her forehead. She'd forgotten all about her cigarette, which rested heavy with a stack of granny ashes on the edge of the sink.

"Will it actually work?" As always, I had my doubts about Melissa's plans. They usually seemed to go fine for her, but somehow I always ended up getting grounded. Sure, Dad was planning to extend my curfew to eleven o'clock on weekends, but I'd get in a load of trouble for trying to use a fake ID.

"My ID always works," she responded reassuringly.

"It's your cousin's ID. It's real, even if it isn't you."

"I cede you a point, madam. A slight family resemblance and the idea that Asians all look alike goes a long way."

It was true, not to mention kind of racist. None of the bouncers in the bars, clubs, and music venues around Louisiana State University seemed to notice the difference between half Cajun, half Vietnamese Melissa and her all-Vietnamese cousin. They barely even looked alike. Melissa had her Cajun dad's wavy hair and hazel eyes, though her facial features were more like her mom's.

"Don't you want to know how I got it?" she asked gleefully. "And how it got to be so awesome?"

Melissa launched into an animated monologue complete with hand gestures, clearly delighted by the devious means she'd had to employ in order to obtain my permit photo from my room by lying to my dad. And then she had to tell me about discovering the perfect forger, a guy named Erik who'd dropped out of our school last year and now worked at Kinko's.

I only half listened as she rambled on. I kept thinking that I was about three minutes and fifty-five seconds into the five-minute break between classes. Even if the ID was so awesome that it would get me in anywhere, Mrs. Bonnecaze might send me straight to the dean of discipline's office if I showed up late to religion. It wasn't a good way to start the year.

"And that's why it's going to be perfect when we go out—"

The bathroom door slammed open, and I froze. Melissa quickly washed the cigarette down the drain, scooping water around the rim of the sink to wash away the ashes, and I slipped the fake ID into my backpack.

"Girls, aren't you running late for class?" I knew that voice. Mrs. Turner, the guidance counselor, stood behind me, sniffing the air through her upturned nose. I hoped I hadn't gotten close enough to Melissa to smell like cigarettes.

A clear-eyed earnestness overtook Melissa's face as she looked beyond me to Mrs. Turner. The guidance counselor had been out to get her since last year's Planned Parenthood/ Suicidal Tendencies incident, because Melissa had illustrated exactly how out of touch Mrs. Turner was with, as she would say in a singsong voice, "today's young people." Mrs. Turner always reminded me a little bit of a long-haired hamster, with round dark eyes whose pupils were indistinguishable from her irises, and brassy dyed-blond hair that surrounded her round face in a puffy halo. She always *acted* warm and friendly, but like those cute, furry rodents, her cuddly exterior hid the fact that she could bite you.

"Athena needed a feminine hygiene product." Melissa pulled a box of tampons from her backpack. Between cigarettes and tampons and fake IDs, Melissa barely had room for her books.

Since Mrs. Turner couldn't see my face, I narrowed my eyes at Melissa. No one said "feminine hygiene product." And it was massively unfair that *I* had to be the one who was supposedly on my period.

Still, it was a stroke of genius. I turned to see Mrs. Turner's reaction.

"Now, Miss Lemoine and Miss Graves," she said, her brown eyes widening with sympathy. It was her favorite trick and served her well when she was trying to get people to cry about their problems in her office. "I understand the *urgency* of the situation, but you really must hurry on to second *period*."

I almost choked at hearing her emphasis on the last word. Did she intend that as some double meaning? I didn't stop to think about it, because she could easily change her mind about letting us go if she saw cigarette ash in the sink. I darted out of the bathroom to the hall, Melissa trailing behind me, as the bell rang.

"Athena, wait *up*!" Melissa said, grabbing my shirt. "Close call, I know, but Mrs. Bonnecaze is, like, the most lenient teacher in school. In terms of lateness anyway. Tell her you had to stop in the guidance office, and you'll be fine. She won't ask for a note, and it's true enough that you saw Mrs. Turner."

I slowed so she could catch up with me, and as we passed the glassed-in walls of the guidance office, I almost stopped completely. The Cute Boy slouched in one of the waiting room chairs, reading a book. He must have been waiting for Mrs. Turner to return and help him pick out his classes—standard procedure for transfers.

"Oooh, new eye candy," Melissa said, following my gaze. "Do you want dibs?"

"Dibs? Are we in fifth grade?"

"Yes," she said, pausing for dramatic effect and nodding. "I think you should have dibs. I've never seen you look at a boy that way."

I didn't think I ever had, either. He was so incredibly cute, with his hair just falling into his eyes as he read. He even made chewing on a pen cap look good, because it made me notice his full, kissable lips. Though he didn't have much competition at our school, which wasn't exactly awash in the finest specimens of the gene pool. Except for Sean, who had the most perfect dark brown skin and friendliest smile I'd ever seen. But while I recognized Sean's attractiveness, it was in a way that you could objectively *know* your brother was the best-looking guy at school, but feel instinctively turned off at the same time.

Melissa looked me up and down, her brown-green eyes appraising me. "Yep, you have dibs. Besides, I have a date with Jason on Friday night."

I knew it. She wasn't being magnanimous—she already had a date with someone else. But if it worked out for me, did it matter?

I stole one last glance at the guidance office and nearly

jumped out of my skin, like a startled cat. The Cute Boy was looking back at me. He smiled, just like he had earlier, and I blushed furiously before hauling a cackling Melissa with me down the hall and out of sight.

3

Sean slouched back against the cast-off floral love seat that his mom had let him drag up to his room when she'd redecorated their living room, his dark brown eyes fixed on his issue of *The Amazing Spider-Man*. Nothing could come between him and Peter Parker, not even me being annoying and asking every five minutes or so whether he knew the Cute Boy. I described him in detail, but "sun-kissed light brown hair," and "gorgeous brown eyes," and "chiseled nose," and "sculpted shoulders and the butt of a Greek statue," and "the most perfect boy, ever" only made Sean roll his eyes at me.

"For the last time, I don't know the guy," Sean said to his issue of *Spider-Man*. "You forget—I'm not in those smart-ass classes with you. I take biology with the rest of the normal sophomores. Now, if you'll excuse me, this is the *thirtieth anniversary issue of Spider-Man*. It's the most important story of our *lifetime*."

He put the comic back up to his face like I wasn't there, though I knew he was half joking. But only half. Spidey was serious business, albeit serious business that Sean revealed to a select few.

Sean's school world was a lot different than mine, and not only because I was in honors everything. People always thought our friendship was a relic of growing up next door to each other in the crappy, boxy townhouses on the edge of Shenandoah, a sprawling neighborhood filled with streets named after Civil War battles and Confederate generals. Or else they thought it was the result of him needing some kind of help from me, like when I'd tutored Sean's ginormous linebacker friend Trip Wilson last year. But that was because no one knew about Sean's comics fetish or the hours he spent scouring flea markets for *Star Wars* toys. If they bothered to look past his football player exterior, they would see he was an even bigger nerd than I was.

And in our private nerd world, it would take a lot more than me pestering him about the Cute Boy for him to put down his comics.

"He's only in my physics and calculus classes," I protested. "I don't know what else he's taking, or his grade! I just thought—"

"You just thought he looked like a football player, right?" he asked, giving me the most annoyed look possible over his comic. "But from what you've told me, he's built like a quarterback. And that's my job, dude."

He said the *dude* in a Bart Simpson voice, so I could tell he wasn't actually offended. Also, Sean wasn't the type to say *dude* for real, under any circumstances. But he was right. They were both tall and lean and broad-shouldered. I hadn't thought of that as a quarterback's build, but of course Sean would.

I suddenly regretted bringing the Cute Boy up. Last year, Sean's promotion from JV to varsity had been viewed as controversial. Or, one could say, laced with a flavor of racism, hidden under a thin patina of suburban-polite questions about a (black) freshman's ability to compete. The absurd controversy finally died down once we started winning for the first time in our school's history. This year, people had started mentioning our school along with the word *championship*, and they weren't being ironic.

I sincerely hoped the Cute Boy wasn't someone's attempt to edge Sean off the football team.

"Sorry," I said. "I'm an ass."

"Come on, Athena, I'm joking." Sean peered at me over the comic. "I really have no idea who that guy is, or whether he even looks like a football player. And I promise, if you let me finish my comic and learn who this Spider-Man 2099 is, I'll help you with your boy problems."

I let him go back to his comic, knowing I wouldn't be able to get his attention again until we eventually wandered over to my house so that Sean could grab a Coke from our fridge—his mom didn't let him have soda, but my dad kept a healthy stock of it—and make fun of Helen, since he didn't have any siblings of his own to pick on.

Until then, I had to find another way to occupy myself. I sorted through my homework, but since it was only the first week of school, I was done in about five minutes. I flipped through my copy of *Sassy* to check out the fall clothes, but I didn't have much use for them, considering how little fall we experienced and how much time I spent in my school uniform.

Juliana Hatfield was on the cover, guitar in hand. I'd liked her album *Hey Babe*, but then she'd started talking about how most women weren't good guitar players and that she wanted to be the exception, which had really irritated both Melissa and me. But she *looked* cool. I pulled my hair up into an approximation of a bob, wondering if short hair would look as good on me as it did on Juliana. It might work. I would ask Melissa for her opinion tomorrow at school, even though she sometimes made fun of me for reading *Sassy*. She'd tried to get me hooked on *Ms.*, but it seemed like a magazine my mom would read. Actually, it *was* a magazine my mom read.

A knock on Sean's door interrupted my reading. Helen leaned casually against the doorway, a giant red cherry slushee in her hand and a bored look on her face. She'd changed out of her school uniform into a belly shirt and short-shorts that made her legs look disproportionately long. A pair of round-framed John Lennon sunglasses sat on top of her blond hair. I don't know who she was trying to impress, unless it was some random guy at the minimart—or maybe Sean, as remote as that possibility seemed to me.

"Shouldn't you be at your house, wearing out a New Kids on the Block cassette on your Walkman?" Sean gave her a teasing smile, but she looked back at him with a world-weary expression.

I shook my head. "Nah. First of all, she's moved on to more adult fare," I told him, as if Helen wasn't even there. "Pearl Jam was the flavor of the summer, and seems to be persisting into the school year, with some competition from the Lemonheads because she thinks Evan Dando is a-*dor*-able. And second, she doesn't use headphones. She uses our stereo because she likes to torture me any chance she gets."

"Veeerrry funny, losers," Helen said, drawling her words. She was acting annoyingly cool, and I wasn't sure if it was to irritate me or get Sean's attention. Either way, she was definitely achieving the former, if not the latter. "Are you two nerds done playing Dungeons & Dragons?"

"That joke is so old," I groaned. "You know comics are nothing like Dungeons & Dragons. What do you want anyway?" Helen often spent her afternoons in our shared bedroom, which was why I usually headed to Sean's place after school when he wasn't at football practice and I didn't have cello lessons.

"Wow, you're so friendly." Sarcasm was Helen's latest favorite thing. I reminded myself that I was trying to be nicer to her, but she knew exactly how to annoy me. "I need to tell you two things. First, Mom called. She's in New York. She wants you to call her back."

Our mom had just started her new job at NYU, which meant we would be spending future summer vacations and spring breaks in New York, instead of Eugene. She was supposed to call us tonight, not right after school, but it didn't surprise me that she called early. She was never very good at keeping track of time.

"Okay. What's the second thing?" I asked impatiently. If I wanted to catch Mom before she got lost in her stack of freshly moved Latin poetry books, I'd need to call her back soon.

Helen gave me a look of smug superiority. "Mrs. Bonnecaze wanted me to ask you to join the pro-life club. She said it was because you're—quote, unquote—'so sweet.' I tried not to laugh in her face."

"I already told her I wasn't interested." It was hard being one of approximately five pro-choice kids in a Catholic school, especially when you were otherwise a model student. Everyone just assumed that you'd *want* to be part of the pro-life club.

Last year, Helen and I had gotten into a huge fight at Sean's house when she told me she was president of her middle school's pro-life club. I'd initially thought Helen had joined the club for popularity's sake, because it didn't fit with our family's values at all. Mom was as feminist and pro-choice as anyone could imagine. And while Dad was a Catholic and had gone to a Jesuit college, he mostly invested in the social justice side of Catholicism. We didn't go to church on Sunday or anything.

Then, after I fought with her about it, I had to deal with her and Melissa continuing the argument. I'd sided with Melissa, of course, and Helen had refused to talk to me for a month. I occasionally tried subtle hints to change her mind—I tossed *Sassy* on her bed, with a dog-ear on an article on abortion. I periodically reminded her incessantly that Eddie Vedder, the singer of her favorite band, had written *pro-choice* on his arm in marker on MTV. She had taped that episode of *Unplugged* and watched it over and over, though she always fast-forwarded through that part.

"I know. I told her that," Helen said, crossing her arms. "Besides, I figured you wouldn't want to get involved with something that your *best friend* Melissa would disapprove of."

"That's—that's so not true! I have my own opinions!" And those opinions were based in empathy, science, reason, feminist history, and a little bit of riot grrrl. I had to give credit to Mom for the feminist history part, but otherwise it was all me. I definitely wasn't pro-choice just because Melissa was, and Helen's accusation rankled me to no end.

"If you say so." She slurped on the slushee dismissively, sucking up the last bits with that unmistakable, airy, loud-straw sound.

I sprang up from the floor and lunged toward Helen.

Sean grabbed my shoulder and pulled me back before I hauled off and smacked my sister. "Whoa, tiger! Why don't you go next door and call your mom back?"

I was practically growling, but I nodded at him. *Yes*, I would go back to our house to call Mom.

"Do you want me to keep her here?" Sean said.

I nodded again, grabbed my backpack, and shot a death-ray look toward Helen.

"I'm not staying with *him*!" Helen said, her voice rising. "He might try to make me read comics or watch *football*." The last word dripped with disgust. One of the few things Helen and I had in common was our disdain for football in a city where everyone rooted for the LSU Tigers.

"You'll stay with me, or I'll tell my mom you went out without telling anyone." Sean nodded toward the empty slushee cup in her hand. He had her cornered, and she knew it. We weren't supposed to leave the house without telling each other, but that slushee had come from the convenience store half a mile away.

Sean grinned at her, somewhere between friendly and evil.

Helen narrowed her eyes. "You wouldn't dare."

"Oh, I would." He gently steered her out the door. "She'd give you what for, and then she'd tell your dad, and then you'd be grounded for a week. And it would be such sweet revenge for that time last year when you 'accidentally' left a box of my tapes in the backyard."

Helen stopped and looked from me to Sean with a measured glare. "Fine. Whatever. And that *was* an accident. You locked me out in your backyard when Leah showed up. So I went home. Not my problem *you* forgot your precious tapes were outside in ninety-degree heat. And it's not like anything good was in there anyway, other than Run-DMC." She tossed the slushee cup into the garbage can by Sean's bedroom door, turned on her chunky platform shoes, and stomped down the hall like an angry, knock-kneed baby giraffe.

"She really knows how to make an exit," Sean said, shaking his head as we listened to her clomp down the stairs. "But…

I should probably go with her, so she doesn't 'unintentionally' wreck something else of mine. And you should go call your mom."

"I think she's gone beyond those unintentional days," I said. "All her acts are *fully* intentional now, no scare quotes about them."

I followed Sean down the stairs. By the time we got to the living room, Helen had already sprawled across the couch in front of the TV, legs extended, so that no one else could sit with a good view of the TV unless they specifically asked her to move. The only bit of courtesy she offered—and it was clearly for Mrs. Estelle, not Sean—was that she'd taken her shoes off before she put her feet up on the couch. Mrs. Estelle was like family, which meant she'd give Helen the same punishment she'd dole out to Sean for disrespecting her couch.

Sean tilted his head toward Helen. "I can handle it from here. I don't think our prisoner is going to make a break for it. Though I can't see why she risked you ratting her out in the first place by sneaking out for a sugar rush. It's not like slushees are that appealing. Unless it's some guy who works there." With widened eyes, he gestured toward his midriff, then pointed dramatically at Helen.

I guess I wasn't the only one who'd noticed Helen's belly shirt. Both Sean and I were still in our school uniforms.

"I can hear you!" Helen shouted from the couch. "And there's no slushee guy! I just happen to like keeping up-to-date with fashion, unlike either of you."

Last night, Helen had been so eager to try her uniform on, and now she couldn't wait to change into something less institutional. But I could figure that conundrum out later. For now, I had to call Mom.

Still, I found myself hovering by the foot of the stairs, alternately shooting looks between Sean and Helen. I wanted to talk this out with him, but I didn't want to talk about my weird feelings about Mom in front of Helen. Despite being so different from each other, Mom and Helen could somehow talk on the phone for hours. But I, the supposed junior feminist, never could figure out what to say to her.

Sean nudged me toward the door. "Go on. Git. Move along, cowgirl. I've got this."

"Can I talk to you outside for a minute?" I sounded conspiratorial, and even though what I wanted to talk about had nothing to do with Helen, she'd probably think it did.

"As long as you're not talking about me!" Helen snapped, right on cue. She never, ever stopped listening to me and Sean.

"Not everything is about *you*, Helen," I replied, rolling my eyes.

Sean followed me outside, closing the door behind us. "Are you sure something isn't going on between you and Helen? Because I'm getting a high level of tension from you two. You're both…unusually hostile, to a point that's made you forget all about that guy you were bugging me about."

I shook my head. "No, I haven't forgotten about him. And it's really not anything more than the usual with Helen." I sighed, dropping down onto one of the two plastic chairs Sean's mom kept on their tiny front porch. "I mean, I guess it is. Sort of. This was our last summer in Oregon, right? Mom's starting a new job at NYU, and something about that makes me feel like we're going to see her a lot less. So maybe it has to do with Helen, too, but not just the two of us. More like Helen and Mom, and Mom and me, separately."

My throat tightened as I trailed off to nothing. None of this should be a big deal. Mom had moved many times before, starting when she went to grad school at Duke. She and

Dad were still married back then, and her academic stint in North Carolina was supposed to be temporary. Helen and I had believed her promises, but anyone who wasn't under ten years old saw where things were really headed.

By now, we should be used to following her to new places. I should be treating her new move as something exciting, because it was *New York*. Instead, I felt as if I was one more step away from Mom's life.

"Anyway," I finally said. "I'm supposed to call her, and I have no idea what I should say. I saw her a few weeks ago, but now she's in New York, and I don't know what to say about that, because I've never been there, and it's not like we can talk about all the fun things we did in Oregon this summer, because we didn't. Do anything fun, that is."

Sean sat down next to me, leaning back in the plastic chair, which creaked as much as plastic can.

"I know how you feel. My dad only lives in Houston, but..." He shrugged, looking out into the empty street. "May as well be Mars. When I went to the family reunion with him in July, he kept calling me by his younger kids' names, probably because they're the same age I was when he and Mom split."

Sean's parents got a divorce the year after Mom and Dad, and his dad had carried out a full do-over on his life, complete with a new wife and a set of twin sons who looked like tiny cloned versions of Sean.

"Oh, man," I groaned. "Mom's always calling me by Helen's name, too. But at least Helen's not seven."

"Yeah, right? Point is, every time I see him, I have to get to know him again," he said. "And I think your phone calls are kind of like that, right? You spent the summer with her, but now she's moved for the millionth time. You're starting over yet again, kind of like me and my dad every Thanksgiving. And family reunion. And birthday."

"So I'm not an emotionally stunted freak for not wanting to call my mom?" Sometimes I felt like Sean was the only person I could voice my inner fears to out loud.

"Nope," he said. "I think it's pretty normal for you to feel weird about it. But I miiight call you out on being emotionally stunted—or maybe just immature—for the fights you get into with Helen."

I smacked Sean's shoulder for the insult, a reflex that proved his point. He smiled back at me with a smug "see what I mean?" look on his face.

"Okay." I nodded at him. "I'm going in."

I walked the few feet to our front door—our houses were attached after all—as Sean went back inside.

Our house felt extra quiet without Helen. I stared at the phone, daring myself to pick it up. I always hesitated before calling Mom. I never knew her teaching schedule, or if she'd be writing, or working on a new translation, or reading postmodern theory. When she'd first told me the term, I'd had no idea what she was talking about, and she'd laughed when I told her I watched a show on MTV called *PostModern*. I think that was why she sent me Foucault's collected works for my birthday last year. Needless to say, I hadn't read them.

I willed myself toward the phone, telling myself that I had no reason to be so nervous. I'd missed her call, but she wouldn't be mad at me for that. It would be fine. I inhaled deeply, placed my hand on the receiver, picked it up, and dialed.

"Hello?" Mom answered.

"Hi. It's Athena," I said. As if she didn't know.

"Hi, baby," Mom said. "I'm in New York!"

"Awesome!" I said, then cringed. She hated when I used

awesome to mean *cool*. She always said it was a bastardization of the word's true meaning. "How's the job?"

"It's fantastic, Athena," she continued. "Lower teaching load, much more research focused, and an extra year on my tenure clock. Isn't that amazing?"

I had no idea what most of that meant, but sure.

"Yeah, amazing!" I said anyway.

"So, your father and I have talked," she said.

When had they had the chance to talk? I didn't even know that they *did* talk. My whole body tensed at the idea of what that might mean, because it couldn't be good.

"Really? About what?" The words came out strangled.

"Oh, it's good news, sweetie," she told me. "He and I have decided that, since I'll be in Rome over winter break for a research trip, you and Helen should each visit me in New York for your birthdays."

"But we were supposed to go to Rome with you," I said. "And my birthday is in November and Helen's is in April. That...doesn't seem fair to her."

The disappointment hit me right in the chest. I should be used to this by now, but somehow it always hurt. And while it didn't explain Helen's outfit change, Mom's decision *did* explain why she was egging me on more than usual. This news sucked for her even more than it did for me.

"I know it's not what you wanted," she said. "But I wanted to make sure I could spend some quality time with each of you individually, and because of my schedule in Rome, I'm afraid that's not going to happen. I promise it'll be better than Eugene. I almost never saw you this summer. The two of you were always off together, plotting something."

I didn't believe for a second that she didn't notice that when we left her house, we generally biked in opposite directions. She was only saying that because it made *her* feel better, not because it would make *me* feel better. She couldn't tell me the truth, which was that she was cutting down our visits because in New York, it would be too hard for her to keep an eye on both of us.

I twisted the phone cord around my finger, trying to convince myself that New York in November for a few days would be as cool as Rome for two weeks at Christmas. I knew if I tried to say something, I would cry. So I didn't.

"You'll love New York," Mom gushed, filling in the silence. "When you get tired of all the wonderful museums, we can go shopping at those stores you're always complaining *aren't* in Baton Rouge."

I snorted a cynical laugh. Mom's perception of teenage taste included lots of bright colors and Italian leather. Even Helen, Queen of Fashion, had balked at the weird patchwork leather clothes she'd sent us from her last research trip to Italy.

I considered telling Mom about the Cute Boy in my physics class because he was the most exciting thing that had happened to me all day. I couldn't do it, though. She'd probably get the wrong idea and send me a box of condoms or another copy of *Our Bodies, Ourselves.*

So I settled in and let her do the talking—it was much easier that way anyway.

4

Melissa's rusty blue Subaru wheezed as she drove me and Helen to dinner after orchestra auditions. We were supposed to be celebrating. My dad, convinced that our Saturday afternoon would yield first-chair victories for the two of us, had given me money to take Melissa out to dinner, as long as we picked up Helen after the auditions and took her, too. Sean was also meeting us at the restaurant for our first group hangout since I'd gotten back from Eugene.

Instead, we rode in miserable silence. Melissa didn't even bother to play anything in the tape deck or turn on the radio. It didn't feel right to listen to music under the circumstances. We had both been robbed, and neither of us wanted to talk about it. Melissa ended up second to Tommy Roberts, violin genius of Baton Rouge, and I was second to Aaron Cormier, Dr. Walsh's favorite orchestra player in the history of ever. I didn't care as much as Melissa, since being second chair to his precious Aaron meant Dr. Walsh would yell at me less. Melissa had been winning competitions since her dad started teaching her Cajun fiddle when she was four, though, and she deserved to beat Tommy Roberts, a Suzuki-obsessed automaton.

By the time we pulled into the restaurant's parking lot, we were the two glummest people ever. Melissa went in to put her name on the waiting list, while Helen and I stayed outside. Helen stood next to me, leaning casually against the building, one of her legs propped up stork-like against the stucco wall.

"Is Sean coming?" Helen asked, staring out toward the road.

That was weird. Helen never asked about Sean.

"Of course. Why wouldn't he?"

She shrugged. "I dunno. Is he bringing *her*?"

"Probably."

We lapsed into silence again.

"She's a bitch," Helen said after an eternity. She shifted uncomfortably next to me, a fidget that turned into a reworking of her slouchy form.

"Yeah, I know. Don't use that word, though. It's sexist."

Melissa and I were trying to weed the word out of our vocabulary, except in cases of irony or humor, and then only with each other, not about other people. Melissa often made an exception for Leah, but as Sean's friend, I tried to stick to the B-ban for her, too. To do otherwise would be hypocritical.

"Whatever. You hate her, too."

My feelings toward Leah rarely approached hate. I classified them more as a studied indifference, with a side of banal dislike and a soupçon of fear.

"What's she done to you?" I searched Helen's face for any telltale signs of trouble. Something about this conversation didn't feel like her normal dislike of Leah, which was usually more obligatory than deeply felt.

She looked at her studded black shoes, as though they would offer some answer to my question. Slouching down the wall didn't help Helen shrink away from the question, and neither did her platforms. From the side, she looked like a stretched-out, curved comma, her legs sticking out far in front of her and her head hanging low.

"Nothing, I guess." Her mopey, quiet reply didn't *sound* like nothing.

She had to be lying. In my head, I flipped through all the things she could lie about. Maybe she liked Sean, despite all of their teasing and back-and-forth jabs that never ended. Or maybe going to school with Leah had brought this out.

"Do you *like* like Sean?" I scrutinized her face for any sign of emotion. She flinched slightly, but that was it. "Oh, my God! You do!"

"Ew!" Helen blurted. "No!"

I didn't *quite* believe her, but something about her posture told me now wasn't the time to press the issue.

"Then what's the problem?" Now that she was a junior, Leah most likely wouldn't pay much attention to freshmen girls, at least not until homecoming court nominations came around. Then again, Helen wasn't an ordinary freshman. She was unusually pretty, and she spent a lot of time with Leah's boyfriend. Two strikes, waiting for a third.

"I didn't want to say anything because it's your audition celebration and all, and I didn't want to make it a big deal," she said, sounding like whatever was bothering her *was* a big deal. "But someone's been saying that I—" Helen looked toward the parking lot, and her voice trailed off. "Never mind."

Leah's purple Mazda Miata had just pulled in. Helen

watched, lips pursed tight, as Sean and Leah climbed out and walked up to us.

As usual, Leah's makeup was one step away from beauty pageant readiness: just enough mascara, just enough blush, and just enough lipstick that she didn't creep over the edge from skillful application to full-on clown town. Platinum highlights streaked her long wavy blond hair. A tight Pepto-pink Ralph Lauren polo shirt exposed a two-inch gap of tanned skin between its hem and the top of her white denim cutoffs, which she'd rolled up to show off her muscular legs.

She looked like an extra on *90210*. Compared to her, in my black T-shirt, frayed cutoffs, and Doc Martens, I looked like an extra in a Nirvana video.

Sean, under Leah's fashion tutelage, looked nearly as preppy as she did in jeans and a baby blue polo shirt that complemented her pink one, a terrible choice for such hot weather. Somehow, I didn't mind the preppy look on Sean, as long as he didn't start popping his collar. It was better than his pre-Leah habit of alternating between Spider-Man T-shirts and LSU jerseys.

With a wave and joking pee-pee dance, Sean rushed inside the restaurant, leaving Helen and me alone with his girlfriend. My brain froze at the thought of conversation between me, Helen, and Leah, especially since my usually talkative sister had clammed up next to me.

In the year since they'd started dating, I'd tried to like Leah. Their whole relationship shocked me at first because Sean and I started high school at approximately the same level of popularity—that is, zero. Leah, on the other hand, had an entire entourage. So when she and some of the other cheerleaders started hanging out with Sean and his football buddies at school, I thought it was an extension of their symbiotically intertwined sports.

And then he asked her out, and she said yes.

At first, she didn't seem that bad. She was much like all the other cheerleaders—interested in football, and rightly insistent that cheerleading was a sport. She seemed totally devoted to Sean, recognizing that he wasn't just talented, but genuinely a good person. I'm sure it also helped that he was hot.

For a few months, she'd treated me as an almost friend—not necessarily someone you'd confide in, but someone you'd go to the movies with or hang out with in a group. I was happy to support her, too, because Leah had lost friends when she started dating Sean. My school didn't have a lot of experience with interracial couples, especially one where the girl was a year older than the boy. People didn't say anything to her, but they whispered. It didn't even matter that Sean had incredible talent.

And then the football team won district. Suddenly she and Sean were the Couple of the Century, and I was back to being Sean's weirdo friend from next door who never got invited to the jock parties, a sad reminder of the geeky life whence she'd rescued him.

"Hi, Athena," Leah said, showing her whiter-than-white teeth in a sharky smile. "How was your audition?"

"Okay." I shrugged. "Second chair. But considering no one else from our school's orchestra made the cut except me and Melissa, that's pretty good."

"Pretty good," she said, like it was the exact opposite. I had to give it to her—her use of sarcasm was much subtler than Helen's. I could feel my cheeks start to burn with embarrassment and failure, solely because she'd uttered two devastating words.

Next to me, Helen sank farther down the wall, stuck in giant comma mode.

"Hi, Helen," Leah said, turning with laser-like precision. "I've heard so much about you."

"I bet you have." Helen didn't look up. "Considering we've known each other for over a year now."

"Ha. I was thinking, like, more along the lines of at *school*."

Helen's face flushed a deep pink that stood out against the sprinkling of summer freckles on her cheeks. I didn't know what had happened at school or why Helen would act this way. Then again, I'd spent the past three days trying to figure out who the new guy in physics and calc was, and no one else seemed to know the answer to that, either. It wasn't that I didn't care about Helen—the latest gossip tended to fly below my radar.

"If you think—"

"Think what?" Leah asked in an overly innocent voice while winding her hair around her finger like a little girl. She was *so* infuriating.

I found myself slouching against the wall next to Helen, trying to figure out if something I could say would make this conversation better. My downward slide seemed to trigger something in Helen. She straightened up to her full height, which, with the giant shoes, reached over six feet, towering over Leah.

"You know, it's not important." She smiled at Leah, broad and confident.

The smile clearly confused Leah, whose rose-red lips pulled into a frown. It confused me, too. Whatever Leah had said or done, it must have not been that bad if Helen could recover so quickly. My sister again looked like her normal, secure self, and Leah backed away.

“Hello, ladies!” Melissa bounded up and hugged Helen and me in an extravagant display for Leah’s benefit. She didn’t really like Helen, but she *hated* Leah. “Our table’s ready.”

I exhaled with relief. If anyone knew how to deal with Leah, it was Melissa. But I couldn’t shake the feeling that Leah was up to something devious. What kind of impossible social chess game were she and Helen playing?

5

There was a goth girl in front of my locker. Or, more accurately, she was by her locker and trying to get it open, but completely blocking access to mine. She wrestled with the combination a few more times before banging on her locker, as though that would help open it up, her teased-out dyed-black hair moving stiffly in time with each loud thump of fist-to-locker. Under her white pancake makeup, her cheeks were red from the struggle.

"Excuse me," I said politely, trying to maneuver around her so I could open my own locker and grab my stuff for physics. Mrs. Breaux didn't accept late work. Last week, she'd even assigned us extra work to keep us occupied while school was canceled for three days during Hurricane Andrew. Thankfully, the storm didn't damage Baton Rouge too much—not like Florida, and some of the parishes closer to the coast—but I still had to finish my homework by the light of a battery-operated hurricane lamp. Mrs. Breaux told us that it was light enough during the day, and daylight hours provided more than enough time to get homework done. She didn't care that most of us had to help our parents clear up yard debris during the day.

So if Mrs. Breaux didn't give us extra time due to a hurricane, she wasn't going to care that I couldn't find my homework folder on a random Friday when the weather was sunny and clear.

"Oh, hey, Red!" The girl turned to me with a bright smile that clashed with her almost-black lipstick and crinkled the corners of her eyes, where eyeliner swooped out like the Death character from Neil Gaiman's *Sandman*. Her full-on goth look was a little outside what anyone could normally get away with in terms of hair or makeup, but the girl's perkiness overrode any sense of the supposed darkness within.

"Hey…?" I didn't know how to finish the sentence. Karen? Kandace? Kelly? What was her name? I vaguely remembered her from last year, pre-goth, but the transformation had overridden most of her identifying characteristics.

"Wisteria," she answered, rocking back on her heels with a nod of finality.

That one was definitely made-up. Like all the goths' names.

"I'm Athena." You would have thought my name was made-up, too. But, no, my mom had definitely embraced her love of the classics when she named Helen and me.

"Oh, I know," she said brightly. "I just like your hair." At least *someone* besides Melissa did. Helen said it looked like I'd been assaulted by the Kool-Aid Man, and my dad had just shaken his head when he saw me get off the plane from Eugene with it freshly dyed red.

Wisteria looked back at her locker. "D'you have any idea

what's wrong with this thing? I never had any trouble last year?"

She said everything like a question, a trait I didn't normally associate with goths. Then again, I hadn't spoken to most of them. They tended to hang out behind the school smoking clove cigarettes and practicing sullen ennui.

I suspected Wisteria's lack of trouble last year came from not actually locking her locker, as most people didn't. I also suspected her current troubles came from Melissa, who liked to mess with people by casually twisting locks as she walked by. Wisteria's proximity to my locker was a dead giveaway.

"Do you know your combination?" I felt obligated to help, since Wisteria's struggle was most likely my best friend's fault. We didn't have much time between classes, but I couldn't just bounce off to next period and leave her to suffer.

She nodded. "Yeah, but it just doesn't *work*."

I was going to have to get back at Melissa for this one. Messing with people's lockers seemed a lot less funny when it was causing stress to someone who seemed like she didn't deserve it. Not that anyone did, really.

"You need to twist right twice before your first number," I told her, "then twist left past zero to your next number, and then right again to the last number."

Wisteria tried again after watching me open mine. "It worked!" She jumped up and down enthusiastically. "Thanks!"

"No problem." I grabbed my stuff for physics and shoved my religion notebook and calc binder into my locker.

Wisteria paused for a second and squinted at me curiously. "Uh, Red?"

"Mmm-hmm?" I half listened to Wisteria as I continued to search through my locker for my physics homework, which seemed to have gone missing among the chaos of my possessions.

"Uh, this is *super* awkward, but, I wanted to thank you and Melissa for all your pro-choice activism this summer?" Wisteria said, leaning in so that her voice dropped to an enthusiastic whisper. "It's a *really* big deal? Because no one in this school *gets* it?"

I stopped my search for my physics folder and turned to give Wisteria my full attention. Two things confused me about this conversation: first, I'd had no idea that Wisteria was pro-choice. In theory, I knew there might be other pro-choice people at our school, but that theory was, until now, unproven. The second puzzling thing was that she had no real reason to thank me.

Everybody knew about Melissa's work on the front lines, but I couldn't take credit for being a badass when my contributions to the pro-choice cause had maxed out at writing an essay for the zine Melissa handed out at the protests and buying a Rock for Choice T-shirt via mail order. Oh, and I also considered keeping Helen away from the protests as part of my civic duty.

I shook my head. "You've got it wrong. I totally support Melissa, but I was in Eugene at my mom's all summer."

"But your sister?" Wisteria looked at me with a face that mirrored my own confusion, tilting her head to one side and scrunching up her face so much that the curlicue eyeliner crinkled in on itself at the corners of her eyes.

"Helen was in Eugene with me all summer?" Now I was doing the question-voice thing, too, and tilted my head to mirror hers.

"Oh. *Oh.*" Wisteria's eyes widened with an epiphany that I

clearly wasn't in on. "Never mind? I think I was given some bad intel?"

Okay, now that my sister was in the mix of a sentence involving "bad intel," I needed to know what it was. I suspected it had something to do with that weird interaction between Leah and Helen almost two weeks ago, but since then, Helen had clammed up whenever I asked her about it, saying it was no big deal. She eventually resorted to putting on headphones and playing CDs on her Discman during Hurricane Andrew's landfall so she wouldn't have to talk to me. Then she'd ignored me all weekend, saying my cello practice was annoying her, and wound up going to her friend Sara's house. Whatever was going on, she didn't want my help.

"Wisteria, can you please tell me what you heard?" I pleaded. I wanted to be patient, but it felt like Wisteria had an aversion to being direct. And while it wasn't Wisteria's fault that I felt so in the dark, I'd had enough of being the only one who didn't know what was going on.

"Really, Red, I think I just got confused," she said with a hesitant smile. "I wouldn't worry about it if I were you!" She paused again, and her smile faded. "It's just—I heard that you and your sister were more, like, *involved* with the protests than that. Like, you may want to talk with your sister." She widened her eyes with emphasis, like I was supposed to understand.

"Oooh-kaay." I shrugged my backpack up on my shoulder. I usually let Helen fight her own battles, but this seemed serious. After school, I'd check in with her to see if she was all right.

But right now, physics—and the Cute Boy—called.

I forgot all about Wisteria's ominous mention of my sister within the first two minutes of physics, when Mrs. Breaux called the Cute Boy to the chalkboard.

"Kyle Buchanan, please work out problem three on page twenty-five."

That's it, I thought. *That's his name!* I'd been trying to find it out since the first day of school, but had so far hit speed bumps during our two classes together. Neither Mrs. Breaux or our calculus teacher, Mr. Loring, took attendance, and since the other students were all at least a year ahead of me, I didn't know anyone except Melissa well enough to ask. Now, finally, at the end of the third week of school, I knew his name: Kyle Buchanan.

Suddenly, the thought that he might be related to Pat Buchanan entered my brain, and my hopes deflated. He couldn't be, though. He was too attractive to be related to that lumpy potato-faced man. I would die if he shared genes with a guy whose speech at the Republican National Convention made Mom so angry she actually stopped working on her book and went on a long, sputtering rant about how the Republicans were priming the nation for a fascist dictatorship.

There was no way this perfect guy was related to a fascist. I watched dreamily as he wrote out the physics problem on the board. His back faced the class, his face shadowed by his hair when he turned slightly to the side. Even from the back, he was the hottest guy I'd ever seen. His white uniform Oxford shirt hung perfectly off his broad shoulders. The shirt was tucked perfectly into the plaid uniform pants that outlined his perfect, callipygian derriere. *Everything* about him was perfect.

But I didn't want to be caught staring when he eventually came back to his seat, so I looked down at my notebook. Then I became acutely aware of how weird and antisocial I must look with my nose two inches from my book, so I tried to look at him, but not too obviously. I didn't want to miss an opportunity to catch his smile, but I also didn't want to seem like a creep. I couldn't seem to get the balance right.

"Where did you go to high school before?" Mrs. Breaux asked when he finished.

"I went to the International School in Brussels for the past two years."

Wow. It wasn't *that* weird to hear of someone who'd spent a few years in Brussels, but it was still intriguing. Brussels was the one international city that kids with parents who worked at Exxon might suddenly go off to, when their dad—and it was always their dad—got a promotion. Most of the kids who came back from Brussels didn't go to St. Ann's, though. They went to St. Christopher's or St. Ursula's, the all-boys' and all-girls' schools, respectively, or even Baton Rouge High. It was always some school with a better respected, Old Baton Rouge pedigree and not the School that Suburban White Flight Built.

"Well, they seem to have been adept at making you memorize formulae. You can sit down now. Caitlyn Comeau—" Mrs. Breaux called someone else to the board, but my eyes were still on Kyle.

He walked back to his seat, three behind my own. As he passed by me, he smiled, and I somehow managed to smile back.

I also blushed.

I told myself not to get excited, but my internal dialogue was in all caps. *HE SMILED AT ME.* The Cute Boy—Kyle—had smiled at me! Maybe he didn't think of me as a complete weirdo after I grabbed his backpack and mistook him for a girl much shorter than he was. It was the best I could hope for.

A tap on my shoulder snapped me out of my reverie. I turned red, thinking for a second it could be a note from Kyle. Then I came to my senses. Melissa sat two desks behind me a row over, and the note was tightly folded into her signature sharp origami-inspired triangle.

As I pried opened the note, my hand slipped. The tearing sound of paper, much louder than I expected, echoed outward from my desk. I held my breath, hoping it couldn't possibly have been as loud as I'd heard it in my head.

"Miss Graves? Please bring that note forward," Mrs. Breaux said.

It *was* that loud. Shit.

Tendrils of heat crept up my cheeks. I walked toward Mrs. Breaux's desk, my black Oxfords squeaking against the waxed linoleum with each step. I didn't know if I imagined the sound, or if, like the ripping note, the shoes were magically amplified due to Mrs. Breaux's presence.

"Would you like me to share your note with the class?" Mrs. Breaux's eyes challenged me from above her oversize red plastic glasses, which took up more than half her face and stood out against her milky white skin and bright red hair.

"No, ma'am," I said, remembering Mrs. Breaux required Southern politeness at all times. That note could say *anything*, from a report on Melissa's date to plans for this weekend to more about this summer's abortion protests. Fear and embarrassment bloomed in me at the thought of her reading it aloud, especially if Melissa had written something about Kyle.

"Then I hope that this won't happen again," she said. "May I please have the note?"

"Yes, ma'am."

Mrs. Breaux unlocked her desk, metal grinding against metal as she pulled the top drawer out. I cringed, more from a sense of impending punishment than from the sound. She placed the note inside the desk and closed the drawer, carefully turning the key in the lock.

"Miss Graves, I will see you after class," she said. "And you also, Miss Lemoine."

I sat through the rest of class facing the ominous certainty of detention. Most teachers ignored note passing, but Mrs. Breaux was a draconian ruler. She didn't like talking out of turn, note passing, whispering to clarify homework assignments, or quiz answers that deviated from the way she taught formula solving—even if the answer was right, and especially if you'd figured out a smarter way to find it.

I shouldn't care about being punished. But the fact was, I did. I didn't want to explain to my dad that I'd gotten into trouble for something trivial. I think he'd be fine if I got into trouble for standing up for my principles, but for passing a note? I'd get a long lecture about taking classes seriously, for sure.

Finally, the bell rang. I walked with dread toward Mrs. Breaux for the second time. Melissa, a defiant look on her face, joined me.

"Ladies, what do you have to say for yourselves?" Mrs. Breaux asked. Her mouth turned down at the corners like an angry Muppet. It would have been funny if she weren't so terrifying.

"I'm sorry," I said. "I shouldn't have been reading a note in class."

It wasn't very riot grrrl–esque to care this much about detention, but my palms were sweating.

"I'm sorry, too," Melissa said. She didn't *look* remorseful, but at least she sounded polite.

Mrs. Breaux scanned the note, her reading glasses slipping down her nose. She held the paper up, using it as a pointer to accuse us of wrongdoing.

"*Yo, Athena*—Now, isn't that a nice way to talk to your best friend?—*Is the point of physics to make us question our existence or to want to end it?*—My, I'm glad you shared that with me!—*I saw the Cute Boy smile at you! Maybe he likes you*—Oh, how touching, young love—*What are you doing this afternoon? Want to come over and help me dye my hair? I want it blue (you're so right about dyeing it that color!) for tomorrow when I go out with Jason. I already have the Manic Panic.*"

Mrs. Breaux eyed Melissa critically. "As if you need any more ways to violate the school's dress code, my dear," she remarked drily, then continued reading. "*Jason and I are going to see whoever's playing at the Varsity. I hope he has a fake ID*—Thank you, Miss Lemoine, for letting me know you are breaking the law! I doubt your father will like hearing about this—*Do you think he does? You're right. He is a bit scholarly. But he's funny, and cute...and a good kisser*—Oh, how I needed to know that, Miss Lemoine—*Gotta go, best wishes for living through this dull class*—Thank you for that kind assessment—*Peace out, Melissa.*"

Mrs. Breaux folded the note sharply in two and glared bullishly over her reading glasses.

"This note is absolutely inappropriate, Miss Lemoine," she said. "Though I'm not surprised it came from you, considering your summer activities. Like many people at this school, I *am* surprised that you're still here this fall, considering our pro-life policy."

She paused to give Melissa a long, withering stare. Melissa's face remained expressionless, but I could tell from her clenched fists that she wanted to talk back. I shook my head at her slightly, hoping Mrs. Breaux wouldn't notice.

"Miss Lemoine, I will see you tomorrow morning for detention."

Melissa nodded, because there was nothing else to do. Mrs.

Breaux had skipped over the reasonable option of after-school detention, which Melissa could avoid telling her parents about by making up an excuse about staying late at school, and gone straight to the nuclear option of Saturday-morning detention. She would *have* to tell her parents.

Then Mrs. Breaux turned to me. I shrank back, certain she was going to give me the same punishment as Melissa. "As for you, Miss Graves, I'm giving you a warning." Relief shuddered through me, followed by a wave of angry annoyance when Mrs. Breaux added, "And I suggest you stop associating with Miss Lemoine, unless you also want to spend more time with me."

Melissa and I rushed out into the deserted hall together. I gulped in the air of freedom, even though it was technically the same air as in the classroom.

"God, she's awful," a voice behind us said.

I turned to see who'd spoken to us. Kyle, the Cute Boy, leaned casually against the lockers, like he'd been waiting.

"What are you doing here?" Melissa asked. "I hope you weren't eavesdropping."

She sounded *pissed*. Guilt crept into my brain. After all, I'd escaped unpunished, but she would be hanging out with Mrs. Breaux tomorrow morning.

"No, I left my books for the next class in there." He smiled at me, but I had a hard time smiling back. Recovering from Mrs. Breaux's threats would take time, even if most of them weren't directed at me. "I didn't know if she'd let me in after lunch."

"Want to eat with us?" The words popped out of my mouth unexpectedly, and I lost my ability to speak for the next few seconds, surprised that I'd managed to say something to the

Cute Boy. It hadn't been a very long sentence, but it was clearly spoken and made sense.

Kyle's smile widened. "Sure. I'll meet you in the cafeteria after I get my books."

His answer surprised me even more. All thoughts of Mrs. Breaux disappeared from my mind as I nodded at him and walked to the cafeteria with Melissa.

6

In the cafeteria, I sat across from Kyle, and Melissa sat next to me. As I looked at Kyle, my stomach flipped and a deathly silence descended on our table.

I was in shock. I'd asked the Cute Boy—Kyle—to eat lunch with us. I reminded myself that it was just lunch. It wasn't a date or anything. He was new at our school, new enough that asking him to eat lunch with us wasn't crossing cliques or an affront to some girlfriend, at least as far as I knew. I had no idea what he did after school, though. He could have half a dozen girlfriends.

I tried not to think about that. Instead, I racked my brain frantically for something to talk about. Since the first day I'd latched onto his backpack, I'd been thinking of all the things I wanted to talk about with him. Now that we were sitting together in the cafeteria, though, they'd all disappeared from my brain. It was like going into a record store, knowing that I wanted a specific band's latest CD, but all memory of what I was looking for vanished as soon as I crossed the threshold into the store.

Instead, my mind buzzed with a thousand boring small-talk topics that would make me sound like the therapist my dad made me and Helen see after he divorced Mom—*So, what's your family like? What does your father do?*—or like a complete freak—*So, it doesn't seem like you've joined any clubs or sports, as far as I know. What do you do when you're not at school?*

So I can stalk you.

"Did y'all see that Ross Perot might reenter the presidential race? That guy's got some straaange ideas," Melissa said, in her version of "How about that local sports team?"

I had to think fast, or else Melissa would dominate the conversation with a political diatribe. There was nothing less romance inducing than your friend going on a rant about the lasting legacy of trickle-down Reaganomics or what she planned to spray-paint on the fake abortion clinic near LSU, which lured pregnant girls in with false pretenses of help but didn't actually offer any medical services. I had to say something.

"Do we have to talk about him?" I asked. I shifted uncomfortably in my chair, which scraped fartingly against the floor. Great. Now I sounded awkward *and* flatulent.

Kyle let out an uncomfortable half-cough sound across from me. He ran his hand through his hair, which was either a nervous tic or something to fill up the awkward pause.

"Who are you going to vote for in the mock election, then?" Melissa asked.

Oh, no. She wasn't letting go of the politics. I wanted to hear the answer, and yet I also didn't. In the fake "open primary" we had last spring, only seventeen people voted for a Democratic candidate. Everybody else voted for President Bush. I didn't think much would have changed in six months. When I told Ms. Boudreaux, my history teacher, that I thought Bill Clinton had better ideas than President Bush, she chided me for "being swayed by his charm." I thought it was super gross of her to imply that I had a crush on him. I didn't, of course, but even if I had, his dorky saxophone performance on Arsenio Hall's show would have killed it dead. There was nothing worse than someone my dad's age trying to be cool.

Except maybe Melissa's obsession with talking politics.

"Melissa," I hissed before Kyle could answer. I accompanied that hiss with an under-the-table kick to her shin.

"Ow! Oh, hey," Melissa said. "Kyle's got the same backpack I do."

She returned my sharp kick under the table. I glanced at the backpack. She was definitely smarter than I was when it came to boys. She was nudging me to ask him what music he liked, something I knew about. *And* there was a Clinton/Gore button, which answered the election question. I let out an audible sigh.

"Oh, yeah," Kyle said. "I meant to ask you about—"

But he didn't get a chance to ask whatever question he had. Just when I thought the relationship gods had smiled on me with the favor of a boy with similar musical and political tastes, doom followed in the form of Leah Sullivan and her ever-annoying sidekick, Aimee Blanchard.

My jaw clenched automatically, and suddenly I remembered something—not any of those things that I wanted to talk about with Kyle, which was fine now that I had a legitimate topic in terms of music, thanks to Melissa's eagle eye—but about Wisteria. And Helen. And, of course, Leah.

Leah slid into the seat to the left of Kyle, and Aimee on his right, forming a sandwich that was like a moldy bun around the most perfectly cooked hamburger ever. I had to get rid of the moldy bun before it spoiled the rest of my hamburger, but I couldn't do that until I found out what Leah was suddenly doing at my lunch table, and what she was doing to my sister.

"Hey, y'all," Leah said cheerfully, as though it was perfectly natural for her to join us at lunch. Her Southern accent lilted with charm and cuteness. She flashed Kyle a smile that sent a hot flame of jealousy through my stomach.

"Aren't you supposed to be at the cheerleaders' meeting?" Melissa asked with a false sweetness through clenched teeth.

"Um, like, we quit," Aimee said. She tried to do a hair flip with her frizzy brown curls, but her hand got stuck in the wiry mess. Aimee had gotten an ill-advised perm over the summer, most likely to look more like Julia Roberts in *Pretty Woman*. People often said Aimee looked a little bit like her, which was true enough if you squinted. "It's, like, too hectic, you know? And Coach Braden is, well, *you know*."

I didn't know if it was one of Leah and Aimee's made-up rumors, or just an odd bit of gossip that happened to be true, but a story was circulating that Coach Braden was, *you know*, a lesbian. It didn't seem like a good enough reason to quit the cheerleading squad, in my opinion. My guess was if Coach Braden was, *you know*, a lesbian, she'd be interested in women her own age.

Back when I was trying to be friends with them for Sean's sake, I never understood why Leah let someone like Aimee hang around with her. She wasn't especially pretty, and she could be way too obvious when it came to trying to manipulate people. But fortunately for Aimee, Leah valued someone near her who wasn't quite as shiny, to make her look better. I should know—it was something she'd said *about me* to Cassie Sanchez last year, to explain why she'd hung out with me during her temporary exile from popularity.

Aimee wasn't creative enough to come up with the lies by herself, or else they'd all be variations on the themes of witchcraft and devil worship. Leah's input was what made the stories stick; she knew instinctively how people worked and what felt realistic to them. Last year, for instance, after Melissa started dating Aimee's ex-boyfriend, Leah and Aimee started a rumor that she was the daughter of a Vietnamese prostitute and an American GI who was then sold to her current parents for fifty dollars—and half the school believed them, despite Melissa's obvious genetic resemblance to her parents.

Of course, that made me even more worried for Helen.

"We wanted to have lunch with our friends," Leah said, flashing Melissa and me a big fake smile. She looked at Kyle's profile, seemingly willing him to turn to her. He was looking at me, but he glanced at her for a moment. Or maybe it was a second more than a glance—was I imagining that he gave her a once-over? It happened so fast, and then he was looking back at me, as intent as ever.

"Well, then, you should go find them," Melissa said. I was thinking it, too, but I never would have said it out loud.

"Ha-ha-ha," Leah laughed in a staccato, leaning across the lunch table to give Melissa a gentle punch on her arm. Melissa scowled back at her. "You are so hilarious, Melissa! Aren't you going to introduce us to your new friend?"

Great. She was planning to be here for the long haul. I would never get to talk with Kyle, and I couldn't tell her off, because she was being insincere in a way that would only make me look jealous if I called her out on it.

"I'm Kyle Buchanan." He coughed nervously after he said it.

"Very nice to meet you." Leah held out a perfectly manicured hand to Kyle. "I'm Leah Sullivan."

Kyle shook her hand, and Leah held it for an extra beat,

stroking her hand across his palm as she let go. I wanted to kill her. She had a boyfriend—who was one of my best friends!—and here she was, *touching* the first boy at our school I had any real interest in. And who had willingly joined me at lunch. And who had good taste in music. I wanted to reach across the table and slap her hand way from his.

It wasn't that I expected Leah to make a real move on Kyle. But I *did* expect her to flirt with any guy near me. Her goal in flirting wasn't to actually capture the guy for herself so much as it was to provide a means of distracting him from me. She did it last year when Trip Wilson, Sean's friend from the football team, was over at my house for algebra tutoring. I'm still not sure if Trip was interested in me—or if I even wanted him to be—but he sure had a hard time concentrating on his algebra homework when she was around.

It was different with Trip, though. Leah had flirted with him in an obvious, over-the-top way to embarrass him. He eventually turned all kinds of red anytime she got close. At first, Sean thought it was hilarious, until Trip told him he didn't think it was funny. Then Sean put a stop to it. Somehow I doubted he'd find it funny if he saw Leah flirting with Kyle the way she was right now.

And, at any rate, *I* didn't want Leah flirting with Kyle. He wasn't a friend of a friend I was tutoring. He was a guy I was interested in.

So again, I was back to thinking about getting that moldy bun away from my hamburger, while also trying to figure out what Leah, and most likely Aimee, were doing to my sister. These two goals had nothing to do with each other, but both made anxiety pulse under my skin. Despite our differences as sisters, I knew that the more important goal here was helping Helen, and I might not get another chance. But confronting

Leah about Helen might make me seem petty and gossip oriented in front of Kyle.

Still, Melissa's strategy of overt hostility wasn't working. I tried something less direct.

"Hey, Leah," I said, trying to sound completely neutral instead of completely rattled by her presence. "What was it that you and Helen were talking about at Superior Grill? You know, when you *and Sean* came to dinner with us?"

I couldn't stop myself from emphasizing Sean's name, even when the goal was to figure out what was going on between her and Helen. For a half second, Leah pursed her lips together like I'd caught her at something, and she needed a moment to make an excuse.

"Oh, that?" She shook her head. "I…heard some *nice* things about her, you know? She's really getting to be *so* popular."

I had to hand it to her—Leah was *good.* Taken at face value and to an outside observer, everything she said could be a compliment, like she was flattering Helen, not tearing her down, no trace of sarcasm in her voice. But I'd been there and seen how she made Helen, usually a fount of confidence, quake in her platform boots.

"What, exactly, have you been hearing?" My voice strained with reined-in anger. I couldn't let Leah know that she was getting to me, but she was more frustrating than Wisteria had been. Especially since I knew Leah was doing it deliberately.

She smiled sweetly. "Oh, you know. And if you don't, you should ask around. I'm sure you'll hear some *great* things. Anyway, I'm sure that Kyle doesn't care about gossip, do you?" Leah turned to him. "I hear you're really good at math and science. Almost as good as Athena. And, actually, I think Aimee and I need a tutor." She pouted at Kyle. "Math is hard."

Seriously? *Math is hard?* Was she that awful talking Barbie?

My throat burned with anger, with all the words I wanted to say but wouldn't let exit my mouth. It would make me look terrible in front of Kyle. To an outside observer like him, I'd look like a catty bitch.

I hated myself for thinking something so antifeminist, but the situation wasn't exactly giving me a lot of options for practicing riot grrrl revolution.

"You know, Athena's a really good tutor." Melissa leaned across the table toward Leah. "Just ask Trip Wilson. He wouldn't have passed algebra last year without her."

"Oh, I'm sure of that," Leah said, ignoring Melissa and me in favor of training her laser-beam attention on Kyle. "Anyway, Kyle, I'll be in touch. It was *very* nice meeting you."

Leah smiled at him again and trailed her fingers over his arm as she left the table, a much-more-than-welcoming, totally unnecessary gesture.

She was diabolical. I needed to tell Sean about this, but he'd never believe me. And even if he did, he'd probably dismiss it as Leah "teasing" me, like she'd "teased" Trip. He always said I could only see bad things about her, and maybe that was true, but he didn't see *any* of the bad things about her, and that just killed me.

"Is she always that friendly?" Kyle asked. An extensive blush spread over his face. I would have thought it was adorable, if not for the fact that Leah had caused it, and that he was nearly stuttering from it.

"Only to guys," Melissa said. "God! She makes revolution girl-style now so *hard*!"

I laughed at Melissa's petulant delivery of the riot grrrl slogan, but I felt a sick mix of jealousy and fear at the back of my throat. I tried to push it down with a reminder to myself about how I shouldn't compete with other girls. Jealousy—especially over a guy—was antithetical to riot grrrl. But Melissa was right. Leah was hard not to hate, especially now that she seemed to be taking aim at Helen *and* at Kyle in different ways.

"Are you okay?" Kyle leaned across the table toward me. "You're pretty quiet."

"Oh, yeah," I said, trying to push down the feeling that Leah was going to ruin every aspect of my life, and, more than likely, Helen's. I couldn't explain any of that to Kyle, though, mostly because I didn't know what exactly she was doing. Besides, she'd been *nice* to him. "It's nothing."

He looked as if he wanted to question me further, but instead he asked, "So, where do you usually hang out?"

"Wherever, I guess," I said absentmindedly. Baton Rouge wasn't particularly exciting. "Depends on who I'm with. Chimes Street if I'm with Melissa, the Daily Grind if I'm with Sean, home if I'm with my sister, Helen."

"What are you doing—"

The bell rang, drowning out the rest of Kyle's words.

"I've gotta go. My Latin class is all the way across the school. I'll be late." I got up from the table, trying to balance my lunch tray and heave my backpack onto my shoulder at the same time. I couldn't wait for this conversation to end.

"Wait! I—" Kyle said.

I was already in the hall when I realized that Kyle was maybe, sort of, possibly in the process of asking me out.

7

"I can't believe I didn't know he was asking me out." I must've repeated it at least forty times, both in my head and out loud, on our way to Chimes Street, the only vaguely cool area near LSU. The street was about three blocks long, its short length illustrating how little coolness Baton Rouge had. Chimes contained Highland Coffees, plus a cool used record store and The Bayou, the one bar that I vaguely aspired to get into. It was right around the corner from the Varsity, the only decent music venue for miles, and Paradise, the best place for new records.

Chimes was also the home of the fake abortion clinic, which Melissa always wanted to spray-paint a message on; a head shop that sold all things related to marijuana consumption; and a used textbook store. Those weren't places I frequented, but they fit the general demographic of the denizens of Chimes Street.

"Look, it's not that bad," Melissa said, squeezing her Subaru into a tight parallel-parking spot like a master. "You should be celebrating! *We* should be celebrating! My mom didn't ground me for getting detention, and you escaped punishment altogether, which I would be mad about, except it's not your fault. But on top of all that, we're going to see Lydia's Dream! The only local band that doesn't suck!"

We planned to give my fake ID some exercise tonight. Lydia's Dream was great, and they were playing an eighteen-plus show at the Varsity. Despite the real threat of being busted if we met up with the wrong bouncer, I was more concerned that I had missed out on my chance with Kyle, and I might not get another.

I wallowed in a haze of self-recriminating thoughts. I didn't know that Kyle was asking me out. I didn't know what Leah and Aimee were spreading about Helen. I didn't know *anything.*

Melissa said I'd definitely get other chances with Kyle, and whatever Leah was up to with Helen was probably something my sister could take care of herself, or else she'd have asked for help. But I'd felt like a zombie all afternoon to the point where I let Melissa pick out my outfit, and now I was wearing a skirt far too short and too tight. Riot grrrl preached body confidence, but I was most confident in slightly looser clothes.

"It's not a big deal," she said, for at least the hundredth time. "I'm sure he'll ask you again. Trust me."

Melissa didn't look at me while she said that, so I had no idea if I should believe her. She sat on the edge of the driver's seat of her car, buckling the high-heeled platform boots she'd bought in New Orleans. The buckles went the whole way up her calf, so she was taking forever. She couldn't drive in the boots, and she couldn't quite walk in them, but she was determined to wear them. She'd paired the boots with a blue minidress and fishnet tights, which was actually an understated look compared to the metallic boots.

"Besides, you won't get another chance to see Lydia's Dream," she said. "They're going on tour soon. And you seriously need to break in that fake ID of yours. But first, I need coffee."

Melissa hobbled in her doom-boots and I walked like a normal person past the darkened shops on Chimes Street toward Highland Coffees.

Under normal circumstances, I loved Highland Coffees. It was better than the rest of Baton Rouge's coffeehouses, if only for the number of cute college boys studying in its corners. But not even the promise of significantly above-average eye candy could make me feel better after the lunch disaster.

Melissa pulled open the door to the coffee shop with a sweeping gesture. A gust of espresso-scented air greeted us from the giant roasters near the front door.

"After you," she said. "What do you want? It'll be my treat."

"I want to restart this entire day," I said. "And not make an ass out of myself in front of Kyle."

"Stop being so negative," Melissa scolded, steering me into the coffee shop. "The night is young. You need to open up to its possibilities. Look around you. And I mean, *really* look around you. Now, what do you want?"

"Ye olde iced mocha, I guess." My enthusiasm should have been at an all-time high: Lydia's Dream, good coffee, cute boys. But I felt deflated. I'd landed Melissa in detention, messed up with Kyle, *and* let Leah get to me. The day had been an utter disaster.

Melissa marched toward the counter. "Open up to the possibilities," she repeated, and I really wished I could, if only to get her to quit with the self-help talk. "Really look around you." As if any of the college guys here would look twice at me.

Past the counter where Melissa was ordering our drinks, Highland Coffees opened up into a large room filled with tables and couches, sprinkled with the occasional solitary armchair perfect for reading. During the day, light flooded the seating area through enormous windows that looked like they belonged in an old-fashioned library. At night, cozy and welcoming lamps gently lit the room. Tonight, the coffee shop was crowded with couples on dates and students with statistics and chemistry textbooks working on problems in their notebooks. A cluster of writers occupied one corner, loudly and pretentiously critiquing each other's work.

As I looked for an empty table, I suddenly realized I knew what Melissa had meant by "really look around you," because there was Kyle, sitting alone at a table, waving me over. He looked almost as enthusiastic and dorky as I must have, and it only took me a second to figure out why. His smile wasn't the half smile he'd given me on his way back to his seat in class, but a full-on grin. I suddenly felt way more at ease, a considerable feat since I was wearing Melissa's super short skirt.

I could feel Melissa standing next to me, radiating victory.

"You noticed." She was grinning, too.

"Yeah. Did you have something to do with this?" I gestured toward Kyle, slightly afraid that he was a mirage.

"Sort of," Melissa said. "Well, yeah, I totally did. It was kind of a gamble. When you darted off to class, Kyle asked what you were doing tonight. So I told him to meet us here."

"Why didn't you tell me? I was so miserable all afternoon!"

Melissa raised her eyebrows and tilted her head.

"I didn't know if my plan would work out exactly as I wanted," she said, the tiniest trace of smugness in her voice.

"If I'd told you, you would have freaked out the minute anything went wrong. So I didn't say anything. Now, go over there before he starts waving like an air traffic controller to get your attention."

Melissa gave me a thumbs-up before she darted toward one of the shop's cushy chairs, as far from Kyle's table as possible.

I took a deep breath to calm my eager pulse. I had a do-over, a chance to redeem myself as someone who could hold a conversation. I would remember the things that had flown out of my head earlier: music, books, where had he been all my life? Maybe not the last one, which was super over-the-top, but I would for sure ask him what he'd been up to before moving to Baton Rouge.

I sat down in the chair across from Kyle. He immediately closed his paperback—J. D. Salinger's *Franny and Zooey*, one of my favorite books. I was impressed. Most of the boys I knew didn't read—well, not anything approaching literature anyway. I almost wondered if Melissa had tipped him off to my reading taste. After all, she had planned all this without telling me, so why not work his side of the equation, too?

"I guess Melissa broke it to you that you weren't going to the show," he said, smiling.

"No," I said. "But that's okay. I kind of want to kill her for lying to me, though."

I wasn't really mad at Melissa—she was an *amazing* best friend for setting this up. But somehow, pretending to be annoyed with her made talking with Kyle a little easier, since the part of my brain that kept questioning everything I said and what to do next had something to focus on.

"It could be worse," he said. "I thought I'd check out the show before coming here, but the bouncer took my fake ID.

Now I'll never get into shows for the rest of my high school career, all for a show I was only going to spend a half hour at."

"It's not like anyone worth seeing ever comes here, so you won't be missing much." I meant for it to sound reassuring, as if the show we were missing right now wasn't that amazing, but then I realized it might come across as too negative, and I was back to worrying a little.

"Oh, come on," he said. "At least those bands tonight sounded pretty good. Or so I thought from the curb after the bouncer kicked me there."

I laughed. The Cute Boy wasn't just cute; he was smart and funny, too.

"I like Lydia's Dream," I said. "But I really wish I could see Bikini Kill. I can't wait until their EP comes out next month. But they'll never come here, you know?"

Music *and* politics. I could talk about both if he knew Bikini Kill, which he should, considering that button on his backpack.

"You like them?" he asked. "My sister goes to school at Evergreen. She's, uh, friends with them. I, uh, don't actually know their music, though. At all." He looked at me sheepishly. "I hope you can forgive me?"

My heart didn't know whether to leap with joy or stop beating. His sister *was friends with* Bikini Kill. I liked Bratmobile and Heavens to Betsy, the other two riot grrrl bands whose music I could actually track down, due to their split seven-inch vinyl record together on K Records. But Bikini Kill was something *more*. Their shows were supposed to be *life changing*. They took turns on different instruments, they had spoken-word events. They did benefits for feminist causes. And everybody in the band was *so* cool. Kathleen Hanna was brave enough to talk about sexual harassment and tried to get girls to come to the front at their shows, and her voice could be a howl of motivating rage. Tobi Vail *pounded* the drums like all the anger in the world was coming out of her arms. Underneath, Kathi Wilcox played simple, but super solid, bass lines. And Billy Karren's guitar somehow unified everything.

All I had was a scratchy, watery-sounding copy of the band's demo cassette, *Revolution Girl Style Now*, and the Kill Rock Stars compilation album with one of their songs, and a couple of zines written by or about the band. Kyle's sister knew them. *She. Knew. Them.*

But Kyle didn't even know the band's music. *That* was a major comedown.

"Then why do you have a Bikini Kill button on your backpack?" I strained not to sound accusatory or disappointed, but cool-girl calm.

A flare of crimson rushed up Kyle's face. He ran his hand through his hair, the same nervous gesture he did at lunch.

"Um, well, it's embarrassing," he said. "And I'll probably lose scene points as soon as I say this, but my sister put the Kill Rock Stars and Bikini Kill badges on my backpack right before she left for school, and I didn't notice. When I called her, she said—and I quote—'it would help me get girls.'"

Now it was my turn to blush. I had noticed him for exactly that pin. Well, that and the fact that he was way better-looking than the other guys at St. Ann's. But now I knew what kind of guy would have a Bikini Kill button—sorry, *badge*—on his backpack: one whose sister had put it there, or one who wanted to get girls. Or both.

"Oh." I tried to hide the disappointment in my voice. "I like Bikini Kill. And Bratmobile. And Heavens to Betsy."

It was so hard to find other people who were into riot grrrl. It wasn't like the bands were on MTV, or their music was easily available at most record stores. It had taken me a month to track down Bikini Kill's cassette, and I listened to it all the time. Even Melissa, the only other person with musical tastes close to mine, didn't really like them. More than anything, I wanted someone to talk about their music with, but that person wasn't going to be Kyle.

"Please don't get mad at me!" Kyle held up his arms in defense. "I swear I didn't notice it was there until like a week into school. I would never, you know, deliberately try to get girls with a badge. And if you like them, then I'd love to give their music a try—maybe you can bring their album over to my house so we can listen to it together?"

Something about his face—maybe it was the blushing, maybe it was the wrinkled-up pleading look—told me he was being honest. He didn't need any help getting girls, but I tried to ignore that thought. And also, he'd just suggested *I could go over to his house and listen to music.* Inside, I was screaming, like that old black-and-white footage of girls watching the Beatles.

"Do you at least like the Clash?" I asked, trying to see if our musical tastes aligned at all, or if I was going to have to bring my entire cassette tape collection with me. To his house. Which he'd invited me to.

"Oh, man! They're my favorite band." If it was possible, the grin across his face got even bigger when he said it, so I knew he wasn't faking it. Not that I thought he would, since he'd confessed pretty readily about the Bikini Kill thing.

I might have loved riot grrrl bands, but the Clash were classic. They were the whole reason I got into punk when I was twelve, when I saw the video for "Rock the Casbah" on late-night MTV. Back then, I didn't realize that "Rock the Casbah" wasn't *real* punk, or that *Combat Rock* was supposed to be a total sellout album. I liked it anyway, and always would, but I wasn't going to lead our conversation with it.

"What's your favorite Clash song?" I asked.

"I think it would have to be a tie between 'London Calling,' for the bass line, and 'Hateful,' because it's catchy," he said.

"London Calling" and "Hateful" were both great songs that passed the punk-points test. At least he knew the Clash for real.

"'London Calling' is the first song I learned to play on bass!" I blurted with way too much enthusiasm. I needed to dial it down from eleven to maybe six or seven.

"Wow!" he said, more impressed than I expected. "It's kinda hard, though, right? Like, to learn as your first song. I play bass, too, and it definitely took me a while to learn that bass line."

"It was a totally dumb idea," I lied. I had played cello for years before I started playing bass, but it seemed easier to agree with Kyle. I inwardly kicked myself for playing dumb. I seemed to forget everything about being a feminist when I was around him.

"Are you in a band?" He was doing that deep-staring thing again. Suddenly I felt like I was the only girl in the world, and sitting across from Kyle was the only thing that mattered.

"Theoretically, Melissa and I are in a punk band where she plays electric violin and I play bass, kind of like the Raincoats, but neither of us have written any songs since last year, so it's become more of a theoretical band than ever," I said with a laugh. "I think we last practiced in May."

"That's better than me," he said. "I was in a band in Brussels, but it was a disaster, since both my French and my Dutch suck. I'm learning guitar now, though. I think I'm going to switch to that."

And then we could be in a band together, I thought. Because no band needs two bass players. Not even Ned's Atomic Dustbin, which actually had two.

I was getting way ahead of myself. It wasn't realistic to think about long-term plans with a guy I'd known for approximately thirty seconds. But it was so, so hard when everything he said seemed to fit so perfectly into my category of "imaginary boyfriend must-haves."

"What was it like in Brussels?" I asked, because "has been to a foreign country, which is more than I've done" was not necessarily a must-have on that list, but definitely checked a bonus box.

Kyle shifted in his chair. A quick, thoughtful frown crossed his face, but then he was back to normal, with a reassuring smile.

"It was...hard to leave," he said. "Don't get me wrong. I don't want to sound like one of those spoiled rich kids who come back and sneer, 'Oh, Baton Rouge is *so dull* compared to my grand European travels.'" He rolled his eyes, as if to further distance himself from those kids, and then he shrugged. "But it was cool to have the chance to go to school with a bunch of kids from around the world, and it was fun to take weekend trips to places like Amsterdam and Paris. And it sucks to have to start a new school junior year."

"I'm sorry," I said, reflexively apologizing for Baton Rouge sucking, as though it was my fault he'd moved from Brussels to a city that had at best one cool street, if you weren't in love with LSU football. And that said nothing about the other flaws with the city, like the blatant racism or the pollution that everyone pretended didn't exist.

"I knew it!" He grabbed my hands across the table half jokingly, half serious, and a shot of electricity ran through my body. "You're a supervillain, capable of making a whole city suck!" He shook his head and smiled. "You don't need to apologize. Tonight was the first time I've had something to look forward to. So far, you've been making up for the rest of the city."

The shot of electricity turned into a flame. I was about to say something, when Kyle suddenly looked up and dropped my hands.

"Ahem." Melissa stood by our table. I hadn't thought of her once since sitting down. "I don't mean to interrupt, but when you two need a ride home, let me know. I'll be in the corner, reading."

Melissa darted back to the prized cushy armchair she'd scored earlier, unaware that she'd interrupted *at the worst time.*

"You know, I could drive you home," Kyle said. "Except I don't have my license yet. It's embarrassing, but I had to get my mom to drive me here and promise I had a ride home. One of the problems with returning from your dad's overseas trip two days before the school year is that you don't have a lot of time to get a driver's license."

"That's all right, because I think we would probably disappoint Melissa if she couldn't act as our chauffeur," I said. "She wouldn't be able to spy on us."

He laughed. I looked at Kyle and suddenly realized that he was looking at me in a way that meant I wasn't just going to have this second chance, but plenty of others with him. And I was going to savor every minute.

8

The Pontiac was hot, despite my dad cranking the air conditioner. It was the first weekend of September, right before Labor Day, and it was already eighty degrees at eight o'clock in the morning. The car's burgundy vinyl interior seared my thighs, but I hardly noticed. I was too busy replaying images from the night before in my head. Kyle across the table from me, laughing at my joke. Kyle telling a joke, and me laughing at it. Sitting in the backseat with Kyle, holding hands. Kyle saying a reluctant goodbye, looking like he would almost kiss me, and then both of us noticing Melissa's rearview-mirror voyeurism.

I'd turned away at the last minute, not wanting my first kiss to be in front of her. Kyle seemed to understand, whispering, "I'll call you on Sunday," in my ear. I could still feel his hot breath against my skin. I shivered just remembering it, a happy feeling of anticipation creeping up my spine.

Dad and I waited for Helen and her friends Sara and Jennifer to emerge from the house. Helen had gotten up the earliest—much earlier than I had—but her friends had stayed up late last night, oohing and whispering when I got in just before my eleven o'clock curfew. Now they lagged behind in the house, busily preparing themselves for their big modeling show at the mall with last-minute cucumber compresses to reduce under-eye puffiness.

I watched Helen as she locked the door to our townhouse. Everything *seemed* normal with her, and I wondered if I was blowing things between her and Leah way out of proportion. It's hard to know how much you should worry when you have no idea what's going on, and Leah knew I was a worrier. Her dropped hints could have been her messing with me. It didn't explain Wisteria, but it had been easy enough to clear up her "bad intel" with a geographic correction.

Helen looked positively buoyant as she darted down the front steps wearing a pair of black wayfarer sunglasses that I had abandoned as too much like Madonna, and not enough punk rock. They worked on Helen, though, like everything else. Her long wheat-colored hair was still wet, but it would probably dry straight despite the frizz-inducing humidity. Swinging her purse by her side, she slowed to a goofy, sashaying model's walk across the front lawn. Sara and Jennifer collapsed in giggly heaps behind her, trying to imitate her.

Jennifer and Sara—I was never sure which was which—tumbled into the car, sliding across the backseat. Helen's two best friends were both conventionally pretty, tanned, brown-eyed brunettes with teased bangs, and neither of them was loud enough to leave much of an impression when Helen was around. I felt a little un-feminist for thinking they weren't much more than Helen's minions, but that was kind of how she treated them.

Helen scooted in last, behind my shotgun seat.

"Are you staying for the show?" Helen asked, poking my shoulder. She'd earned the first and last looks for the show, despite missing summer session at her modeling school. But she was the only one at the school tall enough to be a real model, and one of the most serious about fashion in general, so she tended to get a lot of opportunities the other kids didn't get.

"No. Why?" I'd planned to look for more "going out" clothes during the show, and then, when Helen was on a modeling high afterward, ask her about what was going on with her and Leah. At Melissa's suggestion, I'd pulled out outfits from magazines that I could copy, so I wouldn't end up with another floral baby-doll dress that Melissa said looked like it belonged to a child prostitute or maybe Courtney Love. Or Kat Bjelland, who said Courtney stole her look.

"No one from our family ever stays." Helen pouted. "Everyone else has someone there."

It wasn't exactly true. Dad had gone to her first modeling-class "fashion show" last spring and bought the big package of souvenir photos that he'd dismissed ahead of time as a big waste of money. He went to almost everything we did, no matter how big or small. Last year, he'd been the one to take Melissa and me to lunch after orchestra auditions, the one who'd cheered Helen on at her last middle school softball games. But since Dad started his corporate job, he'd been working late during the week, and spent most Saturday mornings in the office. I could see why Helen felt suddenly alone, because I kind of did, too.

Helen's resentment reverberated in the car, so much that I began to feel way more guilt than I normally would about missing a modeling show at the mall. Sara and Jennifer eyed each other with worry, but Dad just sighed and looked at her in the rearview mirror.

"You know I want to stay," he said, sounding firm. "But I have a court date on Monday. I need to go into the office this morning."

"You always go to Athena's stuff," Helen complained. "It's not fair. You're even letting her go to New York first."

"Helen, we've been over this," Dad said, frustration creeping into his voice. "You're not going to New York with your sister. It's for her birthday. You'll get your own trip in the spring, closer to your birthday."

"But, Dad!"

"Don't 'but, Dad,' me."

Helen and her friends settled into a tense silence. Dad never reprimanded Helen in front of them, and the brunettes wore identical looks of surprise.

I almost felt bad for Helen. No—scratch that—I *did* feel bad. She was right that it wasn't fair for me to get a trip when she didn't. And it sucked that Dad had to work during her big show. Plus, giving me a guilt trip and talking back to Dad were distinctly out of character for Helen. It felt oddly less capable than I was used to from her.

"I'll stay." I wasn't heartless, even if I did think of modeling as a useless hobby. I could always use the wait time to catch up on my English homework—reading *The Scarlet Letter*—while I waited for Helen to rotate through the cast of model kids. Her being first and last in the order made it pretty easy to kill two birds with one stone.

"That's great!" Helen bounced with glee. One thing to be said for her, she recovered quickly.

As soon as we got to the mall, Helen and her friends rushed from the car, propelled by the excitement of showing off the hottest fashion trends that had made it to Baton Rouge. My cynical opinion of the city's ability to embrace trends, whether fashion or, say, social justice, didn't leave me with a lot of hope in that department, but I wasn't going to squash Helen's enthusiasm. I let them run ahead while I leisurely followed the signage for the fashion show's seating.

Aside from a few siblings too young to wander the mall alone, I was the first nonparental audience member in the crowd. Still, I struggled to find a seat with a decent view of the catwalk. The raised stage, complete with a long runway jutting into the audience, had been set up in the large atrium in front of the Dillard's department store, with curtained-off areas to the left and right. Whoever had chosen the spot did a good job, because the skylight above the stage flooded the runway with natural light.

Crowds of girls and a few boys were getting ready along either side of the main stage. They darted in and out of the curtained-off areas, which seemed to serve as dressing rooms. Department store makeup artists piled on foundation to cover up zits, or added sultry, sophisticated eye shadow for homecoming-themed evening looks, and hairdressers pulled unruly hair into ponytails for daytime outfits or teased and curled it into dramatic updos to accompany sparkling, poufy evening gowns.

I couldn't see Helen, but that was probably because she would be the first to enter the runway. Since I had about fifteen minutes before the show, I pulled out my copy of *The Scarlet Letter.* For a book with such a juicy topic, Hawthorne was surprisingly boring, and I had to force myself to concentrate on the crammed typeface.

I felt a jostle from someone sitting in the seat next to me, a nudge of an elbow poking into my arm so hard that my book jerked in front of me. I huffed out my irritation at the person invading my space and nudged back, a passive-aggressive response to a passive-aggressive action.

"Oh, hey there, watch the elbows!" Thankfully, the voice was one I recognized immediately—Sean. I looked right to see him smiling at me. "I love seeing how long it takes to wake you up when you're nose-deep in a book."

I let out a sigh of relief that I wouldn't have to get into an escalating shoving war with some complete stranger or, worse, with one of Helen's modeling friends' relatives. I dog-eared the paperback page and shoved the book back into my bag.

"It's for English class," I said. "I only looked like I was enjoying it. Mrs. Snyder's nice, but everything she assigns is..."

"Boring?" Sean was in regular college-prep classes, not honors, but we both had Mrs. Snyder. She mostly assigned us the same books, plus additional assignments for the honors class.

"You read my mind." Another thought started to worm its way under the relief that Sean, not some stranger, was sitting next to me. This was Helen's fashion show, and he didn't usually tag along to those. Maybe Leah was involved in some way with the show, which might account for the way things were between her and Helen.

I waved at the stage. "So, uh, what brings you here to this fabulous display of...something?"

Sean gulped nervously, but so imperceptibly that any other human who hadn't known him since he was five might not have noticed. "Uh, Helen asked me?"

It wasn't like Sean to sound Wisteria-ish, which made his presence all the more intriguing. I leaned toward him like I would if Melissa was telling me about a juicy date, then backed off when I realized I was getting into his face about my sister.

"When did *that* happen?" I asked incredulously.

Sean put his hands up in protest. "It's not like that! You're always implying things that would get me into trouble with Leah. Who *does* know I'm here, by the way." He raised his eyebrows in a way that might have implied it had been a bad decision to tell her. Or I could have been adding my own unfavorable reading to the situation. "After school yesterday, when you were off doing whatever you were doing with Melissa, Helen told me your dad wasn't going to be able to make it today. She was kind of upset, so I told her I'd come."

"Uh-*huh*." That wasn't exactly Helen asking him to watch her fashion show, but I let it slide. Sean would just dismiss any questions about finer points of who invited whom as me "implying things." And to be fair, I kind of was.

"Hey, don't 'uh-huh' me," Sean said. "By the way, I heard Melissa drop you off after ten last night. And I mean *heard*. She really needs to get her alternator fixed. But you—I didn't think you were the type to break curfew."

I could feel my cheeks turning red. Not because of Melissa, of course, but because I remembered the heat of Kyle next to me.

"It wasn't *that* late. And I didn't break curfew. My dad extended it this year." A giggly excitement began to bubble up inside me. I'd been puzzling out Sean's attendance here, but I had my own news. News so big that it should be shouted by Christian Bale in *Newsies*. Sean was the only one I could really tell it to, other than the people who were already there. "So, you remember that guy in my physics class? Kyle?"

"Oh, is that his name? Mr. Nice Booty?" Sean wiggled in his seat, which didn't quite illustrate "nice booty" so much as "child who needs a bathroom." I smacked his arm, as usual.

"Yes, that's his name," I said. "You would not believe what

happened! Melissa—she's some kind of evil genius, I swear—she arranged for him to meet up with us at Highland Coffees, and then she went off to a corner, and we actually kind of had a date, and he invited me to go over to his house sometime this week, and—" I paused, gulping in air.

"Whoa, whoa! Take a breath before you pass out," Sean said. He raised his hand. "And give me a high five! I've never heard you create a run-on sentence like that before. Must have been some night!"

I giggled again, uncontrollably and totally out of character, as I smacked my palm against his. "It was, but not like that—"

I was about to launch into more detail about how amazing the night had been, when a voice blared over the loudspeakers near the stage: "Ladies and gentlemen, I would like to welcome you all to our Teen Fall Fashion Extravaganza. Remember, our ladies and menswear shows will be held at one o'clock."

A middle-aged woman in front of us turned around to shush us, finger fiercely up to her mouth, but she didn't need to. Sean and I sat up at attention, ready for Helen, our star attraction.

"Up first, we have our casual fall look of a blazer and scarf. Paired with a chambray shirt, boot-cut jeans, and riding boots, the look is an instant classic that'll take your daughter from Louisiana to New England," the disembodied announcer said.

Helen emerged from the curtains at the top of the stage. She strutted down the runway with an intense stare a world away from her goofy prance across the front lawn. The outfit was standard Ralph Lauren, not exactly the hottest teen fashion. But the brown houndstooth jacket and light blue shirt paired perfectly with Helen's coloring, bringing out the blue in her eyes and the pink of her cheeks and camouflaging the smattering of freckles across her nose. She looked older than fourteen, like a more put-together version of a college student hanging out at Highland Coffees. Flashbulbs went off near the stage, where the modeling school's photographer snapped away. Helen would probably con him into giving her the picture for her portfolio for free, even though parents were supposed to pay for them.

"That's our girl!" Sean clapped loudly as Helen got to the front of the stage. "Whoo!"

The woman in front of us turned around again to glare pointedly at Sean, but he just shrugged at her. "She's my friend. And her sister." He nodded to me. "We get to clap for her, as loud as we want."

The woman's glare softened slightly, but I could tell she was the type who enjoyed shushing.

"How much you want to bet she's mad Helen took her daughter's spot?" Sean whispered. "I wasn't being *that* loud."

"Probably," I whispered. "Or she's mad that we're not going to stick around for the adult fashion show at one, and we can't see her glorious Sunday best."

After Helen, each look grew more boring. Boys in polo shirts and jeans—why those needed runway exposure, I had no idea, since they were what 99 percent of the guys wore already—and girls in various short, pleated skirts and babydoll dresses and burned-out velvet holiday wear. None of them wore anything nearly as cutting-edge as the pages that I had torn out of my magazines.

Sean and I clapped for all of them, though, both out of politeness and to cover the snarky commentary we whispered to each other.

Finally, Helen emerged again, the last in a tableau of a homecoming court. She was the homecoming queen, as I had no doubt she would someday be in real life. She would make the court this year, for sure. Her dress was a long forest green velvet number that pooled around her ankles. The neckline plunged low, and the fabric stayed close to Helen's body, tight through her waist before gently skimming over her hips. She could have easily passed for eighteen.

"Whoa," Sean whispered, with enough appreciation in his voice that I would normally call him on it if I weren't rock solid in my expectation of another denial. "Helen should be sending up prayers of thanks your dad isn't here."

"She looks great," I said defensively. "Don't be mean about it."

"Who said I was being mean? All I'm saying is if he saw her in that dress, he'd keep her locked up until she was thirty."

He was right, but that wasn't exactly the point. I felt unexpectedly proud of Helen. She walked the runway like a professional, despite the mall setting and the dozens of other nervous, giggling models who waved to their parents and friends. I could never stand there with so many people looking at me, judging the way I walked and looked and exposing my breastbone for all to see. So Sean and I stood up and clapped loudly as the models returned briefly to the stage, hoping Helen could see us in the audience.

9

“Did you see me?” Helen rushed over to us and plopped down in the empty folding chair next to Sean. With her face scrubbed clean except for some traces of mascara, and back in jeans and a floral scoop-neck top, she no longer looked eighteen. Her enthusiasm and need for approval didn’t add any years, either.

“You were amazing!” I said, surprised by how much I meant it.

“Yeah, fantastic.” Sean took in a breath like he was about to add something else, but his eyes darted somewhere over my shoulder. I turned to follow his gaze to where a big old-fashioned clock hung outside the mall’s nicer jewelry store. It was almost twelve thirty. “Um, I have to go.”

“Now? But I just got here! And Sara and Jennifer are with their families. I thought we could all hang out.” Helen’s smile melted into disappointment. I could relate—Sean had skipped out on my youth orchestra concert last year in favor of going on a date with Leah. It wasn't even a special occasion for them.

Sean stood up between Helen and me, and awkwardly patted Helen on the shoulder. "Good job walking. Keep it up, legs moving forward one at a time," he said in a way that sounded almost dismissive. Helen's crestfallen face must have gotten to him, though, because he switched his tone. "No, seriously, you did great, and I'm sorry I can't stay to help you celebrate. Duty calls."

Sean didn't have to say that "duty" was Leah, and not some randomly scheduled Saturday football practice. He shuffled past my legs to the aisle and darted through the crowds of parents celebrating their kids' successes.

I'd ask him about it later, but I wondered if Leah had given him some sort of ground rules—that he could watch the show, but not hang around with Helen after. She might consider Helen in the flesh too much of a temptation, even though there was no way Sean would ever cheat on anyone, let alone a girl who could ruin him as much as Leah could.

Helen slumped back in the folding chair. "This sucks."

The way she said it got to me—two words so infused with sadness and disappointment. She'd just had her biggest triumph to date, and not only did Dad have to work, but I pretty much had to be dragged here, and Sean had ditched us as soon as the show ended.

"Sucks? But you were so great!" I protested. I'd never understood why Helen had become obsessed with fashion, or why she wanted to be a model instead of, say, a fashion designer. But she was *good* at this, unlike most of the other kids. "I could *never* get up there and do what you did! And you looked great doing it! I think you could really be a model."

"If that's so true, will you tell Dad so he'll let me go to New York now instead of April so that I can audition for real modeling agencies and get a contract so I can do runway work?" she blurted out in one breath.

"Umm, what?" She sounded more desperate than I'd ever imagined hearing her. She'd walked the catwalk like a pro, but now she was collapsing in front of me. I didn't understand how my sister functioned.

"Look, I need to get out of this town," Helen pleaded, scooting into Sean's empty chair and grabbing onto my arm. *"Please."*

"What's going on, Helen?" My stomach sank with a feeling that it had to do with Leah, but I instinctively knew I should let Helen tell me instead of interrogating her. It wouldn't help to start off by saying, *Hey, I know Leah's torturing you, but everyone's been vague about it and then I forgot about it for a whole evening because Melissa arranged a surprise date last night with the boy of my dreams.*

It was honest, but not particularly nice.

Helen's eyes welled with tears, but she didn't let them escape. First, she tried to ignore the tears by looking upward and blinking them back, while holding her breath and then letting it out in controlled bursts. When that didn't work, she moved on to other measures. As soon as a tear welled up, she wiped her eyes, pretending she had something in them.

Getting Helen to a state where she could talk was hard. I needed to calm her down, but I didn't know how. I hadn't seen her cry since she was eight, when our mom said she wouldn't be coming back to Baton Rouge after finishing her master's, and that she and Dad were getting a divorce. Crying in public was the antithesis of popularity promotion. I should know. I'd been branded a crier in elementary school.

"I hate high school," Helen said, letting a few words escape between held breaths and eye swipes.

"*Everyone* hates high school." I tried to sound as kind as possible. "If you like it, you're a freak."

Helen half smiled. But then the tears welled up again, and her face broke into a deep frown. Now I knew why she didn't cry in public. She looked like a baby ogre, with hints of old man around the eyes and mouth.

"What if I want to be a freak?" she wailed. Tears rolled down her face, much faster than she could wipe them away. She gave up entirely and put her head down between her knees, her shoulders shaking. I awkwardly placed my arm around her.

"Then I can't help you," I said quietly. "Because high school isn't easy, not for anyone. Now, can you tell me what's wrong?"

Helen loudly sucked in a breath. After a few seconds, she exhaled with a hiss through her teeth.

"I think Leah's been spreading lies about me," Helen said. "Or at least someone has. And people *believe* them."

"People will believe anything, if they want to." So far, I had escaped Leah's creative embellishments, but it was only because Sean was dating Leah. If that ever ended, it would be open season on my reputation. "What exactly are they saying?"

Helen screwed her eyes shut and wound her mouth up again in that unfamiliar, frowning face. Her tight-lipped tears made it impossible to tell if the gossip was that bad, or if Helen, who had always been popular, just wasn't used to high school's big-league intrigue.

"It started on the first day of school," Helen said through sobs. "I heard someone whispering about me in the hall. I didn't think anything of it, 'cause I'm kind of a giant, and people always gawk at the freakishly tall girl. I mean, I've been five-ten since the sixth grade, so I'm used to it."

She took another breath and continued, her voice thick and raspy. I'd never realized that Helen had been teased—or anything close to it—for being tall. A sudden pang of guilt hit me for missing out on times I could have helped my sister instead of fighting with her.

"But it wasn't just that. I kept hearing the whispers all day, and then the next, until that Friday Jennifer told me what they were. She knew it wasn't true, she said, but she thought I should know." Helen took a deep, shuddering breath. "Someone had been saying that I slept with Drew Lambert over the summer. I've never even talked to Drew Lambert!"

My hand flew up to cover my mouth as I gasped. I didn't want it to seem that helping Helen would be impossible, but this was worse than I had anticipated. Drew Lambert was a racist asshole. He'd been among the loudest to complain when Sean became the starting quarterback last year. He'd used words like *jigaboo* and *jungle ape* and threatened to hold a protest.

"At first, I thought it was because Drew said he slept with me or something." Helen sniffled with each sentence. "Which would have been bad enough. But people kept *whispering* things in the hall when I walked by. And people don't whisper like that for sluts."

I cringed at Helen's choice of words, but I got what she meant, and how much this was bothering her. People would talk, sure, about how *this* girl supposedly slept with *that* guy, but it didn't usually involve outright hallway mockery. My mouth started to go dry in anticipation of something even worse than people saying you were sleeping with a junior-level white supremacist.

She stared blankly at the rows of chairs in front of us, as though she was reliving something she didn't want to tell me. I followed her eyes to the maintenance man carefully shifting the folding chairs back into precise rows for the next show. He didn't notice us. Every once in a while, she'd reach her hand up to swipe away a stray tear or two.

"Helen, we're gonna have to go." My eyes darted from her to the maintenance man. "Do you want to tell me what's going on now, or do you want to do it somewhere else? We can go if you want to."

Her face twisted up again, and she shook her head.

"No, if I don't tell you now, I don't… I don't know when I will." She forced the words out through clenched teeth. "They were saying—I found out from Sara that they were saying it wasn't just that I'd supposedly slept with him, but that I'd gotten pregnant and had an abortion, and you and Melissa had helped me. They were saying I was a *baby killer*." She spat out the phrase. "And Angelle said I should quit the pro-life club, 'cause they shouldn't have hypocrites in their ranks. I told her that it wasn't true, but…" She shrugged, and her face folded back into the angry old-man cry face.

Now I *really* didn't know what to say. Not that I could talk with my desert mouth. These rumors were *bad* at our school, but they fit together like a plot meant to take down all three of us. Helen, for "having an abortion," and me and Melissa, for helping her. There wasn't anything wrong with having an abortion, or with helping a girl get one, but it wouldn't matter. Like all of Leah's best lies, this one was based on personal knowledge. She'd been at Sean's house when Helen and I had our blowout fight about the issue last year. She was aware of Helen's commitment to pro-life causes, and how Melissa and I were pro-choice. This was exactly the kind of gossip she designed for the masses to devour: an ounce of believability, an irresistible dash of political hypocrisy, and a pretty girl Leah wanted to take down.

Even worse, the rumor could potentially get Helen expelled from school. St. Ann's strict pro-life policy meant that any girl who got pregnant had exactly two choices: adoption or become a teen mom. Even then, the options weren't good or fair because pregnant girls had to be homeschooled for the duration of their pregnancy. But abortion? Unthinkable. It was grounds for automatic expulsion if the school administration found out.

But Leah's lies weren't merely designed to be believable and dangerous—they were designed to hurt personally. Helen cared because she was pro-life. Someone like Melissa would easily be able to fire right back and say, "So what if I did?" Helen couldn't do that, though, because it would make her a hypocrite. But, right now, I didn't care what she believed, only that she was hurting. I was going to protect her from this crap.

"Look, we need to figure out what to do about this," I said, squeezing her reassuringly. "But I don't think moving to New York is the answer."

"It would help, though," Helen mumbled.

"Yeah, I mean, sure, it would." I left out the fact that neither of us could deal with Mom long term. "But we need to figure out a way to stop the rumors. Preferably at the source."

"How're you going to do that?"

"Well, for starters, I'm going to talk with Sean and Melissa."

Helen shook her head violently. She had finally stopped

crying, but her eyelashes were clumped together with tears and the areas around her eyes were smudged with leftover mascara from the fashion show.

"Sean's not going to *believe* you," she said. "And what can Melissa do? I don't want everyone in the world to know about this!"

I sighed. She was probably right about Sean, but Melissa had firsthand experience. She'd fought back against Leah and Aimee's rumors about her parents last year, and within a month or so, everyone had forgotten about it. Of course, it helped that she'd ditched Aimee's ex-boyfriend, Matt Bouchard, about two weeks after they started dating. Apparently, he'd said something so gross about Asian girls that Melissa wouldn't even repeat it to me. After that, Aimee didn't have much reason to go after Melissa anymore.

"Melissa's an expert in dealing with Leah and Aimee," I said, trying not to let all those extra factors give me doubt. "She'd love the chance to get back at them."

My suggestion of asking Melissa for advice seemed to calm Helen down. The red drained from her face and the facial contortions stopped.

"I don't get why she'd pick on me," Helen complained. "I'm just a freshman. I'm nobody!"

I laughed. Helen, despite the mean-girl skills she'd honed in middle school, didn't recognize the obvious reasons Leah might want to take her out.

"It's not funny!" Helen was looking teary again.

"You're way prettier than she is, and you spend time with her boyfriend every day," I explained. "It should be obvious why she's doing it. You're a threat."

Helen smiled, as though the only thing that could bring her back from the edge was knowing she was better than Leah.

"She's really fake, isn't she? Like, so fake you don't know what's under all that makeup."

"Totally," I said, absentmindedly agreeing while my brain leaped ahead to other things. If Helen was in this state, Leah's lies must have taken hold with a lot of people—well, more people than I knew about anyway. It would be easy enough to get back at Leah, but so, so much harder to make things better for Helen. Once rumors got out, they were impossible to stop and could reach all the wrong people. And with Leah ten steps ahead of us, what could I possibly do to help?

10

I sat cross-legged against my bedroom wall, my US history homework fanned in front of me on the bed. As I worked, my bed slowly crept away from the wall, and I could feel my butt sinking down into the widening gap. Every few minutes, I had to readjust my bed, my homework, and my posture, but there was no way I was leaving my room now. Literally any other space in the house—the kitchen table, the kitchen counter, even the coffee table in the living room—would have been a more secure and comfortable place to do my homework, but there would have been no privacy. And I needed privacy because Kyle was supposed to call.

It wasn't that I expected to have a super personal call with Kyle, but I didn't want Dad overhearing, then grilling me about Kyle's family, or how well I knew him, or what our plans were. Or insisting that he needed to meet Kyle before I could go over to his house. Or giving me some embarrassing speech about how teenage boys were only out for sex. And I didn't need Helen, who was doing her homework downstairs at the kitchen table, making fun of me for being so obviously into Kyle. She would just distract me, and then I'd say all the wrong things.

And so I was glued to my bed, as awkward as that was, waiting for him to call.

It was now two thirty, and the phone still wasn't ringing. What if he didn't call? He'd said he would call, but he could just as easily *not* call. Boys didn't call all the time. And while it wasn't late in the day, it wasn't exactly early, either.

After every multiple-choice question I answered on Ms. Andrews's take-home history quiz, I looked at the lavender phone I shared with Helen in our bedroom. But it just sat there, not ringing.

I picked up the receiver to make sure it was working. It had a dial tone.

As I set the phone back down, I felt ridiculous. My obsessive phone behavior wasn't going to make Kyle call any faster. Besides, I should be thinking of ways to help Helen, who actually needed me, instead of worrying about whether a boy would call. It was antithetical to the kind of feminist I was supposed to be. I was supposed to be someone who was pro-girl and pro-choice, and helping my sister, who had been victimized by abortion-stigma gossip. But I couldn't help myself, no matter how hard I tried to focus on a very real problem.

I was waiting by the phone for a guy to call.

Kathleen Hanna would be ashamed of me.

I didn't know her, but I *knew* she'd be ashamed of me. Oh, she wouldn't call me out on it—she'd probably write about it in a zine instead. She'd be cool about it, but she'd make a point that it wasn't part of the revolution to care whether some guy was going to call, even if he was cute and maybe liked you back.

Rrrrrrrr. The phone rang. I jumped.

"Hello?" I said, grabbing the phone from its cradle before Helen or Dad might pick it up downstairs.

"Hi." It was Melissa. My pulse slowed to near death.

"Why are you calling?" My voice surged with panic and irritation. It wasn't a fair reaction exactly, because Melissa had no idea Kyle was supposed to call. But I needed to get her off the phone. Yes, we had call-waiting, but the longer I was on the phone with Melissa, the more likely it was that Dad would realize I'd been on the phone for a while and come up to my room to remind me to focus on my homework.

"Nice talking with you, too. I'm the one calling *you* back. You left a message with my mom? She just gave it to me."

I put a hand to my forehead in embarrassment, as if Melissa could see me on the other end of the line. I'd called her yesterday as soon as Helen and I got home, but she'd been at a Cajun music festival in Lafayette with her dad. It was always a fifty-fifty chance her mom wouldn't deliver the message, so I'd planned to try her again after Kyle called me. Which he hadn't.

"That's not what I meant. I'm sorry."

"Ha! You were waiting on Kyle, weren't you?"

"Yeah." Melissa was definitely going to make fun of me for this, and I deserved it.

"You've got to chill. He likes you, or he wouldn't have shown up Friday night."

She was right. But there was a difference between recognizing Melissa's logic and truly feeling it in my bones. And

I didn't feel it. Not because I doubted Kyle, but because no boy had ever paid much attention to me before.

"I know, but..." I stopped, feeling my eyebrows gathering in a frown. "I want him to call."

"Fair enough," Melissa said. "He's pretty cute. Anyway, what else is up?"

I hesitated for a second. "So, you remember how Helen was acting weird when we went out to dinner with Sean and Leah?"

"Oh, God, don't tell me this is about Leah and Aimee and the abortion bullshit." Her voice dripped with disdain.

"Wait—when did you find out?" I didn't try to hide my shock, because this kind of bombshell wasn't something Melissa would usually hide from me.

"Literally this morning, at mass." In contrast to our dad's Christmas-and-Easter Catholicism, Melissa's mom was a devout Catholic. She dragged Melissa to church every Sunday as her sole intervention into Melissa's "wild" behavior. That was, her super liberal political activism. Her dad, on the other hand, golfed every Sunday morning.

"At *mass*?" I asked, horrified, as I imagined a priest condemning Helen from the pulpit for an abortion she didn't have.

"Well, after mass, not during," Melissa clarified reassuringly. "Jamie Taylor pulled me into the youth group room to tell me all about it."

Jamie Taylor was a senior I knew *of*, but had never talked to in my life—she was that level of popular. I didn't know that Melissa knew her, either, but it wasn't nearly as surprising, since they apparently went to the same church. Also, Melissa had a way of knowing everyone.

"And you didn't think to call me?"

"Athena, I'm calling you *right now.* I just got home! You know my mom. We had to stop at the Vietnamese supermarket on the way home because she wants to make pho, even though it's eight million degrees out. I'm cursed to come from not one, but *two* cultures that seem to think soup is for hot weather."

"I'm sorry," I said. "But this has me worried. It's not one of Leah and Aimee's typical rumors. Helen could get *expelled* for this."

Melissa sighed dramatically. "She's not going to get expelled, because it's not like teachers are going to believe this. And even then, your dad can provide proof that Helen wasn't here all summer. But beyond that, this rumor is all based on abortion hype due to what happened this summer. All Helen has to do is show she doesn't care about it, and then it'll go away."

Sometimes, I wanted to punch Melissa for her overly mature "I know how to handle things better than you" attitude. I was glad that the distance of the phone line prevented me from taking physical action I would regret.

"Yeah, but she *does care,*" I snapped. "That's why she came to me, and that's why I'm asking for your help. And I really don't think this is the type of thing that will just go away. Not at our school."

"Okay. So what do you think we can do about it? I mean, can we confront Leah? No. Can we confront Aimee? No. Can we disprove the lies without bringing your dad into it, embarrassing Helen, and making things worse? Probably not."

Melissa was right, but I'd been telling Helen otherwise. I'd held out hope Melissa could help. She always had a solution for everything else.

"We can't do *anything*?" Disappointment settled in my chest, mingled with powerlessness.

"I didn't say that," Melissa said. "But as of now, I don't have any ideas. Whatever you do, though, you shouldn't say anything to Sean."

"Why?" I asked. "He's my best friend!"

"Thanks. I thought *I* was your best friend."

"You know what I mean. Why can't I talk with him about this?"

"Because you're his friend, but Leah's his *girlfriend*," Melissa said, stressing the world of difference between the two.

"Yeah, but—"

"I get it. He's your *oldest friend*." She emphasized the last two words like *oldest* definitely didn't mean *best*. I'd heard it before. It was part of the Sean-me-Melissa dynamic in which I kept the two of them apart as much as possible. "But this is *Leah* we're talking about. No one really likes her, but everyone is afraid of her, except for Sean, who actually does like her *and* is also probably afraid of her."

My mouth was trapped in a quivering space between telling Melissa off and agreeing with her.

"That's all true," I said, finally. I started talking again before she could steamroller me. "But it's Helen. I've *got* to talk with him about this."

"Are you really that oblivious?" she asked incredulously. "Your sister *flirts* with Sean, and he flirts back." I held the phone away from my ear to distance myself from Melissa's suddenly loud voice. "I'm sure Leah has noticed it, even if you haven't. You have no idea what Leah and Aimee have been saying to Sean just to forestall the inevitable on that one. And you know Sean—he's not comfortable with the idea of any kind of impropriety, so he'd never *do* anything other than flirt, but it's way different than last year, when she looked like a weird long-legged golden retriever puppy. He probably feels icky that he's looking at your sister as anything other than a pest, not to mention that he probably feels guilty for looking at any girl other than Leah."

I'd always suspected Helen had a crush on Sean. But it never felt that different from the kind of crush she had on Evan Dando or Eddie Vedder or River Phoenix or Will Smith or Jordan Knight. Sean was cute, therefore she liked him. And I didn't think Sean returned any feelings for her, but he'd acted so oddly yesterday that all kinds of things were suddenly coming into question for me.

"She can't seriously think of Helen as a threat," I protested. "And even if Helen threw herself at Sean, and even if he liked her, he'd figure out some way to reject her *and* save her from embarrassment. And then he'd honorably tell Leah about it. That's who he is."

"It. Does. Not. Matter!" Melissa exclaimed, blasting my ear. "Because of who Leah is! And who Helen is! Helen's not some kid anymore. She's a *babe*."

I wasn't sure why I was arguing with Melissa. All the things she was shouting into my ear were things I thought, too. It shouldn't surprise me that Leah had noticed them, or that her faith in her boyfriend's faithfulness would be less than mine, or that she felt threatened by Helen. And I could understand her insecurity—being Helen's less attractive sister and Melissa's less outrageous friend frequently meant I melted into the background. It wasn't quite the same, but I got it.

On the other hand, I didn't go around starting shit about people.

"So, what now?" Melissa's futility was starting to infect me.

She let out a sigh so heavy and breathy I had to hold the phone away from my ear. "I don't know."

This was the worst thing about Melissa. She was quick enough to make me feel like I was the least observant human on the planet, but she didn't have any suggestions for fixing the problem. This was especially true when it came to Sean.

"There's got to be something," I said. "Think about how *she* works."

"Well, we could spread an equally vicious, probably true story about her to everyone in school. Like that she put out so her doctor would give her free fake boobs."

"That's not what I mean." Melissa could be too much. Like, all the time. "And besides, aren't we supposed to be above all that?"

"Oh! I know! We could start suggesting that she and Aimee are secret lesbians!"

"Oh, come on! That's not funny. Can we please try to find a real solution?"

"That would probably make the most sense." She pretended she hadn't heard me. "They quit cheerleading because of Coach Braden, because she was, *you know*, a lesbian. Maybe it's true that homophobia masks latent homosexual tendencies!" She sounded excited to land on a plausible path to revenge.

But this kind of "solution" made me feel worse. Melissa would never seriously start a rumor about Leah and Aimee that depended on the homophobia of the masses, but even joking about it turned my stomach.

"See? That's what I mean!" I exclaimed. "I know you're trying to point out that Leah and Aimee are homophobic for saying they were quitting the squad because Coach Braden might-could be a lesbian, but it's not working. It just makes *you* sound homophobic. And I need you to focus!"

Melissa was silent on the other end. I almost started to apologize for exploding at her, but another part of me overrode that. She'd gone too far, and I wasn't sorry.

"You're right," she finally said. "I have no idea what to do. But let me think on it. And in the meantime, whatever you do: Don't. Tell. Sean."

Her words echoed in my brain long after I hung up the phone. What was I supposed to do if I couldn't talk with the only person who could possibly help?

11

PopCRACKBzzzt. A painful blast of noise surged from the amp.

"Oh, shit, sorry." I'd plugged in my bass without checking to see if the amp was on. A clumsy beginner's mistake. I would never have done that at home, and I would never have done it in front of Melissa.

I was more than a little unnerved to be standing in Kyle's rec room on a Tuesday afternoon, on what seemed to be a date, still in my ugly school uniform. We'd ridden the bus from school to his house, and now I had a pristine, gorgeous, vintage black-and-white Rickenbacker bass around my neck.

Nothing had felt real the entire afternoon—not the Rickenbacker, which was much heavier than my crappy Squier bass, causing me to hunch over; or Kyle's rec room, with its complete microphone setup, a ton of amps, collection of vintage guitars, and full drum kit. The overly bright afternoon sun bounced off the whole room, making me feel like I'd entered into a fantasy world of dudedom.

The room was fully decked out, ready to be the ultimate classic rock bro space. On the walls hung posters of different generations of dude bands. The Sex Pistols. Nirvana. The Beatles crossing Abbey Road. The giant Rolling Stones mouth. A poster from a Led Zeppelin live show. Eric Clapton in guitar-orgasm face. The Who.

This was some kind of teenage boy dream room, if one of those teen boys was now in his forties.

Oddly enough, the rest of their house looked like the movers had arrived, dumped the furniture, and run away as quickly as possible. We'd passed through the living room, where everything was either in a box or covered in padded moving blankets, and the only seating was a set of metal folding chairs positioned in front of the TV, which was on the floor. It looked like Kyle's mom had been wrestling the kitchen into order right before we arrived. The glass-front cabinets displayed all their dishware, but several boxes labeled "kitchen stuff" were unopened on the counter, and one of the drawers had been left open with half of the silverware placed inside. The rest of the silverware sat in the dish strainer by the sink.

I hadn't asked him why this room got so much attention, which clearly made it special, and then I made a rookie mistake with the amp. It was like everything real disappeared when Kyle was around, including my sense of musicianship.

"It's okay." Kyle checked that my bass was plugged in before turning on the amp again.

"I'm not normally that clumsy," I apologized. "I mean, I *am* that clumsy, just not with musical instruments." I wasn't sure which was making me more nervous:, being alone with Kyle or holding the Rickenbacker. Aside from Melissa's ridiculously expensive violin, I'd never touched an instrument that cost more. My cello didn't come close, and the other instruments here would have laughed my Squier out of the room.

"Um, are you sure it's cool that I'm playing this? It seems like this room is..." I gestured vaguely to the walls and the amps and the guitars.

"A lot?" He smiled. "Yeah, it's my dad's first love. He moved all this stuff out of storage as soon as he got back to the States. He started his job a month before Mom and I got here, and it was the first room he unpacked. Mom hasn't been able to catch up with him since."

"And she's okay with that?" As soon as I said it, I realized how it might have come across. That the abandoned kitchen signaled something like giving up, especially in the face of the boy-town band room.

"I think so?" Kyle shrugged, and his guitar bounced against his chest distractingly. "I know the kitchen's driving her up the wall, but she wouldn't have wanted my dad to touch anything in there before she got here. Same with the living room. She lives in terror of the day he buys a huge leather couch and ruins her aesthetic. In fact, she's out right now looking at couches in New Orleans because nothing in Baton Rouge works for her."

He rolled his eyes a bit at the thought of going to New Orleans for a couch, but something about the way he said it reminded me of his hedged answer about Brussels. He didn't want to say Baton Rouge sucked, and that he didn't want to move here...but Baton Rouge really did suck, and it seemed clear to me that he hadn't wanted to move here. But I could also tell he didn't want to talk about it, and so I felt like I was getting to know only the parts of him that he wanted me to see.

Or maybe I was overreacting. Maybe *this moment* was when I should be getting to know him, instead of jumping ahead to assume that because he didn't tell me something within three seconds of knowing him, it would forever remain a mystery.

One solution to this would be to tell him something about myself, in hopes of getting him to share more. But I didn't have any international travels under my belt—thanks, Mom—and the big things in my life were things I wanted to escape from today: Helen and the abortion gossip, and Leah and Sean.

I chewed on my lip for a second, trying to figure out if I should try to dig deeper or ignore it all in favor of playing music. I justified to myself that playing music was, in fact, a good way to get to know someone.

"Anyway, what song do you want to jam on?" Kyle asked, noticing my indecision.

The word *jam* made me cringe inwardly, and I found myself involuntarily wrinkling my nose. Unless it was a specific reference to the Jam, who, coincidentally enough, played Rickenbackers, I wanted nothing to do with it.

"What, don't think I can play?" Kyle asked. He leaned close to me as if the question had been a challenge. The deep caramel of his eyes and every dark eyelash stared back at me. I almost couldn't breathe.

I hiccuped a nervous laugh. "No, it's the word *jam*," I said quietly, feeling the heat emanating off him—or maybe my own temperature was rising. Either way.

"Too much like Phish?"

"I was going to say the Grateful Dead, but yeah."

"So, what did one sober Grateful Dead fan say to the other?"

"Umm, I have no idea. I didn't know there were any."

"This music sucks." He looked at me with his face slanted away, trying to maintain some element of coolness. A half-wicked smile spread across his face.

I laughed. It was a groan-worthy joke, but he looked so cute telling it. Damn it. I couldn't think about how hot he was without losing track of everything else that should be in my head.

"So, what do you want to play?" he asked. "Do you know 'Smells Like Teen Spirit'?"

A sarcastic "Who doesn't?" popped into my head, and if it had been anyone else, I would have said it out loud. But Kyle's stint in Brussels probably prevented him from understanding what a big deal Nirvana's "Smells Like Teen Spirit" had been in the US. Melissa got so annoyed with Nirvana's popularity that she'd trashed her copies of their records. Before that, she and I had arranged the band's songs for violin and cello, but neither of us could get through a song without laughing.

"Ah, the hit of the year." I nodded. "Let's do this."

Kyle crashed through the abrasive opening chords, his golden-brown hair flopping into his eyes. He screwed his eyes up tightly when he played, and I was so busy watching his facial contortions and flailing hair that I nearly missed my entrance. I recovered barely in time, entering with the solid eighth notes of the song, *duh-duh-duh-duh-duh-duh-duh-duh.*

The song's simple bass line started to bore me. Maybe not bore, exactly, but I couldn't focus on it. Without noticing I was doing it, I started playing the alternate bass line I'd made up for my band with Melissa, a swooping counterpoint to the vocal melody that twisted and turned but still held down the rhythm. It wasn't that hard—it was still eighth notes—but it had a lot more fill-ins in the melody.

Kyle stopped the song after the first chorus. I kept playing my contrapuntal line for a few seconds, lost in the simple rhythm of the song.

"You're really good," Kyle said.

I held my breath. I hoped he wouldn't add "for a girl." The last time I'd played with a guy—one of Melissa's endless parade of boyfriends—he'd said that, and I felt a smoldering flame of humiliation fester in my chest. But the phrase never arrived, and Kyle just kept staring at me in amazement.

"How long have you been playing?" he asked.

"About a year, but it's not hard," I said, shrugging. "It's an easy song."

Kyle raised his eyebrows. I didn't notice the expression of surprise and disbelief so much as how warm his amber-brown eyes seemed.

"You weren't playing the bass line, though," he said. "You came up with something that sounded like Bach's invention on a theme by Nirvana."

A mess of embarrassment dropped on my head. I had gotten caught in the one lie I'd told him. I hadn't told him I'd played anything else before picking up the bass. I'd acted like a dumb girl, and I never did that.

"Yeah, I play the cello," I said. "Lots of Bach there." And, over the summers, I took counterpoint lessons. And theory. But I didn't want to seem like I was bragging. Besides, my bass line wasn't that complicated. Certainly not Bach level.

"Wow," he said. I wished his eyebrows would return to a normal position on his face. I was worried they'd freeze in that position.

"It's not a big deal."

"No, you're like a musical genius or something."

I looked down at the bass, with its perfectly smooth black

finish. It suddenly felt like my own personal, very expensive albatross. I knew what that sentence meant. Once a guy put me in the smart-girl category, he didn't see me as a girl anymore. The next thing I knew, he'd start asking me if Melissa or Helen were single.

"Is something wrong?" he asked.

I avoided his gaze. No sense in staring deeply into them now anyway, even if those eyes were so deep and brown. "It's the g-word," I said. I slouched backward, feeling the weight of the Rickenbacker pulling me down. Albatross.

"You're mad that I'm calling you a genius?" he asked. His eyebrows finally migrated down to their normal position, but now his face was all scrunched up with concern.

"No, not mad exactly," I said. "It's just that anytime anyone uses the word, they kind of stop hanging out with me."

"You're kidding, right?" he said. "I seem to recall Melissa calling you a genius the first time I met you."

"That's different," I said, trying to look him in the face and failing miserably.

"Athena, I didn't mean it like that," he said. "I think it's hot that you're a genius."

I jerked my head up to look at him. Boys didn't say that. Before I could process what was happening, he was right in front of me. I felt his hand lift my chin, and I instinctively closed my eyes.

I was about to have my first kiss, with the Cute Boy. I couldn't process that, either, but somehow, it was happening.

Krrrngggccchhhnnnggg. Neither of us had noticed that we still had guitars around our necks, and the two instruments scraped together with a loud burst of amplified metal on metal.

Kyle popped the strap from the end of his guitar with an efficient motion and grabbed the neck of the Rickenbacker, helping me lift it over my head. Cupping his hands around my face, he pulled me in for a kiss, hard and awkward, and then another that was hard but not awkward, and then another that wasn't either hard or awkward, but soft and warm and perfect. I thought of my favorite Catullus poem and *The Princess Bride* and every girl group song I heard on the oldies station, and still nothing compared to that moment. My entire body felt like it was on fire.

We stumbled over to the rec room's aging leather couch. I felt completely out of control, but, maybe for the first time in my life, I truly didn't care.

12

The digital clock on my bedside table blinked 4:10 at me, a glowing red reminder that Sean was late for our usual Wednesday comic book excursion to Steve's Cards & Comics.

Steve's occupied a storefront in an aging strip mall close to the edge of the wrong side of town. Every week, our comic book experience was pretty much the same routine: I'd buy one or two things, usually something like *Love and Rockets*, while Sean got his "pull" of the eight to ten comics he'd preordered. He would double-check that everything made it into his pile while I'd browse the indie comics sequestered in one tiny corner of the store, looking for any new trades that might be worthwhile, and then flip through the back issues that lined the walls in plywood bins.

Wednesday comic shopping was the only guaranteed time we'd spend together during football season, between his practices and my youth orchestra and chamber music rehearsals. So Sean's lateness rubbed at my nerves, but not because I thought anything had happened to him on his way home from practice. Instead, I was worried because if, for some reason, I didn't see him today, I'd likely end up waiting a whole extra week before I'd have another chance to talk to him about Leah and Helen.

For the past two days, Melissa and I had brainstormed every chance we got—on the phone on Labor Day, at lunch, at school orchestra practice, in carefully coded notes passed in the hall, but not in Mrs. Breaux's class. We'd come up with nothing. Meanwhile, I'd started hearing whispering in the hallways. Yesterday, Jackie Rodriguez stopped talking as soon as I walked into the girls' locker room to change for gym. Half the class surrounded her with shocked faces leering at my arrival, none of them bothering to play it off.

And so, without a real plan, I decided I was going to talk with Sean about it. Only the longer he took to get home, the longer I had to think about how bad of an idea that was, and the more likely I became to chicken out. My mouth started to go cotton dry with worry.

I threw myself on my bed. I was a *terrible* sister, and kind of a lousy feminist. I'd spent yesterday afternoon at a boy's house, making out, not thinking about anything other than being at a boy's house and making out. When I got home at seven, Helen had shot me a look so fierce I nearly disappeared in a pile of ash. Today, at least, her after-school modeling class meant I didn't have to deal with her impatient judgment.

I looked over at the photocopied Bikini Kill flyer I'd pinned to the corkboard over my desk to remind me of their official debut vinyl EP release next month, which I'd already mail ordered from Kill Rock Stars. What would Kathleen Hanna do? She wouldn't sit around, getting steadily more nervous about talking to her friend. Or Tobi Vail? She had a shriek like Yoko Ono's. I couldn't imagine Tobi letting injustices slide by.

I needed some inspiration. I turned to the Bikini Kill demo cassette that had lived in the tape deck of the stereo I shared with Helen since we got back from Eugene, fast-forwarding and rewinding it until I could get to the exact starting place of the song I wanted to hear. I felt chills as the record started.

"We're Bikini Kill, and we want revolution girl-style now!"

It was always the same with "Double Dare Ya." It was like hearing it for the first time, every time, chills included. Kathi's bass thudding in time, Billy's guitar picking up the descending pattern, with Tobi's propulsive drumming driving the whole thing forward. Kathleen's vocals on top, all lungs and power, beckoning whoever was listening with an energetic "Hey, girlfriend!" and a laundry list of the most awesome dares. Not playground dares, but *feminist* dares—to stand up for my rights to be who and what I wanted.

It felt like it was directed at *me*. Well, not *just* me. I wasn't *that* obsessive. I was tethered to reality. But a girl like me anyway.

A girl who *wasn't* Kathleen or Tobi or Kathi. Or Billy, but he was a guy. Or, for that matter, a girl who wasn't Melissa. The kind of girl who *needed* to be dared. Who needed to be reminded that she could stand up for her rights, stand up for something. That she *had* rights in the first place. That she didn't have to be boring and good and smart and all the things that I was. Or even if she was boring and good and smart, she could still make a difference.

It was *my* anthem. Other girls might find solace in Heavens to Betsy's "My Secret," or identify with the pain that Kathleen sang about in "Feels Blind," or revel in the seedy but fun underbelly of "Carnival," but "Double Dare Ya" was for *me.*

I'd always wondered why Melissa didn't get into Bikini Kill, other than she thought their music was overly simple, but now I *got* it. She did stuff of her own volition. She was political to the point of self-righteousness, and she didn't need anyone to dare her, let alone double dare her.

But maybe that wasn't true, either. Even Melissa was dragging her feet on the Helen thing.

But *that*—the Helen thing—was something I needed to be double dared to do. I couldn't let it fester and explode. I wasn't ready to confront Leah, but I *could* talk to Sean. Not about my rights, exactly—he wasn't a sexist jerk or anything like that—but I would need to get him on my side to stop Leah's rumors before they took on a life of their own.

The song took about two minutes, and then, like a true punk song, it was over. I considered rewinding it so I could infuse my entire being with double-dared-ness, but then the doorbell *finally* rang.

I grabbed my purse and darted down the stairs so we could leave right away, before I lost my courage. When I opened the door, Sean stood slouched against the door frame, car keys in hand.

"Hey! What's the rush?" he asked as I grabbed his arm and dragged him to his car.

"You're late!" I said, trying to sound normal. Anxiety propelled me forward. Excuses floated up inside me, like cowardly ghosts: *You shouldn't talk with him about Leah. You'll sound accusatory. He'll say it's because you two don't like each other.*

"I'm not that—Athena, slow down!" He trotted up next to me as I got in the passenger side of his car, a used Volvo that Mrs. Estelle had bought for him because it was built like a tank.

Until this year, Sean's mom had driven us over to Steve's every week, so that we could keep up with the latest releases. But Sean had gotten his driver's license as soon as he turned fifteen at the beginning of the summer. Like my dad, who thought sixteen was a more magically appropriate age for a driver's license, Mrs. Estelle had been against the idea, but Sean's dad had taken him to the DMV on one of his visits to Baton Rouge, because he loved to be the good cop to Mrs. Estelle's bad cop. Since Mrs. Estelle couldn't exactly undo the driver's license, she'd put embarrassing restrictions on Sean's driving instead—namely, he wasn't allowed to drive after dark, which meant Leah did most of their driving on dates.

Fortunately, our weekly trips to Steve's had made Mrs. Estelle's list of approved driving destinations, and because of that, there was no better time for me to have this conversation with Sean without fear of interruption.

"Sorry!" I tried to calm myself down, but some primal part of me kept planting the thought that the sooner we got in the car, the sooner I could ask him about Leah. But that same part of my brain wouldn't let me ask him on the lawn, because it feared that he'd clam up and demand that I go back inside, and then I would never get anywhere, literally or figuratively.

"Why are you acting so weird?" He squinted at me through the aviator sunglasses Leah had given him for his birthday.

"I don't know." *Melissa is right. You shouldn't ask him anything*, the voices of doubt said.

"Okay, weirdo," he said, falling into silence as he concentrated on driving. Baton Rouge had developed into a massive suburban sprawl of strip mall after strip mall, most of which were accessed by tiny service roads that provided another terrifying layer of traffic.

"Um, hey, can I talk with you about something?" I mumbled, looking out the window. So much for my riot grrrl courage.

"Oooh, did something happen between you and that Kyle guy?" He glanced at me from the driver's seat. "If you need to talk about the birds and the bees, I'm happy to direct you to my mom, who is sure to be both factually correct and is *not me*."

I groaned loudly, covering my face with my hands. Yes, Kyle and I had made out, but I didn't need sex ed for that.

"No, I'm good." I couldn't talk with Sean about Helen now, not while we were on the topic of Kyle. And I *did* want to talk about Kyle with Sean. The undermining voice wheedled in my brain: *You can talk about normal things before you get to the Leah stuff.* "But I did have a lovely afternoon."

"'Lovely'?" he asked, eyebrows wagging.

"Okay, we made out and it was great and now that you know we can never speak of it again, because it's too embarrassing to talk about." I sank down in the passenger seat so far that I could barely see out the window. I couldn't look at Sean, so I stared at the glove compartment in front of me.

"Well, look at you! My girl Athena's all grown-up!" He laughed. "You should see yourself." He swiped at the corner of his eye dramatically, even though he hadn't laughed anywhere near hard enough to make himself cry.

"Anyway," I said, taking a deep breath to refocus. "That's not quite what I wanted to talk with you about. It's something more serious."

"Oooh-kaay." Sean drew the word out, signaling that he understood I wasn't joking.

"It's about Leah...and Helen," I said, watching his face for a reaction.

As he pulled into the parking lot of Steve's, his mouth turned into a frown and his arms stiffened. The sudden chill from him pushed at me so much I almost gave up and apologized.

"Go on," he said, letting out a big hiss of air saturated with doubt. "Tell me what you think is happening. But let me get my pull first."

The way he said it—tell me what you *think* is happening—seeded even more doubt in me, and so did his prioritizing his comics over the conversation. Technically, that shouldn't surprise me, as focused as he was on the accuracy of his pull list, but it felt like a jab. As he got out of the car, he jerked ahead of me into the store and pushed the door open so forcefully that it swung back toward me with a hard bounce against my hands.

"Hey!" I said. "It's not like that!"

"Pull list," he said over his shoulder, and marched to the counter. He turned his back on me to face the eponymous Steve, who leaned down with a sigh to get Sean's comics from the cabinet under the counter where he stored regulars' comics.

Sean's shoulder formed a wall between me and the counter, and I knew better than to interrupt him at this point. I drifted toward the wall of indie comics, hoping I could keep up my courage until Sean finished his thorough review of every book he was supposed to have, and their condition. This part could take forever.

I didn't get it. I hadn't even *said* anything yet. We'd been having a good time, and then, as soon as I mentioned Leah and Helen, he'd flipped. Maybe I should have phrased it differently, not involving Leah, but focusing on the rumors instead, and their impact on Helen. Or not asked him right before we got to the comic shop. Or led him in more gently, by talking about how it was great that he came to support Helen, but that she'd cried in front of me after the show. He would have to care about that. He'd cared enough to show up for her after all.

I circled the shop aimlessly until Sean finally nodded at me, silent and stern, like an angry stone monument come to life. I swallowed hard as I walked over to where he was standing next to a crate of old *Batman* comics in the back corner of the shop. He'd chosen a location with the fewest eyes and ears—far enough from the counter that Steve couldn't overhear, and out of direct sight of the other guy working there, who was diligently stocking the shelves along the opposite wall with this week's comics.

"What's going on?" he asked, facing me with arms crossed.

"I don't know," I said, which was partially true and partially not, since Helen had told me about the abortion rumors. I *did* know, but I didn't know how to talk about it, or which way might possibly not offend Sean. "But something's been festering for a while—"

"Oh, come on." Sean scoffed, shaking his head. "'Festering'?"

I sucked in a sharp breath. I didn't understand what nerve I'd just pressed on, but it was clear that I'd hit something. I couldn't give up, though, because now I had *two* goals: first, figure out what I'd said that bothered him so much, and second, talk with him about Helen.

"Yes, *festering*," I said. He raised his eyebrows at me with cynical disbelief. "This isn't the usual thing between Helen and Leah." I tried to sound serious and measured, but landed somewhere closer to desperate and whiny. "It started back when we went to dinner at Superior—"

"And Leah tried to talk with Helen about the pro-life club?"

"Wait, what?" I asked. "That's not how the conversation went." I replayed it in my mind. Had I misinterpreted the whole thing? Had Leah "heard" *good* things about Helen, or her involvement in the pro-life club, and I'd created something out of nothing? No, no way. Even with my unfavorable view of Leah, I'd seen her effect on Helen. And then there was Leah's interruption of my lunch with Kyle. I'd asked her directly what was going on between her and Helen. If she'd had a real reason involving the pro-life club, she would have said it then.

Sean sighed and leaned against the crates of back issues. "Look, I understand you two don't like each other. And that Helen doesn't, either, because she follows whatever you do—"

"Are you kidding me? Helen doesn't follow whatever I do!" My sister had her own backbone, much more than I did.

Sean gave me a slow, blinking pause, illustrating his lack of patience with me. "I know you don't think that," he said. "And maybe I phrased it wrong. But she does value your opinion, more than you think. Otherwise she wouldn't be constantly stealing shit from you."

Sean's words reframed everything, at least in terms of my sister. Definitely not for Leah, but I could see why he'd feel that way. I let his words sink in as he flipped through the back issues in the crate he was leaning against.

"Is something going on with you and Leah?" I asked. "I don't get why you're mad at me. I wanted to talk with you about Leah and Helen because their conversation seemed super weird to me, that's all."

"Is that really all?" The dubious, raised-eyebrow look was back.

"Yes and no, because there're other things that I'm worried

about with Helen, and I didn't get to that yet. It's a…separate issue." Despite double daring myself, I couldn't bring myself to connect the dots with Sean. He was already mad at me for even alluding to the possibility of Leah's viciousness toward Helen, so I couldn't exactly come out and say that I thought his girlfriend had started gossip about Helen that could get her kicked out of school.

Sean nodded, which didn't tell me if he already knew about the abortion gossip or if he was willing to back down for half a second. He didn't turn away from *Batman*, though.

"To answer your question, no, there's nothing going on with me and Leah," he said, sounding deliberately bored in a way that was clearly put-on, but effective enough at upsetting me. "Like Helen, she has her own problems to deal with, though. And I wish you'd be a little more sympathetic about those before jumping on her case."

"What's going on with Leah?" I tried to sound casual. Instead, my voice came out strangled. I knew from the silence that followed that it was exactly the wrong thing to say—too prying, not enough sincerity.

Sean let out a long, frustrated sigh. "See, this is the problem. I want to tell you because you're my oldest friend," he said. "But the two of you are like oil and water, and I'm always in the middle, and so I can never figure out if you'll be supportive or not. What happened? You guys started out as friends."

We were never friends, I wanted to say. And when I thought we might be, Leah stabbed me in the back. Or at least started talking about me behind my back.

"She's not… She never wanted to be friends with me," I said, remembering how much it had stung to hear that she'd told everyone how boring and stuck-up I was. "She treated me like a human stopgap for a few months, that's all."

Sean slumped against the old comics. He didn't have to say that he felt like giving up. I could read it all over him.

"And she basically says the same thing about you," he said, pointing at me. "That as soon as you realized Melissa didn't like her, you chose a side, and it wasn't Leah's."

That wasn't fair, I wanted to protest. But I didn't because there might have been a grain of truth in there. It wasn't so much that I'd dropped Leah because Melissa didn't like her, but that Melissa not liking her helped me feel better about being dropped by Leah.

None of it made me feel good about myself. Also, none of it mattered now. Both of us could be at fault for being jerks to each other. But I'd also never said anything about Leah that I wouldn't say to her face. And I would never do anything to anyone at our school—no matter how horrible I thought they were, or how deserving—that could get them expelled.

"You don't like each other, and there's nothing I can do about it," he said, frustration in his voice. He dropped the *Batman* in his hand back into the bin, where the bagged-and-boarded back issue hit the plywood bottom with a firm *thunk*. "But I don't want to fight with you about it."

"I don't want to fight with you, either," I said, resisting the urge to back down entirely. "But I wish that you'd believe me when I say I have real concerns about Leah and Helen."

He turned to me and smiled, suddenly and a little sadly, like he wanted everything to be normal, but wasn't willing to give an inch on the possibility that his girlfriend had done anything wrong to Helen, or possibly ever to anyone.

"I do believe you're worried," he said. "But I really don't think it's what you think it is. And so we're back to where we started, full circle."

I leaned against the bin next to Sean. Maybe I couldn't

get him to stop Leah. Maybe no one could. And somehow she had gotten into my head, too, via Sean, so that I started to doubt my version of things. I even started to reconsider bringing up the rumors about Helen because he'd probably tell me I was wrong about that, too.

Double dare ya. Yeah, sorry, Kathleen. And sorry, Helen. I failed you both.

I couldn't fail Helen, though. Sean had to at least care about *her.* He'd been so proud of her at the fashion show, and that was just a few days ago. I had to turn this around to be about her, not Leah, if I wanted to get anywhere. And not have him pissed at me for months.

"Sooo." I took a deep breath. "Someone's been spreading the most awful lies about Helen."

"And you think Leah has something to do with it." Sean turned to look at me. His eyes were flat again, like he couldn't have been more disinterested. "Yeah, I know that's what you and Melissa think. That's exactly what Leah said you'd say."

Heat flushed my neck, a flare of frustration that our conversation kept circling back to the simple fact that I didn't like Leah and never went anywhere more productive, like toward Helen, whom I was trying to help.

"That's not what I said! Don't get pissed off at *me*," I said, holding up my hands defensively. "I'm worried about *Helen*, and I thought you would be, too. That's why I wanted to talk to you. Look, leaving Leah out of it for one second—just one—can we agree that something's going on with Helen? Because I have a feeling you know what it is."

Sean let out another big sigh and slumped against the comic bin, his body weighted with futility.

"Of course I heard about it." He looked me in the eyes.

"Leah thinks Helen started them herself in order to get sympathy. You know, the whole 'no publicity is bad publicity' thing."

"Are you kidding me?" I asked, incredulous. My voice crescendoed as I launched into all the reasons Leah was wrong. "You know Helen. Has she *ever* started a rumor about herself? And if she did, it would be about a modeling contract or something else that made her look *good*. Why the hell would she want people to think she had an abortion? You know how stubbornly pro-life she is! And you know how everyone at our school is! And even if abortion was suddenly a cool new fashion trend, *and* Helen changed her views, *and* she was into gossip, she's not dumb enough to start a rumor that could get her kicked out of school."

The comic shop stock boy, Brad, glanced over at us. I guess he could hear my diatribe, but I didn't care. Sean needed to hear how flimsy Leah's reasoning was, because surely he wasn't so dazzled by her charms that logic couldn't pierce his brain. He might defend Leah, but saying Helen made the rumors up *about herself* was ridiculous.

Sean's shoulders dropped with acceptance. He nodded slowly.

"You're right about that." At another time, I might have savored a moment of Sean saying I was right. In this one, though, I was waiting for a "but," and invariably, it came. "But Helen's strong. She survived middle school. Hell, she *thrived* in middle school. I'm sure she'll get through this fine."

The problem was, Helen wasn't fine. It had taken me a while to see that, and I didn't have Leah trying to convince me up was down.

"Yeah, I don't think so." I thought back to how Helen had crumbled, how desperate she'd seemed. "She was super upset after her fashion show. Snotty crying and everything."

Sean's eyebrows went up in surprise, and then a look of deep skepticism followed. "Helen? Crying? The last time I saw her cry was when she was seven and I scalped her Barbie."

"She wasn't faking. Then or now." I could feel the annoyance rising in my throat. He was taking Leah's side. Melissa was right.

Sean looked at me like he was trying to weigh the thought of Helen crying on a scale of possibility. Anything I said would probably be a weight in the wrong direction, so I waited.

"Look, what people are saying about Helen is terrible." He chose each word with care. "But no one believes it. And Leah has nothing to do with it. Trust me. She's got enough of her own shit right now."

I leaned against the plywood bin next to Sean. This conversation hadn't resolved any doubts, and it made the gulf between me and Sean a lot wider because people *did* believe what was being said about Helen. Enough anyway.

"So what *is* going on with Leah?" I asked again, trying to get us back onto steady ground.

Sean pursed his mouth together. I knew that look. I'd seen it enough in middle school when Sean's parents were splitting up. He never just came out and said something—he had to sculpt it in his head, turning it over until it formed the right shape, so he could eventually push it out of his mouth.

"Her parents are getting a divorce."

In a way, that wasn't major news. About half the people I knew had divorced parents—mine, Sean's, tons of people. But Leah's parents were the kind of rich people who stayed together and had affairs on the side because it was easier than dividing the assets.

"Oh, that sucks." My voice was hollow from holding myself back from what I actually wanted to say—which was that her parents splitting up wasn't a reason for Leah's sociopathic rumors about Helen.

"Yeah," Sean said. "It's a mess. Her mom cheated on her dad with his *brother*. And now her dad is trying to make sure her mom doesn't get anything in the divorce—no money, no property, no custody rights to Leah or her younger brothers, nothing."

"Wow." I could see where Leah was having a tough time, but it didn't excuse a lot of her behavior. Or any of it, really. "But you know her dad can't do that, right? Louisiana's a community property state. Her mom would have to be really awful. And she's not, right?"

"No, lawyer girl, she's not." Sean shook his head at me. "Her mom's fine, which you'd know if you had ever given Leah a chance." I held my tongue at Sean's dig. I felt like this was a test to see if I had any empathy for Leah, and I wasn't going to blow it. "And that's part of it. Her mom and dad had a huge fight about cheerleading, and now that she's not on the squad, she's kind of lost. The reason… Well, it sucks. Her dad pulled her off the squad, saying it was bad for her grades to spend 'too much time with the football team.' I guess that means me."

So the whole "Coach Braden is a lesbian, so we have to quit" scam was a cover for Leah's dad making her quit. I could understand why Leah wouldn't want people to know her dad had so much power over her, but she didn't need to drag Coach Braden into it. Just like any girl could be expelled if the school found out she had an abortion, teachers could be fired for being gay.

And, unfortunately, Sean's suspicion about Leah's father's motive felt spot-on. Leah's father didn't like Sean, or the fact that St. Ann's was trying to bring in more black kids via scholarships, since our school's runaway success as an institution was largely the result of many white parents pulling their kids out of public school to send them to Catholic school after integrated busing started about ten years ago. Last year, at a football game, he'd shouted for our football team to "beat those n-words from West St. John." Only he hadn't said *n-word*, but the actual word. Sean never said anything, but I knew it bothered him.

"Well, you know that never works," I said, trying to sound reassuring. "Seriously, if you tell a girl not to date some guy, she's going to want to date him more. It's like crack or something. The whiff of rebellion is a very powerful aphrodisiac."

But even as I said them, I knew my words weren't true. If Leah's dad could make her quit the cheerleading squad, which she'd loved for a long time before Sean came along, he could make her dump Sean.

Sean smiled weakly, his brown eyes filled with a hurt that he would never talk about. I hoped that I was wrong about Leah. For his sake—definitely not mine.

"You know girls better than I do," he said.

That was exactly what I was worried about.

13

"Wait, so you're telling me that you told Sean about the rumors? And you were surprised that he got mad at you? And, oh, my God, are you telling me Leah's mom cheated on her dad?"

Melissa looked up at me from the piano bench. Her back was to the piano keyboard, pressing down a dissonant trio of keys that had long since stopped ringing out. Her relaxed position was a sharp counterpoint to the astonished look on her face. Her hands absently plucked at the violin in her lap, turning one of our serious orchestra pieces—Wagner, which also made it self-important—into a jaunty, pizzicato tune.

Our Thursday orchestra rehearsal wouldn't start for another hour and a half, so we were theoretically practicing for our chamber group. But a string quartet works best with four people, and since Jessica and Derek were both sick, we were hanging out in one of the LSU music building's soundproof practice rooms. It was the perfect gossip capsule. I had expected her to want details on my after-school date with Kyle, but she'd homed right in on Sean and Leah and Helen.

"Yeah, and no, and yeah." I kind of regretted telling Melissa the whole story now, especially the part about Leah's parents getting a divorce. Despite being the least important, it was the juiciest fruit of the conversation. "You were right. But he was already primed to be mad at me. Leah had already planted the seeds of 'oh, Helen made this up herself.'" I rolled my eyes, which didn't nearly convey how angry it made me that Leah would expect anyone to believe that, even Sean. "Anyway, I think I got through to him a little by the time we left Steve's."

Melissa's nose wrinkled at the mention of the comic shop. "I still don't get why you go there with him."

"You know I like comics, too." Melissa could be so judgy when it came to Sean, and that sometimes leaked over onto me.

"Yeah, I know." She shrugged, but her hands kept fluttering on her violin. I *think* she'd switched to the Shostakovich, but without actual bowing, I couldn't say for sure. "Still, you shouldn't be surprised that he's on Leah's side. I told you he would be. Sean's super into her, God knows why."

"So, what now?" I must have looked as sad as I felt because Melissa's expression suddenly softened, and she finally put the violin down on the piano.

"Hey, if it'll make you feel better, we can go do something really dumb to take your mind off things, like try to find the worst clothes of the seventies at the thrift store, or call KLSU from Dr. Walsh's office and ask to send out a dedication to him for a Dead Milkmen song or something."

The thought of dedicating a song like "Punk Rock Girl" or "Bitchin' Camaro" to our cranky, white-haired orchestra conductor might, under normal circumstances, be kind of funny. Not that he'd ever hear it, but enough people in orchestra might, and they'd definitely laugh when he took to the podium. And he'd never know why.

But this wasn't a normal day. At least not for me.

"I don't want to do something dumb." I spat out *dumb* with proportional ferocity to my frustration over having failed Helen. "I want to do something that *matters*."

Revelation spread across Melissa's face. It started as a light in her hazel eyes, and then a small flicker of a smile that bloomed into as toothy a grin as she ever got. "I've got it! You want to do something that matters."

I stared at her. "Yes, that's exactly what I just said."

"Yeah, so." She grabbed her very expensive violin and waved it in my face to shush me. I backed away, putting myself out of range. "I have the perfect thing. You know how we always talk about spray-painting the fake abortion clinic?"

"You're not serious!" I told her. "It's only five thirty. It's September. It's *daylight*. There's going to be eighty-seven million people on Chimes Street. We can't spray-paint the fake abortion clinic *now*."

"I *know*." She grinned maniacally. "That's why we're not going to go with our original plan." She said it with another dismissive wave that did nothing to reassure me. "We're going in."

"You're joking, right?" Even as I protested, part of me thought she might stop pushing me to help her spray-paint the place if we did this. And I *was* a little curious. I'd like to know what kind of inaccurate science they were touting as human biology.

"Hear me out!" She was packing up her violin like it was a done deal, gently laying it in its case. "We go in posing as volunteers. True believers, you know?"

I was fairly certain my face looked the same as it did when I was trying to figure out the Saturday *New York Times* crossword puzzle before the caffeine hit me.

"How is this going to help Helen?"

"I don't know what it will do, but..." Her voice trailed off for a second, and then she bounced on the piano bench. "Look, we need insight, right? Everything that they say seems like it's the first cousin of truth, you know? It's the same at the clinic, you know? We could learn from them. Something anyway."

None of this was really related to Helen, other than the associated topic of abortion. I weighed going to the clinic in relation to the theoretical vandalism that Melissa always suggested. The risk was proportionate to the payoff. That is, not all that much, if I could keep Melissa in check.

"If you promise that we'll be back in time for rehearsal." I looked at her, trying to appear as stern as possible.

She clapped her hands. "We will! I promise! We'll be back *at least* fifteen minutes before Dr. Walsh raises his baton."

The fake abortion clinic—otherwise known as the River Rouge Choices for Women—was in an old frame house in the middle of the block on Chimes Street, nestled between a used textbook store and a head shop. In sharp contrast to its neighbors, the clean clapboard was painted a cheery yellow, and white shutters framed the windows.

On the way over, we'd rehearsed our roles. We were going to pose as members of our school's pro-life club, which we knew enough about from the incessant invocations of its name every time the topic came up in religion class. In case they knew the officers of the club, we were going to be recent converts.

"Okay, we're solid, right?" Melissa asked, doubt inching into her voice as we got to the front porch of the building.

"I *think* we're solid." For once, I sounded less nervous than Melissa. I didn't have anything to lose in this scenario, whereas she'd been on television pulling girls into an abortion clinic. On top of that, she was far more recognizable than I was. There weren't a ton of purple-haired half-Asian girls running around Chimes Street, but there were at least a half dozen generic white alternagirls like me within two blocks at any given time.

At the door, she paused and turned to me one last time. "Let's do this, Graves."

"You got it, Lemoine."

She pulled the door open and gestured for me to go in first.

The waiting area looked like a cross between a doctor's office and my grandmother's wood-paneled living room. A row of beige chairs lined one wall, while a large squishy off-white pleather couch occupied another. All around were posters of smiling babies, held by happy mothers, with testimonials underneath. In one, a slightly older couple snuggled a baby, thanking the birth mother—presumably in the room—for giving them the opportunity to be parents. Another poster featured an African American girl thanking the organization that ran the clinic for "keeping her and her baby off welfare." Its offensive stereotyping stood out from the others, with their generic, smiling white people and lack of assumptions about motives.

We stood in the center of the room, uncertain. We'd expected someone to be at the front desk, but it was harder to focus on our plan in a deserted room.

Finally, a petite youngish woman with curly black hair and a long prairie-print Laura Ashley dress walked out from the back. She had an upturned nose and an air of Cabbage Patch cuteness. When she saw us, she stopped and clasped her hands almost prayerfully. A sad smile was on her face, as though she knew exactly why we were here. In her mind, one of us needed an abortion, which she was absolutely not going to let us get.

"Welcome, welcome," she said softly. She shook her head, and her shiny curls bounced in time. "So young," she muttered. "So, so young."

Melissa bristled, her mouth twisting briefly into a frown. Then, remembering why we were there, her face cleared into a wide-eyed, shocked expression.

"Oh, uh, no, ma'am," she said. "I mean, we *are* young. But we're not here for counseling. We're, um, from the St. Ursula's pro-life club."

It was a brilliant bit of improvisation to say we were from St. Ursula's, the all-girls' school across town, instead of St. Ann's. We knew maybe ten people in the entire school, and none in the pro-life club, so it was a gamble. But at least the visit wouldn't be traced back to us.

"Oh, did Reagan send you?" The woman clapped her formerly praying hands with such a loud slap that the lace cuffs of her sleeves shook around her slender wrists. Melissa jumped at the sound. "Are you out of materials already? That's so wonderful!"

Melissa looked quickly toward me. I nodded, first to Melissa, and then—convincingly, I hoped—to the woman. "Yes, we're *all* out," I lied.

"Oh, then, just let me run and get a stack of brochures for you." She was already swooshing out of the room, her long floral dress swirling around her feet. "Such a wonderful, good girl, that Reagan," she said over her shoulder.

When the woman vanished down the hall, I turned toward Melissa. "Do you know Reagan?" I whispered.

She shook her head. "No, and the less we say now, the better."

My stomach tensed as minutes passed while the woman was in the back. After what seemed like an eternity, during which Melissa and I couldn't talk out of fear of giving ourselves away, the woman returned. She struggled with a large box, her tiny body bending backward under its weight. When she got to the desk, she dumped the box with a *thud*. Her face was red and sweaty from the effort.

"Do you girls think you can carry all this? I don't want you to run out again so soon." She gestured toward the box, which was packed tight with at least three types of pamphlets. From where I stood, it looked like one was for women entering abortion clinics, "Do YOU know the consequences of abortion? A primer for mother and the unborn child," and another was for girls like us, "How can YOU bring the fight for life to YOUR school?" The third I couldn't quite see from where I stood because the woman was now leaning over the box in an attempt to catch her breath.

Melissa shook her head with faux sincerity. "Oh, no, ma'am. We weren't expecting this many pamphlets. Could we, um, maybe take half? And, um, would it be possible to get a tour before we leave? Reagan was talking about how much good work you do here, and we'd love to see for ourselves."

Melissa was *good*. If we got through the next few minutes without messing up, this day would go down in our personal books as legend: the day we tricked a fake abortion clinic worker into showing us how their whole operation worked.

"Oh, girls, I would be delighted." She dabbed sweat from her forehead with a tissue from a box on the desk. I imagined the tissues were for girls in the waiting room, and a pang of sympathy ran through my chest for all the girls who probably didn't find the help they wanted here. "But it will have to be short, I'm afraid. We're about to close, and there's a patient in one of the rooms."

Melissa flinched at the word *patient*, but kept the broad smile on her face. I hoped the woman didn't see Melissa's true reaction as she led us down the hall past rooms that looked like any other doctor's office. Except, I noticed, there were a *lot* of posters about fetal development. Here a fetus, there a fetus, everywhere a fetus. Fetuses that didn't look like the nebulous tadpole creatures I was used to seeing in biology books, but baby-like. Even the tiniest of fetuses looked like a chubby newborn.

The woman stopped directly across from the only exam room with a closed door. She clasped her hands together in the same sanctimonious motion she'd used when she first saw us.

"It is my great pleasure to show you these rooms," she said, projecting her voice across the hall. "It is such an *important* part of our work. In exchange for attending our counseling sessions, we help the girls with whatever they decide. If they want to keep the child, we help them sign up for assistance programs. But, more often, we help them find loving homes for their babies with good Christian families." She paused for a moment and bowed her head dramatically. "Of course, THEY NEED TO KEEP COMING TO COUNSELING SESSIONS TO GET ANY OF THIS," she bellowed toward the closed door. "AS EVIDENCE OF THEIR REPENTANCE."

I jumped back at the fire and brimstone. I glanced at Melissa, who under other circumstances would probably tell the woman that Planned Parenthood did all the same things without requiring repentance.

"Um, what if they decide that they want an abortion? How do you keep them from that?" Melissa asked in a pinched voice.

The woman blinked and frowned so deeply that her whole face seemed like it was composed of nothing but a downturned mouth. "Oh, sweetheart," she said, shaking her head. "We can't even let them *think* about that. Their *souls* would be in mortal danger from taking a life, and that's the foremost thing we must stress. But for those who don't believe as we do, it's our duty to let them know of the…*other* consequences."

She said the last sentence conspiratorially.

"What do you mean the, uh, 'other consequences'?" I asked, trying not to look at Melissa. She had to be hanging by a thread.

The woman widened her eyes. "Oh, you must be *very* new. Reagan is *very* well-informed about the biological consequences that girls can face if they go through with an abortion. I'm surprised she hasn't told you."

I finally looked at Melissa. Behind her smile, she looked volcanically angry, like the time last year when our biology teacher dismissed evolution as "only a theory." A twitch appeared at the corner of her mouth, and her hands were shaking. I shot her a look, and she crammed her hands into the pockets of her jeans.

"Oh, no, ma'am, we're *so* new," I said apologetically. "Just went to our first meeting a couple of weeks ago. We haven't *learned* everything yet."

The answer seemed to satisfy the woman, and she nodded.

"Well..." She gestured for us to follow her down the hall. "There's an increased risk of breast and uterine cancer—" Melissa shook her head behind the woman's back "—and an increased risk of infertility—" Melissa rolled her eyes "—and a whole host of complications that can arise from such a dangerous procedure, *especially* if the woman has VD."

None of this was scientifically accurate, or even remotely true. I'd looked up the statistics before I wrote the medical essay for Melissa's zine.

Beside me, Melissa let out an angry, strangled sound. She tried to play it off as a cough, but the woman turned around abruptly as we got to the final room.

"And this is our headquarters, though Reagan probably told you..." Her voice trailed off as she took in the sight of Melissa's red face and uncomfortable grimace of a smile.

"Sooo, uh, this is where you organize for protests?" I interrupted, trying to get the woman to look at me instead of Melissa.

"Oh, yes." Her gaze flitted to me for only a moment before returning to Melissa. "Do I know you from somewhere?"

This was it. "Oh, no," I said, shaking my head. "Like I said, we, uh, just got into the cause. You know, it became *so* important after this summer."

The woman nodded, scrutinizing Melissa.

"You know." She narrowed her eyes. "There have been a lot of *interesting* converts lately. Some whose *motives* I suspect. You wouldn't be the first ones—or even the first ones *this week*—who don't seem to know as much as you should. And I don't think Reagan is at fault."

We were at the back of the building, trapped behind enemy lines, with a long, long walk to the front door.

"Oh, no, ma'am, she isn't." I could feel the heat of my lies creeping up my face. I grabbed Melissa's arm and started pulling her backward through the building.

"Wait." Melissa jerked her arm away from me. She faced the woman with an almost—but not quite—contrite look, the way she looked at Mrs. Breaux when she tried to get out of detention. "I'm sorry. This whole thing is...overwhelming. I just wasn't prepared for some of the more, uh, graphic imagery. Um, did you say that *other girls* came here this week for materials?"

The woman's prairie dress and hair-sprayed curls jiggled as she nodded. "Oh, of course," she said. "It *can* be overwhelming." She clasped her hands prayerfully, for at least the third time. "Those girls. All they wanted was the posters we take to protests, which are *so* harsh by necessity. I can see that you're different from them now. You're so tenderhearted that you're barely able to stomach the truth. I can't imagine you'd want those posters, at least not yet."

The idea of Melissa being tenderhearted, along with the idea that this was a "friendly" space, was absurd, almost funny. But the general panic of the situation kept me from laughing.

"No, ma'am, you're right, we're not quite ready for those right now. We should probably just take those pamphlets you got for us and go." I tugged on Melissa's arm.

The woman nodded sagely. "You know, the box is *very* heavy. I can have one of our boys deliver the pamphlets to your school tomorrow."

"That would be so wonderful, thank you!" I nudged Melissa to get moving. Her face had gone from contrite to sour after the woman called her tenderhearted. As we retraced our steps to the front office, she grimaced at every poster, threw double birds at false medical charts, and snarled silently at the woman behind her back. We had maybe thirty seconds before she would blow up.

We'd almost reached the front door when Melissa turned to face the woman.

"I want you to know something—"

I shoved her through the door, hoping the woman couldn't hear the flow of angry medical fact-checking coming from Melissa.

"Thank you very much!" I shouted.

The woman looked at me, shook her head sadly, and closed the door in my face.

14

I shoved my cello case through the door of our house, dropped my backpack to the floor, and tossed next month's copy of *Spin* onto the side table.

Trying to maneuver everything at once felt nearly impossible.

I should have put the magazine in my bag, but this edition of *Spin* was *Important*, with a capital *I* and italics. Melissa subscribed, so even though this was the October issue and it was only mid-September, she already had a copy. She'd given it to me after our Friday afternoon private instrument lessons, and when I flipped through it as she was driving me back to my house, I immediately saw why: Eddie Vedder, Helen's favorite hot guy of grunge, had written a pro-choice essay.

I didn't think the essay would help change Helen's mind about abortion—she was too stubborn for that—but I hoped it might make her care a little less what other people thought about her. She *hadn't* had an abortion, and she *wasn't* a slut, but neither of those things should be a reason to judge somebody anyway. If I could convince her that Eddie Vedder didn't think abortion was a life-ruining event, I might also be able to convince her to ignore the masses who did.

It was worth a shot. Easier, anyway, than convincing Leah to call off the dogs.

I shoved my cello into its spot in the dining room just as Helen came walking down the stairs from our second-floor bedroom. Sara and Jennifer trailed behind her, looking like an innocuous teenage version of the twins from *The Shining* in their school uniforms and swinging ponytails.

Helen stopped halfway down the stairs, her foot hovering above the next step like I'd caught her committing some heinous act like hiding a body in the woods. She had a small overnight bag clutched in one hand and her sleeping bag tucked under her other arm.

"Where are you going?" I asked curiously.

"Sara's. I have a Saturday modeling class tomorrow, remember? Dad knows I'm spending the night." She said it a little too quickly, which sent up major warning flares.

I eyed her suspiciously. "You're acting weird. Is there something else going on at Sara's house? Like a party or something Dad doesn't know about?"

"No. No parties," Helen said, staccato and almost shouting. "Besides, it's not like anyone would invite me to one of them these days."

I couldn't tell if her anger was at me, or the jerks at school who'd decided to ostracize her over an imaginary abortion. But I'd hit a nerve, which I should have realized was there. Still, even taking everything into consideration, her behavior felt off—though it was hard to judge what was normal now for Helen.

"I'm sorry," I said. "I didn't mean it like that."

Helen's hand unclenched from its death grip on her overnight bag, and she started down the stairs again. Remembering what I had to give her, I grabbed *Spin* from the side table and held it up as she dropped her pile of sleepover accoutrement near the front door. Sara gave Jennifer a silent shrug as they followed her.

"I brought you something to read." I flipped the magazine open to the Eddie Vedder essay.

She squinted at me. "Are you a Jehovah's Witness now? Or maybe a Mormon?"

"It's just *Spin*, Helen. There's an essay by Eddie Vedder I thought you'd like to read." I tried to sound friendly, but I sounded like a bad actor doing a terrible line reading. I guess we weren't very good at this "being nice to each other" thing. Also, maybe it wasn't so nice that I was trying to subtly convert her via pro-choice essays by a guy she had a crush on.

She looked from me to the magazine in my hand. "Angelle told me about that essay," she said with a withering stare. "I ask you to help me, and this is what you do?" Her voice rose in volume with the question, and her sneer landed somewhere between disbelief and disgust. "I shouldn't have told you anything. I knew you wouldn't be able to help me. I bet you haven't even tried."

"I *have* tried," I protested. "It's only been a week since you told me, and I've been working on trying to figure something out every day. I asked Melissa for help, and she couldn't come up with anything, so I talked with Sean, and—"

"I *told* you not to tell him!" she shouted. Sara and Jennifer backed away from us, looking scared. Helen and I had fought in front of them before, but usually Helen was antagonizing me with sarcasm. This was different. She was *mad*. I don't think that any of us had ever seen her like this.

"Of course I told him!" I was shouting back at her now. I could feel my face growing red with shame and failure. Nothing I had done had helped, and I might have made things worse by talking to Sean. If he told Leah about our conversation, she might retaliate in ways I didn't expect.

"I don't know what you wanted me to do," I said, exasperated. "I'm not good at manipulating people or combating gossip or whatever. You're the one everybody instinctively adores, so if you can't fight this, what am *I* supposed to do?"

"I don't know! You're smart! You've been around Leah more than I have—you must know something I could use against her! Something like what she did to me!" Helen threw her hands up in anger.

"That's not going to work." I shook my head. So *that* was the only reason she'd asked me for help. She wanted dirt on Leah. I *did* know something we could use against Leah, but it would mean betraying Sean's confidence—and I wasn't about to go that far. Guilt already nagged at me for telling Melissa.

The last thing I wanted was to get into a continual one-upping with Leah, and not because she was way better at figuring out how to destroy people and could easily add me to her list. And it wasn't because I would ruin the remnants of my friendship with Sean, though that was certainly something to be considered.

No—it was just plain *wrong*. Wrong in the sense that I felt an in-the-bones betrayal of riot grrrl principles even thinking about it. Tearing down another girl by sharing all the messy details of her parents' divorce wasn't feminist; it was the exact opposite.

Helen glared at me, and I swore for a second that her eyes

were filling up with angry tears. But then she blinked, took a deep breath, and turned to Sara.

"Where's your mom?" she barked. "I can't *wait* to leave."

Sara jumped back at Helen's command. Her brown eyes were wide with surprise.

"I'm sure she's on her way. Are you all right?" Sara's eyes darted from Helen to Jennifer to me, like she was afraid Helen and I would start throwing punches.

"No, of course I'm not all right!" Helen rolled her eyes. "Everybody knows that." She waved toward Sara and Jennifer, who exchanged worried looks. "But I thought you actually cared enough about me to help."

"I do care!" I shouted. "But I can't help you. Not this way, at least."

A honk came from the driveway outside. Helen nodded her head at Sara and Jennifer and snatched her things from the floor.

"Come on," she said to her friends. "I need to get out of here."

"Helen, wait—" I tried to come up with something to keep her here, but she was already out the door, followed by Sara and then Jennifer, who closed the door softly behind her.

If Helen had been alone, I'm sure *she* would have slammed it.

I dropped onto the overstuffed couch in our living room. Everything I did to help turned out wrong. Though I probably shouldn't have shoved *Spin* in her face like that—Helen would have been mad at me regardless, but I really stepped in it.

I needed a break from Helen's problems. Calling Melissa or going over to Sean's was out of the question, since they would inevitably remind me of my failure to help Helen. Instead, I did something I never would have seen myself doing a week before.

I dialed Kyle's number on the phone next to the couch.

We were supposed to go for dinner and then to the movies tonight, but he wasn't picking me up for another two hours. I hadn't seen him today because his mom took him to get his driver's license, but maybe if I caught him now, we could go out earlier—and I wouldn't be stuck in my house thinking guilty thoughts for an extra few hours.

His mom answered. "Hello?"

"Um, may I please speak to Kyle?" I asked, sounding ridiculously formal. The phone greeting my grandma had taught me rushed out before anything less rigid could take its place.

"I'm sorry, but he's…tutoring someone right now, and I'd hate to interrupt," she said. "Can I take a message?"

"Um, sure. Can you let him know Athena called? He has my number."

"Okay, dear. I'll let him know."

After I hung up the phone, something nagged at me. That pause. *He's…tutoring someone.*

I was reading too much into things. He'd signed up for the same volunteer peer-tutoring program that I'd belonged to last year, where I'd helped Trip. But because Leah had said she wanted him to tutor her in math, in my mind, he was "tutoring" *her*, and whatever they were *really* doing gave his mom a reason to pause.

Now, in addition to worrying about Helen, I was worried about Leah and Kyle. Probably for no reason. Even if *she* wanted to make a move, he seemed to like me. We were going on a *real* date in a few hours, not just hanging out under the guise of tutoring—if that was even what was going on between them. And it was just as likely that he was innocently tutoring someone else from the program, and his mom's pause meant nothing.

I shook my head furiously. All this speculating was ridiculous and getting me nowhere. I just needed to keep myself occupied until it was time to get ready, and everything would work out fine.

I tried practicing my cello, but I didn't have enough focus to work on my orchestra parts or the Bach piece I was studying in my individual lessons. My arms were stiff and jittery, and my eyes kept losing track of where I was in the sheet music. Practicing required being in the zone, and I wasn't even in the same universe as the zone.

Finally, after an hour of torture, the phone rang. I crossed my fingers and said a little prayer that it was Kyle before I answered.

"Hello?"

"Hey, Athena." It *was* Kyle. "My mom said you called. What's up? We're good for tonight, right?" He sounded concerned that *I* might be canceling.

"Oh, yeah!" I couldn't let him think I was anything less than excited to see him. "I actually wanted to see if you could come over a little earlier. I was thinking we could go to Albasha for shawarma before the movie. It gets crowded on Fridays, though, so I figured we should probably book in some waiting time."

"Sounds great! I didn't know Baton Rouge had a shawarma place," he said. Then he paused in such a way that I could feel a *but* approaching. "But my mom insisted on a family dinner tonight now that she's finally got the kitchen in order. We're still on for the movie, though." His voice dropped to a whisper, making me think his mom might be nearby. "And bring your fake ID, just in case. *Fire Walk with Me* is rated R."

"Sure thing!" I bit my tongue so I wouldn't add, "Baton Rouge has a lot of shawarma places!" No matter how brightly I said it, I'd sound like a jerk for pointing out that our city wasn't a completely uncivilized backwater. Besides, Kyle sounded genuinely into the idea, even if it wasn't going to work out for tonight. And we were still going to the movies, which meant that we were having a *real* date. This wasn't just a coordinated coffee or an after-school music playing/make out session.

I went upstairs to get ready and tried to put everything else out of my mind. Helen. Leah. Sean. Kyle's mom's weird pause. But no matter how excited I was, those things kept creeping back in. During my shower, I remembered how I'd gone against Melissa's advice. And how Sean dismissed everything I said as a consequence of bad blood between me and Leah. And how upset Helen was when she left.

By the time Kyle finally rang the doorbell at 8:02, I had officially undermined my excitement. Sure, I looked *great* because I'd had so much time to get ready. I'd borrowed another going-out outfit from Melissa. This time, it was a short-sleeved plaid dress with a fitted bodice and a short, flared skirt, plus a pair of velvet Mary Janes that she'd bought in New Orleans. They'd never really fit her very well, but they were perfect for my half-size-smaller feet.

"Wow!" Kyle said, looking me up and down in a way that set my entire body on fire. Maybe he *was* the right person to distract me, to get me out of my head. "You look great!"

He was just wearing jeans and a Mudhoney T-shirt, but he looked great, too—not because he'd made any special effort, but because he was superhumanly attractive.

"I'm glad I got my driver's license in time for our date," he said as we walked to his car. "I was a little nervous that I'd have to ask Melissa to drive us again, which would make everything super awkward."

He walked around to the passenger's side of his brand-new Geo Metro and opened the door for me. The car was an extremely sensible parental choice that no boy would make—not showy, not cool, not sexy. No girl would choose it, either. But it was a *new* car. Most of my friends had gotten used ones, even Melissa, whose parents otherwise showered her with expensive items. The car was so tiny and low to the ground that I had to crouch to get in, and it felt like it could be blown off the I-10 bridge over the Mississippi River with a strong breeze. But again, *new.*

"Dad really knows how to pick the wheels, right?" Kyle squeezed his lanky frame into the driver's seat. "He has some grandiose idea that I'm going to learn how to work on cars with this thing. He thinks it's, and I quote, 'a valuable skill for every young man to have.' Personally, I'm just glad that he didn't buy the used VW bug on the lot that he got nostalgic over. Dad's a little too into the fact that he went to Woodstock."

I giggled nervously, not because I thought hippies were funny, but because I couldn't think of any response that properly modulated *This car is so unsubstantial and tiny, and all the rest of the cars on the road are minivans or trucks* with *Wow, your parents bought you a brand-new car within weeks of moving back to the States.* Somehow, my verbal acuity kept seeping out of me as soon as I got near Kyle, which I hated, but couldn't seem to control.

"I'm looking forward to seeing *Fire Walk with Me,*" I said, hoping that I could push the conversation away from cars and toward David Lynch movies, a subject I actually knew something about, since Melissa was obsessed with *Twin Peaks* and Kyle MacLachlan. "I'm sure it'll be creepy and weird and not make much sense, but—"

"—it'll still be awesome!" Kyle interjected, then launched into a monologue about David Lynch movies. I should have piped up because I knew at least as much as he did—I'd seen nearly all his films during sleepovers at Melissa's, when I got to watch movies my dad would never allow in our house. At first, I was a little relieved not to have to talk. I nodded and *mmm-hmm*'d my way through as he talked about *Blue Velvet* and *Eraserhead* as masterful demonstrations of Lynch's avant-garde abilities. I'd seen both, but somehow couldn't find a way to insert myself into his observations.

As I stared out the window and watched the strip malls go by, I thought about how Kathleen Hanna would know how to put herself into a conversation about David Lynch. Or about anything, really. I wished I was more confident, like her.

Finally, we pulled up to the theater on Siegen Lane. Kyle grabbed my hand as we walked toward the ticket booth. Near the front of the line was a large group of kids from our school: Cady Jenson and her boyfriend, Tommy Fabre, who were both in my honors English class. Jenny Broussard and Todd Aucoin, who were maybe going out but always got into disagreements in religion class, so who even knew? Spilling out of someone's van nearby was a group of juniors wearing our school colors—basically, the kids who would otherwise be at a football game on a Friday night, if that game wasn't forty-five minutes away in Donaldsonville.

Cady waved me over. We didn't normally run in the same circles, but we'd worked together on some school projects last year. She was surprisingly and consistently friendly for someone who spent most of her weekends in the cutthroat world of beauty pageants. I smiled and waved back, but next to me, Kyle stopped abruptly. He dropped my hand and patted his shirt.

"Oh, uh, just a second," he said. "I've got to run back to the car. Um, wait here? I'll be right back."

Kyle jogged to his car as I walked up to Cady. At least her waving me over meant I wouldn't have to stand awkwardly by myself near the box office. She met me halfway and pulled me away from the crowd, toward the posters that lined the side of the building. Her eyebrows—expertly plucked by her ultimate pageant mom into chestnut arcs—met in a worried crease, and tension built in my shoulders. I had the sinking feeling that I knew exactly what she was going to say, and I didn't have any idea how to respond.

"Hey, so I don't want to seem like one of those people who stirs shit for nothing," Cady whispered. Her eyes darted back toward the group of people she was with. "But yesterday in gym, when we were taking down the badminton nets, I overheard Aimee telling Casey that she'd seen some freshman named Helen going into the abortion clinic this summer during protests—not as a protester, but a patient." She watched me carefully for a moment, then added, "And then she said *your* name, and I don't know if she was saying something else about you, but… I'd just watch your back, okay? You can't trust her or Leah."

"I *know* that," I blurted. Cady backed away so fast that her ponytail bounced. I hadn't meant for my anger to sound like it was *at her*, pushing her away. "I'm sorry. I'm not… It's just that Helen's my sister, and I don't know what to do about any of this. The rumors aren't true, and I really want to do something for her, but…you know how Leah and Aimee are. It's impossible."

I couldn't believe I was talking with Cady about this—someone I hardly knew—but the words fell out in a steady stream. Or maybe it was *because* I didn't know her very well that I felt comfortable unburdening myself—after all, if she came up to me to tell me about this, it was because she understood how major it was.

"Oh, wow, she's your sister?" Cady widened her eyes, like everything was clicking in her brain. "That explains a *lot.* Ugh, Aimee is the *worrrrsssst.* If it's any consolation, she's a shit badminton player. She might fail the unit because she can't even get the birdie over the net on a serve."

Unfortunately, that bit of gossip, true as it was, barely chipped away at the feeling of being trapped in emotional quicksand in front of Cady.

"I just wish I knew what to do," I said, letting out a big sigh.

Cady's brown eyes darted between my gaze and her friends at the box office. Tommy was waving her back over.

"I'm really sorry, but Tommy..." She trailed off, grabbing my hands in a genuine, comforting squeeze. "I wish I could help more, but I'll make sure word gets around gym class at least that Aimee's full of shit about your sister. And I'll throw Leah under the bus for good measure, because wherever Aimee's spreading smoke, there's a fire set by Leah."

I nodded gratefully. A lump was forming in my throat, both because Cady was being super nice to me and because, as kind as *she* was, one gym class wasn't going to make much of a dent in things. I watched Cady dash off to her friends, who all looked impatient to get into whatever movie they were seeing—I didn't think they were the type to have fake IDs to get into *Fire Walk with Me.*

I watched them file into the movie theater, and then I was awkwardly alone, worrying about Helen.

When Kyle finally rejoined me, his face was red with exertion, which was kind of weird. The car wasn't *that* far away, just on the other side of the building, but he'd been gone for a good five minutes. Something about it bothered me, but I couldn't figure out what, so I put it out of my mind.

"You're never going to believe this," he said, looking at his Converse for dramatic effect. "But I, uh, just now remembered that the bouncer from the Varsity took my fake ID. And, um, I don't think we can get into the movie without it."

Twin Peaks: Fire Walk with Me was definitely an R-rated movie, and Siegen wasn't the easiest place to sneak into. Maybe if we were seeing it at the Broadmoor or Bon Marche, but those were second-run theaters and wouldn't be showing it this week anyway.

Still, I wasn't thinking about the movie anymore. Aimee and Leah took up so much space in my mind with their attacks on Helen. It felt relentless, like a thousand small cuts chipping away at her reputation.

"Are you okay?" Kyle asked, peering into my eyes. "It's not the end of the world if we don't see *Fire Walk with Me.* I can be up for something else." He squinted at the board near the box office with the times. "I'm, uh, not sure we can make it to *Honeymoon in Vegas*, though. Starts in five minutes, so it might be a stretch. And…everything else is an R."

"It's not that." I tried to sound far more upbeat than I felt. "I'm okay if we do something else."

He let out a *whoof* of relief, a little exaggerated for effect. "That's great! I thought you were going to hate me because you couldn't experience the cinematic mastery of David Lynch." I let out a small laugh, but my heart wasn't in it. He leaned closer to me as we walked back to the car together. "Wait, did something happen when you were talking to that girl? Isn't she from our school?"

So he'd seen me talking to Cady. From where, though?

"No…not exactly. It's just…"

We stopped right in front of his car. "You can tell me what's wrong," he said, opening the door for me. "I don't judge."

My heart ached a little. I wanted to find a solution to helping Helen, but telling Kyle felt like spreading the rumors further. And I knew if I talked to him about it, Helen would be mortified. Also, more selfishly, I wanted so much to keep the gossipy bullshit away from Kyle, to keep him as the one part of my life that wasn't infected by the rot Leah and Aimee were spreading. But that was never going to work, not if our relationship was going to be something real.

I slumped into the passenger seat as he drove us out of the parking lot. "Cady didn't do anything wrong," I said. "She just… Well, Leah and Aimee have been saying awful things about my sister behind her back." I left out what those things were, because if he didn't know, I didn't want to be the one who told him. "And Cady wanted to warn me that she'd heard them, too."

Kyle's hands seemed to grip the steering wheel more tightly. Maybe he *was* tutoring Leah. Maybe he thought she was nice. Maybe he was like Sean in that respect, and wouldn't believe me.

"Are you sure it's not just *Cady* spreading shit?" he asked, not taking his eyes off the road. "She could be egging you on. Getting under your skin by making sure you know that people are talking about your sister. Seems pretty manipulative to me."

I considered it for half a second. I didn't know Cady that well, but I *did* know she wasn't a liar or manipulative. She'd held up her end of our group project last year, unlike everyone else. You can tell a lot about a person from how they act during group projects. Plus, Leah had been taunting Helen for a while, and Aimee was a known gossip. They were the obvious choice over someone who was consistently nice and honest.

"Yeah, no," I said, toning my voice down to sound less combative than I was feeling. "Cady's great. Leah and Aimee, not so much."

Kyle and I drifted into silence. This was exactly what I *didn't* want to happen. I could tell he thought I was one of those girls who hated other girls, and was constantly immersed in gossip. That wasn't who I was *at all*, or at least wasn't who I was trying to be. Revolution girl-style… I was trying.

Then he turned to me and smiled. "Why don't we forget all about it? Someone in one of my tutoring sessions was telling me about a place where we could get beignets and hot chocolate. It's across town, but—"

"Coffee Call?" My voice lit up. I was a sucker for beignets. Melissa and I used to go to Coffee Call a lot after orchestra practice, but we hadn't been there in a while. "I'd be into that."

Our conversation drifted toward beignets, and how they were different from European doughnuts, and I pushed our talk about Helen out of my head. I needed to get to know Kyle better before I could expect him to understand what was going on with her. And that wasn't going to happen if I made it sound like I was obsessed with getting revenge on Aimee and Leah. He knew I cared about my sister and was trying to help her, and that was the important thing for now—right?

But no matter how much I told myself that, I still felt like I was letting Helen down.

15

"Athena, where's your sister?"

Sunlight blazed through the window as I blinked myself awake and focused on the figure in the doorway. Dad never woke us up, not since we were little. Helen was a natural alarm clock.

"She's at Sara's." I yawned, rubbing my eyes.

"Sara's mother just called. Helen and Sara were gone when she woke up. They aren't at modeling class, either."

That was odd. Helen *never* missed modeling class. I looked at Dad, who hovered in the doorway in sweatpants and a grubby T-shirt, as though crossing into the room would violate my personal space. Sara's mother had probably woken him up, a suspicion supported by the way his curly brown hair was mussed and twisted in all directions.

The wrinkles on Dad's forehead deepened with concern.

He looked exhausted, more than usual for a Saturday. Last night, I'd been genuinely surprised that he wasn't awake when I got home fifteen minutes past my eleven o'clock curfew. He was a lot more lenient now that his job was so much more tiring.

"I'm sure she's fine," I said, trying to sound casual and positive.

"Athena, if you know anything..." Dad's voice trailed off as he looked at me over his glasses.

I didn't. At least, I didn't know where she was right then, at that moment. I *knew* she'd been acting suspiciously yesterday, though, but she'd only had an overnight bag. And I knew she wanted to go to New York to stay with Mom, but I didn't think she was desperate enough to run away. I doubted she'd take Sara with her, either.

Dad stood there, eyeing me like he suspected I was hiding something, and I willed myself to think harder.

"Have you called Mom?" If Helen was trying to get to our mom's house, she'd probably prepped a lie for Mom as to why she was on her way.

I was fairly certain that if he was my age and a girl, Dad would have rolled his eyes at me. His adult version, a reflexive frown, made it perfectly clear that he thought Mom had nothing to do with this.

"I'm serious," I insisted. "I think Helen might try to visit Mom. She asked me a couple weeks ago if I would trade my spot with her, but I said no."

True enough, and I didn't bring in anything about the abortion rumors. If we could find Helen—*when* we found Helen—I would force her to tell him. Until then, gossip was irrelevant.

"I'll call her." He left the room, walked down the hall to

his bedroom, and closed the door with a firm finality. He never called Mom, unless one of us was sick or injured, like when Helen broke her arm falling off the monkey bars. Or if one of us had done something exceptionally well, like when I scored an eight hundred on the verbal section of the SATs or when Helen won the science fair.

Actually, now that I thought about it, he called her quite a bit.

I got out of bed and crept down the hall to listen.

"Margaret," I heard him say. "It's Alan. Have you talked with Helen recently?"

A long pause while Mom said something. If I had to guess, that something was only tangentially related to Helen's disappearance.

"Mmm-hmm. And you told her that she could visit in the spring, closer to her birthday?"

Another long pause. I wished I'd been savvy enough to pick up my bedroom phone and simultaneously hit the mute button. Dad's side of this conversation was more questions than answers.

"And you heard from her this morning?" he asked. "Okay, okay, I'm writing that number down. I'll call you back."

That sentence gave me the signal to dash back to my bedroom and pretend I'd heard nothing. I sat on my bed with a bounce and tried to act like I'd been sitting patiently the entire time.

"Athena." Dad took up his post in the door frame again. "Your mother told me she heard from Helen this morning. She said that I'd finally agreed to let her visit sooner, and she said something about getting a modeling contract today. But your mom didn't ask Helen what she meant."

It figured. I couldn't remember the last time my mother

listened to the specifics of a conversation when it didn't involve a long-dead poet. The "modeling contract" piece made some sense, at least given the things Helen had told me after the fashion show, but where would she have gone to try to get one?

I thought about Helen's modeling friends. If Sara had gone with Helen, Jennifer might still be a source of information.

"Do you or Sara's mom know if Jennifer went with Helen and Sara, too?" I asked Dad.

He raised his eyebrows in sudden recognition.

"She's the other brown-haired one?" he said. "I forgot about her." I trailed him down the stairs to his small half office near the kitchen, where he kept a Rolodex with the names of our friends' parents. Today, I was glad my father operated in the strict-to-overprotective zone.

Again, I could only hear one side of the conversation. This time, I sensed Dad's growing impatience with the fourteen-year-old who'd answered his call.

"Jennifer, please," he said. "No, no. I'm not going to yell at you. No, you're not in trouble."

He held the phone away from his ear. Jennifer's hysterical blubbering came out of the phone at warp speed. I couldn't tell what she said, and I don't think he could, either.

"No, they're not going to be in trouble," he said reassuringly. "I just want to know where they are. I need to know they're safe."

Jennifer's sobbing subsided, and Dad put the phone back against his ear.

"She went to a casting call in New Orleans?" This time, he really did roll his eyes. "Okay, thank you, Jennifer. Can you put your mother back on, please?"

I didn't stick around to hear Dad talk with Jennifer's mother.

Back in our room, I looked over at Helen's bed. She kept her side of the room far neater than I kept mine. She hadn't taken anything with her other than maybe a change of clothes and her toiletries, so it didn't seem like she'd be gone for long.

Eventually, Dad reappeared in the doorway. I'm not sure he'd seen the inside of our room so many times in one day since I got the flu last year. He didn't look nearly as worried this time.

"I called the modeling school director, Mrs. Brouillette," Dad said. "Apparently, this casting call is legitimate, at least as legitimate as those things go. Only girls with signed permission slips were supposed to go, and Helen apparently forged my signature. Sara must have forged Mrs. Lewis's, as well. Why the hell Mrs. Brouillette didn't tell Sara's mom about this when she called the school earlier this morning, I don't know. That woman hasn't got an ounce of sense."

"So you think Helen went to New Orleans?"

"I know she did," he said. "Mrs. Brouillette called the casting office to confirm after she spoke with Mrs. Lewis. She was very excited that Helen was the only girl to get a callback from the Ford rep. I don't understand *why* she's so excited, considering she let Mrs. Lewis and me think Sara and Helen had run away. And there's no way I'm letting my daughter model swimsuits at car shows."

I laughed for the first time this morning. "Dad, Ford is a modeling agency. One of the big ones." Helen had been obsessed with them since she found out they were Christy Turlington's agency.

"How big?" he asked in a measured voice, as though weighing the twin options of letting her benefit from a trip that she'd taken without permission and grounding her for the next six years for putting him into a state of panic. "Big as in Sears and Roebuck, or big as in *Vogue*?"

"Vogue," I said. "She could be a real model, and not just one at the mall. *Brooke Shields* is one of their models." I surprised myself. Somehow, I'd absorbed enough from Helen's fashion obsession to know this random fact. She knew which agencies, like Ford and Wilhelmina, represented all the big models, but Brooke Shields was the only one Dad might know.

"Do you know why she'd do this?" he asked, shaking his head. "It seems like a foolish risk, and that's not like her at all. She could have at least asked me."

I cringed inwardly. Telling Dad about the rumors would betray Helen, but not telling him meant lying.

The weight of the decision pushed down on me. Helen didn't want Dad to know, and I didn't want to tell him, either. She'd come to me for help, and I'd tried. I hadn't been super effective, but I'd tried. Bringing Dad into the situation would inevitably make things worse—he might be able to confirm to the school that Helen had been abortion-free all summer, which would prevent her from being expelled, but a parental intervention sent a signal of weakness to the student population, a drop of blood in the sea for all the swimming sharks. *That* was what Helen didn't want, and I wasn't going to put her in that position.

But that was before she disappeared. Waiting to see if things got better, trying to find other solutions—those things hadn't worked. And lying to Dad might make me feel solidarity with Helen, but it wasn't going to help her in the end, either. Or me, for that matter, if he found out I'd lied.

"Yeah." I sighed. "I do. I think she feels desperate."

I told Dad the stories circulating about Helen. That Leah and Aimee first told people that Helen had sex with Drew

Lambert, then embellished with the abortion story. That it cost Helen her spot in the pro-life club, which caused another eye-rolling episode, since he landed somewhere to the left of Al Franken on the political spectrum. I told him everything, including trying to get Sean to help, going to the fake abortion clinic with Melissa, and failing to get Helen to read what Eddie Vedder had written.

I'd never had such a one-sided conversation with Dad before. By the time I reached the end, his face had frozen with his mouth turned down and his eyebrows drawn together.

"Why didn't you tell me sooner?" he asked once I'd finished.

"Helen asked me not to," I said. And besides, Leah can't be stopped, I thought. Not when she trades in believable lies.

"You know that's not a good excuse," Dad said, giving me one of his patented stern-father looks. "You say this Leah girl's responsible for it. Why haven't you two gone to the guidance counselor or the dean of discipline about her?"

Ah, Dad, so naive. Parents always thought that bullying had some easy solution.

"Because we don't have any proof," I said, exasperated. "And because we didn't think anyone would believe us. Helen hoped it would just go away." That wasn't technically true, since I knew she wanted to get back at Leah in some way, but Dad didn't need to know that. "*I* hoped it would, too, but it hasn't yet."

Dad looked at me and sighed. Then he frowned and bit his lip, a habit both Helen and I had inherited.

"I know it's easy to think that I couldn't have done anything," he said. "But you should have come to me."

I shrugged because any answer I could give him would be rude. He was saying what a good father was supposed to say.

But what Dad didn't understand was that getting the school involved wouldn't end things. Leah would deny everything, and people would still whisper about Helen. And chances were Leah would find some way to make things even worse.

"Why don't you go down and put some coffee on?" Dad gave me a half smile of encouragement, since I must have looked as sullen as I felt. "I'm going to call your mother. She deserves to know that we've solved part of the mystery."

"Are you going to tell her about the abortion stuff?" I asked, worried. "I think it would be better if Helen told her."

Dad shook his head. "Sorry, but the time's long since past when Helen should have said something."

The smug adult wannabe in me knew he was right. But it didn't seem fair that Helen hadn't gotten to tell either Dad *or* Mom what she was going through, because I had ratted her out. She might not forgive me for that. I wasn't sure I could forgive myself, either.

I went down to the kitchen to put the coffee on, made some toast with butter and cinnamon sugar, and tried to read the newspaper. When Dad finally came back to the kitchen after his second call to Mom, he quizzed me for a while about all the modeling agencies in New York that Helen had her eyes on. But my knowledge base was like Lake Pontchartrain—wide and shallow—so it took about two minutes. After that, we mostly waited for her to get home.

Part of me worried Helen would take the agent's card and head straight to New York on a bus after her audition. Dad probably felt the same way. He hadn't showered or changed out of his pajama pants and T-shirt, and every few minutes, he looked nervously at the clock on the microwave. He stayed on the front page of the newspaper so long that I had to ask him for it when I finished everything else. He hadn't read a single word.

When I finally heard Helen's key in the lock, I looked at Dad, half expecting him to tell me to go upstairs. Instead, he motioned for me to sit down in the living room. I sank into the couch and tried to look natural, but the overstuffed chenille didn't really lend itself to anything but slouchy TV watching.

Unaware that Dad and I had been waiting for her for two hours, Helen bounded down the hall and into the room, punching the air with excitement. She had no reason to expect us to be home. On a normal Saturday, Dad would have been at the office, and I would have been at Melissa's or Sean's, or upstairs reading and listening to music.

When she saw Dad, she froze and her eyes widened. When she saw me, she narrowed them. By sitting next to Dad on the couch, I had unforgivably crossed over to the side of parental authority.

Dad cleared his throat and gestured for her to sit. Helen flopped into the oversize armchair that matched the couch. She tried to casually swing her legs over its arm and failed. She was too tall, and her legs hung over the edge and her back curved uncomfortably. She had to hold on to the back of the chair so she wouldn't slide off and ended up looking ridiculous instead of nonchalant.

"Is something wrong?" she asked.

Dad sighed for the fortieth time this morning, and I suspected that any chance he would go easy on her had just vanished.

"Helen, I know you went to New Orleans," he said. "But before discovering that, I had no idea where you were. We spent the entire morning thinking you and Sara had been kidnapped or run away."

The innocent, inquisitive, wide-eyed gaze on Helen's face faded, replaced with an ashen, bunched-up look. She sat up from her casual slung position to an alert, straight-backed posture, but said nothing. She was smart not to.

"I finally got ahold of Mrs. Brouillette and heard that you were at a casting call with some other girls," he said. "I didn't give you permission to go. You didn't even tell me about it, in fact."

Helen looked at Dad, her face expressionless. She might have been weighing what she should say, or she might have been planning what she would *do*. Now that she had broken a really serious rule, she might have more reason to run to New York.

"On the other hand, I hear you got a callback from an agency," Dad continued. "And from what Athena tells me, it's a pretty big one."

Helen's blue eyes flashed with the slightest flicker of hope. Her fingers tightened around the arms of the chair. Dad could, at any point, snuff out that tiny flame.

"This puts me in a very bad position," he said. "If I punish you, you miss out on a good opportunity. If I let you go to New York, I'm rewarding inconsiderate, rude, and immature behavior."

Helen shrank back into the cushions. Dad had never been so angry with her, at least as long as I could remember.

"My question to you, before I decide on anything, is why did you do this?" he asked.

The answer would determine Helen's punishment. He could ground her for a year, or he could revoke modeling classes or the New York trip or anything else. But I knew something Helen didn't. Dad already knew about the rumors. Knowing him, though, he wanted to hear it from her.

"I don't know," she said. "I wasn't thinking."

Dad waited for Helen to say something more substantial, but his hands relaxed for the first time today. I think he was weighing whether to bring "disappointment" out from his arsenal. That would be the surest way to maximize Helen's guilt. It certainly worked on me.

"It's pretty clear that you weren't thinking, and that's not like you," he said, shaking his head. "Why didn't you ask for my permission to go? You had every opportunity to, but you didn't."

Helen looked at her hands, which was an improvement over her looking at me like it was my fault she'd been caught. I could understand his question because he probably *would* have let her go. But maybe probably wasn't enough for Helen.

"I didn't think you'd let me," she said quietly. "You hate my modeling. You wouldn't let me do it at all if Grandma wasn't paying for it. And if I'd asked you, and you'd said no, I would have missed my chance. I wouldn't have been able to sneak out. You'd have kept me on lockdown the whole weekend."

Dad shook his head, but I had to agree with Helen. If he didn't want her to go to a modeling call he knew about, there was no way she would have been allowed to spend last night at Sara's.

"Putting aside what I think of your modeling class, I'm disappointed in you." There it was, the big word that neither of us could stand. It was hard for me to watch Helen as she shifted in the chair. I could tell she was struggling not to cry. "You didn't know if I'd say yes, so you decided to preemptively sneak out?" he said. "That's not the kind of behavior

I expect from you. What were you going to tell me about the callback?"

Helen shrugged. "I was going to say a scout came to our modeling class."

"And you expected me to believe that?"

Red crept up Helen's neck to her cheeks as she realized how silly the notion sounded. Dad frequently voiced his opinion that her class was mostly made up of kids whose parents had delusions of grandeur about the opportunities modeling school might bring their precious babies. He had a point about that, but Helen stood out among them. Still, it would have been hard to believe that a scout would show up there to discover her.

"Is there something you need to tell me about school?" Dad asked.

Helen shot me a quick look of hurt betrayal that hit me right in the chest. I wasn't happy with myself, either, but what other option did we have? Everything else we'd tried hadn't worked.

"What about school?" she asked, shifting on the chenille chair, a little squirm that told me she was thinking about lying. "Things are—" She stopped, seeming unable to bring herself to say the word *fine*, because they weren't. "Actually...things are... Things aren't fine at all."

She paused for a second. I hoped she wouldn't cry. Helen's crying in the mall had left me feeling helpless, and I'd felt helpless since then. So far, I'd been needed this morning, and it kept me from thinking about Sean or Leah or anyone else. I wanted to keep it that way.

Helen didn't cry, though. She just sank back against the chair in defeat.

"Athena told you?" she asked. She looked at me, but she didn't seem mad. Not like earlier anyway.

"Yes," he said. Dad looked defeated, too. "Can you please tell me why you didn't come to me when you started having trouble?"

Helen shrugged. Maybe she was relieved not to have to tell him the rumors herself. I wouldn't want to tell him if people had been saying that I was having sex with a racist freak and then had an abortion. There was always a small chance he would believe some tiny seed of the stories. I couldn't handle that, and I doubted Helen could, either.

"It was too embarrassing," she said. "And I didn't think you could do anything. Leah and Aimee are unbeatable."

Dad sighed. I'd never heard him sigh as much as this morning. I thought he was about to give up on parenting.

"We're going to talk with your principal," he said. Helen opened her mouth, but he put up his hand firmly. "Don't argue. Monday morning, I'm calling him."

Helen looked to me with pleading eyes. We both knew talking with Principal Richard would be disastrous.

"As for modeling," he added, "I have to discuss that with your mother. But for now, you are *grounded.* That means no more modeling sleepovers, no parties, nothing. If you want to go *anywhere* after school, you have to go with your sister or with me. Otherwise, you'll be here, doing your homework."

Helen's shoulders relaxed almost imperceptibly. She knew better than to complain. Being grounded sucked, but it wouldn't be forever, and there was still a chance she'd get to attend the callback. And as for Principal Richard, well… I hoped things wouldn't turn out as badly as we both feared.

16

Mrs. Bonnecaze read a passage from the Bible in her slight Southern drawl. I wasn't paying attention. She could have been reading from the *Kama Sutra* and I wouldn't have noticed, because I knew that right then, Dad and Helen were in the principal's office. Or maybe they had shuttled Helen into the guidance counselor's office by now, where Mrs. Turner or Mr. Roget would grill her about the rumors. Of course, they would say things about how important it was to let an adult know as soon as possible when someone spread gossip or acted like a bully, but they wouldn't actually do anything to help. With those two, the burden of proof lay squarely on the victim, like last year with Melissa's Suicidal Tendencies patch.

"Please send Athena Graves to the guidance office. Mrs. Turner needs to see her," a secretary announced over the classroom intercom.

Twenty-two pairs of eyes swiveled to look at me as I stood up from my desk. No one liked being called to the guidance office, unless you were a senior and they had good news about scholarships. I wondered if anyone had seen Dad marching Helen, unwilling and miserable, into the principal's office this morning.

I grabbed my books. I might not return before my next class. Mrs. Turner tended to keep students in her office until she got the information she wanted, and it was almost never about the kind of things a guidance counselor should focus on. If you went in for scholarship advice, she might ask what boys you were dating. If you had a crisis at home, she would pry and push, testing multiple angles until you revealed every detail about your life and the lives of everyone around you. All of this was supposed to help, but it usually felt like an interrogation.

My walk through the empty hallways brought echoes with every step. I didn't know why they would ask *me* to go to the office. I didn't have anything to do with Leah and Aimee's lies. But I supposed they *had* to ask me about them, since I was Helen's sister.

When I pushed open the door to the main guidance office, I was relieved to see that no one else was inside. I didn't really feel like making small talk with other students who might also be waiting for our school's form of "guidance."

Finally, Mrs. Turner, wearing a flowing purple blouse, emerged from her back office and smiled at me, her black eyebrows pulled together in an expression of concern above her button-round dark eyes. She rushed to my side and pulled me in for a hug. I almost leaped out of her way, but I didn't have time, so I stood there passively instead, my arms pinned down by her embrace.

"Athena, I am *so* sorry to hear what's going on with your sister!" Mrs. Turner exclaimed, loud enough for the entire office to hear, which thankfully only meant the department secretary.

"Thanks." I didn't know what else to say, because I didn't

trust her hugs or her voiced concern. I'd heard too many stories of how people had told her things in confidence and she'd somehow betrayed them under the guise of "helping."

Mrs. Turner led me into her office and motioned for me to sit down in the supposedly comfortable chair across from her desk. Its itchy orange upholstery and awkward wooden armrests never offered anything but restless irritation. I think she bought the chair so that anyone sitting in it would confess to their wrongdoings sooner, like a spotlight in a prison cell. Even Sister Catherine, the dean of discipline, didn't have such an uncomfortable chair in her office.

Mrs. Turner flexed back on her own chair, a bonded leather thing that could have graced the office of a high-powered CEO. She sighed heavily, paused, and sighed again, her face never letting go of that look of heightened concern.

"Now, Athena, I'm sure you're wondering why you're in here."

I would guess it's because my dad forced my sister to talk about the crap she's been facing since school started last month, but that's just me. I thought of a few other snarky responses, too, none of which I could possibly say aloud, and instead listened to her reasons.

"Your father has some concerns about your sister's well-being." She looked at me with a very serious expression. "She's much more withdrawn than when school started. According to Mrs. Bonnecaze, she's dropped out of the pro-life club, even though she was the leader of her middle school club and had been so excited to join."

"She didn't drop out," I said, ready to fight for Helen. "She got kicked out. Angelle said—"

Mrs. Turner put up her hand, and I shut up. "I think we know that our most reliable source in this situation is Mrs. Bonnecaze, and she said Helen quit. I'm going to take *her* word for it."

Even if Helen had "quit," it was only after Angelle had strong-armed her, after everyone had told her how *embarrassing* it was for them to have her in the club. "But—"

"That's enough, Athena." Mrs. Turner pursed her lips at me. "I am not here to argue with you. I'm here because I am worried about your sister. Do you understand?"

I nodded, trying to show that I, too, was concerned about Helen. I didn't quite buy Mrs. Turner's "worry," but arguing with her clearly wasn't going to work. And Mrs. Turner required visible signs as "evidence" of caring, like head bobbing and extreme frowns, and *ah*s and *mmm-hmm*s, that I had to remind myself to perform.

"Now, Athena, people have been telling me things about your sister," she said. "And your father seems to think these reports stem from the malicious intentions of another student. I know this is a very difficult thing to ask of you, and please forgive me, but is there any truth—*any* truth at all—in what people are saying? It will help Helen *so* much if you can be honest with us."

I started to frown for real. That "seems to think" didn't sound like Mrs. Turner believed my dad, and neither did her suggestion of my helping Helen by "being honest." She thought I knew something, and, much worse, she definitely believed the gossip—not Dad, and certainly not Helen.

"You're joking, right?" I dug my fingers into the arms of the chair, trying to contain my anger. "Helen's *fourteen*. She's home every afternoon after school. Mrs. Estelle—Mrs. Mitchell, Sean's mom—makes sure we're home every day. And there's no way she could have been seeing Drew Lambert last summer. We *both* spent the whole summer with our mom in Oregon."

Mrs. Turner looked at me with an unwavering frown, her

forehead a tier of wrinkles and her small lips pursed together. Finally, she took in a deep breath.

"Now, Athena, I know you want to protect your sister, but I'm concerned about what these behaviors she's been exhibiting say to me," Mrs. Turner said. "Her skirts are *quite* short. And she has a lot of male admirers. Isn't it possible she went too far with one of them?"

I couldn't believe what I was hearing. Helen's skirts weren't short; she was *tall.* My sister was being called a slut because she had giraffe legs and Dad wasn't on top of back-to-school shopping. And she'd only worn my spare skirts for maybe a week until her special order came in! I searched Mrs. Turner's face, trying to find a glimmer of genuine concern in her almost-black eyes.

"I know you don't want to think it," she continued. "But her behavior is consistent with someone who is feeling a tremendous amount of regret. The withdrawal from activities, the acting out. Your father told me about her desperate attempt at running away. Can't you see this is a cry for help?"

I took a deep breath, held it, and counted back from ten. I never, ever said anything snotty back to a teacher, or a guidance counselor, for that matter. But none of them had ever said anything as upsetting as Mrs. Turner just had. I asked myself what any member of Bikini Kill would do in these circumstances. I tried to channel their ability to stand up to authority—"You. Do. Have. Rights!" was as good a reminder as any.

"I don't think it's a cry for anything other than help with some malicious girls spreading lies about her." Waves of anger vibrated through me, and my grip on the arms of my chair was the only thing preventing my hands from balling into fists. "And if you think Helen's hiding something, go right ahead. Frankly, I'd be withdrawn, too, if the whole school was whispering lies about me." I looked the guidance counselor straight in the eye. "You might want to look at *yourself*, Mrs. Turner, because if you're willing to treat an innocent student this way, it might just be that you don't want to bother with the *real* problems at this school."

Mrs. Turner's mousy round eyes opened wide. I think she'd expected me to crack under the gentle pressure of shaming Helen, not to tell her how to do her job. She took what felt like an hour to reply, letting my words fully rebound off the walls.

"Now, Athena," she said, rocking back in her executive's chair. "I know you *believe* your sister is the victim of idle gossip, but we've already heard from two other students who are concerned about your sister. And they say she confessed to them about her indiscretion this summer."

Leah and Aimee. It had to be. I couldn't believe that they had gone so far as to talk with Mrs. Turner. Spreading rumors among the student body was one thing, but whispering them to one of our guidance counselors took things to a whole different level.

"I bet they did, and I can guess exactly who they were. Why are you so determined to believe the worst of Helen?" I demanded, shaking my head in disgust. "You haven't even questioned whether Leah or Aimee might have made it up, or if this supposed affair was even geographically possible. We were at our mom's house all summer. *Really*."

Mrs. Turner rested her chin on her interlocking fingers. She looked more and more like a rodent, maybe a squirrel eating a nut. Her ersatz concern never left her face, but something I'd said interested her.

"I can't tell you who brought the information to me," she said too calmly. "But I do take it very seriously."

"I just told you who brought the information to you. I

already know." I sat back in the chair and crossed my arms, seething.

"As you know," she continued, gesturing to the student handbook on her desk. "It's our school's policy to support life at all times. Should anything come to light supporting the veracity of these assertions, Helen will be expelled. Because there's no proven evidence about your sister *so far*, I doubt Mr. Richard and Sister Catherine will take any action. However, for her sake, we will be banning her from participating in clubs for now, and we are communicating to the student council president that her name be disqualified from the upcoming homecoming court ballot. After all, if this is mere gossip, as *you say*, it will do her no good to subject her to that level of scrutiny."

Mrs. Turner smiled sweetly at me.

I didn't know Helen was in consideration for the homecoming court ballot, not that it surprised me. But the dance was a month away, so blocking her now seemed more like punishment for what she hadn't done than protecting her from what had been done to her.

I gripped the wooden arms of my chair again, afraid that if I let go, I would punch Mrs. Turner in the teeth.

"You need to go back to class. You wouldn't want to miss any more religious teachings," Mrs. Turner said. She wrote out a pink slip for me to return to class. "Perhaps you can help guide your sister back to the correct path that Mrs. Bonnecaze is kind enough to present to you."

I yanked the slip from her hand and let the door slam behind me on my way out of the guidance office.

Religious teachings. Mrs. Turner probably missed a few.

17

I seethed through the rest of religion class. Through Mrs. Bonnecaze ending the period by leading us in a prayer for the federal appeals court to uphold Louisiana's abortion ban and save the unborn, which she'd never done before and suddenly seemed like it had extra meaning. Then through Mrs. Breaux showing us a video of Galileo's gravity experiment at the Tower of Pisa in physics class. Through her rewinding it, and showing it again, because that was her thing she did when she didn't want to teach from the book and the video was too short.

Everything Mrs. Turner had said made me want to punch her, or whatever easy target was in close proximity. I should have been able to convince her that Helen hadn't had an abortion. I should have been more direct about how wrong she was. I should have said something as I left.

My anger kept on burning all the way up until lunch. I

stomped angrily through the cafeteria, my lunch bag a crumpled mess in my hand. I was supposed to meet Melissa for another brainstorming session, but I didn't see how I could be productive around other people in this state. I was glad that Kyle had a photography club meeting during lunch today. I didn't want him to think that I was mad at *him*.

It was finally cool enough to sit outside for lunch, and after my encounter with Mrs. Turner, I was in no mood to socialize or deal with the inevitable situation of someone trying to ask what was wrong. My plan was to sit in the school's outdoor amphitheater, where we were allowed to eat on sunny days—and where I hopefully wouldn't be bothered.

Melissa, unfortunately, wasn't willing to leave me alone.

"Athena, wait up!" she called after me, struggling to keep up while carrying her tray of industrial pizza.

I pushed ahead through the double doors that led to the amphitheater and marched up the concrete steps. It was more crowded out here than I'd expected, but it was the usual crowd of theater kids and a couple clusters of band kids. They were the kind of people who were either enmeshed in their own drama or too nice to care about yours. I climbed past everyone, all the way up to the top step, where I sat forcefully, anger making my hands tremble.

"What's going on?" Melissa asked, wheezing out a few harried breaths. She dropped down next to me, her backpack sliding down one arm as she struggled to keep the tray balanced with the other.

I shook my head. Tears sprang to my eyes, and my voice shook. "This school. I've had it. Mrs. Turner believes Leah and Aimee's version of events, and now Helen's being punished for *no reason*. And I'm done."

I wasn't articulating what had happened with Mrs. Turner

very well, but Melissa caught the rage wafting off me. She didn't make a joke or say something political and snarky. She waited for me to tell her what happened.

"You know, I *wanted* to believe this school wasn't run by hypocrites and assholes," I said. "But no, Mrs. Turner has somehow decided Helen can't be on the homecoming court, even though it's supposed to be a student-designated event, because she believes that Helen had an abortion. It's not *fair.*" I sounded like a five-year-old, but I couldn't stop my frustration from coming out in an angry stream. "Can you believe that? *And* she's making it even worse—Helen can't do any extracurricular activities *at all.* Who would do that? And how can she—she's just a guidance counselor! She *shouldn't* have the authority to do that, but she's probably talking to all the teachers right now to make sure it happens."

Melissa sighed. "I hear you." Using her hand as a visor to shield her eyes from the blinding sun, she squinted at the far corner of the amphitheater. "Is that your sister and her entourage over there?"

Sure enough, Helen, Sara, and Jennifer sat in a little huddle by the amphitheater's far column, nearly disappearing into its shadows. They'd picked a much more secluded spot than Melissa and I had, which meant they'd gotten here much earlier. Knowing Helen, she'd already planned her hiding spot by the end of her own talk with Mrs. Turner.

"C'mon," Melissa said, grabbing her tray with one hand and pushing herself up from the ground with the other. "We're going to help Helen. We're the smartest girls in school. If we put our minds together with your sister's freaky social skills, we can come up with something. It'll make you feel better. It'll make *her* feel better. Hell, I think it'll even make *me* feel better."

Helen's eyebrows first went up in surprise when she saw Melissa and me. Then her eyes narrowed in an ungenerous squint, and I shrank back from the power of her daggers. It was clear she blamed me for this morning's events.

"Why are you here?" she asked, her voice sour and defensive.

"We've come to extend our help," Melissa said, gesturing like a dignitary entering into parley with a foreign delegation.

"You've done enough damage, Athena, don't you think?" Helen said to me, not looking at Melissa.

"I'm sorry," I said, holding her gaze. "I never thought Dad would drag you to Mrs. Turner's office. Maybe to Mr. Richard's office, but not Mrs. Turner. Anyway, Mrs. Turner told me Leah and Aimee had already visited her, so it was bound to happen at some point even without my telling Dad."

Helen looked at Sara and Jennifer, who nodded like bobbleheads in a moving truck, and then back to me. She motioned for Melissa and me to sit down.

"Damn it," she said, her shoulders falling. "We were right. So what's the plan?"

"To get complete and utter revenge on Aimee and Leah," Melissa said imperiously. "And to restore Helen's honor."

"Can you cut the medieval crap?" If this was going to work, Melissa needed to take things seriously. I gave her a look, and she seemed to get it.

"Right," she said, backing off. "We need to be smart about this."

"What's the *plan*?" Helen repeated. She looked suspiciously from me to Melissa over her cheese sandwich. "Everything you've done so far hasn't worked. It's just made everything worse, and you've done it all behind my back. So I need to know what you're going to do next."

I didn't have a plan, but Melissa's face lit up.

"We need to think like PR people." Melissa gestured at Helen excitedly with her cafeteria French bread pizza. "All of us."

She turned from Helen to Sara, Jennifer, and me. I guess we were "all of us." The way she said it made me uncomfortable, like she and Helen were the leaders of a rebellion, and Jennifer, Sara, and I were mere foot soldiers. Or possibly minions. At any rate, not on equal footing. I couldn't imagine it made Jennifer and Sara happy, either.

"We have certain advantages," Melissa continued, looking at each of us in turn. "We have a fair amount of talent, and a large network of friends, if we act together. There are as many people who want to see Leah and Aimee get taken down as there are people who believe them."

I didn't like the way this was going. After all the riot grrrl zines I'd been reading, I didn't want our focus to be on taking Leah and Aimee down—even though a big part of me *did* want to take them down. But that wasn't the way to win.

I interrupted Melissa before she could go on a rant. "I don't want to take them down."

"What? Why not?" Helen asked, throwing up her arms like she couldn't believe what I was saying. Part of me couldn't believe what I was saying, either.

"I don't want to be like them," I said, shaking my head. "They suck, I know. But do we want to be just like them? Like, is this *about* something, or is it just more bitchiness back and forth? We need to make sure that we're fixing things, not just turning into mirror versions of them."

Melissa looked at Helen, who looked at Sara, who looked at Jennifer, who looked at me in a round-robin of looks. I wasn't sure if they agreed with me, or if they were just humoring me. But they were at least listening.

"Fair enough. That might be a better strategy," Melissa said. She was probably disappointed in my decision not to, say, go light Leah's locker on fire. "Helen?"

Helen nodded, which cued Jennifer and Sara to do the same. They looked a little scared of me and Melissa, though.

"As long as people stop thinking I'm a super slut who had an abortion, I don't care," Helen said, more than a little flippant. I cringed, knowing exactly what was going to come next.

"Ugh!" Melissa slammed her hand down on her lunch tray so hard that her plate jumped. "How many times do I have to think this in my head before I explode? It doesn't matter. So what if you did? It shouldn't matter if you *did* sleep with Drew Lambert or whoever, or if you had an abortion. There's *nothing* to be ashamed about!"

Helen sat in stunned silence for a moment. Then a defiant look filled her eyes, and she squared her shoulders.

"Melissa, I'm pro-life," she said firmly. "That hasn't changed." She looked at me. "No matter how many magazine articles you throw at me."

I didn't throw *it at you*, I stopped myself from saying.

Melissa took a deep breath. We had to find some common ground, or this wasn't going to work. Helen couldn't fix her problems alone, or with just my help. But Melissa had a lot less patience than I did, and Jennifer and Sara were unknown quantities. We all hated Leah and Aimee, yes, but that was the entire basis of our alliance.

We were super screwed.

"I'm not trying to change your opinion," Melissa said. "But if you knew Jennifer or Sara had had an abortion, you'd forgive them, right?"

"But they wouldn't," Helen said, shaking her head. "They're both in the abstinence club."

They both nodded, this time Jennifer enthusiastically, Sara, a little less so. Sometimes, I wished Helen would be a little less stubborn. I wished she and Melissa had something in common.

And then, the perfect thought hit me.

"Eddie Vedder," I said, remembering a cutout of a certain grunge babe plastered in Melissa's locker last year.

"What?" Helen and Melissa turned to me.

"Ed-die Ved-der," I said, more slowly this time. "You both love him. Melissa, don't lie. I know you still have those pinups of him. Helen, you know he wrote in *Spin* about his girlfriend getting an abortion. I know you didn't read it before you ran off this weekend, but I left the article on your bed this morning. And you can be mad at me about that if you want." She opened her mouth to protest, but I kept going. "But you listen to his music *all the time*. You have to have some connection to what he's saying."

I had her in a corner. It was practically the only thing she played on our stereo, to the point that I had placed a moratorium on listening to Pearl Jam in our room. I would never be able to talk to a guy named Jeremy again without wondering if he had been a violently aggressive child.

Helen scowled at me. She hated when I was right.

"I guess so," she said slowly. "But liking what he says in some things doesn't mean that I'm going to suddenly be pro-choice."

"Here's the deal, though. You can be pro-life and still respect that other people, like Melissa and me, are pro-choice." I glanced around the group. Jennifer looked scared, but Sara was nodding. Melissa was about to jump in, so I shook my head at her and turned back to Helen. "You don't have to be pro-choice to think Mrs. Turner—and the rest of the school—is wrong," I continued. "They're punishing you for something you didn't do, and for something that shouldn't be their business. Besides, what kind of message does that send to the guys? They just get off scot-free?"

Three months ago, Helen would have led the charge against a girl who supposedly had an abortion. Now I could see her weighing the fairness of it all in her mind. Finally, she shrugged.

"Well, no one's going to let Drew Lambert on the homecoming ballot, ever," Helen said. "He's a guy. And if guys were allowed on the homecoming court, he'd be too ugly."

She'd sailed right past the point into the shallow waters of appearance and reputation, without considering how or why her own reputation landed on those same shoals. For her, this was about the fact that she didn't do it, not a question about the fairness of punishing someone who'd had an abortion.

"That's true," Melissa said. Her calm tone surprised me. I'd thought she was about to turn this into one of her political soapbox rants, but she sounded like she was following *my* lead for once. "But think more about Athena's point. What kind of message can *we* send, to counter it?"

She looked at me, expecting me to support her with some miracle words. I didn't have them. I had managed to get Helen to stay for a few more seconds, but I didn't have a lot of hope that we could find neutral political ground. Not now, and maybe not ever with this topic.

"Eddie Vedder," Jennifer said, repeating what I'd just said. Her face turned red as we turned and looked at her. She slammed her hand against her mouth. After realizing we weren't going to stop looking at her, she removed her hand

and sighed. "He wrote *pro-choice* on his arm on *Unplugged.* It's a message."

"But I'm *not* pro-choice!" Helen howled, her face red. Sara shrank back into the column's shadows, like she was trying to get out of range of Helen's voice.

"You don't have to be," Sara said in a calm voice that wallpapered over the giant fissure in our political opinions. "But we can do something like that. Like those girls in *Sassy.* I think they're called riot grrrls? Write on things. Maybe not our arms, but on things."

The girl was good at moderating what she said to make it sound less threatening. She had to be, if she'd managed to stay in Helen's inner circle for this long. But she was onto something—*if* we could agree on a message.

"That's...a really good idea," Melissa said. She took out her composition notebook, flipped it to an empty page, and clicked the pen in her hand. We were about to get down to business.

Writing on things at school, like walls and lockers, seemed like a bad idea to me. The idea of visibility, though, I could work with. A tiny plan started to gather in my head, like productive storm clouds.

The last few times I'd tried to think fast had been a disaster—witness my first lunch with Kyle. But he'd had the Clash patch, and Bikini Kill and Clinton/Gore buttons on his backpack, so I knew what kind of person he was, and where he stood on things. I'd been wrong about his interest in Bikini Kill, but the rest told me something.

I smiled as the idea formed. *Buttons.* Nothing against them in the dress code, as long as they were on our backpacks and not on our actual uniforms.

"Melissa, do you have a button maker?" I asked.

Melissa snorted. "Do I have a button maker? *Of course* I have a button maker. Who do you think I am? I'm a *political activist.*" Helen winced at the words *political activist*, because we all knew it meant political activism she didn't agree with. But Melissa kept going. "Plus, my mom was a Girl Scout troop leader until I quit last year. We have anything you want for any kind of arts and crafts project. Screens for printing! Puff paint! Fabric scraps! Plain white T-shirts! Lanyard string for friendship bracelets!" She emphatically counted each option out on her fingers. "What do you have in mind?"

"I don't think we need friendship bracelets," I said. This wasn't middle school. "I was thinking more along the lines of guerilla campaign buttons. We can figure out what to put on them later. But people would see them. We'd have to make them ambiguous enough that the school wouldn't realize what they're about, but we could gradually add more, and then get people on Helen's side, you know?"

Helen and her clique nodded in agreement. All their nodding would have annoyed me, except now, they were nodding at me—no, *with* me.

"I like the way you think, Graves," Melissa said. She turned to Helen et al. "And it gives me some ideas. Four o'clock, my house. In the meantime, think of some slogans. Try to keep it simple. We're going to war, and we need propaganda."

18

Melissa had turned her room into a DIY command post by the time I got there with Helen, Sara, and Jennifer. She'd fanned out our supplies in a wide circle, with different staging areas for the various kinds of propaganda production.

In the corner near her desk, she'd covered the floor in a layer of newspaper and set up a screen-printing station, which waited for someone to cut the transparencies with an effective slogan. Beside the screen-printing frames, she placed a stack of fabric scraps, which would become patches for backpacks and wherever else we could get people to put them. Same thing with the button station on the opposite side of the room, near her fluffy pink satin-covered canopy bed. Melissa had apparently begged her mom for that princess bed when she was five, but now it stuck out in a room that otherwise screamed punk rock rebellion.

Melissa had stopped at a craft store on the way home to get more button supplies. From the looks of it, she planned to make about five hundred. I don't know where she thought she would find that many people to wear them.

To complete the scene, she'd propped a large dry-erase board up against her vanity mirror. The board gave us our first task: find a slogan. Melissa leaned against the vanity as well, dry-erase marker in hand, dressed in military fatigues. She'd gotten them from one of the army surplus/hunting stores in town, and she wore them every time she did anything messy, like screen printing, making signs for protests, hair dyeing, or helping her dad outside. Paint covered the camo fatigues, but she looked the part of a general rallying her troops.

Except she didn't have a slogan. None of us did. Everything we'd thought of sounded too preachy or too vague, or wouldn't fit on a one-inch button. So the construction paper stayed in stacks by the button maker, and the fabric squares sat in their tidy pile by the screen-printing station. And every passing minute made me think maybe this wasn't such a good idea after all.

"This isn't going to work," Helen said. She sat on the floor, Jennifer and Sara flanking her. I was starting to be able to tell the two of them apart, an easier task now that they'd changed out of their school uniforms. Sara wore an oversize Pixies shirt. Black Francis's head was bigger than she was. Jennifer, on the other hand, took fashion cues from Helen, from her black floral shirt with roses to her cutoff jeans to her black tights, down to her black platform Mary Janes.

Jennifer and Sara exchanged a worried glance. They probably didn't feel any more comfortable than I did, and they certainly weren't used to Melissa's take-charge demeanor.

"Propaganda should be short and memorable, like Loose Lips Sink Ships, or Make Love, Not War," I said, trying to sound encouraging. "We should try to think of something that maybe rhymes, but isn't cheesy. Or that plays off other slogans we already know."

Helen and her friends looked at me like they'd never heard the expression Loose Lips Sink Ships. Okay, so it was old, and also, they weren't in American history yet. And there was no telling if they'd even get that far in the course—judging by how far behind my class already was after one month, we would be lucky to get to the roaring twenties, let alone more modern history.

"Are there any slogans we liked that were too long, that maybe we could shorten?" Melissa searched the crossed-out phrases on the dry-erase board.

No one answered. My muse had left for a year's vacation the moment I suggested the propaganda campaign. Saying "Eddie Vedder" again wasn't going to work, either.

"I liked Forgiveness," Jennifer said, looking toward Helen for approval. They'd been in the pro-life club together. It figured she would like the least direct slogan.

"That's too vague," Sara said, shaking her head. "No one would know we were talking about Helen."

Plus, it was super preachy. *Forgiveness?* No one was going to put that on their backpack. I could imagine how it would go over with the cynical crowd, like everyone in the junior and senior classes. Or someone like Trip Wilson. He was nice enough, but I couldn't see him or any of the other football players wearing something that said Forgiveness.

"And then they would think that I *did* it," Helen said, crossing her arms.

She had a point. *Forgiveness* implied that Helen had done something wrong. Plus, if our campaign—at least, from Melissa's perspective—was to say the punishment was wrong even if Helen *had* had an abortion, it didn't help to be sanctimonious.

"God, so what if you did?" Sara exclaimed suddenly. "It doesn't matter! It's none of their business! And it seems jerkish that anyone is talking about it at all, like, no matter what, they're in the wrong. Isn't *Roe v. Wade* about privacy anyway?"

Everyone turned to stare at Sara. Melissa's eyes were wide, and Helen's glare could have turned Medusa to stone, instead of the other way around. Jennifer blinked hard, like she didn't believe this was reality.

I was just as shocked as the rest of them. The speech could have come out of Melissa's mouth, except she would have laced it with an extra creamy center of profanity and a sprinkling of disgust for Operation Rescue or President Bush. I wondered if there was more to Sara than I'd thought. But then again, maybe she was substituting Melissa as her new leader instead of Helen. Helen's warning glower told me I wasn't the only one who thought this.

"I don't want anyone to think Helen *did* it," she said, backing away from *Roe v. Wade* as fast as she could under Helen's disapproving gaze. "It's just that what's wrong here is that people are talking about her *at all.* Like, they don't really care if it is true or not, they're just in for the gossip."

"So what if I didn't, either, right?" Helen's glare transformed into a look of muted disappointment. "They just keep saying it. It almost doesn't matter."

Melissa wrote *So What?* on the dry-erase board in small neat print without adding to the argument. I was glad she didn't, because she might have ruined the whole thing if she stepped between Helen and Sara. Or she might have ended up with a freshman follower.

"I think we need to work around this," I said, pointing to

the board. "So what if you did? But also, so what if you didn't? The school is punishing you either way, right?"

Helen relaxed against Melissa's bed. She no longer looked poised for a fight for her innocence, but I was starting to worry that she was giving up.

"I could get behind something like that," she said, looking at the floor. "I guess."

"Write that down, Melissa," I said. "How about 'So what if she did?' and 'So what if she didn't?'"

"Those are way too long," Melissa said. "I like So What?, just by itself. It's simple, yet defiant."

Melissa *would* like the most punk rock version of the slogan, but I didn't see Helen going along with anything that didn't lead to clearing her name. Fighting abortion stigma by flipping the bird to it wasn't on her agenda.

Helen shook her head violently, her blond hair whipping around her face, her eyes closed tight in a childish protest. She hadn't made that expression since she was five and Mom told us she was moving out to go to grad school at Duke, but it made me a little less worried about her giving up.

"No," she said. "No. It has to imply I didn't do it. I get what you're saying about 'so what if I *did* do it.' But I want people to at least *think* for a minute about why they believe the gossip in the first place."

Helen had a point, and it was only fair to let Helen decide, since the rumors were about her.

Jennifer raised her hand like she was in class. She hadn't said anything since liking Forgiveness. "Do we have to do just one?" she asked.

"No, there are no rules here." I felt too much like a teacher calling on her, not just because she had her hand raised, but because she looked up at me with terrified eyes like I was going to yell at her. "And you don't have to raise your hand."

"Well, I think that 'So what if she did?' and 'So what if she didn't?' could work as a pair," Jennifer said. "So that both sides are represented."

Helen looked at Melissa, whose leaning posture remained casual. Helen, though, looked anything but casual. Knowing my sister, she had major doubts about the potential success of our campaign, but her own attempts at regaining her reputation—not to mention her modeling escapade—had backfired. So she sat there listening for a lot longer than she normally would have.

"They aren't that great, are they?" Helen asked, looking at the board like she could find a better slogan among the ones we'd already rejected.

"No, but they're memorable," Melissa said. "In that it's pretty ballsy to say 'So what?' to anything at our school."

With their twenty clubs each—well, before Helen got kicked out anyway—the three of them weren't the type to say "So what?" to anything. But Helen nodded in agreement, and Jennifer and Sara followed as expected.

"Okay, so we're going to do the pair of them," Melissa said, underlining them both on the board. "Correct?"

"But what about the buttons?" Sara asked. "They're kind of small. And it's not like initials would work. They don't spell anything. And they're the same for both."

The room let out a collective sigh. Just when we thought we'd had something.

I couldn't let the momentum disappear.

"How about So What? on just the buttons?" I asked. "And the longer ones on the patches? Helen, would you be okay with that?"

"It's not ideal," Helen said with a sigh. "But I could live with it."

Finally, we had our slogans, which nobody really loved. But we had them, so we got to work at the assembly stations. Melissa showed Jennifer and Helen how to cut out letters on the transparencies for screen printing on patches. Jennifer turned out to be a natural at creating hand-drawn fonts.

While Melissa worked with Jennifer and Helen, I taught Sara how to make buttons. I think we were stuck on the least messy duties for a reason—Melissa was also cleaning up a jar of paint that Sara had knocked over earlier, which no doubt made her skeptical about Sara's potential for screen printing. But helping Melissa with all her various political projects in the past two years meant I could make buttons in my sleep, and even if Sara wasn't a natural at it, I could fix any mistakes she made.

After demonstrating how to make buttons, I took Sara upstairs to Melissa's dad's home office, where we photocopied Jennifer's tidy So What? on colored paper. We printed some with white letters on a black background, too. Those were my favorites. So stark. In your face. Perfect.

"How do they get the names for the homecoming court ballot?" Sara asked after we returned to Melissa's room.

The question felt really out of the blue, but the way Sara asked it, I could tell she had an idea that she was holding back.

I didn't seem like someone who would know, but, weirdly, I did. Last year, Melissa had been nominated and tried to withdraw her name because she thought the homecoming court was an exercise in sexism that encouraged girls to compete with each other for shallow reasons. But they wouldn't let her withdraw, so she campaigned on behalf of the other girl, who ended up winning.

"The student council nominates them," I said. "I don't

know how they decide who gets nominated, exactly. There were two girls each on the ballot for freshmen and sophomores, four for the juniors, and a massive eight seniors. After the election, one freshman, one sophomore, two juniors, and four girls from the senior class make up the homecoming court. No one knows which of the four seniors will be the homecoming queen until the homecoming game. And then they all wear their sashes and prance around like princesses at the dance."

Sara pushed down the button maker with an angry *whump*.

"That's a stupid process." Sara's tanned skin had grown red from effort. "Why let a dozen kids make decisions for the whole school?"

"Most people would agree with you."

"It's gross anyway, pitting girls against girls in a popularity contest," she said. "And why aren't there boys on our homecoming court? Don't most other schools have a homecoming king, too?"

"I have no idea." I was more interested in the quality control of our stack of buttons than the court's gender imbalance. But she had a point. Our school treated the homecoming court like a beauty pageant.

"Is there any way to get someone's name on the ballot for sure?" Sara asked, pushing down again with a great, heaving *wham*.

"Not unless you bribe the entire student council," I said. "Where are you going with this?"

Sara blew her hair out of her face absentmindedly. She was growing her bangs out from the poufy style that everyone had stopped wearing last year, and they were at that awkward stage where they were too short to pull back, but long enough to be annoying. At least they made it easier to tell her apart from Jennifer.

"I was just thinking... Homecoming's a big deal, right? What if we tried to do something there? You know, to help Helen?"

If we wanted to get our message out to a lot of people, homecoming could be the ideal place—if Helen was okay with that. Our school was less than a decade old, so we didn't have that many alumni who theoretically made homecoming a real "homecoming." But last year, because the football team was the best in the history of the school, it had become the central focus of the fall. The homecoming court had been featured in the newspaper alongside the winning team, and the dance had turned into a party celebrating that the team had enough victories to guarantee a spot in the district playoffs for the first time. This year, with the team undefeated so far, we'd have a huge crowd and lots of attention.

"That...seems like a great idea," I said, as the realization that I'd grossly underestimated Sara dawned on me.

"Jennifer's the freshman girl representative on student council," she said. "I know we can't get Helen on the ballot, but do you think we can try to stock the court with our friends? Then we can maybe do something with the slogans?"

I froze, scissors and paper in hand. The girl was a genius. If our propaganda didn't catch on, we could figure out a way of getting our message across on the homecoming court. Somehow.

"Do you think Jennifer could do that?" I asked.

"I know she seems quiet," Sara said, shrugging. "But she's a member of debate club. She's surprisingly good at being persuasive." She leaned in closer to me and lowered her voice to a conspiratorial whisper. "But we're going to have to persuade Helen first."

19

Kyle held my hand as we walked toward the football stadium at Greenlawn High, the public school where we had home games, gravel crunching under our feet. The feeling of my hand in his sent a frisson of excitement tingling up my arm. I was holding hands with a boy I liked, and every step brought us closer to a crowd of people, who—and I tried not to think like this, swear on my stack of *Sassys*—would see us as a couple.

A guy might make out with a girl and never call her again, or he might make out with her on a lot of occasions and never acknowledge it in public, or he might make out with her and tell his friends what a slut she was. But it meant something to go to a game together, to hold hands in public, to be recognized as a unit.

I felt like a bad feminist for caring that people saw I was on a date with a hot guy. It was absolutely antithetical to riot grrrl, where every zine told me I shouldn't care about the kinds of double standards buzzing through my brain. Even aside from feeling my personal political inadequacies, though, a feeling of dread lurked under my happiness as we got closer to the bleachers. I might not be a perfect feminist, but I *was* feminist enough to be in touch with my feelings—and my feelings were that I absolutely *did not want* to go to this football game, despite what such a public date with Kyle meant to me.

Under normal circumstances, I only watched our team's games to make sure Sean didn't get hurt. But these weren't normal circumstances—tonight was a series of land mines. Leah and Aimee would be there, cheering on Sean and spreading more lies. Sean would be in the spotlight because the team was doing well, and so I'd have a constant reminder that he was ignoring me. And I had a backpack full of buttons and patches that I *should* try to hand out, but I knew I would feel demoralized when only stoners and slackers who embraced So What? as their personal motto wanted them.

Why was everything so complicated? Why couldn't I have a normal, stress-free date at a football game like half the other people in the crowd? I snuck a look at Kyle's perfect profile, his light brown hair falling in front of his face like an angelic skater boy, and sighed, loud and long.

"What's wrong?" Kyle asked, looking at me from the side. "You don't seem super enthusiastic to be here."

"I'm really not into football." I tried to tell the truth without getting bogged down in the details. "I usually only go because I'm friends with Sean. But I'm supposed to, you know, hand out these things." I jiggled the backpack. "Or at least try to."

Kyle abruptly stopped walking. He looked at me with those amazing amber eyes, very seriously, for about two seconds before launching into a stream of disbelief. "You don't love football? But you live in Baton Rouge! Tiger country! Are you sure you're not a pod person?"

"Nope. Not a pod person," I said warily, fully expecting a lecture like I'd gotten from everyone else in my life. From Dad, who went to LSU for law school and rooted for them, even though they were in the middle of their worst year in history. From Melissa, who watched LSU games with *her* dad and who had an undying love for our school's team, even when they sucked. Last year, she'd even cut the necklines and hems of the school booster club's bulky Beefy-Ts, sewn in new, tightly fitted side seams, and turned them into a fashion statement, all because she *cared about football.* And then of course from Sean, who was, after all, the quarterback.

Everyone wanted me to like football.

"You know, we don't have to stay here," Kyle said, nodding toward the stadium. We'd stopped short of the entrance to the bleachers, and a few latecomers looked at us quizzically as they passed us on their way into the game.

"You don't like football, either?" I'd never met a boy who didn't like football. It didn't seem possible.

"Not really," he said, casually dismissing football with a shrug. "I kinda dig English football, which you play with your feet. I might go out for the 'soccer' team this spring." He used air quotes on *soccer,* which made me happy. I'd never understood the use of the name *football* for a sport that was mostly about throwing and tackling.

"Then why did you ask me to go to the game tonight?"

"Well, I wanted to go with *you,*" he said, like it was the silliest question in the world. "And this seems to be the place that people go on dates. But if you don't want to be here, who says we have to stay? Why don't we go on an adventure instead?"

"What're you thinking?" I felt a twinge of guilt at the

weight of the buttons and patches in my bag, but I pushed it out of my mind. I would have plenty of time to hand them out at school next week. Besides, Melissa had recruited a couple more juniors to help us, so I wasn't essential to the operation. And no guy had ever asked me out on an *adventure* before.

"I was thinking we could steal a golf cart and drive around the golf course." His eyebrows went up and down with the suggestion.

"What? Really?" I liked Kyle. A lot. But there was no way I was going to steal a golf cart from the country club where Melissa's dad and our principal played every Sunday.

"No, but that *would* be an adventure," he said with a grin. "Why don't we just go for a drive? I still don't know where anything is in this town."

Driving around wasn't exactly an adventure, but I considered for a minute that his suggestion might be code for "going somewhere to make out," which honestly wouldn't be that bad of an option compared to watching the football game.

We headed back to his car and drove around for a while, aimlessly, listening to KLSU, the university's distinctly weird radio station. Finally, Kyle smiled at me, turning away from the steering wheel for a moment. We had reached the corner of two main streets, neither of which led to anything other than boring strip malls and office parks.

"Left or right?"

"Right?" I said. "I guess. There's not a lot out this way."

Kyle grinned. "I think I know what we can do for our adventure."

He turned off the main street into a gravel parking lot next to an unfinished, abandoned building near the campus of Jimmy Swaggart's bible college, which the cooler public school kids from youth orchestra referred to as "The Building." It had attained semi-legendary status after someone realized that security patrols almost never came by to check on it. The building was the most popular make-out spot around. It was also a haven for the kids who liked to smoke pot and the artsy types who wanted to practice their tagging.

"We're going to explore that building," Kyle said. "C'mon, it'll be fun. It's really cool and decaying. We'll be urban explorers."

The building loomed up in the darkness, a sense of foreboding oozing from its unfinished concrete frame. I tried not to look at the fungus-covered concrete or exposed steel beams, or the empty darkness of the glassless windows. It screamed "HORROR MOVIE DEATH TRAP" instead of "cool, romantic date." And sure, this was my third date with Kyle, but I'd seen enough *ABC Afterschool Special*s and horror movies to know that you probably shouldn't follow the hot guy into the abandoned building. Either the guy was going to do something terrible to you, or some creep in a mask would show up.

Kyle grabbed a flashlight from the back of his car. He clicked it on and off, testing its battery power, and grabbed a few other items: a camera, a detachable flash, tripod, and a blanket. I let out a huge sigh of relief. Photography was a normal hobby, and somehow reassuring in both its illustration of creativity and its heavy equipment that could be used to fight off an attacker.

As I followed Kyle through the broken chain-link fence, I heard nothing but the loud crunch of gravel under my feet. My heart pounded as we crept through the building. On the first floor, someone had left behind an ancient charcoal grill, but it looked like no one had used it in months. We entered the stairwell, which smelled of a mix of pee and chemicals and things I didn't want to think about, and I started gagging slightly. I worried that my footfalls were going to echo throughout the building as we walked, but I told myself to calm down. I'd always wanted to know what was in this building, and now I was finding out.

With every floor we walked up, I could see the suburban sprawl of the city starting to spread out beneath us through the unfinished walls of the upper floors. Finally, we stopped at the twelfth floor. Outside, streetlights created lines and winding paths and semicircles of cul-de-sacs. Clumps of trees interrupted the lighted patterns with spots of indistinct, inky darkness. The traffic on the highway produced a high-speed line of white and red lights.

I sucked in my breath. Baton Rouge had never looked so amazing.

"It's nice, right?" Kyle had that goofy grin on his face again.

"It's beautiful!" I sighed.

Kyle's flashlight traced an interior wall of the twelfth floor, where graffiti bloomed across the concrete. Blocks of letters outlined in red merged into orange and then yellow in a three-dimensional rendering of someone's tag. Next to it, someone had painted psychedelic three-dimensional images of tropical flowers in bright blues and yellows, something I had never seen in graffiti. On another wall, Tom and Jerry duked it out in black and white. In some places, vandals had scrawled simple tags over the more elaborate drawings, which made me sad and angry for the waste of work that the artists had put into the wall. Even though it was all graffiti, there was a difference between creating something beautiful amid the ugliness, and simple destruction for the sake of it.

"Can you stand there?" Kyle asked. While I'd been gaping at the walls, he'd set up the camera on its tripod.

"Why?" I asked suspiciously.

"I want to take your picture," he said. "C'mon."

I didn't really want him to take my picture right now—I was sweaty and gross from climbing twelve flights in a building without air-conditioning—but I let Kyle position me in front of the camera anyway. From the angle of his tripod, I could tell that whatever picture he took would capture some of the suburban lights and some of the wall of psychedelic flowers. I felt ridiculous and self-conscious in front of the camera. Just when I thought I'd gotten over being awkward around Kyle.

"What am I supposed to do?" Helen would know how to pose, and at this point, I think she might even offer me tips. But she was stuck at home, grounded—until the end of time, most likely.

"Just look out the window," he suggested. "Pretend that I'm not here."

That was impossible, especially since looking out the window meant he'd be shooting me in profile, which made me more nervous than anything. I hated the bump on my nose and the way my chin jutted out. My mother said those things gave me a "strong profile," and riot grrrl preached body positivity, but somehow I could never extend that courtesy to my nose.

Kyle set up the camera on a long timed exposure, so I held my pose for an excruciatingly long time. Then he moved me again. I felt like a doll, and I wondered if this, too, was something that Helen experienced when she modeled. I made a mental note to ask her tomorrow.

"Okay, I'm going to do a few with the flash now," he said. "It'll be really cool with the contrast."

The light from the flash burst out, bouncing off the walls with a sudden, blinding brightness. I'd gotten used to the dim light of the electricity-less building, and I involuntarily squeezed my eyes shut in a ferocious blink.

"Uh," Kyle said. "Maybe not."

He adjusted the flash, bouncing it off other objects so that it wouldn't flare so brightly in my face. After a few minutes, panic seized my chest.

"Kyle," I said hesitantly. "Do you think people can see that flash from the street?"

Kyle's eyes widened. We both rushed to the window. The street below was empty…except for a tiny set of headlights coming up the building's access road. Shit.

"Yeah, we should get out of here." With a remarkable level of efficiency, Kyle popped the camera from the tripod shoe, collapsed the tripod, and tossed everything into his bag.

I struggled to keep up with him as we headed down the stairs. It wasn't like we heard alarms or footsteps, but we were twelve stories up and the building had only one exit. A thousand fears of getting caught swarmed in my head. We were in an abandoned building, trespassing, breaking the law, no "oh, gee, Officer" way around it.

We rushed out of the building toward Kyle's car. I gulped in the night air, much fresher than what had been in the building. Or, if not fresher, at least without the stench of pee. I'd been feeling out of breath for the last three floors, both because I was running so fast and because the stairwell smelled like a broken toilet.

As we reached the car, I saw headlights in the distance creeping toward the building. I couldn't tell if the car was coming toward us or simply using the street as a shortcut. Kyle motioned to me to get in. The driveway made a U-shape the whole way around the building, and we were parked in the back, so no one could see his car from the street. I crossed my fingers that we would have enough time to get to the street before the other car saw us. Kyle drove, slowly and without headlights, around the far side of the abandoned building, so that we were on opposite end from the other car, which was approaching from the front. Finally, Kyle sharply executed a turn onto the narrow road that led away from the building.

I turned around as we picked up speed. Kyle's driving had worked. I could see the other car's headlights through the empty skeleton of the building, but without our lights on, it was doubtful the security guard—or whoever it was—could see us.

About a half mile down the road, Kyle turned on the headlights and started laughing. I wasn't sure if he'd been playing to my fears all along, or if he was as relieved as I was. I giggled, too.

"That was great," he said. "What was I thinking? A building that dark—a flash that bright…"

"I didn't think about it, either," I admitted.

"Until I blinded you."

"Yeah," I said with a laugh. "I guess you're right. Me and my squished-up face, blinking from the flash."

"Never complain about your beautiful face," he said. "Especially when your giant blink made us both realize that we could get caught."

For the third time tonight, I felt my cheeks grow red, and it wasn't just from running down twelve flights of stairs. He'd used the word *beautiful* in connection with my face.

"But see?" he asked, grinning broadly. "Adventure. Definitely better than a football game."

20

After an all too brief make-out session in the car, there was really only one thing we could do to follow up almost getting arrested at The Building—a trip to Denny's.

Actually, Denny's was the only answer to any question about late-night activities. Where do you go after a football game? Denny's. Where do you go after prom (not that I'd been yet)? Denny's. Where do you go after a rare all-ages show at the Varsity? Denny's. Where do you go after the movies? Denny's. What's the only place open after 10 p.m. that didn't require an over-eighteen ID? Denny's.

Kyle held the door open for me as I walked into the brightly lit restaurant, which spread out in a series of plastic booths and shiny fake-wood tables. An elderly hostess with gray hair in tight roller curls led us into the main dining area, and I froze. The entire football team was spread out in one corner of the restaurant, sweaty and gross from their game. Judging by the general excitement emanating from them, it was clear that they'd won, and Sean was holding court in the middle. He smiled, telling a joke that I couldn't hear, and everybody around him laughed.

Trip was on one side of him, red-faced and giant. His messy blond hair stood out in all directions, like an artful punk hairdo someone would spend hours trying to achieve, but was likely the result of towel drying his hair after taking off his helmet.

On the other side was Leah, nestled under Sean's outstretched arm. She smiled at every one of his jokes, and almost, but not quite, flirted with the guys surrounding her. She had a way with boys, including Sean, that baffled me. The other guys were totally thrilled to have her attention, but Sean never seemed remotely bothered by it. Of course, they were his football friends, and if any of them ever tried anything with Leah, it would destroy the team. Plus, Leah Sullivan was not the type to be known as the girl who brought down the potential state champs of 1992. Still, it amazed me that Sean put up with all the flirting.

My stomach tensed. I felt an absence in my heart that I hadn't even known was there. Sean was supposed to be one of my closest friends, but I'd never been invited to any of these after-game hangouts. Leah and Aimee seemed to be the only girls in the group. Since they'd left the cheerleading squad, were the rest of the cheerleaders now banned? Or had they never been to one of these hangouts before, either?

Kyle nudged my elbow. "Hey. Our table's ready." I was frozen in place beside him. He looked from me to the table of football players and back again. "Or..."

"Or what?" I watched Leah laugh at something Sean said

while my stomach turned into a rock quarry. She thought it was her job to ruin my friendship with Sean. She thought it was perfectly fine to destroy my sister.

Helen had nearly run away from home, and half the school had ostracized her for an imaginary abortion because Leah felt a tiny bit threatened. Our So What? campaign hadn't taken off, and so Leah was perfectly fine, going on with her life as though she'd done nothing wrong.

Did I dare say something to her in front of everyone? Did "Double Dare Ya" come into play here, or would it be smarter to wait it out instead of shooting myself, not in the proverbial foot, but in the face?

"Or we could go somewhere else?" Kyle's voice ended on an unsure note as he looked at the crowd of football players.

"I—" I was about to agree with him.

"Hey, Graves! What's up?" Trip's voice boomed from across the restaurant. He waved excitedly. "Come on! Bring your guy over! It's a party!" Next to him, Sean shook his head subtly, but Trip didn't see. He was too busy gesturing for me and Kyle to join them.

I shrugged at Kyle. "I guess we're going to have to say hi. At least."

We walked over to Trip, who continued to shout excitedly at me the whole time. "What a game, right? I mean, I have no idea what it looked like from up the stands, but, *man*, that last pass was like something out of a movie!" He grinned broadly at me. Trip's enthusiasm almost made me want to like football *and* made me feel bad that we'd missed the game.

Trip turned to Kyle. "What did you think, buddy?"

"Uh..." Next to me, Kyle was caught in a huge lie. He glanced at Sean and Leah. Leah's hand was brushing up against Sean's face as she pulled him in for an ostentatious public display of affection. "Yeah, it was a great game," he said, smiling back at Trip. "Awesome game."

I appreciated Kyle lying for both of us. I hadn't seen as much of Trip this year because I wasn't tutoring him anymore, but I couldn't bring myself to lie to him. Everything about Trip was so honest, from his earnest efforts with algebra to his unironic love of *Wheel of Fortune*—which, he explained to me, he'd watched with his grandma all the time when she'd lived with his parents after she broke her hip.

I looked at the rest of the crowd of football players, spilling out of a corner booth across a few shoved-together tables. There was no room for us. Thank God.

"Well, we're going to go grab our table," I said, trying to muster up some less awkward vibes. "Nice seeing ya, Trip." I smiled at him and turned away.

It was a nice escape. Almost.

"Oh, Athena! I didn't see you there." Leah's voice carried over the football players' steady rumble. "Why don't you and Kyle come over here? It's *always* good to see you two!"

She smiled at Kyle in a way that made him flinch. I couldn't believe this was happening in front of Sean, who was now busy talking with Trip. It had shades of that first lunch I'd had with Kyle, but it *shouldn't* bother me. It shouldn't mean anything, even if she *was* doing it in front of a bunch of people, and even if I was obviously on a date with Kyle. But, in the eternally valid words of Han Solo, I had a bad feeling about this.

"Good to see you, too," Kyle said. He shifted nervously next to me. "Uh, Athena and I are kind of hungry, so…" He trailed off, not moving from his spot, with a confused look on his face.

I grabbed Kyle's hand, desperate for a physical connection. I felt like something was off, but I didn't know what. The look she gave him wasn't her usual playful, flirtatious glance. It was different, somehow more intense.

She must have read my mind, because she broke her gaze on Kyle and switched to me.

"Oh, Athena," she said, all feigned innocence and big, Margaret Keane–painting eyes. "I feel *so* bad about what's happening with Helen. I hope your little badge and button campaign works. It's *such* a bummer that she's not in the pro-life club anymore. We all miss her so much at our meetings."

An involuntary snort erupted from my nose. "Really?" I asked, rage bubbling up my esophagus. And then it finally happened. I was taken over by the Spirit of Riot Grrrl or some other feminist instinct or maybe pure anger. "You didn't seem all that interested in the pro-life club until your lies got Helen kicked out. You weren't even a member last year. I didn't think you were enough of a sadist to colonize the part of her life that you destroyed, but I guess I was wrong."

My entire body tensed as I waited for her mean retort. But Leah just stared at me, her overlarge brown eyes slowly but surely welling with tears.

"I...I thought we were friends. I can't believe you'd think I had *anything* to do with that! Why would I want to hurt your sister?" She looked at me with a mouth open in shock, as though my accusation came from out of nowhere, and was based on nothing.

I couldn't believe this was happening. Everyone was looking at me now, from Sean to Trip to the benchwarmers in spotless uniforms and everyone in between. I must have lost contact with reality, that my version of the world was being warped into some through-the-looking-glass truth.

"Are you serious? *Friends?* You've never been my friend! And all you do is spread shit about people! You're petty and jealous and mean, and..." Panic surged through me as all logic and argument slipped away, and I realized that everything I said made me, not her, look bad. I scanned the faces around me to see if they believed her. Trip looked worried that he'd been the one to call me over. Sean stared at me with the same blank, disengaged look that he usually gave to the opposing team before and during a football game. I didn't know a lot of the other guys, but Matt Ambeau and Paul Guillory were looking at me with wide eyes, as though I'd confessed to working with the Unabomber to support Bill Clinton to win the election as a Nixonian Republican—which is to say that they were looking at me like my actions made no sense.

But next to Leah, Aimee hid a silent laugh behind a greasy wadded-up paper napkin. So I *wasn't* wrong about the real state of things. Leah was gaslighting me and everyone else.

"Are you kidding me? Look at her," I snapped, pointing to Aimee. If the guys saw her, maybe they'd believe me about Leah. She dropped the napkin on the table and struggled to keep her mouth in line. "She's *laughing* at this. She thinks it's hilarious that her best friend over there is ruining my sister's life." I turned dagger eyes back on Leah. "You can pretend like you didn't do anything, or that I'm somehow at fault, but I know what's going on. I know what you've been saying about her, about Drew Lambert and some fake abortion. And you know as well as I do that it's not true, just as well as you know that it *shouldn't fucking matter* whether or not she had an abortion. But it matters to *her*. And you two are... You're—"

"Athena, I think you should go," Sean said, interrupting me with a cold voice. "You've done enough."

His eyes were flat and distant again, but I wasn't some lineman on another team that he had to dodge. I was *sup-*

posed to be his friend. My chest suddenly hurt, and I thought I would cry.

"Done enough?" My voice wavered as a lump gathered in my throat. "I can't believe you, Sean! I thought you cared about Helen! I *thought* you were my friend. I thought you of all people would see that I haven't 'done' anything. *I'm* not the one who's at fault here."

I burst into tears, unable to continue. I couldn't keep making accusations, not when Leah was so good at pretending.

I saw myself through the eyes of the guys staring at me. I was a drama queen. A shit stirrer. A "crazy girl" who couldn't get over the fact that her friend didn't need her now that he had a girlfriend. "Crazy girls" like that didn't exist—as riot grrrl reminded me, it was just an excuse for guys not to deal with girls' emotions.

And right now, no one wanted to deal with mine. They probably thought I was jealous that Sean was dating Leah, that I wanted him for myself. But that wasn't true at all. I missed having a real friendship with him. I missed being able to trust him. I missed *him* trusting *me*. But that wasn't part of our current reality.

Sean stood up and nodded to Kyle. "You need to take care of her, okay? Get her out of here. She's upsetting my girlfriend."

The words were like a gut punch. Not *to* me, but *about* me. Like I was a misbehaving child who needed to be dealt with.

Sean knew me. He *knew* literally nothing else he could say would make me more upset. Make it all about a guy being able to "calm" me down, to "take care of" me. Really dismiss me. Make me feel small. Push me to explode with feminist rage, so they could all dismiss my righteous anger as some scene caused by "that crazy girl."

Kyle grabbed my arm. "Co—"

I jerked my arm away. "It's all right. *I'm* all right. I'm leaving."

I turned, but not before I saw Kyle shrug at Sean out of the corner of my eye. Rage boiled inside me. What was *wrong* with guys that they didn't see how manipulative Leah was? How was I the one in the wrong here?

I bolted back out through the Denny's as fast as I could, with Kyle following silently. I'd fucked everything up, and I didn't know what to say. Or do. Or if I even wanted to talk to him right now, after his display in there.

Back in the car, Kyle pressed Play on the cassette player and turned it up loud. I sniffled in the passenger seat, looking out the window. I was fuming from all the things I wished I'd said to Sean, to Leah, to the whole damned football team—and even to Kyle, because who agrees to "get their girl out of there"? *I* didn't want to strike up a conversation with *him*. I wanted *him* to break the silence to talk with *me*.

He'd put in Faith No More earlier, and I'd said nothing about disliking them. It wasn't that they were terrible musicians—they were technically awesome—but every asshole misogynist in our school was into them. If I held up a boom box playing "Epic" in the style of John Cusack in *Say Anything*, every wannabe muscled goon within a five-mile radius would show up and worship at my feet.

The song on right now was "Midlife Crisis," which started out with a loopy, groovy drumbeat. And then it was fine through the verse—typical angsty dude stuff. Whatever. But then it got to the chorus, and I decided I'd had *enough*.

"Is he seriously singing about a woman on her period? Are you fucking kidding me? What *is* this bullshit?" Yes. I was going full-on feminist rage at this point.

Kyle sighed. "You could just ask me to turn it off. Don't get mad at me because of what happened back there." I could practically read his mind: he was thinking I was mad about a dumb menstruation line because I was PMSing, and now he was trying to placate me. He reached over to the passenger side and grabbed a case of tapes. "Pick something out that you like."

The case was full of bands that were supposed to be what you listened to if you were a guy with good indie rock taste. The Clash, whom I obviously liked. The Replacements, who were vastly overrated and apparently disastrous live, even though I'd never seen them. The overly pretentious Elvis Costello. Nirvana, including *Bleach* for DIY cred. Dinosaur Jr for indie cred. Pavement for boring indie cred. Fugazi, who at least had done some shows with Bikini Kill over the summer. Lemonheads, which meant Kyle had something in common with Helen. The fucking Screaming Trees. Who would even buy their album? Soundgarden, almost metal grunge. Pearl Jam, now super popular mainstream grunge.

There were no women. Not even critically acclaimed ones, like Throwing Muses or Tori Amos or PJ Harvey. None of the rocking ones like L7 or Hole or Seven Year Bitch or Babes in Toyland. No Lush or Sinead O'Connor. No Sugarcubes. Not even the Pixies, who had Kim Deal.

This is what the tape collection of a guy who wore a Bikini Kill button—sorry, *badge*—looked like. The same as every other indie rock boy.

I grabbed Sonic Youth's *Dirty*, because at least the band had Kim Gordon. I pushed it into the tape player and hit Play.

"Good choice." Was it supposed to make me feel better to be validated by a guy's agreement?

"Humph," I said, not quite acknowledging him.

He turned the stereo down. "What's wrong? Why are you mad at me? I didn't do anything back there."

I glared at him for two seconds, and then realized that I wasn't that mad at him, at least not for what had transpired at Denny's. The jury was still out on his music collection. He'd been trying to help in the only way he could see, not playing into some patriarchal conspiracy to make me seem like a stereotypical "crazy girl" in front of the football team.

"I'm not," I told him with a sigh. "I'm just mad in general. Leah thinks she can get away with ruining Helen. This pin and patch thing hasn't gone anywhere. No one cares. I know it's been less than a week, and I shouldn't expect so much, but… People would rather continue to speculate on the status of Helen's uterus."

Kyle was quiet for a while, but he didn't turn up Sonic Youth again. Finally, he cleared his throat. "Are you sure that's it?"

"Well, mostly, yeah."

"Mostly?" Something about his voice worried me. Like he didn't trust me. In just one word, I sensed an ocean of doubt.

"Yeah," I said. "Leah's been one step ahead of us this whole time, always dropping hints about 'things she's heard' or leering in front of Helen and asking, 'oh, how are you doing,' or taking Helen's place in the pro-life club…" I trailed off.

"That's not what I'm talking about." He was hinting at something, and it bothered me that he didn't come out and say it.

"So what *are* you talking about?"

He couldn't look at me because he was driving, but it felt like he didn't *want* to look at me, either.

"What's going on with you and Sean?"

"Wait. What? Why would you think anything is going on

with us?" Though of course I knew *why* he would think that, after the way Leah had managed to spin our confrontation off as me being mean to her. It was what a girl jealous over a boy might do, even though it had nothing to do with that, at least not in the sense Kyle seemed to be thinking.

His shoulders slumped. "It's just that...back there...you seemed like you were more upset about Sean's reaction than Leah's."

"Of course I was!" I protested. "We've been friends since we were three! I'm upset he basically erased that in favor of believing his girlfriend and her cackling apprentice!"

Kyle sighed again, louder than the first time. It felt like he didn't believe me, either about Leah's culpability or about my lack of romantic feelings for Sean.

"Have you ever considered that your dislike for Leah *might* be coloring your opinion of who started those rumors about your sister? I didn't want to say it, but—"

"I am absolutely certain that she's behind it," I said, trying to sound serious but calm and not completely angry that he'd doubt me. I was, however, utterly livid at him now, too. "She's practically been holding up signs over her head claiming responsibility every time she talks to me."

"I know you think that, but..." Kyle paused for a second. His mouth was at war with itself—firmly set until it looked like he was about to say something, then repeat. Finally, he found the words. "I need to know that it's not something else."

"Something else?"

"Do you *like* Sean?"

My heart pounded. I could lose Kyle, right now, if I answered wrong. I didn't *like* Sean, not like that. But I understood why people got confused. There wasn't a whole lot of precedent for a girl being close friends with a guy at our school. Or anywhere, really.

"No, Kyle," I said. "I don't. I like *you.* It's been hard to lose Sean as a friend, but honestly, I think we've been slowly growing apart for years. It's just that this thing with Helen has brought that fact to the forefront of my life, you know? But it's not about being jealous or whatever."

Kyle let out a long exhale as he slowed the car to a stop in front of my house. "Are you sure?"

"One hundred percent," I said earnestly.

He turned and smiled at me. "I like that percentage."

Then he kissed me, long and slow, and I finally felt like he believed me.

21

After a week, our campaign had halfway worked with the lowest strata of the school. The So What? buttons popped up among the freshmen, and they had a strong appeal with the stoners. But no one seemed interested in the patches, which had our real message.

"Give it time," Melissa said. From the sound of her voice, she was reassuring herself as much as the rest of us. She liked being our de facto leader, but that meant she had more to lose if we failed. Not as much as Helen, obviously, but enough to make her nervous.

Jennifer, Sara, and Helen stared down at their sandwiches. We were going to need a miracle to make this work.

I looked at my own sandwich with defeat. Not only had I lost faith in our ability to get the right kind of attention on Helen, I'd had that huge fight with Sean at Denny's. I couldn't even put words to what happened. I kept trying to tell Helen about it, and had even reached for the phone to call Melissa, but somehow the whole episode embarrassed me so much that I didn't want to talk about it. I'd meant to come off as strong, to stand up for what I believed in. Instead, everyone had looked at me like I'd set the Denny's on fire while vowing to destroy Leah.

I couldn't tell them. At least not yet.

"Good afternoon, girls."

Oh, God. Mrs. Breaux towered above us in a paisley polyester dress that flowed around her pantyhose-covered calves. She smiled pleasantly and said, "Melissa, Helen, Athena, could you please come with me?"

We hadn't done anything. I could see her seeking us out if our campaign had been successful, but it wasn't. Still, the self-satisfied expression on her face didn't bode well for us.

I put my sandwich back in my bag, hoping I'd have the chance to eat it before the bell rang for my next class. My stomach rumbled, a complaint at the unfairness of Mrs. Breaux interrupting us during our free time, especially when Melissa and I had just come from her class right before lunch. If she was going to "catch" us at something, she should have done it fifteen minutes ago.

But whatever she wanted to catch us at remained a mystery for now. Melissa shrugged as she got up from her spot, while Helen's mouth was a thin line of consternation. I was sure I'd complained about the physics teacher in front of Helen before, but since she was only a freshman, she hadn't yet fully experienced the wrath of Mrs. Breaux.

The three of us followed Mrs. Breaux through the empty corridors toward what I thought was our final destination—the principal's office. But when she got near Melissa's locker,

Mrs. Breaux stopped. She rubbed her hands together, satisfied that she had uncovered some secret wrongdoing.

"Please open your locker, Miss Lemoine," she ordered.

"Why?" Melissa asked. She crossed her arms and stood in front of her locker, blocking access.

"You know why." Mrs. Breaux crossed *her* arms, matching Melissa in defiance. It occurred to me from Mrs. Breaux's answer that maybe *she* didn't know why she was doing the search. I looked at her face for clues that I was right, but it was hard to say. Her manners were usually so put-on that it was impossible to tell what was genuine indignation and what was a knee-jerk response to Melissa's question.

"No, really, I don't," Melissa said. "I don't know *why* you want to search my locker, and I don't think you have the authority."

The patches and buttons weren't in Melissa's locker, and besides, they weren't against the rules to have—though obviously we didn't want to have to explain them to the principal or the dean of discipline, because it would likely undermine our rebellion before it had a chance to take off. At any rate, Sara was carrying them in her backpack, which, in theory, teachers weren't allowed to search. I'm not sure that those search parameters mattered to Mrs. Breaux, though, since she wasn't supposed to search our lockers, either.

"Just open it," Mrs. Breaux barked, her face red above her high-necked dress. Her aggression seemed way out of line for mere buttons and patches. Melissa flinched as the physics teacher leaned toward her. "I can assure you that Principal Richard is aware of this search."

Melissa squinted at Mrs. Breaux with a quizzical look, then shrugged and twisted her locker combination, throwing open the locker door in seconds. She had nothing in it except a neatly arranged row of books and binders, plus some pictures of Suede's Brett Anderson pasted on the inside of the locker door. According to *NME*, where Melissa got the photos, Suede was Britain's next awesome band or something, or else Brett Anderson wouldn't have made the coveted spot. He was one pretty man, though.

Smiling, Mrs. Breaux rifled through the locker's contents for a good three minutes, destroying the perfect order. But when she found nothing, her face turned to a pursed-lip frown within seconds. She shut the locker door and marched us down the hall.

"Miss Graves." She looked at me over her red plastic reading glasses. I suspected she wore them only for the purpose of intimidation, but it wasn't working on me at the moment. I couldn't figure out *what* she thought we were hiding. All this drama felt too great for buttons and fabric scraps.

"Which one?" Melissa asked in a tone that came right up against a line of disrespect, but didn't quite cross it. "You brought two of them into the hall."

Mrs. Breaux pursed her lips together again. She alternated between three expressions: smug smile, pursed lips, and wrinkly scowl.

"Remember your detentions with me, Miss Lemoine." She turned to me. "Please open your locker."

We walked the remaining fifteen feet to my locker. Mrs. Breaux wouldn't find anything there, but I had the tiniest fear that Aimee and Leah had somehow broken in and planted something there. It was possible they'd figured out my combination. Or paid some kid to break the lock.

I wiped my suddenly sweaty hands on the polyester of my uniform skirt. I shakily turned the lock's combination, 36-10-28. The lock clicked open, and I slumped with relief.

My locker had nothing out of the ordinary, just books and papers and binders. A little messy, but nothing incriminating. On second thought, it was a *lot* messy. Mrs. Breaux huffed unsatisfactorily, lifted the mess of crumpled papers that sat on top of my stack of books, and took out a desiccated apple that was supposed to be part of my lunch last week. I didn't much like apples, and I'd meant to throw it away, but forgot.

Taking note of the apple with a disapproving sniff, she repeated the rifling process, as though going through the mess of my locker again would manifest whatever sordid object she was looking for. Finally, she slammed my locker door shut without saying a word and turned to Helen. Just in case, I turned my lock quickly, making a mental note to trash that apple the first chance I got.

Mrs. Breaux ushered us down the hall toward the freshman lockers. By now, people had started to trickle into the hall from the cafeteria, grabbing forgotten books or trying to make sure they got across campus in time for their next class. A small crowd gathered to watch us as we stopped in front of Helen's locker.

"Miss Graves, please open your locker." Mrs. Breaux clasped her hands together with the command.

"No," Helen said. She looked paler than usual, but her voice was firm.

"What?" Mrs. Breaux tried her intimidation trick of looking down at Helen over her glasses, but Helen stood a good three inches taller than Mrs. Breaux, so the woman found herself looking up instead. The effect wasn't quite the same.

"No, ma'am." A lilting politeness returned to Helen's voice. "According to the student handbook, only the dean of discipline or the principal can ask a student to open his or her locker. I'm happy to wait for Sister Catherine or Mr. Richard, but, until then, I politely decline your request."

"Open your locker," Mrs. Breaux demanded, her face growing sweaty behind her glasses. "Or face detention."

Helen smiled, a more triumphant reaction than I would have expected from her. Leaning against her locker, she seemed much more confident than the rest of us. Or maybe this was her way of buying time. Either way, she was getting as much as she could out of the moment.

"I am happy to oblige," she said. "But you do realize that you open the school up to a lawsuit if you knowingly violate my right to privacy and the terms that you agreed upon in your teaching contract."

I gasped. Helen sounded *exactly* like our dad when he was on the phone with an opposing counsel. I couldn't tell how much of her talk was bluffing and how much was based on the actual student handbook, and I had no idea what the teachers' contracts stated—I'd never seen one. But something she'd said made Mrs. Breaux back away. She recrossed her arms in front of her dowdy paisley polyester dress, an act of firm self-assurance that made me suspect she didn't know what was in the handbook or her contract, either.

"Stay right here," she said, walking toward the nearest open classroom door. "I'm getting Principal Richard."

I rolled my eyes. Apparently she needed to find someone to watch over us. The nearest door belonged to Ms. Hebert, the biology teacher. Mrs. Breaux, gesturing in our direction and whispering about our misdeeds, pulled tiny, disheveled Ms. Hebert into the hall by her arm.

"I'll be right back," Mrs. Breaux said. "Don't let them move a muscle."

Ms. Hebert's eyebrows arched up stealthily. Newer teachers

weren't supposed to show dissent to the senior faculty members. But we'd all been perfect students in Ms. Hebert's class. In fact, Helen should have been about to enter her classroom now for biology, but was instead trapped near her locker.

"Helen, why don't you let the poor woman have a look?" Ms. Hebert said. "Surely your books aren't the products of some terrorist plan."

Ms. Hebert sounded so reasonable and calm, but Helen still shook her head. I was surprised, since Ms. Hebert was one of Helen's favorite teachers.

"I'm already being punished for something I didn't do," she said angrily. "I've been forbidden from doing any extracurricular activities for the rest of the semester, and if they come up with some kind of 'evidence,' I'll probably be expelled. I'm not going to make it easier for her."

Ms. Hebert put her hand on Helen's arm and squeezed it, a tiny gesture that seemed far more genuine than any of Mrs. Turner's hugs. Ms. Hebert wasn't like some of the other teachers, especially not Mrs. Breaux. I wouldn't say that being young made her more relatable, but she lacked the bitter finishing note of the more hardened teachers. Her brown wavy hair hung well past her shoulders, and she wore informal clothes—tunic shirts and long, swishing broomstick skirts and jangling bracelets. She wasn't old enough to have been a hippie, but she looked like a kind, sober Janis Joplin.

None of us said anything until Mrs. Breaux returned, Mr. Richard in tow. From halfway down the hall, we could see her gesturing angrily to the principal, who shook his head as he waddled toward us in his too-big suit. Mr. Richard always looked like he was shrinking inside his clothes, which went along with how some of the teachers ran right over him. I hoped he'd informed Mrs. Breaux that teachers couldn't look in students' lockers without consent, and that Mr. Richard would back Helen up.

"Miss Graves," Mr. Richard said, clearing his throat. "Please open your locker."

Evidently my hopes were for naught.

Her hands shaking in anger, Helen opened the lock with a short half twist that meant she'd never locked it in the first place. As soon as she opened it, she let out a gasp and raised her hands to cover her mouth.

Someone had papered the entire inside of her locker with full-color photos of aborted fetuses. The posters were full of blood and gore, with *baby killer* scrawled across each one in Sharpie. Larger pictures, on poster board, were taped to the walls of her locker, while smaller photos were taped to the covers of her books and notebooks. Whoever had done this had left no surface empty. And the pièce de résistance—a pig fetus stolen from the biology lab, stuck in a jar of formaldehyde—was placed right in front.

My stomach turned at the display, and my heart ached for Helen. Only some kind of monster would do this to her. First, to break into her locker with all this hateful crap. Then, to make sure Mrs. Breaux got tipped off that *something* illicit was in one of our lockers, and that she needed to be the one to root it out. She was the only teacher I could think of who'd be so aggressive.

I peered into Helen's locker for a closer look. I knew those posters—they were from the fake abortion clinic on Chimes Street. The ones the woman had thought were "necessary" at the protests. Melissa and I hadn't seen them that day—just the pamphlets and the lighter propaganda—but the woman had said that some girls had come in for them specifically.

But I'd seen them elsewhere before. Some of the members

of the pro-life club got a stack last spring to protest at Delta Women's Clinic even before Operation Rescue announced its "Summer of Purpose." But Sister Catherine said the tactics were against school policy, so she took the posters and locked them up. So whoever had visited the clinic before we did must've vandalized Helen's locker, because it sure wasn't Sister Catherine.

Melissa nudged my arm. "Fake abortion clinic," she whispered.

"Shh. I *know*."

Around us, the small crowd turned into a near mob with everyone clambering to see the "evidence." Some of Helen's former pro-life friends covered their mouths in horror like she had. A handful of students laughed, and still others stared with car-wreck fascination.

"See! Look at the evidence!" Mrs. Breaux boomed, stretching her arms wide, certain the crowd's shocked reaction meant she'd found something truly incriminating. She stood with her back to the locker, never even turning around to see what was there. Her words implied an altogether different kind of wrongdoing—that she'd found something scandalous, and we were finally on our way to getting the punishment we deserved.

"You're a sick lady, Mrs. B!" someone shouted from the crowd. It sounded a little like Trip Wilson.

When a few more people shouted more vulgar things from the safety of the masses, Mrs. Breaux's triumphant glare melted into a blend of confusion and anger.

"This is unacceptable! You all have—"

"You *might* want to turn around." Mr. Richard quietly steered her toward Helen's locker.

As she turned, Mrs. Breaux let out a small shriek of surprise.

Her mouth seemed to get stuck in the shrieking position, making her look like Munch's *The Scream*, once the sound faded.

"This has gone on long enough. Helen, why don't you go into my classroom?" Ms. Hebert pushed her way to Helen's side. "I'm sure Athena and Melissa can clean out your locker for you."

Helen's defiance melted into tears as she looked at the locker full of pro-life propaganda again. She grabbed her biology book from her locker, ripped the fetus-paper cover off, and jammed it into her backpack. Without saying a word to Mrs. Breaux or Mr. Richard, she stomped into Ms. Hebert's classroom.

"People, you need to go to your classrooms," Mr. Richard said. But for a man who prided himself on his disciplinary qualities, he didn't have much effect. Dozens of juniors and seniors kept standing there, watching Melissa and me clean out Helen's locker.

Mrs. Breaux had already disappeared. Some people just didn't know how to apologize.

I approached my own locker with suspicion at the end of the day. I had locked it after Breaux's search, but I felt like it was smart to remain wary.

Wisteria was already there, shoving her black-covered textbooks and purple-and-black composition notebooks in and out, doing the homework shuffle.

"That was *so* mean, what happened to your sister," she said, shaking her head. Today, her black-as-night hair was pulled into a ponytail, and her bangs fell straight across her forehead like Bettie Page, or a goth Veronica Lodge. She leaned in close and dropped her voice to a whisper. "So, um, can I get a button? Or a patch? You know, maybe make the full statement? 'So what if she did?' I think that one is the *best.*" She bounced with more enthusiasm than I thought appropriate, considering the subject matter.

"Sure." I fished one out of my backpack and handed it to her. I'd been giving the few people who'd approached me a choice from whatever I had on hand, but after today's incident, I wasn't about to put my stash on display.

"Awesome!" She proudly pinned it to her backpack. "Thanks, Red!" She looked up behind me, and her Cleopatra eyes widened. "Oh! You've-got-company-gotta-go-bye!" Wisteria rushed off, faster even than her words flew out of her mouth.

I turned around, hoping to see Kyle and fearing to see Mrs. Breaux or Mrs. Turner. Kyle and I hadn't talked much since our date on Friday, since I'd been spending so much time with Melissa and Helen and her friends.

But instead, I found Trip towering over me, six-feet-plus of muscle encased in a layer of protective linebacker bulk. "Biscuit muscle," Melissa called it. A blush crept up his face when I looked up at him.

"It's, um, really crappy what happened to your sister's locker today." He leaned down, dropping his voice to almost a whisper. "And I, um, think it's also really crappy what Sean said to you the other night. I'm not a huge Leah fan, and if you think she's behind what's going on with your sister, well... Let's just say I'd believe you over her anytime."

I felt an urge to hug Trip. Which I didn't do, because it would be weird. I wasn't a hugger, and we weren't close enough friends for that.

"Thanks, Trip," I said gratefully. "Do you maybe want a patch or a pin? I don't have that many left right now, but I think..." I dug into the bottom of my backpack, trying to fish out the few remaining things, but Trip smiled and tilted his backpack toward me. Front and center, he'd pinned a bright orange So What? button.

"That's so awesome! You're the best!" And then I hugged Trip anyway. After a day where the grossness of humanity had been on full display, it just seemed like the right thing to do.

After I let go of him, Trip stood awkwardly in front of me, blushing, like he wanted to say something more, but then he caught sight of something over my shoulder.

"Oh, hey, your boy's here," he said less than enthusiastically. "See you soon?"

"Of course!" I wondered if I'd upset him by hugging him—sure, we weren't *hugging* friends, but it was a friendly hug, not a boundary-crossing or sexy hug.

As Trip waved goodbye and practically ran away, his face beet red, I turned to Kyle with a smile.

"Want a pin or a patch? I bet we have something that'll look great next to that Clinton/Gore button," I said, hoping to build on the good that had happened today, instead of focusing on the bad. I hadn't seen Helen yet, but I hoped she was getting the kind of positive response that I was, or at least starting to feel better. I dug in my backpack for the gallon-sized plastic bag with all my campaign supplies. "Sara and Jennifer have most of them, but..."

"Oh, that's okay," he said, reaching out to pull my arm back from my search. He gave my hand a squeeze before letting it go. "I'll get one when you have a better selection, okay?"

"But you don't even know what I have." I couldn't hide the disappointment in my voice. He didn't have any reason *not* to take one. Wisteria and Trip had been enthusiastic. Why not Kyle, who, as far as I knew, was the only other surefire liberal person around?

He must have read my face, because he backed up a little and gestured to my backpack with a grin, as if to make up for hurting my feelings. "All right, let's see what you've got!"

I glanced down the hall, making sure that no teachers were in sight. When the coast was clear, I tugged the bag up from the bottom of my backpack and pulled out the three So What? pins I had left. "Take your pick!"

Kyle grabbed the one in the center, black on bright green. "I think this one'll do."

"Excellent choice," I said, smiling up at him. "Now, put it on. I bet it'll look great with the rest of your collection."

He put it on his backpack and gave it a light tap, like it was something to be proud of. Which, to me, it was.

"I think it looks good," he said, brightly enough to make up for whatever slight I'd perceived earlier. "So, um, about tomorrow…"

"Oh, shit," I interrupted, grimacing. Tomorrow, we were supposed to play music again, and this time maybe work on writing some songs together, instead of blasting through covers. But after years of never having anything social on my Wednesday schedule except the now-canceled comics shopping with Sean, I'd made separate plans with both Kyle *and* Melissa and Helen. "I…double booked."

I worried for a second that he was going to be annoyed. "But I think I can change my plans with Melissa and Helen?" I offered. "Or, rather, they can get along without me." As soon as I said it, though, I wasn't so sure. They could do the work without me, of course, but whether they could *get along* without me was another question. "We were going to plan out the rest of our campaign…"

I trailed off. Instead of looking disappointed, as I'd expected, Kyle looked relieved.

"You don't need to cancel with Melissa and Helen," he said, squeezing my shoulder. "You guys are doing important work! And besides, I was about to say that I have someone coming over for peer tutoring tomorrow, so I was going to need to switch things up anyway."

"Oh." I could fit a lot of things into that "oh." Disappointment, confusion, and the tiniest bit of suspicion about why he said "peer tutoring" instead of naming whomever it was he was tutoring. I couldn't justify my suspicion, but I kept having the nagging feeling that *something* was off about Kyle's tutoring plans.

He gave me a quick kiss on my forehead, which wasn't exactly romantic, but it *was* a public display of affection at school, so I took it as a good sign.

"Ah, don't be so dramatic," he said with a smile. "We're still on for Friday, right? And it's not like we won't see each other at school before then."

Except we *didn't* really see each other at school, I wanted to say. We'd now gone on three legitimate dates, plus the Melissa-arranged coffee-shop meet up, but barely spent any time with each other at school. He was always going to lunchtime photography club meetings or had some other excuse not to sit with me and Melissa. Though I kind of understood not wanting to sit with us, because Girltown, USA, could be a little overwhelming. And it wasn't like we could talk in class. But I knew it would be wrong to point all that out—it would make me seem paranoid. And jealous, which, again, was something a self-professed riot grrrl should be weeding out of her personality.

"Yeah, you're right," I said, trying to emulate the kind of girl I wanted to be. "I'm just a little bummed that we're delaying our songwriting a bit." I grinned up at him, projecting as much confidence in myself and our relationship as I could. "But I'll get over it."

"You're the best," he said, squeezing me in a tight hug. "Thanks for being such a cool girl."

"No problem," I said, returning his hug. Maybe if I kept acting like a cool girl who wasn't jealous for no reason, I would eventually turn into one.

22

The next day, Jamie Taylor, a senior girl I barely knew, grabbed my hand and pulled me into the girls' bathroom. As a senior, Jamie moved in a completely different world than I did, even though I was in calculus with her. She was one of those girls who managed to be smart *and* nice *and* pretty *and* popular, all at the same time. Everybody liked her, to the point that Leah and Aimee wouldn't even try to go after her with gossip, because no one would believe them.

Jamie gripped my hand as she pushed open the door, as though she was afraid that I'd be swept away into the crowd of everyone rushing home after school. Then, like Melissa feening for a cigarette, she checked under the stall doors to make sure that no one else was in there with us. Even while she was performing such an undignified task, Jamie's chestnut hair fell in a perfect, elegant cascade over her shoulder.

Finished, she let out a sigh and briefly closed her eyes. A bit dramatic, I thought, but with the way my week was going, not entirely unexpected.

"Athena, you're one of the Gang of Five, right?"

"The *what*?"

Jamie sucked in a deep breath and her brown eyes flew open, frozen in fear.

"So you're *not*?"

"Jamie, I have zero idea what you're talking about," I said, shaking my head. "The Gang of Four was a name for either an English post-punk band or a group of four people during the Chinese Cultural Revolution. I'm obviously not part of either of those."

Jamie frowned, and then she nodded, like she'd suddenly thought of something.

"But you're friends with Melissa, right? And your sister is Helen, that girl who got the abortion?"

Helen would hate the way Jamie said that, like it was so certain. Not "the girl those rumors were about," or "that freshman whose locker was plastered with anti-abortion propaganda," but "that girl who got the abortion."

As pro-choice as I was, I felt the need to offer a bit of correction.

"Uh, no." Jamie started looking even more confused, so I continued quickly, "I mean, yes. Melissa is my friend, and Helen is my sister, but she'd just about die if she thought you actually believed she had an abortion." Jamie flinched. I didn't know what I'd said to provoke that reaction, so I continued, "Not that there's anything wrong with that—it's just she and I don't exactly see eye to eye on the issue, you know?"

Jamie gave me a half smile—the kind that is part of a

conversation, like a *like* or an *um*, but that doesn't exactly indicate happiness—and nodded.

"So you *are* part of the Gang of Five," she said. "At least, that's what everyone's calling you… Melissa told me that you had some patches I could get. You know, for my backpack."

This was the first time I'd heard us being called anything, or that anyone cared about who I was in relation to other people. Since she was into post-punk *and* constantly annoyed when people mistook her for being Chinese—or worse, called her a Chinese commie for her liberal political activism—Melissa had probably created the name as some kind of ironic homage. But while the Gang of Five clearly had her fingerprints on it, other people were embracing it, too, including girls like Jamie, apparently.

A small thrill ran through me at the thought. I was part of a gang—a girl gang. Maybe not riot grrrl, but definitely something great.

"Yeah, that I can do," I said, excited that I could help her out. Jennifer had given me a stash of patches and a bag of buttons in a clandestine hallway handoff between sixth and seventh periods. She'd muttered something about being freaked out by the demand and ran off before I could thank her. It didn't exactly make me feel confident in Sara's assertions that Jennifer was our great hope for finding a way to stock the homecoming court with Helen's supporters.

I fanned out a selection of patches on the tile ledge of the bathroom window. There were gingham ones, and some on T-shirt fabric, and a few on white muslin with a border of our school's uniform fabric, to emphasize the connection. Those were all "So what if she did?" Melissa's idea of pushing the political envelope.

Jamie's hand hovered among the choices. Her pink-lipsticked mouth was back in a frown, and I had a flash of fear for a minute that she was going to change her mind and maybe even rat me out to Sister Catherine. So far, the dean of discipline had left us alone, and I wanted her to be blissfully unaware of our plans.

"How much do these cost?" She studied the piles of patches.

"Cost?" I blinked. We'd been giving them away for free—that was the whole purpose of propaganda, right? To get everyone to do it. I'd never thought we could charge for them, even though that would help with costs for more supplies if we ran out. "They're free, of course."

"Oh, yeah," she said, nodding slowly. "Like the buttons at the protest last summer."

I nodded back, confused. Melissa hadn't said anything about anyone else from our school being at the protest. While Melissa liked being a leader, she wasn't the type to erase anyone else's work. Plus, someone else from our school being a clinic defender—well, that was *major* news. "You were there?"

Jamie pursed her lips again. "Yeah. Melissa really…showed me the ropes, I guess you could say."

That surprised me. Miss Super Nice National Honor Society President didn't seem like she'd put herself in danger at the clinic. Melissa *liked* riding the edge of what she could get away with in terms of out-of-school activities. Jamie, from the little I knew of her, seemed like the exact opposite.

"Wow. I didn't know."

"Yeah. It was intense." She was looking at the patches, not me, lost in thinking about last summer. I hoped she'd pick her patch soon—I had to go find Helen. I put out a tidy pile of buttons next to the patches, in case she wanted one of those, too. Maybe she would get the picture and pick something already.

"I guess you're happy to hear the good news, then, right?" Yesterday, the federal court had struck down the state's abortion ban. It was all Melissa had been able to talk about at lunch today.

Jamie stared at me blankly.

"The law? It was struck down. Operation Rescue's protests didn't work."

"Oh, yeah," she said, addressing the patches again. "It was hard, you know." Her voice echoed around the bathroom. "There were so many protesters. *So* many. Screaming about killing babies and holding signs like the ones in Helen's locker." She looked up at me, and I was surprised to see that she was on the verge of tears. "I saw that yesterday. No one deserves that, whether or not they've had an abortion."

"Yeah, and a fetus at that age doesn't really look like any of those posters..." I trailed off. Jamie didn't need to hear my scientific, biological explanation. She'd been in the trenches, on the front line, and any other military analogy I could think of. All I'd done was make some ambiguous buttons and patches with my friends.

She shrugged. "Yeah. I guess. Anyway. It wasn't an easy experience, but I'm still happy I did it."

"Yeah, Melissa said it was rewarding to help everyone."

Jamie gave me a strange look for half a second. Then she smiled wanly. "Oh. Yeah. Definitely. It was."

Something about the way Jamie was talking about the protests itched at my brain. Melissa's letters to me in Eugene had been filled with incandescent, righteous anger and a sense of obligation to the girls and women she'd escorted. She'd written about how the patients coming to the clinic were all types of women, some young, like us, and others who were older. All races, from all walks of life. She knew that she was helping them get what they needed, and she'd worked hard to be a kind face for them in the sea of protesters. She'd been there to protect the patients, and whatever epithets the protesters had yelled at her became fuel for the next day of helping patients.

Jamie's reaction…wasn't like that. It was more like she'd felt the protests were directed at *her*.

Things clicked into place in my mind. If she felt that way, and Melissa had never mentioned her, could she have been a patient at the clinic? The question was too big for me to handle—not something I could ask a relative stranger, and not something I needed to know. I wouldn't feel right asking Melissa, either, because she obviously hadn't told me about it for a reason. But I cringed at my earlier fetus-poster talk. If Jamie *had* had an abortion, I probably reminded her a little too much of how she was treated on the way to the clinic. But she couldn't have…could she?

She picked up our most risqué model, the one with the school-uniform trim. "I think I'll take this one."

"Good choice," I said encouragingly. "Be bold."

"You know it. Thanks, Athena." Jamie squeezed my hand and, as quick as she'd pulled me in there, she was gone. I shoved everything else into my backpack and headed out to find Helen.

23

The next morning, I was startled to find Sean waiting at my locker before homeroom, slouching in such a way that I could practically hear Mrs. Estelle's voice in my head telling him—and me—to stand up straight. Come to think of it, she said it to me far more often than to him.

"Hey, Athena." He inhaled a sharp breath, like he wanted to say more, but didn't.

I scowled. I'd moved beyond feeling like *I'd* been the one to mess up our friendship and now firmly believed that Sean wasn't being at all fair to me. I wasn't the one who couldn't talk about my feelings until things exploded all over the place.

Like now. Why couldn't he just say what he was going to say, instead of making me *ask* him what was wrong? When had he asked *me* what was wrong lately? And beyond me—us, our friendship—why had he stopped caring about Helen, who'd always been like a little sister to him, too?

No, I'd moved *far* past feeling like I was at fault to feeling like Sean had been *beyond* unfair.

"Hey," I said with more than a little bit of impatience. "I'm going to be late for class."

"I just—you know, I—Leah and I..." He paused and looked at his feet. "You know what, never mind."

"Why do you always have to be this way?" I asked, all the anger I had at him bursting out at once. Which didn't make me much better than him, honestly. "You want me to ask you what's wrong, and that's not fair!"

As soon as the words left my mouth, I couldn't believe I'd said them. *That's not fair.* No matter how true it might be, I still sounded like a five-year-old whose toys had been taken away during dinner.

Sean looked at me like I'd slapped him. "I'm not always—" He stopped himself. "Okay, that's fair. I do take forever to talk about the things that really matter. But this is...important."

I could feel my resolve fading. I never ignored Sean when he had something big to say—mostly because he almost never shared his feelings about certain things with me, or really anyone else.

But he'd been *such* a jerk. I could still feel the shame and embarrassment of him telling me off in front of everyone. Of making it seem like I'd been out to get Leah, and not the other way around. I blinked back tears, trying to steel myself for whatever he was going to say. I couldn't get any words out, so I just nodded for him to continue.

"I wanted to explain to you what happened," he said. "The last time we saw each other—it made me realize a few things. And I don't like how I acted... And Leah..."

He stopped, and I waited. When he didn't continue, I could feel the anger building up again inside me.

"An explanation isn't an apology, Sean," I said through gritted teeth. If I ungritted them, I knew I'd collapse into tears.

His eyes met mine, and I could see the genuine regret in his gaze. "I know. I just—look, I want you to know that I *am* sorry. I got into a huge fight with Leah afterward, and—"

"So now that you've gotten into a fight with her, *that's* why you're apologizing?" I swiped my hand up my cheek to push away the tears that started rolling down. "That's not a great reason."

"I—you're right." His shoulders sank. "I guess I'll just see you around, then. Okay?"

"Fine."

He turned and walked down the hall.

I told myself I didn't care. He owed me much more than he'd offered just now. But guilt crept into the back of my mind, making me wish for a moment that I'd tried to be more patient with him, tried to listen.

I shook my head and pushed the guilt away. No—he was in the wrong, and he needed to find a way to make things right again between us.

I needed a real apology before I could find it in myself to forgive him.

24

Another day in physics, another tightly folded note tapping on my shoulder. After our last note-passing debacle and the impromptu locker inspection, I was surprised Melissa would risk Mrs. Breaux's wrath. It must be something urgent.

I quickly grabbed the note and sent a surreptitious glance toward the front of the room, where Mrs. Breaux was bent over with her back to the class, busily fiddling with the VCR. She was trying to rewind a videotape about Galileo and Copernicus, but it seemed to have gotten stuck in the VCR. We'd already watched it once, but she seemed to have forgotten. Everyone around me was half-asleep.

I unfolded the paper as quietly as possible and saw that it wasn't a note from Melissa after all—it was a gift certificate to Michaels for craft supplies. I flipped it over, completely puzzled.

Thought you could use this.
—Lissa

I turned around. Lissa Jaubert, one of the seniors in the class, waved from the corner of the room. She gave me a thumbs-up and pointed to her backpack. She had one of everything from our campaign, like a mini advertisement for our line of protest wear.

I mouthed *thanks* and stuffed the gift certificate in my backpack before Mrs. Breaux had the chance to notice and take it from me. It was dangerous to have anything that might give her certain proof that I was part of the Gang of Five.

The kindness of Lissa's gesture was enough to buoy me through the rest of physics. Someone outside our tiny circle *cared* about our campaign, enough to give us twenty-five dollars. That was five dollars more than my grandma usually gave me for my birthday. It could buy us a lot of buttons, and plenty more screen-printing paint.

When the bell finally rang, I rushed over to Melissa so we could walk to lunch together, as usual. As soon as we were in the hall, I proudly showed her the gift certificate from Lissa.

"I almost want to thank the assholes who did that to Helen's locker," Melissa said, looking at the gift certificate in my hand. "It's only been forty-eight hours since Mrs. Breaux went nuclear, and I'm completely out of patches."

I'd never had a huge stash to begin with, but mine were gone, too. A couple random freshmen had asked for my last patches when I was waiting in line to pee in the girls' bathroom earlier. If Leah and Aimee had meant to ostracize Helen further, their plan had certainly backfired. The meanness of it all had generated a wave of sympathy toward Helen, and the

Gang of Five—which everyone really *was* calling us, despite its dubious connotations—was now an open secret.

"I wonder how the kids are doing," Melissa said, nodding toward where Helen, Sara, and Jennifer were waiting for us in our now-usual lunch spot in the amphitheater.

I bristled a little at her calling them "kids," because they were only a year younger than me. I was dangerously close to being tarred by the same underclassman brush.

"Hey, girls!" Melissa said as she sat down. "Looks like our revolution is working. I know we planned to make more patches and pins tonight, but I think I have a better idea. Who's up for a field trip? Athena, show 'em what you've got!"

I held the gift certificate up proudly, like a riot grrrl Vanna White.

"Y'all in? We could go to Michaels after school, and..." Melissa trailed off. "Helen...is something wrong?"

I turned to my sister, who was glowering at the two of us. She remained silent, chewing her veggie-and-cheese sandwich angrily, which for Helen meant slowly, deliberately, and silently. Meanwhile, Jennifer stared at her lap and Sara shrugged at us like she didn't know what was going on.

I couldn't see a reason for her to be upset, especially since things were now in our favor, but I didn't have a lot of patience historically for her silent treatment.

"Okay, spit it out," I said. "Why're you mad that we're succeeding?"

She put her sandwich down—again, slowly, deliberately, silently—and swept her gaze across Melissa and me.

"What. Do. You. Two. Know. About. My. Locker?" Anger simmered in each syllable of her question. Next to her, Jennifer picked at the chicken nuggets on her cafeteria tray while Sara pretended to read from her lit textbook.

"What? What are you talking about?" I asked, horrified that she could even think I'd had something to do with it. I might've been mean to Helen on occasion, fought with her on others, but that was normal sister stuff. The stunt with her locker involved public humiliation and deliberate meanness, and whatever issues we had with each other, we were never *that* kind of mean.

"Why would we know anything about your locker?" Melissa asked at the same time.

Melissa and I exchanged a look. Her forehead was wrinkled in confusion, and I knew she had to be feeling the same bewilderment I was, even if she didn't necessarily share my fear of losing the fragile, new kind of relationship we'd all been forging in the past few weeks.

Helen seemed to relax a thousandth of a percent, her scowl not so deep as before. But she didn't back down.

"I heard from Angelle, who heard from Reagan at St. Ursula's, that two girls visited Choices a few weeks ago and asked for a bunch of pamphlets. Angelle said Reagan said Miss Laurel Anne said they were interested in a tour of the place, but that one of them—" She paused and looked at Melissa with daggers in her eyes. "*One of them* was a girl with purple hair who freaked out near the end of the tour. And the other—" this time she looked at me "—was a redhead who couldn't hide the fact that she didn't want to be there."

It certainly sounded like us. As in, exactly like our trip to the fake abortion clinic. I wasn't surprised that it eventually got back to Helen, considering her connections.

"Helen, I would never do that to you," I said, hoping that she'd believe me. I was telling the truth, but with how she'd been treated lately, I would understand if she didn't trust anyone. "We went there, yeah, but that was before we started campaigning. And it wasn't to do anything that would hurt you. I may not always be so great at it, but I've been trying to help you all along."

She looked at me for a long time, judging me, before she said anything.

"Okay," she said, relaxing even more—at least toward me. "I believe you. You're a terrible liar, so if you'd done it, or if you'd known that Melissa was planning something, I know you never would've been able to keep quiet about it. You'd have been sweating bullets by the time we got to Melissa's locker. And you were as confused as I was."

I wanted to protest, but she was right.

Helen turned to Melissa.

"But I'm not sure about *you.*" She paused dramatically and resumed her glower. "Number one, you're deeply committed to pro-choice causes, and plastering my locker with dead babies makes the pro-life side of things look bad. Number two, you were at the clinic, and Miss Laurel Anne said that the girls had asked about the posters. And number three, you mess with people's lockers *all the time.*"

Helen had amassed a respectable level of circumstantial evidence: motive, opportunity, skill set. Even I could see how Melissa could have done it. But I didn't believe for a minute that she *would*. At least not now.

For someone who normally traveled in the land of the self-righteous, Melissa looked surprisingly hurt at Helen's accusation.

"We didn't take anything from the clinic," Melissa said, never breaking eye contact with Helen. "I swear." She shook her head. "I mean, we did go. But that was before we all got together and started campaigning. And the woman—Miss Laurel Anne, did you say?—she got some pamphlets for us to pass out at school, which, yes, we told her was St. Ursula's, but we didn't take them with us. She said she'd send them over with some guys. We were in and out in about five minutes, and never even got close enough to touch those horrific posters."

I could tell that Melissa was holding herself back from calling the posters scientifically inaccurate, or talking about how Miss Laurel Anne had been a jerk to the "patient" waiting in one of the "treatment" rooms, which wouldn't help her case with Helen. But what she was saying was all true. I'd never gotten a good look at the posters, and neither had she.

Then I remembered something that could clear our names, if Angelle was a decent person and not deliberately undermining us.

"You know, Miss Laurel Anne told us that there'd been two girls who visited before us," I said. "Specifically looking for those posters."

Helen looked at me with a measure of distrust. "That sounds awfully convenient."

I sighed. "I know it does. But you think I'm a terrible liar—which I am—but even if you don't believe me, I think you should ask Angelle. Or call Miss Laurel Anne yourself. I'm sure she doesn't know enough about a bunch of gossip at St. Ann's to take sides with anyone."

Next to Helen, Sara perked up. "Oh! I can call her," she said. "She used to be our youth group leader at church, before she started working at the fa—I mean, Choices."

Melissa's eyebrows shot up. She'd heard what I had—Sara was about to call it "the fake abortion clinic," which meant a significant shift in our group. I knew better than to say anything, but it gave me an idea.

"Okay," Helen said. She looked at me. "You *are* a terrible

liar, so I'm going to believe you. But until I hear from Sara that Miss Laurel Anne says *other* girls visited, the jury's still out on you, Melissa."

I cornered Sara in the hall between sixth and seventh period, grabbed her by the wrist, and pulled her into the girls' bathroom.

Hey, it worked for everyone else.

This time, I was the one checking the bathroom stalls for spies. I put my finger to my lips as I leaned down to check for feet.

"Athena, what's going on?" Sara looked worried. "Did you and Melissa...?"

It dawned on me that I probably seemed more like I was feeling guilty instead of cautiously conspiratorial.

"What? No!" I protested. "I'm still hoping you can clear things up with the fake abortion clinic woman so Helen will believe us, too."

Her face squinched up. "Then, uh, what's this about?"

I could see why she was confused. Aside from helping her with button production, Sara and I rarely spoke.

"So, remember when we were talking about that idea for homecoming?" I said. "Well, the student council is going to announce the nominees in less than a week, and we've done *nothing* about it. Do you think we have time to convince Helen *and* the members of the student council?"

Her brown eyes lit up, and she nodded enthusiastically. "Oh, wow," she said excitedly. "Yeah. I've been thinking about it since we started handing out patches. It's not much time, but I know that Jennifer has a meeting about it before school on Monday, and I know of at least a couple of other girls who would be totally supportive if we got them nominated."

Sara dug in her backpack, pulled out a notebook, and flipped it open. She shoved it in front of my face, not rudely, but eagerly. I took it from her hands and looked at what she'd been working on.

"Look, I made a list," she said, pointing to the page in front of me, where she'd written down first names and last initials. "Whenever a girl approaches me, I've started thinking about what level of popularity she is, and if she's the type of girl who could actually be on the homecoming court in terms of votes and support. And I have at least one name for each year, and a *ton* of seniors. Like, they're my most loyal customers. So if we can come up with a list of names in time, Jennifer should be able to lobby for them."

Sara's ranking system was *brilliant*, but keeping this list in a notebook that someone might find was not. Although we'd structured everything so that we *technically* weren't breaking any rules, we couldn't know what might be used against us if anything fell into the wrong hands.

"Okay, two things," I said. "First, that list is great. Second, for the love of God, keep it at home from now on. We don't want anyone in there to become a target."

Sara turned red with embarrassment. "I didn't think—"

"It's okay," I assured her. "Just leave it at home tonight. But let's talk this through. Our plan is to stock the homecoming court, and then what?"

Sara bit her lip. "See, that's the part I'm not sure about," she said. "We need to bring in Melissa, I think, and Helen—"

I interrupted her with a wave of my hand. "Leave Melissa to me. But Helen's not going to agree to anything until we can clear up the mess with Miss Laurel Anne."

"I'll call her as soon as I get home from school," Sara said eagerly. "Like I said, I know her from youth group—I'm sure she'll be willing to talk to me."

I smiled at her gratefully. "Thanks, Sara. That would be amazing." I looked down at her list again for a moment, then made an executive decision. "We'll come up with the purpose of Phase Two later. We know we want do *something* at homecoming, and you have a brilliant list of girls who are popular *and* sympathetic. So let's run with that for the moment."

"But we don't have any idea of what the *something* is," she said with a sigh, slouching against the bathroom sink.

"Doesn't matter." I shook my head. "The important part right now is that we get the court stocked with sympathetic people. Then we'll have, like, two weeks to figure things out. But we're running out of time to get this rolling—when did you say the meeting was again?"

"Monday," Sara said. "First thing. Then the nominees are announced Tuesday morning at assembly."

"I know you're planning to call Miss Laurel Anne, but do you think you can get the final list together tonight, too?" I asked, trying to sound way more confident than I actually was. When I said it aloud, the task felt impossible. It was already *Thursday.* We basically had one school day and then the weekend to figure this out. "Hopefully we can convince Helen tomorrow, and then call everyone on your list on Saturday to see if they want to participate? Maybe do a phone tree? That is, if Helen and Melissa are behind the idea. And Jennifer is willing to be our voice."

Three days wasn't nearly enough time, unless everything worked precisely as planned—and we still didn't know *exactly* what we were going to do at homecoming. But for now, the more pressing issue was how to get everything done in time for the meeting. Melissa and I had youth orchestra practice tonight at LSU. I had a date with Kyle tomorrow after my cello lesson, and Melissa had *two* dates with two different guys—one from St. Christopher's, the other an LSU freshman she'd met at Highland Coffees. She was testing out who she wanted to ask to our homecoming, which required some research on her part. Plus Helen, Sara, and Jennifer had modeling class on Saturday morning, which Helen would *never* miss, especially now that Dad was going to meet with Mrs. Brouilliette about her callback from Ford. They were trying to figure out whether Helen should fly up to the New York offices so she could do her callback there, or if another scout would visit New Orleans.

Then again, Sara had been putting together names all this time. Maybe she could pull this off faster than I knew.

Sara nodded in fierce agreement, soothing my doubts somewhat. "I can do it. I'll start calling people tonight. And Helen *has* to say yes when we tell her. She knows So What? has its limits, and as soon as we give her another option, I know she'll do it. We just have to present it in a way that doesn't make her feel like she's losing ground."

Sara really *got* my sister, maybe more than I did. I crossed my fingers that Jennifer would surprise me as much as Sara had. Then maybe we'd have a fighting chance.

25

Angelle was waiting outside the door of Mrs. Bonnecaze's religion class before first period, hands held awkwardly in front of her, almost like she was praying. Her dark ash-blond hair was permed in a wavy style that hung heavily around her shoulders in a way that made me think of the Virgin Mary's veil. Or maybe I only read that in Angelle's image because she was such a big part of the pro-life club.

The last time she'd spoken with me, I'd been a freshman, and she'd tried to get me to join the pro-life club because it *would be good for my college applications.* When I told her I didn't plan to go to a Catholic college, she got huffy and told me I had no principles. Of course, one could argue that joining the pro-life club in order to get into a certain college was deeply illustrative of said lack of principles, but when I told her so, she got huffier.

Now she was looking contrite and polite, almost saintly. I

wondered if she was planning to give our class a pro-pro-life speech—it seemed like a good time to do it, given the circumstances at Helen's locker. But when Angelle saw me, she waved me over to her.

"What's up?" I asked, half expecting her to tell me I was going to burn in hell for being pro-choice. Or maybe she wanted to try to dissuade me from the So What? campaign, because it might actually make people think for themselves for a change.

"I wanted to say it's awful—just *awful*—what those creeps did to Helen," she said. "If there's anything I can do…"

"You kicked her out of the pro-life club," I said flatly before I could stop myself.

"That's not how it went," she insisted. "I never wanted to kick Helen out, I just wanted to make sure that she hadn't… you know…"

"You mean you wanted to make sure she hadn't had an abortion?" I rolled my eyes. "You can say it." I gave Angelle the fiercest look I could muster. "I don't know why you think you can now say, 'Oh, it's so awful what those creeps did to her,' when you could have ended this yourself a month ago by standing by her and believing her."

Angelle shrank back, like my words were personally wounding her, instead of an accurate description of what had happened. I felt a momentary burst of satisfaction that I'd gotten to her, and then a pang of regret because I was pretty sure Mrs. Bonnecaze had overheard.

"I…did believe her," Angelle whispered. She pulled me closer to the lockers, out of earshot of the kids filing into the classroom. "It's just… Look, even before someone started saying it was Helen, like, literally the first day of school, I heard that *someone* had seen *someone* on the way to the clinic. And not like Melissa, either. *Not* 'protecting the clinic.'"

She did air quotes around the last part, like no one should ever protect an abortion clinic. But what Angelle said reframed everything, including that conversation I'd had with Jamie. It felt like a thousand puzzle pieces snapping into place in my brain, or that feeling when I kept messing something up on the cello, but finally, on the thousandth try, gotten right. The rumors about Helen were super believable to people because they were true—but about someone else. If people had already heard that *someone* had an abortion, it was easy enough to match a random name to it. Leah and Aimee had taken advantage of something that was already there.

Still, if I was right, there was no way I was going to betray Jamie—not even to save my sister. She didn't deserve to be the focus of everyone's gross judgments, any more than Helen did. There was a reason we'd made the "So what if she did?" patches.

"That's no excuse," I hissed back, anger simmering in every word. "No one deserves what's happened to Helen. No. One. And you were part of that, whether you admit it or not."

Angelle sagged against the row of lockers, her curly hair covering her face. She stared down at her hands, looking regretful enough that I began to wonder if maybe she actually *had* believed Helen. Maybe I'd gone too far—or maybe she'd just needed the reminder I'd given her. I wasn't sorry, in any case.

"I know," she said. "I…just don't know how I can help. At this point anyway."

Her regret barely cut into my anger. Angelle could have stood up for Helen at any point, but instead she stood by and let the rumors fester. But I realized there *was* one thing she could do now that might help—not Helen directly, but something that might repair our fractured alliance.

"If you really are sorry, there is something you can do,"

I said, softening my tone a bit. "Helen seems to think that Melissa and I might have had something to do with what happened to her locker, because we visited that fake abortion clinic that one time." Angelle cringed at my name for the place, but I kept going. "The one that has those posters? Well, we didn't take *anything* that day, and we need to confirm it. Could you get in touch with that woman—"

"Miss Laurel Anne." Angelle fidgeted against the locker, like she was afraid I was going to ask her to put out a hit on Miss Laurel Anne.

"Yeah, her," I said. "All I want is for you to confirm with her that Melissa and I had nothing to do with the garbage in Helen's locker. Sara's supposed to call her, too, but I feel like Helen will believe it even more if the news comes from you."

Angelle's whole body relaxed. "Oh, yeah. I can do that, for sure. I thought for a second you were going to ask me to go to the clinic and do something mean to Miss Laurel Anne. She's so good to us."

And now I was back to being angry with Angelle.

"No. Do you seriously think I would do that?" I stared at her with disbelief. She shrugged back at me, looking sheepish. "I just want you to do the right thing." I didn't add the *for once*.

"You want me to call Miss Laurel Anne and confirm that you and Melissa didn't take anything. That's it?" Angelle squinted back at me, like she couldn't believe that I'd gone relatively easy on her.

"Yes." My eyes darted to the classroom doorway. The hallway was nearly empty, and the bell would ring soon. Sure, Mrs. Bonnecaze was the teacher least likely to get mad if you were late, but I had no excuse because she'd likely seen me standing outside the classroom.

"Anything else?" she asked. "I…feel like I should do more to help."

I reached inside my backpack for a "So what if she didn't?" patch. Under normal circumstances, I'd consider it a huge risk to do a handoff right out in the open hallway, but I was down to my last one and you can't get caught with what you don't have.

"Here," I said. "If you really support Helen, you can wear this. It's the most pro-life, anti-gossip thing I have."

I pushed past Angelle and into the classroom, not waiting to see her reaction. I rushed to my desk and leaned over to tuck my backpack underneath. When I sat up, Mrs. Bonnecaze loomed over me, taking up my personal space in the way that all the religion teachers at my school did. Her necklace—a large but simple cross on a gold chain—dangled above me as she bent her willowy frame to my level, serving as a reminder that she was the Voice of God in this classroom.

She knelt down to get a better look at my bright turquoise "So what if she did?" patch, which stood out against the red nylon of my backpack with eye-jarring contrast. Her long purple skirt added an extra layer of clashing color.

"Athena, I don't think that patch conforms to uniform guidelines," she announced.

"I'm sorry, ma'am, but I think it does," I said, trying to sound confident and knowledgeable. I'd been able to boss Angelle into submission in the hall, but Mrs. Bonnecaze was a teacher. Still, I *knew* that the patch conformed to the guidelines. It was all part of our plan—rebel in a totally visible, absolutely legitimate way in order to maximize exposure and minimize risk. "The rules say—"

"I know you want to support your sister." Mrs. Bonnecaze dropped her voice so only I could hear. "And I personally believe that sweet, sweet girl is innocent of the terrible things people are saying about her. But you *cannot* think that suggesting abortion is anything other than a sin will do you any good."

"But I thought the So What? campaign wasn't really *about* abortion?" I said, trying out the lines that we'd prepared for this inevitable situation. I sounded almost like Wisteria. "As far as I know, it's more about getting people to think—"

"I know you might think that," Mrs. Bonnecaze said, interrupting me again. Impatience crept into her rushed tone. "But that is *not* the signal it sends. And, at this school, you *have* to uphold the pro-life policy. Especially in times like these, when our country's courts have seen fit to get rid of a law meant to protect the unborn. For students, that means you cannot suggest, however indirectly, that abortion is a good choice. It simply *isn't.* It's not good for the baby, it's not good for the mother, it's not good for society—"

"That's *not* what this is about," I repeated. "We're trying to—"

"I'm only going to say this once." She leaned into my face so that I could see every pore, the light dusting of powder, the strong line of blush she applied to her cheeks. She was so in my face that not only could I smell her perfume, but I felt like it was transferring onto me. "You have to take that patch off, or I'm sending you to Sister Catherine's office."

I'd never been sent to the dean of discipline's office before. Sister Catherine had the power to suspend me, or worse, if she wanted. I definitely didn't want to go see her, but I also wasn't about to take off my patch. I closed my loose-leaf binder and stuffed it into my backpack, then pushed up from my desk so that I was thoroughly in Mrs. Bonnecaze's space. I wasn't trying to be aggressive, but since she was so thoroughly invading mine, it was kind of unavoidable.

"I guess I'm going to Sister Catherine's office, then."

Mrs. Bonnecaze backed up, holding her hand to her chest with dramatic shock. "Athena, we should talk about this."

"No, you're right. I'll get confirmation that I can have the patch—or not—on my bag, and it'll be over," I said, holding out my hand. "Just give me a note to give to her, and I'll be on my way."

Everyone was looking at me. *Everyone.* My heart pounded. This wasn't like talking back to Mrs. Turner in her office or getting caught with a note by Mrs. Breaux. This was about standing up for something in front of everyone, with all the risks attached.

Mrs. Bonnecaze blinked hard. "If that's what you want." She grabbed a pad of pink slips from her desk, scrawled some writing on it, and handed it to me.

I grabbed it roughly from her hand, more from nerves than anger. If I made it through this, then our campaign would be able to go on. If not, everything would be over. And either way, I'd have to face Helen and Melissa. Either of them would be better at this than I was. Helen had determination, and Melissa had principled rudeness. I wasn't sure what I had.

With everyone now staring at me, I hoisted my backpack onto my shoulders and walked out of the classroom. The only thing that kept me going was the adrenaline buzzing in my head, along with the steady reminder that I was doing something important. I was standing up for something I believed in.

I walked through the empty hallway to Sister Catherine's office, all while trying to figure out what I was going to say to her. I'd never had much cause to interact with her before, so I had no idea how she was likely to react to the situation.

As I walked in, I noticed that it looked a little like Mrs. Turner's office, but sparser and—paradoxically—much more comfortable. Two polished oak chairs with appealingly curved backs were lined up in front of her oak desk, and a bookcase filled with religious books and a ton of family photos stood behind it. I didn't know nuns *had* families.

Sister Catherine didn't notice me standing by the door at first. She sat behind her desk in yet another polished wooden chair, her forehead creased with concentration all the way up to her gray habit. She was studying an open file folder through her reading glasses. Unlike Mrs. Breaux, she didn't peer over the glasses as a means of intimidation, mostly because she didn't have to. Her job title was enough.

I tapped gently on her open door, and Sister Catherine looked up.

"Oh, hello, Miss Graves." Sister Catherine closed the manila folder on her desk and pulled the glasses from her face. I wasn't sure if she usually called students by their last names or if she didn't know my first name. "What can I do for you?"

I wiped my palms against my uniform skirt. The fate of our campaign now rested in my sweaty hands.

"Um, Mrs. Bonnecaze sent me. She wanted me to take a patch off my backpack. But I don't see why."

Sister Catherine peered at my backpack from her seat behind her desk. "Hmm. 'So what if she did?' I see. Well, you're not specifying *what*, so I don't see what's wrong with it."

"Really?" My voice was a high-pitched squeak. "It doesn't violate the pro-life policy?"

As soon as I said it, I wanted to kick myself, because she was either unaware of the controversy surrounding Helen—which I doubted—or giving me a free pass for reasons unknown. Either way, I was shooting myself in the foot.

Sister Catherine studied me for a good long time. I could practically see her thoughts forming in her head, except that I didn't know what they were.

"I think its meaning is in the eye of the beholder," she said very deliberately. She raised her eyebrows at me meaningfully, and I felt a small surge of hope at the gesture. "If someone *perceives* it to be about something, such as—but not only—abortion, I can see why they might think it violates the policy. But as long as no one fills in that last blank on his or her patch, I won't make the student in question remove it. Do you understand?"

I did. Loud and clear. Stay ambiguous, and everything would be fine. Make a direct statement, and it would all be over. And that was perfect, really—I doubted Helen would be happy if we came out and used *abortion* in our campaign anyway. We were trying to clear her name, not cement an association between her and abortion in people's minds.

"Can I tell that to Mrs. Bonnecaze?"

Sister Catherine shook her head. "You can't. But *I* can." She grabbed a pad of pink slips from the corner of her desk and scrawled a note. She handed it to me with a flourish. "Now, get back to class. I don't want to see you here again."

I gulped hard, and then I saw that she was smiling. I guess nuns have weird senses of humor. I smiled back at her, hoping we had formed a bond.

She waved me away. "What are you waiting for? Get back to class, Miss Graves."

She didn't have to tell me a third time. I practically sprinted out of the hall, thankful I'd missed out on whatever punishment that Mrs. Bonnecaze had imagined Sister Catherine might give me.

26

I looked at the pink hall pass to see what Sister Catherine had written.

Athena Graves has not violated the dress code, nor have other students with pins and patches of the same kind. As Dean of Discipline, I offer no opinion as to the supposed political content of the message.

She had also written the wrong time on the paper, giving me fifteen extra minutes before I had to rejoin Mrs. Bonnecaze's class. I didn't go back to her office to let her know. She'd given me a break, and I would take it.

Instead of heading back to religion class, I went to the most isolated place on campus: the library's study carrels. Raised up on a platform, but behind some of the stacks, I would see and hear anyone coming long before they saw me.

Almost as soon as I sat down, Coach Wilson's sociology class filed through the doors of the library. Coach Wilson, a former army brat and Trip's dad, usually took discipline seriously, but that ended as soon as his class got through the doors and scattered to all corners of the library. Once everyone was out of his direct line of sight, he abandoned his teaching duties to flirt with Ms. Clapton, the librarian. I hunched down behind my carrel, hoping no one would notice me.

I froze when I saw Kyle walk in, followed by Aimee. Aimee's scarlet-lipsticked mouth bobbed up and down as she said something to Kyle, whose face alternated between disbelief and nodding understanding. They walked together toward the back of the library, where the sociology section abutted the stairs to the carrels. In other words, right below me.

I ducked farther down and pulled my legs up onto the chair. I couldn't leave now, not when they were so close. I wouldn't be able to get past them without Aimee noticing. Plus, I had to know what she was saying to him. I silently thanked Sister Catherine for those extra fifteen minutes.

"Did you find anything yet?" Aimee asked.

"No. I think they were all checked out by the first-hour class," Kyle answered. He sounded bored. They were probably assigned to work together.

"Oh. Well, like I was telling you before—"

"Look, if you're going to tell me some more crap about Athena, you can stop now."

What did she say about me? Or really, what *had* she been saying, since he'd said "more"? At least he sounded like he didn't believe whatever it was.

I wrapped my arms around my knees and kept listening. I felt so tense I could explode.

"Don't get mad or anything," Aimee said. "All I'm saying

is, if you're going to ask someone to the homecoming dance, please, ask Leah. She *needs* it."

Wait, what? Why would Leah need a date to homecoming? I thought back to my brief conversation with Sean and wondered what he'd been trying to tell me. He'd mentioned a fight with Leah—what had they fought about?

And also, shit. Fuck. All the swear words couldn't encapsulate what I was feeling. Kyle and I had been out together every Friday night for the past three weeks. He'd kissed me in the hall here at school more than once. It might not have been "official" that we were dating, but it wasn't unofficial, either. Maybe we hadn't had a "what is our relationship?" talk, but I didn't expect him to *not* ask me to homecoming. And why would he ask Leah, of all people? He knew what she'd done to Helen.

A book slammed shut, making me jump, and Kyle sighed.

"Let's just concentrate on the project," he said. "Have you found the book on homelessness in major cities since the 1980s? Or the one on homeless Vietnam vets?"

Homelessness. I wasn't sure how far away that was from my perch in the carrels, but I hoped it would be close enough that I could still hear them. I *had* to know how this conversation would end, but I couldn't exactly go creeping around the library like some stalker.

"I think that Leah really needs someone right now," Aimee said. "You know why she had to break up with Sean."

What? They'd broken up? Since when? That *must* have been what he was trying to tell me. I kind of wished I'd listened to him, but he'd been so indirect, and I couldn't deal with it. He owed me a straightforward apology. Still, I should have heard him out, instead of being so impatient.

"Leah said they grew apart." Kyle sighed loudly—again.

"Oh, I guess she was afraid to tell you. Well, you know." Aimee paused. "Sean…well…you know…"

"Know *what*?" He sounded impatient, like maybe he wasn't really ready to believe anything Aimee said.

"Well, Sean's a very… He was a bad boyfriend, let's just say that." Damn, Aimee was *good*. "Bad boyfriend" could mean anything, from cheating to being an abusive boyfriend to just ignoring Leah and her feelings.

But Sean was never a "bad boyfriend," not in *any* kind of way. If anything, he'd been almost too understanding of Leah's problems. He'd stuck up for Leah when she friend-dumped me last year. He'd dismissed any thoughts that Leah had said anything bad about Helen. And he'd always excused any mean thing she did as a mere misunderstanding. You couldn't get a more supportive boyfriend than Sean.

I might be in a huge fight with him at the moment, but that didn't change reality. If I managed to get out of the library without suffocating myself to death or screaming out loud… Well, I had about a dozen different ideas churning in my mind. I would confront Leah about what she was trying to do with Kyle. I'd ask Sean about their breakup.

And as for Kyle, I'd… I didn't know what I was going to do about Kyle. A big gaping hole at the center of my feelings opened up, and what filled it would depend on what he did next.

"Look, I don't know much about Leah's relationship with Sean," he told Aimee. "But I've had a thing going on with Athena, and then this whole deal with Leah came up. I didn't think that she was going to break up with Sean. You see how hard this is for me."

A "thing" with me? I didn't know what that meant. Was it good, bad, passing? My heart told me that it *had* been good, but apparently something had changed for Kyle. And honestly, everything added up, if I looked back. His mom's weird pause on the phone. His suspicion of me and Sean. His "tutoring" plans yesterday.

A lump formed in my throat as I pushed back the sob that wanted to exit my body, but couldn't.

And how hard it was for *him*? What the hell, Kyle? My stomach clenched at the thought of what might have "come up" with Leah. Like Aimee's judgment of Sean as a "bad boyfriend," Kyle could have done *anything* with Leah, from flirting with her to things I didn't want to imagine, but automatically did.

"Athena will get over it," Aimee insisted.

"Look, this isn't an easy decision for me. And no matter what I do, I don't want to hurt Athena's feelings." Kyle slammed a book shut.

"Honestly, I really don't think she'll care. She doesn't like you that much anyway," Aimee said. "I heard her and Melissa talking, and she said you were cute but arrogant, and that she could never seriously date you. Besides, everyone knows she's been trying to steal Sean from Leah for months now."

Bile rose up my throat, and my stomach churned. I was going to be sick. Everything made sense now. They—Leah and Aimee both—had probably been planning this since day one.

"Really?" Kyle sounded like he had the smallest gap in belief, and I knew Aimee could now swoop in there and plant not just a seed, but a big old tree of mistrust about me.

"Yeah," Aimee said. "You know you're only second best to her, right? As soon as she and Sean make up, you'll be out of the picture. You know, they weren't always *just* friends.

Everyone knows they secretly had a thing going before Sean started dating Leah."

My voice froze in my throat. If I opened my mouth, I was sure that something closer to a wail than a word would pop out. This wasn't happening. It couldn't be.

Kyle didn't say anything, either. Why wasn't he saying anything? Shouldn't he say something? If he wasn't saying anything, he was listening to her. And maybe believing her.

"And you've just got to compare the two," Aimee continued, like it was really no comparison and I was *nothing*. "You've been tutoring Leah, right?"

I felt the floor drop out from under me. He'd been really careful to *not* say who he'd been tutoring, and now I understood why. The longer he let her talk, the more it seemed like Kyle was weighing his options on a scale of favor: me or Leah. Leah or me. Aimee's words put a thumb on that scale.

"Have you ever really talked with Athena? All she's useful for is math equations or chemistry homework or English vocab. She can't carry on a real conversation about anything else. Then look at Leah. She's much more of a person than Athena is. Athena's a freak. She's not even pretty."

"Athena is *not* a freak," Kyle said, though not nearly angrily enough, I thought. It sounded like she was wearing him down, and that was wearing *me* down in ways I didn't want to think about. Another book slammed back onto the shelf. "I like her. She's cute."

Cute? Bunnies were cute. Leah, I knew, was *hot*. My entire body felt like a tensed spring, pushed into place by Aimee's lies. I could barely breathe.

"Sorry. I didn't mean for it to sound like that," Aimee said quickly. "But it's like I said before, Leah needs you right now. Athena doesn't. You have to decide between them."

"Come on, Aimee. Athena needs me, too. You know what's going on with her sister, right?"

Aimee sucked in a breath. "That… I get it, but Helen brought that on herself."

The ensuing silence went on for far too long. I was sure I was breathing loud enough for them to hear the quick, panicky breaths that telegraphed all my fears. That Kyle didn't like me. Had never liked me. Hadn't wanted to hang out with me much at school because that might imply a real relationship. Had only seen me as a stopgap make-out girl until he could secure something with Leah.

"And besides, Leah's *really* into you. Athena isn't. You know Leah wants to go to homecoming with you," Aimee wheedled. "You're not her second best. And you know how much she needs you right now."

More silence, more feeling like I was going to throw up. The weight of all that silence pushed down on me. I'd had my doubts about Kyle's feelings for me, but now I could feel his doubts about me, too. Aimee and Leah had probably made it seem like every time I tried to help Helen, I was really trying to ignore him or something. That my lunches with my friends were part of me limiting him to a small corner in my life.

"I'll think about it," Kyle said.

My heart exploded.

"Please," Aimee pleaded. I wanted to strangle the girlish whine right out of her.

"Oh, all right," he said, relenting. "You're right… I need to make a choice. I'll go to the dance with Leah, but I have to break it off with Athena first. So don't go prancing off to rub it in."

In that one sentence, all my hopes vanished. "Needing to make a choice" didn't imply that he was going to homecoming with Leah *as a friend*. It implied that Leah and I had somehow, until this very moment, been on some kind of equal footing. That meant that something beyond tutoring had been going on between them. I didn't know the boundaries of what that something was, but I suspected it was likely as far as I'd gone with him—which meant that Kyle wasn't the boy I'd thought he was. He'd barely considered my feelings for him, and had so easily allowed Aimee to persuade him that I didn't care. He wasn't at all worried about breaking my heart. He was worried about telling me before being *found out*.

I had to get out of there. I ran down the steps of the carrel area and through the stacks. Maybe Kyle and Aimee saw me, maybe not. Either way, it didn't matter.

I didn't get it. Why would Leah do this? She'd already had Sean, who adored her, and I'd always thought she'd cared a lot about him, too. Why did she have to take Kyle from me?

And then I realized, if he could be taken that easily, he wasn't ever mine at all.

I bolted back to religion class, making it just in time to hand Mrs. Bonnecaze the note from Sister Catherine before the bell rang. She took one look at me, saw that I was shell-shocked, and read the note. Then she read it again, because the look on my face told her it was bad news—which the note wasn't.

"I see you have permission for that patch." She pursed her lips together. Sister Catherine's permission slip also applied to everyone, and not just me, which likely didn't make Mrs. Bonnecaze any happier. "But it looks like whatever Sister Catherine told you has gotten you to think seriously about some things."

I stared up at her blankly. I should have been celebrating my small victory against the administration, but instead I felt like my heart had been pulled out of me and stomped on.

"Um, yes." My body was screaming at me to run away from her—not because of anything she'd done, but because I couldn't handle human interaction right now. "I have a lot to think about. See you tomorrow."

It didn't matter that all the things I had to think about were related to Kyle, and that they'd temporarily stopped any other thoughts from entering my head. I don't know how I made it to calculus, when the buzzing swarm of a haze that had surrounded me in the library refused to lift. I shoved my books under my desk and put my head down. I didn't look up when Kyle passed me on his way to his desk—I could not, *would* not, gratify him with my tears.

"Hey," I heard Kyle say. "You okay?"

He stood by my desk, so close I could feel him. If I didn't look at him, I'd come across as the antisocial freak that Aimee described. If I did, then I would show how much he'd hurt me.

Fine. He needed to know, if only to prove Aimee wrong.

I raised my head and looked at him. His amber eyes held a look of genuine concern, but maybe I only saw what I wanted to see. Apparently, I had misjudged him in so many other respects.

"I was in the library the whole time, Kyle." The calm in my voice surprised me, but I was sure he could tell I had been crying. Saying the words felt empowering, but they didn't change anything. Except now he knew, and if he had any bit of conscience left, he'd feel guilty. Which he deserved.

"Oh, shit," Kyle said in a low voice. "I didn't mean—"

"Kyle Buchanan, please take your seat," Mr. Loring, our calculus teacher, said as he walked to the front of the room to start his lecture.

Kyle glanced down at me and bit his lip, then continued down the row. I put my head on my desk again.

"Miss Graves, is something wrong?" Mr. Loring paused by my desk, peering at me through his round John Lennon glasses.

"I'm not feeling well."

Mr. Loring looked at my eyes, which I was sure were red and puffy.

"Do you want to go to the nurse's office?" His expression seemed like he might be thinking my eyes were red because I'd suddenly decided to join the stoners out behind the school for a joint.

"Umm, no," I said, my mouth quivering. "I just want to stay here." I couldn't bear the thought of getting up from my desk and everyone watching me as I exited, sobbing. And the nurse would probably send me to Mrs. Turner, who was the last person I wanted to see.

His expression softened. "All right. Just let me know if you change your mind, and I'll write you a pass." I nodded, and Mr. Loring turned back to the board.

"Okay, everyone, we're going to start with chapter five today," he said, thumping his book onto his desk.

I'd done my homework, but I had no interest in chapter five—though I found that my book did make a pretty good pillow when it was open. I couldn't remember what chapter five covered, let alone concentrate on Mr. Loring's lecture. Nothing compared to the crushing weight pressing against my chest right now.

How could Kyle ditch me for Leah? What had I done wrong?

Every fear I'd ever had about dating a boy had come true at once. He'd never *said* we were dating—he was just using me as a warm-up to someone else, and I felt stupid for thinking our dates meant something. For believing that some perfect unicorn boy was real.

And I was *angry.* I was angry at myself for not realizing Aimee and Leah would target me next. I'd given Leah far too many reasons. I'd embarrassed her in public, at Denny's, though she'd turned that one around on me, too. Along with Melissa and the gang, I'd made too much headway in confronting her gossip about Helen. I found myself wondering if Leah even *liked* Kyle, or if she only wanted him because he'd liked me, and the fact that I didn't know either way made me angry. I was angry with Aimee for lying to Kyle, and I was angry with Kyle for believing her.

But mostly, I just hurt.

The bell rang, and I went to physics, where I ignored Kyle some more by counting the polka dots on Mrs. Breaux's blouse. Then, suddenly, the day was more than half over. Knowing that I only had three more classes, none of which Kyle was in, offered the tiniest bit of relief. If I could just avoid Kyle, Sean, Leah, and Aimee in the halls, I would be okay. As soon as I realized the enormity of that task, the relief disappeared, replaced with a certain sense of doom.

By the end of physics, I wanted to go home. Instead, I went to lunch—and the inevitable interrogation by my friends once they caught sight of me.

I darted toward the classroom door, trying to lose anyone who might follow me. Or who might comment on my puffy eyes and snotty face.

"Athena, wait up!"

I pivoted on my heel automatically. I shouldn't give Kyle time to explain, but I couldn't stop my body from turning toward him. Like in the library, I had to hear what he would say.

"What do you want?" Melissa asked. She pushed herself between us, her arms crossed, like a club bouncer. I hadn't noticed her following me. I looked at her gratefully, knowing she would defend me, so I could turn and walk away.

"Please, Melissa, I've got to talk to Athena," Kyle said. "I can explain."

I paused, even though I had no great faith in Kyle's explanation. He couldn't possibly make this better. Not after that conversation I'd overheard. Still, right now, part of me wanted Kyle to say something magical, to make this all go away and rewind to an hour or two ago.

"It's okay," I said, looking at Melissa. "This shouldn't take long. I don't think there's much more he can say."

I couldn't believe those words actually came out of my mouth. I had nothing left to lose except a small shred of pride, which I held on to for dear life. I wasn't going to cry. I wasn't going to yell. I was going to listen to him, calmly, and then I was going to walk away.

Melissa took up a post leaning up against a row of lockers, absently turning locks. She heaved a large sigh and rolled her eyes in an elaborate display of impatience every time Kyle opened his mouth to talk.

"I'm sorry you heard what Aimee said in the library, but that was what she said, not me, and I don't agree with it," Kyle said. "I like you." He paused, a little too long. If he stopped there, maybe he could erase the conversation that I'd heard in the library. Maybe he could redeem himself, come up with something that would give me faith in him again. "But I have a connection with Leah, too. She's been going through a lot, and I *get* it. But it's not like what you think. I was just friends with her until now. Really."

Just friends *until* now? I felt my fist tighten and a hot bolt of anger run through me. I didn't believe him. He wouldn't ditch me if he didn't already have something going on with her. It made no sense. She was "going through a lot"? That was the most paper-thin excuse I'd ever heard. Like I was going through *nothing* lately. My sister was in trouble with the school, and one of my best friends hated me.

Leah was behind both of those things, and Kyle knew it. He *knew* it. We'd talked about it. I'd given him the So What? pin. I glanced at his backpack. Sure enough, it was gone.

"If you're going to the dance with Leah because of anything Aimee says, then you're more gullible than any other guy at this school," Melissa said without looking up from her locker tampering.

"This isn't your business," Kyle said, turning his attention to Melissa. "I—"

"You're a jerk." She finally looked up from her lock twisting and faced him with crossed arms. "Yeah. An *asshole.* I overheard Aimee and Leah talking about their strategy this morning. If you'd ever taken a second to ask yourself who has more interest in lying to you, you wouldn't for a second doubt how much Athena likes you. And her feelings for you *never*—not now, not then, not ever—had anything to do with making Sean jealous. Unlike Leah."

Kyle's gaze dropped to the floor near his feet. He seemed to stop talking forever, but he didn't leave, despite Melissa's fierce stare indicating the conversation was over.

"I really like you, Athena," he said eventually, looking at me. "I want you to know that. But I like Leah, too. I didn't expect that to happen. She and I have a lot in common, with our parents both having problems right now. I just… I thought if I talked with you beforehand, you might be okay with me going to the dance with Leah. As friends. She needs more friends."

"That's *bullshit*," I said, shocking myself almost as much as Melissa and Kyle. Maybe he was right that Leah needed more friends, because Aimee was terrible. But Kyle was in a lot of denial if he thought I'd believe he wanted to be "just friends" with Leah after what I'd overheard. "That's *not* how your conversation went with Aimee, and you know it. You don't have to 'make a choice' about someone if you're not already messing around with someone else."

The crazy thing was, I didn't even care about the dance. Until Mrs. Turner used the homecoming court as a punishment for Helen, I hadn't thought about it at all, and now, I was mostly thinking about it as a tool to help Phase Two of the So What? campaign. But these things *did* matter to Leah. A homecoming date with Kyle would send a signal to everyone that whatever Kyle's thing with me had been, it was now over, once and for all.

"I…" Kyle trailed off uncertainly, glancing from me to Melissa and back again.

"It's not okay," I said. "You believed Aimee, not me. You sounded like you didn't care about me at all. And you've been messing around with Leah the whole time, haven't you?"

Kyle looked like I had slapped him.

"Athena, I'm sorry," he said. "It didn't start out like that. But you have to see there are two sides to this. I wasn't—"

"No," I snapped. "I don't have to 'see that there are two sides.'" I made air quotes with my hands. I could feel the anger rising in my chest, along with a ferocious humiliation. "Good luck with Leah. Something tells me you'll need it."

I turned away from him, a wave of disappointment filling my entire body. I had to get down the hall without turning back. I *had* to. But my legs didn't work, and I stayed planted in the spot.

Then I felt Melissa's hand gripping my arm, pulling me forward.

"Steady, girl," she whispered near my ear. "You did good."

I held on to her as we walked down the hall. And I didn't look back—not once.

27

Melissa steered zombie me toward the cafeteria. A weird, vibrating feeling coursed through my body and showed no signs of stopping. Some small part of me categorized it as an excess of adrenaline, but my mind was rebelling against logic and reason. It was a weird, vibrating feeling. That was all.

"Do you have your lunch today?" she asked, linking her arm with mine.

I nodded. I couldn't make any words come out of my mouth. My lunch bag was lodged in my backpack, or at least I thought it was. Not that it mattered—I wasn't going to eat anything anyway.

"Okay, we're going to sit near the theater kids and wait for your sister," she said. "Maybe they'll have some way of helping. Helen certainly owes you one."

I didn't think Helen owed me anything, because Angelle

hadn't come through yet, but I was too numb to protest. I followed Melissa down the hall and through the cafeteria, trying not to look at anyone along the way. By the time we reached the amphitheater, my breathing had returned to normal. We sat down on the concrete steps. As usual, the theater kids were too busy running lines to notice us. I loved them for their obliviousness.

Within a minute, Helen showed up clutching her lunch bag, Sara and Jennifer trailing behind with lunch trays piled with questionable "Mexican" food. A month ago, Helen likely would have seen me crying and kept on going because my tears weren't her business. Now she rushed over and put her arm around me.

It felt kind of weird, but I appreciated it.

"What happened?" Melissa asked. "I mean, I got some of it from your conversation with Kyle, but I'm still confused."

I shrugged. Recounting the whole story would either totally transform me into a detached zombie or immerse me in a pool of stinging embarrassment, so I kept my explanation as short as possible.

"You heard most of it," I said. "Kyle's been hanging out with Leah, probably making out with her for a while, I dunno for sure, but it seemed like that to me. Aimee persuaded him to ask her to the dance instead of me, and he doesn't seem to have any remorse about it. Asshole."

"Athena!" Jennifer exclaimed. "Language!"

I started laughing, a snotty, gross laugh that mixed in with the tears I couldn't hold back. "Oh, God, Jennifer, grow up! *Asshole* is pretty tame, considering what he deserves. Something like *shitbag* or maybe even *motherfucker* would be more appropriate. Or how about *motherfucking asshole*?"

I never swore, at least not like that, but the curse words gave my anger an escape valve I desperately needed right now.

Helen squeezed my shoulder. I couldn't see her face, but she must have given her friend a look of death, because Jennifer sank down sheepishly. Really, I should have been the one apologizing because now *I* was the one being an asshole. Jennifer had been nothing but supportive of our team efforts and had stuck by Helen even before that.

Melissa pursed her lips together. "You know," she said. "We've been taking the high road for so long. Maybe we need to think about how to fight back. Really go on the attack. Leah and Aimee deserve it."

I shook my head violently. The last thing I wanted was to play some version of Leah's game to win Kyle back. Leah had the home court advantage now. If we tried to match her, she would undoubtedly win with Kyle, like she'd won by ruining Helen's reputation.

"I don't *want* Kyle back," I said. "He's lied to me the whole time. I feel so..."

I couldn't finish telling them how I felt, because it was a lie. I *did* want Kyle back. Well, maybe not exactly. I wanted who I thought he was, someone who would never dump me for Leah. I blinked back tears in the strong sunlight.

Melissa leaned back on the concrete steps. "I know it's awful," she said, waving her hands like she was trying to erase the implication that I wanted Kyle back. "But there's got to be some way of turning our humiliation into triumph. Something beyond buttons and patches."

Sara had been kneeling across from me, but she suddenly jerked up with attention. She looked at me with dark eyebrows raised and expectant, waiting for my approval to say something. She was probably hesitating in case I insulted her like I'd done with Jennifer.

And then I remembered. We'd been so excited to come up with Phase Two of our plan, and today I couldn't string two words together without them coming out as a burst of angry profanity.

I nodded at Sara. "We actually *do* have an idea," I said, my voice still thick. "It isn't going to make me feel any better about Kyle, I don't think, because it has nothing to do with him. But it's a good idea, and we don't have much time. Sara?"

Now that I'd gotten the words out, I *knew* it wouldn't make me feel better about Kyle, because the lump had returned to my throat. Nothing would, but especially not a plan organized around homecoming, which was the theoretical impetus for ditching me—because Leah "needed" a date. *Asshole.*

Sara rocked back down to the ground. "Okay, so." She took in a deep breath. "Yesterday, after we agreed to get in touch with Miss Laurel Anne from Choices, Athena and I talked about what we could do to continue, especially if some of the teachers find a way to have the patches banned."

"They won't," I interrupted Sara. "Sister Catherine said it was fine for me and everyone else to have the patches, as long as we don't imply it says anything one way or another about abortion. She gave me a note—"

"I, uh, hate to tell you this," Melissa said, interrupting me in turn. "But I don't think whatever she said will last very long. Principal Richard told my dad when they were at the driving range after work yesterday that Mrs. Bonnecaze has talked with the *other* religion teachers in the school, and *they* put in a call to the diocesan school board. So now he's getting pressure from the diocese to shut us down, and banning the

So What? propaganda will probably seem like the easiest way. Mr. Richard is, after all, the laziest human on the planet."

We heaved a collective sigh. Getting a break from Sister Catherine might stave off the inevitable for a day or two, but not forever. As soon as Mr. Richard let the teachers know that he approved of the ban, all the patches and buttons would vanish from the halls of our school.

"So what's our next step?" Helen asked, taking a swig from her can of Coke. "If So What? gets banned, we've got to maintain our forward momentum. We can't let them win." She gave me a sympathetic glance. "Especially not now."

Sara looked at me for approval again. We hadn't told Helen about the student council plan yet, mostly because we were worried she might get upset. Homecoming was *her* dream, not ours.

"Well...umm," Sara said, glancing back and forth between Helen and me. "I thought we could try to get you nominated for homecoming court anyway. And if that doesn't work, because they won't let you on it, we can try to stock it with the rest of us."

"And then what?" Helen bit her lower lip, a small sign that she hadn't yet made the decision to pout or to congratulate us. Homecoming mattered to her, and Mrs. Turner had yanked that possibility away. But whether she'd see the big picture of us trying to do some mass demonstration at homecoming or not... I never knew which way my sister would go.

Sara nodded to me. It was my turn.

"Well, we thought we'd figure out something dramatic to do at homecoming," I said, looking at everyone in turn. Sara and I hadn't worked out this part of the plan, and I hadn't had time to brainstorm with Melissa, either. "I've been thinking about doing something with our slogans on the dresses, but I don't have anything like a solid idea yet." I paused, trying to work through what might work, and what would 100 percent get us expelled, or at least suspended, if the So What? ban became a concrete, diocesan-enforced thing. "I mean, they make the girls wear those sashes, right? And we have slogans. Might as well put them to good use. We can put the slogans on the sashes, and—"

"Bam! Flip them over when the girls are in front of everyone at the dance!" Sara finished. I'd been thinking that we'd do it at the game, but the dance was even better. At the game, it would be a silent protest, which could be effective. But the problem was, we'd be far enough away that a lot of people wouldn't be able to see us. At the dance, we'd be within a few feet of everyone. The protest would *matter.*

Across the lunch circle from me, Melissa nodded in agreement. Her face told me that she was already thinking of how she might be able to spin this plan out, make it go further, because she knew it was a good start. But she wasn't the one I needed to convince.

I hoped it was enough for Helen. The truth was, homecoming was a big deal, and even if our plans were *for* her benefit, she wasn't going to get to participate in them.

"Part of me thinks that it's going to suck if I don't get to be on the homecoming court," Helen said, weighing each word with a rounded importance. "And part of me thinks it's brilliant. Actually, most of me thinks it's brilliant."

Sara's shoulders drooped with relief. She'd worried that Helen would reject our plan outright. Sara pushed her overlong brown bangs back from her face, tucking them behind her ears. They fell in her face again anyway, but she spoke with too much excitement to notice.

"So the plan," Sara said quickly, "is to get as many of our

people onto the homecoming court as possible. Nominate you, if we can. If not, then me. For the sophomores, Cady Jenson. She's wearing a 'So what if she didn't?' patch right now, and she even handed out some So What? pins of her own design, which are really cool…but anyway, back to the point." She paused for a moment, flashing a look to Melissa and me. "We're not sure of the second person. I asked Erica from the pro-life club, who also has a 'So what if she didn't?' patch, but she's going to Disney World with her mom and stepdad on homecoming weekend, so—"

"Do we have *any* other pro-life people?" Helen asked. I could see her getting antsy. If she didn't think we'd at least *tried* to find pro-life people, she'd never go for the plan.

"Yes!" Sara exclaimed. "I'm getting there. For juniors, Melissa and Missy Bordelon. We're probably not going to be able to stop Leah's nomination, but I thought our fourth nominee could be Angelle. And there's a ton of seniors nominated, but their entire class seems to be pretty sympathetic anyway. Like, they've all got at least one patch of some sort."

Nominating Angelle seemed like a *terrible* idea to me, but I knew the notion would appeal to Helen.

I snuck a covert glance at Melissa, who had been stunningly quiet about the Phase Two plan so far, which I could only guess was because she didn't want anything she said to cloud Helen's opinion. I could tell that holding back was killing her, though, especially now that Sara had mentioned both Angelle and the sympathetic seniors—who were all, coincidentally, friends with Jamie. Melissa kept inhaling these sharp little breaths, like she was going to launch into a long speech, and then, each time, stopped herself and returned her focus to Helen.

Helen did her lip-biting thing again. No wonder the girl

had such perfect, bee-stung lips—they must've been swollen from all the chewing.

"The only definite pro-life person is Angelle?" she asked. "And we don't know about the seniors?"

Sara's eyes darted between me and Helen again. "Yes, and you… Or me, if they don't let you. But we really *don't* know what the seniors think, or why they've been so supportive."

Melissa shifted uncomfortably, like she was holding back some really important news. I almost asked her why she was acting so weird, as a way to get her to spill, but it felt wrong. If my suspicions were right, the news she was sitting on shouldn't be told without the right person's permission, and that person wasn't Melissa.

"The meeting's Monday before school, right? And then the announcement's during morning assembly on Tuesday?" Helen asked.

"Yeah," Jennifer said. "And…um, Sara talked to me about it last night, and I think I can do it. I just…need some help coming up with a pitch for everyone else on the student council." Her voice cracked slightly. "I shouldn't have trouble convincing the girls on the council to vote for the girls we've picked, but…I don't know about the boys. They just vote for who they think is hot, and…"

Jennifer didn't sound like she had a lot of confidence in the boys, or in her ability to convince them to vote for the extended So What? crew. She twisted the napkin on her lap into a tight rose, turning the stem over and over in her hand until the paper started to shred.

"Right," Helen said. "Okay, Jennifer, we're going to go practice. You're going to give me arguments, and I'm going to pretend to be a jerk boy."

Helen got up and signaled for Jennifer to follow her. Sara

stayed behind, but that didn't seem as weird as it would have a few weeks ago. Her staying with us seemed less like a further attempt to impress Melissa than a means of not violating Jennifer and Helen's space.

"Helen always coaches Jennifer on her debates," Sara told us. "She's really good."

"Helen or Jennifer?" Melissa asked. She'd said little the entire lunch. I think she had doubted Helen would go for our plan and didn't know exactly what to do now that Helen seemed fine with it.

"Both—once Jennifer gets over her initial stage fright," Sara said. She pushed her hair back behind her ear again in what I now recognized as a nervous habit of hers.

It did nothing to reassure me of our plan's success.

28

On Tuesday, Sister Catherine paced in front of the two long folding tables from which the student council ruled every assembly. A red cloth with the school's crest hung at the front of the tables, giving the student council an air of authority. Everyone else sat on the gym bleachers and awaited the news of the homecoming ballot.

Sister Catherine's main function at these events was to legitimize the student council's authority and to tamp down any rebelliousness from an audience with a significant percentage of slackers who might reject the decisions of sixteen people they viewed as even nerdier than I was. She did her job well, standing with her hands clutched at her waist, seriousness embodied in her gray veil, crisp white blouse, and below-the-knee gray A-line skirt.

"Ladies and gentlemen," Sister Catherine boomed into the

microphone. "Please remember that this is a *respectful* process. I realize there has been some...*controversy* going around the school, and I want to remind you that the student council's goal is to be accountable to the entire student body—not to any one student, or, for that matter, the faculty."

Sister Catherine stepped away from the microphone, nodding toward the student council president, Eric Boileau, the preppiest boy in the history of prepsters. If this had been a free-dress day, he'd be decked out in so much Polo. He usually managed to pop the collar of his white Oxford uniform shirt, and—when he could get away with it—wore his regulation loafers without socks.

"Hi, everyone!" Eric's voice carried a little *too* much enthusiasm, and he punctuated each sentence with an emphatic Bill Clinton–like hand gesture. I didn't envy Eric's job, because most assemblies involved some bit of heckling at him. But the homecoming announcements were the rare occasion where he had everyone's attention, at least until the crowd decided if the girls were nomination-worthy. "Before we announce the 1992 homecoming court nominees, I want to remind everyone to get out and vote! Not just for the court, but *also* for our final mock presidential election tomorrow! Let's see if our school's votes match the nation's!"

Half the student body groaned because they weren't here for a Clinton/Bush debate. And anyway, they were all going to vote for Bush in the mock election, if they voted at all. In terms of the homecoming court, though, the student council was oligarchy in action, under the guise of representative democracy. They tended to nominate girls from within or adjacent to their social circle, which was why it was such a surprise when they nominated Melissa last year. People like

Eric held our fate in their hands, and I couldn't imagine any of them saying, "So what?"

Jennifer sat with the rest of the council, calm and serene, displaying none of the nervousness she usually exhibited around me and Melissa. Maybe she was in her natural habitat, or maybe the calm wouldn't last, but for now, she exuded confidence. Her hair was pulled back from her face with barrettes, instead of her usual perky ponytail. Something about the hairstyle made her seem older and more mature, but that could have been wishful thinking on my part. I wanted to take her composure as a sign that our plan had worked, but I didn't want to read too much into it, either.

"Now, without further ado," Eric said, "the ladies of the student council will announce this year's nominees!"

I crossed my fingers that the announcement would feature all our friends on the ballot. If anyone had told me a month ago that I would wind up caring so much about homecoming nominations, I would have laughed at them.

The girl representatives from each class walked in single file to the podium. The boys escaped the glare of the spotlight, but—if you included the officers—they actually made up the majority of the vote. Patriarchy in action went along with the oligarchy, I guessed. Jennifer approached the microphone first, slowly and steadily. If she was afraid, it didn't show on her face.

"Darcy Kendall and Sara Lewis, please come to the podium," she announced, steady and strong.

Okay, so Helen was out, but Sara was in. I didn't recognize Darcy Kendall, and I tried to figure out from Sara's reaction if she was a good or bad option. When she reached the front of the gym, Sara assumed one of the straight-backed poses she'd likely learned in modeling class with Helen. Her face held nothing but a vacuous smile that hid whatever she was thinking about Darcy Kendall.

Erica Johnson, a tall girl with frizzy strawberry-blond hair, walked to the microphone to announce the sophomores. I crossed my fingers that Cady Jenson made it through. I wasn't sure how Erica felt about our campaign. She was treasurer of the pro-life club, but she'd been among the first to say that she believed Helen. She wasn't a button wearer, though—"So what if she did?" didn't represent anything close to her ideals.

"Cady Jenson and Athena Graves, please come to the podium."

A wave of chills swept over me. I didn't just hear my name. I couldn't have heard that right.

But I had, and now everyone was looking at me. The feeling that coursed through me was closely related to the one I'd felt when I'd told Kyle that I'd heard his conversation with Aimee. I had to make myself get up, remind myself that I had feet and legs and that they provided mobility.

Somehow, I got to the front of the gym, and, pointing to her own faked grin, Sara signaled to me to smile. I tried, but the most I could muster was an uncomfortable grimace. Everyone was staring at me, and I felt like such an imposter. I wasn't homecoming court material, and they all knew it. I wasn't popular—I was just a proxy for a sister who was. How could the girls have done this to me?

I didn't hear the rest of the nominations, but by the time the assembly ended, Melissa, Leah, Angelle, and Missy Bordelon stood to my left, along with a gaggle of eight seniors who stood with their arms interlocked, each wearing So What? buttons on their uniform skirts.

As I left the assembly to go back to class, I felt a hot hiss in my ear and sharp nails digging into my upper arm. "Athena Graves, in my office, *now*."

There were no tortuous hugs, no pained faux concern, no "Now, Athena" this time from Mrs. Turner. She marched me toward the guidance office with a grip on my arm like she was afraid I'd bolt for the doors if she relaxed her hand for even a second.

"Sit," she snapped, almost throwing me into the uncomfortable chair across from her desk. She fumbled for her own chair, knocking over her mug full of pens and pencils and skewing a stack of papers. Her round face was no longer the dangerous but sweet hamster, but a beet-red mask of rage.

I shrank back in my seat. I hadn't done anything to provoke her wrath. Well, maybe that wasn't true. She wouldn't be the first to be angry about our So What? buttons and patches. But this anger was far too immediate to have been inspired by a campaign that was last week's news.

"Now, Athena," she said, sucking in a deep breath. "When I said it was *irresponsible* for your sister to be on the homecoming court, I wasn't implying that you should *immediately* take her place!"

"But I—"

"No, missy, you do *not* get to interrupt me," she ranted. The red in her face was dangerously close to heart-attack territory, and her hands were clutched into tiny tight fists. "You are drawing *far* too much attention to yourself *and* your sister with all this plotting you're doing." She unclenched one fist long enough to point at me with her sharply manicured nails. "You should know better!"

With a swift jerk of her arm, Mrs. Turner opened her desk drawer. She pulled out a near-bursting accordion file and dumped its contents on her desk. In the pile were dozens of buttons and patches, most of which we'd made and some that other people had done, inspired by ours.

"Do you see this?" She held up one of the "So what if she did?" patches. "And this?" she added, gesturing to a So What? button.

"Now, Miss Graves—" *that* formality was new "—I fully expect you to be honest with me," Mrs. Turner said. She tented her fingers and pursed her lips. "I know that you're a smart girl. But you have no idea what kind of harm you've caused with this…this *riot grrrl* stunt!"

I blinked hard, pushing down a laugh that I knew would *not* make things better for me. I didn't know what Mrs. Turner knew about riot grrrl, but whatever it was couldn't be good or accurate.

"Yes, you heard me," she spat. "I know all about that disgusting group of young women, and I cannot for the life of me understand why you would want to be a part of it." She paused dramatically to hold up an illustrated pamphlet that looked like a Chick tract, only presumably not anti-Catholic, but with the same level of religious fervor. Its cover issued a dire warning against riot grrrl: *The Dangerous New Movement Undermining Girls' Piety.* "You and your friends have the superintendent of diocesan schools looking at our institution with a sharp eye. And you have made your sister's situation no better in my eyes, or in the eyes of many faculty at this school. Now, I know you have something to do with these—" she pointed to the patches "—and I don't think your parents would approve of you using your position on the homecoming court to further an extremist political agenda."

Mrs. Turner clearly knew nothing about my mom, who wouldn't approve of me being on the homecoming court *unless* I used it to further a political agenda. Or my dad, for that matter, who always told us to stand up for our ideals.

Mrs. Turner sat silently, fingers tented again, waiting for

me to say something that would indicate my guilt and implicate my sister. I had to think fast, because all I wanted to do was go back out to the assembly, hunt down my friends, and yell at them for nominating me to the homecoming court. I was halfway tempted to rat *them* out, but I wasn't that kind of person. Still, the thought did give me the idea to tell some of the truth, in just the right dose to make her leave me alone, preferably permanently.

"Mrs. Turner, I've only ever wanted to stick up for my sister," I said as contritely as possible. There was a huge chance she wouldn't believe me, since she always seemed to want to believe the worst thing possible. "But I had nothing to do with the student council nominating me for homecoming court."

The thought of having to parade in front of everyone at the football game and the dance sent flames of heated worry through my chest, along with a simmering anger. I knew I'd panic and do something embarrassing, probably in front of Leah or, even worse, Kyle. Or worst, Leah *and* Kyle.

I started to tear up a little, and I wasn't sure if it was in anger or what. Kyle was such a jerk. Every time I'd forgotten him for a second, the humiliation of him sneaking around with Leah came back. How had I been so oblivious?

Once he slipped into my thoughts, I couldn't get him out.

And I started to cry.

In front of Mrs. Turner.

Ugh, there was *nothing* more humiliating than this.

That thought made me cry even more.

"Now, Athena, there's no need to get upset." Mrs. Turner suddenly seemed to forget that she'd spent the past ten minutes screaming at me. She reached across the desk to grab my hand. "We can still work this out."

I didn't trust her for a second, but my feelings of distrust for her were much smaller than the flood of emotions about everything else—anger at my friends for doing this homecoming court stunt behind my back, fear of embarrassing myself, a renewed mortification over the whole Kyle thing. But I needed to focus on Mrs. Turner, not on the things that would only matter once I got out of here.

"I'm sorry." I grabbed a tissue from her desk with shame. I couldn't believe I was crying in front of her. She was eating it up, though, her dark eyes now filled with ersatz concern. "I just… I don't *want* to be on the homecoming court."

Mrs. Turner's eyes lit up, and she leaned toward me.

"I believe you," she said. I recoiled. Something about her believing me was worse than her grilling me. It meant she was about to ask me for something, and it was guaranteed to be something I didn't want to give. "Now, Athena, I think we can work together."

My stomach churned. I didn't want to work with Mrs. Turner. She was the enemy. She'd threatened Helen, over and over again.

I nodded anyway, but inwardly I was screaming about loyalty to my friends and my sister. I had to think of something. Crying because that was what happened every time I thought of Kyle would only work once.

"You don't seem like you want to be on the homecoming court," she said, a practiced look of concern on her face. "But we can't have you withdraw from the election. That would draw even more attention to the situation, and, as I said, we do *not* want the diocese to intervene. That would be *very* bad news for your sister."

My stomach flipped again. That was a threat as much as it was a warning.

"Now, Athena, here's what I propose." Mrs. Turner leaned

back in her seat, pausing for effect. "Instead of campaigning like the other girls, you need to let this whole homecoming thing—" she gestured to the air around her head "—die on the vine. After all, it's not like you're your sister, who's managed to convince the whole school to rally around her. You don't *want* the attention, and unless you go after it, people won't give it to you."

She looked me in the eyes, and I knew she was right. I wasn't like Helen, and everything that had happened to me in the past week had been a stark reminder of that fact. I couldn't even keep the attention of one guy.

My shoulders fell. If I didn't campaign, no one would notice. It would be an easy way out, but it didn't make me feel so great, especially on the heels of Kyle dumping me for Leah.

And then I was crying all over again, when I should have been raging at Mrs. Turner for shoving my supposed inadequacies in my face.

"You're right," I sobbed, a numb feeling in my chest. "I won't campaign. It's the easiest way out."

A smile crept across her face, the first honest one I think I'd ever seen on her, and I started to feel the rage I should've been feeling all along.

"Good girl!" Mrs. Turner said approvingly. "I knew I could count on you, Athena. You'll see. This is the *right* choice—for you and for Helen. Remember, we don't want or need attention from the diocese. There's a strict policy about abortions, and the circulation of these patches here practically confirms her guilt. And even if no one can *prove* your sister had an abortion, you have violated the school's dress code *and* the pro-life code, *and* disrupted the selection of the homecoming court."

"But we didn't!" I insisted. "I swear, the student council—"

Mrs. Turner held up her hand to silence me, her nostrils

flaring. “I know your sister got a bit of sympathy for that incident at her locker, but I cannot see how you or Melissa Lemoine got nominated without help.”

I opened my mouth to point out that Melissa had been nominated last year, but Mrs. Turner held up her hand again, adding a pursed mouth to her flared nostrils.

“I am *not* finished,” she said. “These are gross interferences with the student council’s processes. If you do anything else, I will go *around* Sister Catherine to Principal Richard, or to Superintendent Guidry, and your sister will finish out her freshman year at Greenlawn. And you know how our public schools are.”

I suspected if I answered, *Yeah. They’re crap because they’re underfunded due to racism*, I wouldn’t get very far with Mrs. Turner. At any rate, this was very effective blackmail. If I campaigned, Mrs. Turner would use it as an excuse to boot Helen from school, and I didn’t want to be responsible for that. Helen would never forgive me for separating her from her friends.

“I…I understand,” I said, my voice hollow. “I, um, need to get back to class.”

“Oh, yes, of course.” Mrs. Turner reached for her stack of hall passes with a smile. “I’m so glad we came to an agreement. Then, as I said, let’s just let this die on the vine, shall we?”

I took the note from her, but my mind was already somewhere else—trying to figure out how I could possibly explain to everyone that I would have to let them all down.

29

That night, Dad sat down with us for dinner at the kitchen table. He'd rearranged his work schedule at the law firm to keep a closer eye on Helen, which meant an earlier departure time for work in the morning and later nights in his home office. I think he was still worried she might run away to New York. He hadn't yet decided on a concrete plan for Helen's modeling callbacks, but I knew he'd been in touch with the Ford scout. He kept giving Helen just enough details to know that he was working on it, so she didn't get any ideas about going off again on her own, but also controlled the flow of information enough so that he didn't seem to be rewarding her while she was grounded.

The effort of balancing it all was starting to catch up to Dad, though, and he'd fallen asleep on the couch earlier while the tuna-noodle casserole he'd prepped for dinner was in the oven. Needless to say, his ill-timed nap hadn't worked out very well for the casserole. The smell of burnt tuna lingered in the air, mingling disgustingly with the scent of Chinese takeout now wafting from cartons on the table.

I concentrated on piling lo mein onto my plate and avoided talking to or looking at Helen. Every once in a while, I thought I caught her looking at me, but I averted my eyes just in time. I'd avoided everyone all day, which included eating lunch by myself in the yearbook room. I couldn't figure out how I was going to tell her about Mrs. Turner's threats, and I didn't want to do it in front of Dad. Helen would probably understand, but she might not. Plus, somewhere underneath the fear of Mrs. Turner's threats, another feeling kept creeping up. I didn't want to say it—or even admit it to myself—but I was angry that my friends hadn't told me they were going to put my name in. Helen *had* to have at least known about it—she and Sara had coached Jennifer through the plan and plotted out who to lobby for.

Dad looked back and forth between us, trying to figure out if our silence meant we were up to something, or if we'd gone back to our usual nonassociation with each other.

"I got a call from Sister Catherine today," Dad said, letting the words drop out casually.

"Oh?" Helen asked, the slightest bit of alarm creeping into her voice. She put down her fork and placed her hands in her lap. The memory of Dad marching her to Principal Richard's office probably wasn't that far from her mind.

"What I want to know is why one of you doesn't come to me when you have problems, and the other doesn't tell me when she has good news," Dad said, pointing his fork at me. "Sister Catherine called to tell me Athena was nominated for the homecoming court."

"But it's not good news!" Bile was rising in my throat. I shoved the lo mein away. I wanted to forget I'd been nominated, because I had no way out from Mrs. Turner's bargain. And Mrs. Turner was right. Even if I campaigned with all my heart, I'd never be seen as anything but a low-rent version of my sister—who was a *freshman.*

"Why not?" he asked. Now all of us had our forks down, and Dad and Helen stared at me in disbelief. Dinner, ever the awkward meal in the Graves household.

"Yeah, why not?" Helen echoed. "I don't get it. You were in on our plan to stock the homecoming court, and you knew we needed another sophomore girl. I mean, *I* would have wanted to be part of it. Besides, I thought you had some sort of *politics* you believed in."

I could feel tears welling up in my eyes. Stupid, stupid, stupid waterworks. I couldn't tell her the truth about Mrs. Turner, at least not in front of Dad, but I could tell another truth.

"I don't want to be on the court," I mumbled, staring down at my plate. If I looked at them, at least one would suspect a deeper truth.

"What's this 'plan'?" Dad eyed Helen. Despite his diligent parenting over the past few weeks, he didn't know anything about the Gang of Five. "You two aren't going to do something that will require Sister Catherine—or, God forbid, Mrs. Turner—to call me again, are you? I was hoping I'd heard the last of *her* for a while."

Helen and I sighed simultaneously. I glanced at her, blinking back tears, and she shrugged.

"No, nothing like that." Helen didn't have the look of panicky getting-caught-ness she'd had when Dad had been waiting for her after the New Orleans trip. Instead, she slumped back in her chair with just the tiniest hint of frustration on her face.

"Well, then, what is it?"

"We just wanted to stock the homecoming court with our friends," she said. "In protest against me not being on it."

It was Dad's turn to sigh. This one was less exasperation, more relief. For the first time, I noticed that he had a bit of gray in his brown hair. I wasn't sure if it was his new job or our drama giving him the gray hairs.

"Well, I can understand that, I suppose," he said. "As long as neither of you does anything that requires me to speak with Mrs. Turner for the rest of the year, you have my support."

Helen squealed with joy. Neither of them seemed to notice that I didn't look very happy about the nomination.

"Athena, pleeease?" Helen wheedled. "Can you do it for me?"

"I don't know," I said, not wanting to fight or to give an explanation. If I *really* campaigned, I had no doubt Mrs. Turner would make good on her promises. Helen needed to know about that, but I couldn't tell her *now.* Dad would march me straight to Principal Richard's office, and Mrs. Turner would deny everything. "I'm not going to drop out. That would be weird. But I don't want to stand in front of a bunch of people in an evening gown."

"I'll go shopping with you and do your makeup and get Melissa to do your hair and it'll be perfect, I promise." The words rushed out of her like an enthusiastic, burbling brook. She bounced in her chair at the prospect of painting my face with a dozen kinds of makeup.

Her eagerness to help made me feel extra guilty for the bargain I'd made with Mrs. Turner. I had to talk to her as soon as Dad went into his office after dinner.

"Helen, we'll let Athena decide if she wants to cross that bridge when we come to it," Dad said.

Helen nodded, but excitement still lit her eyes. I turned back to the lo mein on my plate, now soggy and cold. It didn't matter. I didn't want it. Another ruined meal, thanks to Mrs. Turner.

Bzzzzzzzt.

The back doorbell rang. No one rang our back doorbell except Sean and sometimes his mom, if she was working in their garden. But Sean and I weren't speaking, and it was dark, so Estelle wouldn't be working in the garden.

Dad glanced at me, clearly expecting me to open the door, since I was closest, but I froze. I didn't want to see Sean.

Helen pushed her chair back from the table with a groaning scrape against the floor. A few weeks ago, she would have said something like "The nerd king is here," or simply "Ugh, you again?" But once I'd told her what Sean said to me at Denny's, that all changed. I think she was even more mad at him than I was.

Helen peered through the small diamond-shaped window in the door. "It's Sean." She turned back to us. Her lip curled like Billy Idol's trademark sneer.

"Helen, let him in," Dad said distractedly, intent on his plate. "Don't be rude to your sister's friends."

Dad didn't know Sean and I weren't friends anymore. I hadn't told him about our fight at Denny's.

Helen yanked the door open with a huff, and, ignoring Sean, plopped back down at the table with a *thud*. She rolled her eyes at me, annoyed with Sean for daring to show up, or maybe with Dad for making her open the door. Or possibly both. Her actions were overly dramatic, but I appreciated her solidarity. *Take that, Sean.*

Sean stood in the door holding a large garlic-emitting pizza box. His eyes scanned quickly around the room, landing on the cartons of Chinese food.

"I could smell the burnt tuna from next door, so I ordered you a pizza," he said. "But I guess you've already fixed that problem."

I suspected the pizza was his attempt at a peace offering, but the Chinese takeout on the table kind of spoiled whatever plan he'd had. I had to admit that the pizza smelled much better than the greasy lump of lo mein on my plate, though.

When none of us responded, Sean turned to leave. Helen kicked me under the table, a sharp jab to my shins. I swallowed hard.

"Hey, wait," I said. "Why don't we have a slice in the backyard? You know Chinese isn't my favorite."

I hoped Dad wasn't offended, because I'd said I was fine with Chinese food when he asked what we wanted for dinner. I followed Sean into our tiny backyard, which Dad kept tidy, but boring. We didn't have Estelle's flowers and vegetables, but we did have a decent patch of grass.

Sean sat down next to me and carefully placed the pizza on the lawn between us.

"I don't really know where to start, except to say that I'm sorry," Sean offered.

"Yeah." All the anger I'd held on to suddenly turned into sadness. "So'm I."

We looked at the grass instead of each other. I felt a lump in my throat. He'd been mean to me at Denny's, but that had been the final straw, not the entirety of our fight. Things had been rocky for a long time, and we'd both ignored that.

As if reading my mind, he said, "I don't know why I acted like that at Denny's."

I shrugged. "You wanted to support Leah because that's what good boyfriends do."

"Yeah, but I wish I could take it back. I feel like such an asshole." He sighed.

I snorted, with a little bit of tear-induced snot in the background. He *had* been an asshole. But he'd been my friend for much longer. I picked at the cool grass next to me, trying to find something to say that could encapsulate the guarded forgiveness I felt, while at the same time knowing if I did start to talk, I might cry.

It wasn't easy to find the right words for a feeling that went something like, "Hey, I want to be your friend again, and I've missed you, not just recently but for a long time, but you hurt my feelings and I needed you to be there for me these past couple of weeks, you asshole," without a loud bang of emphasis landing on *asshole.*

"Anyway, that's what I wanted to say." He started pushing himself up from the grass, but I wanted him to stay so we could talk things out. It was never easy to do that with Sean because it was so hard for him to open up, but I was determined to do it.

"That's it?" I asked, my throat tight. "I mean, I'm ready to accept your apology, but there's a whole pizza here, and we have a lot to talk about."

Sean lowered himself down again and leaned back on his elbows. He looked up at the sky, searching for answers—or, more likely, avoiding my eyes.

"I don't know where to start," he said.

"Me, neither," I said. "But I'm starving, and I don't want to go back inside. Apparently, the Gang of Five have some terrible idea about me being on the homecoming court, and

Helen's far too excited about the prospect of dressing me up like her own personal Barbie."

I left out the part about Mrs. Turner for the moment. It was too hard to explain in one sentence. Without that added layer of drama, though, the whole thing sounded ridiculous, like I was angry at Helen for transferring her homecoming energies to me. But I wasn't sure I was ready to talk with Sean about more serious things like Mrs. Turner's blackmail, or, even touchier, the garbage pile of Kyle and Leah. But maybe if we talked about the dumb things first, we could eventually get around to the things that mattered.

"I've missed a lot, haven't I?" Sean asked. "It's weird to see you get along with your sister. You and her, together at last, in the Gang of Five."

"She's gotten better," I said brightly. "But not so much that I don't want to kill her on a regular basis."

Sean laughed. For a second, I felt a glimmer of how easily we'd interacted in the past, and then it was gone, replaced by that lumpy-throat feeling. I wanted things back to normal so much, but I didn't know quite how to get there. It felt like trying to pull a train back to the right tracks, but having no way to switch it over.

"Well, there's this pizza." He struggled to sound enthusiastic. "And, if you need me to, I'll go with you to the homecoming dance. It'll give Helen and Melissa something to talk about."

He didn't say anything about Leah or Kyle, though we both knew they would be there, too. But if he wanted to avoid that topic for now, I could handle it. I was hungry and tired of how many times I'd skipped lunch or dinner over the past few weeks. Every time someone wanted to talk about something serious, it just *had* to be over a meal, sending my stomach into knots only an experienced sailor could untangle.

"Who knows?" I said, forcing a laugh. "Maybe Helen will finally confess her true love for you."

Two months ago, my remark would have passed in a second. Now, it seemed to echo in all the wrong ways.

"Then at least somebody would." He cleared his throat and looked at the ground. Not that it mattered in the darkness. Dad had forgotten to replace the floodlight at the back door for months, like a lot of other maintenance that had slid since he'd started his new job. Estelle's mosquito zapper gave off the only light, an eerie blue glow in the darkness. I was silently thankful for that missing floodlight, though, which at least took away one awkward hurdle. If he was crying, I couldn't see it, and he didn't need to be embarrassed.

"I think Leah really loved you at some point, you know," I told him. "As much as she could love anyone but herself anyway."

Hardly a ringing endorsement. Sean snorted. He looked down at the grass again and let out a huge sigh.

"Leah," he said. "Yeah. I don't want to talk about her."

"Sorry." So much for saying the right thing.

"It's okay. You know, you were right about her all along. And I got mad at you for being right about her, instead of seeing her for the opportunistic bitch she is."

"Mmm-hmm." I didn't know how else to reply. I was so used to having to curb my words about Leah around Sean. It felt like a trap. If they got back together, anything I said now would echo for months.

"I don't know what happened to her," he said, shaking his head. "I mean, she always had her faults—"

I held back a rude, rueful laugh, because I wasn't the type to say "I told you so."

"—but she had her good qualities, too. She *always* believed in me, even when no one else did. I mean, I know you believed in me, but your knowledge of football is..." He held up his fingers about a quarter inch apart, which was fair enough.

"What changed with you two?" I asked, both because I cared about how Sean felt and also because I wanted some insight—*any* insight—into why Leah might have decided to go after Kyle, even though Sean was clearly a far more faithful boyfriend than Kyle. That jerk.

"I'm not sure," he said. "I keep going over and over it in my mind, analyzing it like it's a series of plays. If I'd paid attention to this, if I hadn't ignored that. I don't want to absolve myself of anything, but..." He shrugged. "I can't think of anything *I* did. All I can think of are the things in her life that changed, and that maybe they were too much for her. She's living with her dad now, and since we're not dating anymore, I can finally say this about him—he's a racist dick."

The words pretty much exploded out of his mouth. Sean *never* talked with me about the racist things people said about or to him, and I was never sure if that was due to some flaw in our friendship—because he thought I wouldn't understand—or if he just didn't like to talk about them in general because ignoring them made them seem less terrible.

"Do you think that had anything to do with how she's acting?" I kept my question as vague as possible because I didn't want Sean to close off how he felt from me. Again.

"I dunno," he said. "I don't think it's the *only* thing, but I do think it probably got a lot harder for her to hear a litany of bad things about me from her dad when her mom wasn't around. Plus, she was super pissed at her mom for what she did to her dad, so if she's siding with her dad on that one..."

"Then every awful thing he says about you becomes more reasonable to her," I finished the thought.

"Exactly. You know, she always said you were jealous because you didn't have a boyfriend," he said, looking up again at the cloudy sky. "I think it's pretty hilarious that as soon as you got one, *she* turned jealous and had to steal him."

Had Kyle been my boyfriend? We'd been out on a bunch of dates, but we'd never had any kind of conversation cementing things. In retrospect, it seemed almost like Kyle had intentionally kept things ambiguous—just like it now seemed a little fishy that we'd never made it inside the football stadium for the game, and we didn't go to *Twin Peaks: Fire Walk with Me* because he'd conveniently remembered that he didn't have a fake ID once we'd spotted people from school. And he somehow never had time to eat lunch with me at school, even before the Gang of Five stuff really got going. Besides, if he'd asked me, I could've taken a break from that to eat with him.

I wondered if Aimee and Leah had been working on him the entire time—or if he had been working *her* the entire time, keeping his options open. If that was the case, then I'd never really stood a chance. He was probably making out with Leah right now in the boy-music room at his house—or maybe she was in his bedroom by now, on his bed with the plaid comforter. I tried to block the images from my mind, but I knew that the same ones probably floated through Sean's mind, too, except with Leah's bedroom filling in the details.

"He wasn't my boyfriend." It was my turn to look awkwardly at the grass, as though it held some answers to our problems. But it didn't. It was just grass.

"Oh, come on," he scoffed. "For weeks, he was all you

would talk about. You were unbearable. Don't act like you didn't like him."

I had. But that wasn't the point. It didn't matter how much I'd liked him. All that mattered was he didn't like me enough, at least not enough to believe in me over Leah. He had that much in common with Sean, actually.

"I did like him." I left the rest of my thoughts out of the conversation.

"Hey, you know, let's not talk about them," Sean said, nudging me with his elbow. "Cold pizza is fine and all, but it's so much better when it's hot."

"And we're not locked outside this time," I said, finally opening the box and grabbing a slice. "Like when the door closed behind us that time we snuck out to pay the pizza guy when we were twelve because we didn't want to eat the left-overs my dad reheated for us."

"Not unless Helen gets some ideas," he said, taking a piece of pizza for himself. "You should have seen the look she gave me when she opened the door."

"I still say she loves you." This time, Sean laughed.

It took about three hours for us to circle back around to talking about Leah and Kyle, and I couldn't stop crying long enough to get the story out coherently. When I finally got to the part about what Aimee had said in the library, he tried to make me laugh. Even though all I managed was a small sardonic wheeze of air barely related to a laugh, it was a start. And then I asked him for advice about Helen, and it wasn't exactly like the old days, but in a good way. Instead of cracking jokes about her, he told me I had to be honest and deal with Mrs. Turner's blackmail thing.

By the end of the night, I felt a hint of our old closeness coming back, a weight lifted now that I'd have someone else to talk with in case this whole homecoming thing failed miserably.

Afterward, I crept up the stairs to my room, not wanting to wake Dad. I hoped Helen was still up, though, because my Sean-induced courage would wane if I waited until morning.

The bedroom light leaked out from under our door, and I exhaled. She was awake. At least I could have our uncomfortable, impossible conversation now, instead of sometime tomorrow after school.

When I opened the door, Helen bolted up in bed, her copy of *Vogue* sliding off the comforter next to her.

"So are you going to forgive Sean?" she asked eagerly.

"That's a little direct," I said, without thinking of how it would come out. Old habits died hard, and part of me wasn't yet used to Helen caring what was going on in my life. "I mean, it's fine. Sorry. It was a long, weird conversation. I *think* it's going to be okay, but..."

I crashed onto my bed. You never knew about these things. Maybe he'd get a new girlfriend in two months and he'd disappear again. Or maybe things weren't ever going to be the same anymore, since we weren't in the same classes, didn't run in the same circles, and hanging out at each other's houses after school every once in a while didn't feel like a real friendship.

"It's going to be *fine*." Helen leaned forward on her elbow and yawned. It was nearly midnight, and we had to get up at six for school.

"That's a change from earlier," I said, raising my eyebrows. "You practically chased him out of the house."

"Yeah, but that was before I eavesdropped on you guys for an hour. Or two."

I choked out a laugh. *That* was the Helen I knew. But somehow, I didn't mind it so much. At least I didn't have to condense a three-hour conversation into a five-minute summary for her.

"Just how long did you listen?"

"Long enough to know why you freaked out at dinner," she said, punctuating the sentence with an angry *harrumph*. "And to know we've got to step up because I am *not* letting Mrs. Turner kick me out of school. But don't worry—we can do it."

"But she said—"

"What? That I'm guilty in some way? That no one's going to vote for you? That she has *any* power over us? Because, you know, that's *not* true." Helen's voice was getting louder, and for a minute I worried Dad would walk across the hall and yell at us, mistaking our conversation for one of our many arguments.

"No, I—maybe? I know she's not right about you, but maybe she's right that no one would vote for me—" Helen opened her mouth to protest, but I continued, "If none of this had happened, I would *never* have been nominated to the court, and you know it. But I don't think that's true now. I *do* think that a lot of people would vote for me. But Cady's also on our team, and it might be better to campaign for her, like what Melissa did last year, than to make *me* into the ideal candidate. It kills two birds with one stone, you know? Mrs. Turner won't know that Cady's on our side—she's too self-involved for that—but it'll take the heat off *us*."

What I said sounded a lot smarter and more logical than what I'd *planned* to say, which was that I didn't think most people would vote for me regardless. As much as Helen wanted to think our campaign was about rumors and not a political stance, at least half the people who were into it had joined us because it was vaguely rebellious. We couldn't count on that lasting if people had to stand up for something real, though.

Helen frowned. "You might be right. And that would work. But I don't like that you think Mrs. Turner is right about you losing just because you're not me. That's bullshit."

She was totally wrong. I would never have been nominated under normal circumstances. But I was suddenly okay with that, and even if I won—which was incredibly unlikely—I'd be okay. I wasn't some second-best Graves sister who stood in for the pretty one. Our mom's obscure-ish Greek names for us didn't have to *mean* anything—I didn't have to be the smart one, and she didn't have to be the pretty one. I hadn't been a second choice because she'd been forbidden from being nominated—I had been the *first* choice for helping my sister.

And the best way to do that was to help Cady win.

30

I pushed my way through the crowd at the front of the school, like every morning. Staying up late the night before talking with Sean was good, but it was going to be a long time until we were truly best friends again.

Staying up even later to talk with Helen after meant I'd only gotten about three hours of sleep. Now I faced the morning's classes with a groggy discombobulation that no amount of coffee could improve. I hadn't done my homework, either.

"Hey, Red! You're famous!"

Oh, Wisteria. She was so sweet and cheerful, but why wouldn't she use my name? I leaned against a row of beige lockers to let others pass while I waited for her to catch up. In her school uniform, she still looked every bit a member of the Gothtastic Four: florid eyeliner, black lipstick, and, most recently, the bleach-blondest roots with the dyed-blackest ends—

like Terri Nunn of Berlin, if her roots were only about two inches long.

"What are you talking about?" Yesterday's news that I'd made the ballot for the homecoming court didn't qualify me as "famous" by any stretch of the imagination. She wasn't saying it in a bad way, though, so that meant Leah and Aimee hadn't struck again. They'd been surprisingly blasé at the announcement yesterday.

"No, look." She pushed a flyer into my hands.

Whatever, I thought through my haze of tired. Melissa was probably trying to expand the So What? campaign to highlight our mutual nominations for homecoming court, or else she'd picked up on the fact that I was ignoring her and wanted to make it right. Or maybe Helen, Jennifer, and Sara did something to support me.

I looked down at the photo on the flyer, and my stomach lurched when I realized that this wasn't the work of any of my friends. So much for not campaigning.

It wasn't exactly a flyer, at least not a cheaply photocopied one with crappy contrast. Someone had taken their time with these—it was printed on expensive paper, and the image was a high-quality reproduction from a laser printer. I immediately recognized it as one of the photos Kyle took that night of the football game. I'd thought that I must have looked tired and sweaty and gross in all those pictures, but this one had turned out surprisingly well. The photo had been carefully cropped down to my face and the night background, so the lovely but incriminating graffiti disappeared. My face was turned in three-quarter profile, with the city lights behind me, and I was halfway smiling at something.

I looked cool and mysterious and almost beautiful. I never looked like that in real life—did I?

The text below read Athena Graves for Homecoming Court. Nothing else. No carefully crafted slogan, no mention of the Gang of Five. Nothing but me looking far better than I did on a daily basis.

"Red, they're *everywhere*," Wisteria said. "I have no idea how, either. There aren't half as many for anyone else. Someone really likes you. And you look *fantastic*. I want whoever took those photos to do my album cover. They're, like, super punk rock."

Photos, *plural*? There were more? At least Wisteria assumed someone else had done it, because it would seem super egotistical if I'd done this myself. As I walked through the halls, my face looked back at me—half smiling, posted on lockers; fully smiling, three-quarter angle, on corkboards; in profile, on the concrete columns. Wisteria was right. My face dominated the campaign space, so much that I had a hard time finding a picture of Cady or Sara or Leah. And they were the best photos I'd ever seen of myself.

Had Kyle done all this? These were his photos, but I didn't really think that he was committed to doing me any favors. For all I knew, Melissa could have strong-armed him into giving up his negatives. After all, she knew about our adventure to The Building, photos included, and she had a hookup at Kinko's. It wasn't unbelievable that she'd do that to—or, in her mind, *for*—me. Besides, Kyle hadn't said a word to me since I'd confronted him in the hallway last week. I pretended to adore calculus and that I was in love with my physics book whenever he walked by my desk now. In physics yesterday, he'd hesitated near me for the slightest fraction of a second, and I'd held my breath, waiting to see if he would do something. Apologize, hand me a note, tell me to go to hell. But he hadn't said anything.

Now I had to rethink everything. Wisteria wasn't rocking

the hyperbole. She was serious about how many copies of the photos lined the walls. It seemed like far too many for Kyle to have done himself, and not like something he'd do so soon after choosing Leah over me. Yes, him feeling this degree of regret and guilt over what he'd done would give me a lot of satisfaction, but life rarely worked that way. It seemed much more likely to me that Melissa was somehow behind this. But even if Kyle hadn't created and put them up himself, he'd done *something* of a good deed in my direction by supplying the photos.

Except that this good deed was *awful*. I was elated that he—or maybe Melissa and the gang, but someone—had tried to make me look good, and I wanted to throw up at the same time. Because even though I hadn't done this myself, Mrs. Turner would see it as a reason to make good on her threats. I could almost feel her grip clawing into my upper arm already.

"You are *so* dead, Graves," a voice near me threatened. Aimee.

I turned to see Leah's permed companion, a ripped-up copy of Kyle's picture of me in her hands. She was going for full-on sinister, but only managed an incompetent menace.

"Yeah, I bet." A few weeks ago, I'd have been terrified of what she and Leah might do to me. Now she seemed pathetic. "So what'll it be? Are you going to start a rumor that I'm into witchcraft? That I snort coke off Chippendales' asses?"

I shocked her into speechlessness for a moment, but she recovered quickly, sending me a smug smirk.

"You really have to make everything all about *you*," she sneered, crumpling the photo in her hand. "You wrecked Leah's relationship with Sean, and now you're trying to turn the homecoming court into some lame political stunt. But you'll always be a loser."

She turned dramatically, trying to toss her hair over her shoulder for effect. Instead, it looked overwrought and soap-operatic, an impression that was only further emphasized when she threw the crumpled flyer to the ground and stomped on it.

Whatever she and Leah were planning, I thought, the Gang of Five would be ready for it.

"So you've decided to join us again for lunch?" Sara looked up at me brightly as Melissa and I arrived at our usual spot. Not that long ago, Helen would have shot her a look of death for sounding so eager to see me, but right now, she looked relieved that I'd decided to show up after ignoring everyone yesterday for nominating me to the court, and then avoiding them after Mrs. Turner decided to blackmail me.

I nodded, sitting down between Jennifer and Melissa. It was about all I could do, considering how tired I was. Meanwhile, Helen looked sprightly and excited and fresh as ever, despite also staying up late. Maybe she'd managed a quick nap while I was talking with Sean, or maybe she had some secret to staying awake that I didn't know about. I'd have to ask her later. Right now, I could barely keep my eyes focused on my turkey sandwich.

"We need to talk about the posters," I said, trying to muster the remaining energy I had left into some kind of confrontation. The fear of Mrs. Turner's blackmail was the only thing propelling me forward. Well, that, and the can of Coke I'd gotten from the cafeteria vending machine. I gulped down a giant mouthful of it, hoping the caffeine and sugar would hit me soon. I waved the can at Melissa. "Did you have anything to do with that?"

Melissa looked guilty—which she *should*, if she'd done anything to promote my candidacy. She knew I was so angry about the surprise announcement that I'd eaten lunch alone in the yearbook room yesterday, which essentially involved breaking and entering into a space that I knew would be empty until the second half of the first semester, which was when the yearbook staff—of which I was a member—would actually have something to do. I was done seething for now, but the real threat of Mrs. Turner loomed over my head.

"Well, yes and no," she said, as hedgily as anyone had ever hedged anything. "I… Well, I want nothing to do with that turd Kyle, *as you know*. And I honest to God didn't set out to talk to him. But I *happened* to be at Kinko's last night to photocopy my zine, because Erik was working and he gives me free copies. And Kyle *happened* to be there, and I *happened* to see those were particularly good photos of you, and I *happened* to get Erik to tell him which ones were best, and I *happened* to get him to shuffle Kyle over to the super high-res copier and only charge him the shitty copier price, so he had a lot of flyers by the end of the night. But as for giving him the idea to make flyers of those photos and post them everywhere—or even talking to him—no, I did not. The flyers were all his idea, and, as for his reasoning or motive…" She shrugged exaggeratedly. "You'd have to ask him. Only I wouldn't, if I were you. He's an asshole, and his cowardly attempt at showing how awesome you are doesn't count as an apology."

Her explanation was the most Melissa-sounding thing I'd ever heard in terms of her possibly engineering things from afar. I was the kind of tired where my eyeballs felt like they were going to fall out of my head, and thinking about Kyle's strange behavior and what it might mean paled in comparison to the fact that the flyers were sure to piss off Mrs. Turner.

"Don't worry," I said, taking another hit of caffeinated sugar. "I want nothing to do with him, and I don't want his help." I glanced at Helen, debating how much I needed to rehash Mrs. Turner's blackmail. I knew I should tell everyone, but I burned with humiliation every time I thought of it. It also didn't feel wise to talk about it out in the open. "At any rate, we need to start campaigning for Cady because I *do not* want to have to ride around in a convertible waving like the queen."

I wasn't lying, exactly, but I *was* hiding the real reason I wanted to campaign for Cady. Helen started to say something in protest, but I shook my head in warning. Fortunately, no one else seemed to notice our exchange, or if they did, they didn't know what it was about anyway.

"Awww!" Sara let out an overly loud sound of disappointment and wrinkled her face into a pained wince. "It's going to suck if I have to be up there by myself, if I get it. I don't want to do this any more than you do, but we had more trouble thinking of freshmen and sophomores than juniors and seniors. For whatever reason, the seniors *love* our campaign. But I don't *know* them, and I don't really know anything about Cady, other than she picked out a 'So what if she did?' patch on the first day of the campaign, even before…"

Sara glanced over at Helen. I could tell what she was about to say, and I didn't *think* Helen would get mad, but… "Even before someone trashed Helen's locker, she told me that she thought the rumors were, and I quote, 'fucking hypocritical garbage,' thought up by 'the tackiest human alive.' And again, that was before everyone else jumped on the bandwagon, so…"

I almost spat out my Coke at the words *hypocritical garbage*. I didn't know Cady *that* well, but it was promising that she was so blunt in her support. She was one of those girls whose mom had pushed her into beauty pageants when she was younger. She somehow ended up rebelling against it by developing a sailor's mouth, but never looked anything but pretty and put together.

"I dunno, Sara," I said. "Sounds like you've tapped into the essence of Cady Jenson. I think you'll be fine."

"Yeah. I guess it's fine." Sara's face said it was the opposite of fine. "But I'd rather be up there with you and Melissa."

I wanted to sink into the concrete steps. The gang hadn't picked me for the homecoming court in order to make me miserable, or because I could be a half-assed substitute for Helen. They'd picked me because I was one of them, and now I was going to have to let them down.

Along with every other girl nominated for the homecoming court, I sat on the gym bleachers after school, half listening to Sister Catherine's long list of rules for the upcoming week. I didn't need to hear this. We were going to campaign for Cady, who supported us *and* who'd been second runner-up at Miss Teen Louisiana last year. In a normal year, even without politics, she'd be the obvious choice. Everything was going to be okay.

My head drifted downward, sleep taking over. Melissa poked me, sharpest elbow in the world digging into my side. I jolted awake.

"Miss Graves, please sit up." Sister Catherine looked at me with the kind of stern face only a nun could muster.

I forced myself into an upright position, but I was still too tired to pay attention.

Melissa's presence on my left buffered me from Leah somewhat, but I could feel her smug vibrations radiating toward me at Sister Catherine's correction.

"Good luck beating an actual beauty queen," Leah sneered. It was meant to make me nervous, but I had an entirely different reaction. Somehow, after Leah's comment, a tiny vengeful kernel within me wanted to win. If only to beat *her.* And then I remembered that I wasn't running against Leah, but Cady, and I *wanted* Cady to win.

Sister Catherine droned on with more rules and regulations. The winners got to wear not one, but *two* non-school-uniform outfits for homecoming. We were supposed to wear "age-appropriate business casual dresses or skirts" to the football game. Hillary Clinton pantsuits and Barbara Bush pearls were the only kinds of business clothes that came to my mind, and I kept pondering what "age-appropriate business casual" was while Sister Catherine reiterated the rules for the selection process, described how we should act when we heard the announcement of who made it into the court, and stressed our proper comportment for the football game and dance.

After Sister Catherine finished her lecture, she made us walk in pairs across the gym to a row of folding chairs opposite the bleachers, where we were supposed to sit like ladies for the announcement. I think "proper comportment" translated into Sara's rod-straight posture, because Sister Catherine smiled approvingly at her while scowling at the rest of us. Despite her repeated warnings about sitting nicely, I more or less collapsed into my folding chair. I could barely keep my eyes open, let alone my spine rigid.

When I wasn't nodding off, my mind drifted stubbornly toward the flyers with my face on them, and Kyle and Leah. Kyle hadn't said anything to me about the pictures, and I'd started to suspect Melissa had more to do with it than just getting Erik to steer Kyle toward the better copier. But it also wasn't like her to not take credit. So my mind kept circling back to Kyle, and what any of this was supposed to mean. If it meant anything.

"Ladies, be sure to cross your legs. Miss Graves, please sit *up.*" Sister Catherine's words yanked me back to the gym. I kicked myself internally for thinking about Kyle. It wasn't like I was still interested in him anyway. Right?

"Sister Catherine! So glad I found you!" Mrs. Turner darted delicately across the gym floor, her kitten heels clacking the whole way.

It only lasted a moment, but I swear I saw Sister Catherine grip at the rosary at her waist like some cognitive behavioral therapy tic before turning to face the guidance counselor.

"Yes, Mrs. Turner?"

Mrs. Turner took Sister Catherine's acknowledgment as encouragement to scuttle closer to our group. Her gaze raked over us, and she flashed her tiny pursed-lipped smile before settling into a look of stern approbation.

I looked left and right. Melissa shook her head at me. Leah smirked. Angelle looked eagerly at Mrs. Turner. Everyone else looked bored.

"Now, ladies, there is every reason to take this seriously," Mrs. Turner said. "But you might be aware of some, shall we say, *inappropriate* campaigning going on." She looked squarely at me, her round black eyes full of fury. "If I catch any of you wearing *anything* inappropriate or passing along any *illegal* materials, I'll make sure Sister Catherine knows. And you will be off the court."

She nodded her head with great finality, unaware that Sister Catherine was standing next to her, shaking her head. Her hand had wandered back to the rosary at her waist. She had to be praying for enough patience to not smack Mrs. Turner.

"Mrs. Turner, I'm sure you mean well," Sister Catherine said, an edge creeping into her usually level voice. "But none of these girls has done anything inappropriate. Each has produced tasteful campaign materials within the school's guidelines. And do I have to remind you that *I* am the dean of discipline?"

Mrs. Turner flinched but quickly recovered. The tight smile was back. "Now, Sister Catherine, I do, as you said, mean well. And I believe you are unaware of the *emotional* impact that the more *questionable* elements of this campaign have had on the girls. Addressing that sort of thing *is* my job, and several girls have already told me how threatened they feel."

The idea of anyone feeling threatened by the actual content of any of the homecoming posters was ridiculous. The So What? campaign wasn't threatening anyone, either. The only threatening thing that had happened in any campaign was Mrs. Turner threatening me and Helen—and Aimee threatening *me* in the hall.

"I'm sure you're prepared to handle their emotional stress when and if they do come to you," Sister Catherine said, as though she wasn't all that sure anyone would willingly enter Mrs. Turner's office. "But as long as they are maintaining their current standards of behavior in their *exemplary* campaigns, I don't see what the problem is."

Mrs. Turner pressed her lips together again. "I see. Well, ladies, I wish you all good luck. I'm sure Sister Catherine is a good judge of your campaign tactics." She started walking toward the door, tiny shoes *clack-clacking* against the wooden floors. Midway across the basketball court, she turned, and a bright, gloating smile stretched across her face. "And I'm sure Principal Richard will intervene if anything else comes to light. We wouldn't want there to be a scandal, would we?"

Sister Catherine's face turned bright red against the light gray of her habit, but she stayed quiet. Letting Mrs. Turner have the last word was the only way to get her out of the gym.

31

On Friday afternoon, Helen shoved me into an overcrowded dressing room stall in the juniors department at Maison Blanche and slammed the door shut before I had the chance to bolt. Over her arm, she'd slung a huge stack of dresses—some shiny, some silky, and one a hideous blend of lace and animal-print crushed velvet that made me think she'd lost her solid sense of fashion.

I'd been campaigning for Cady since Monday, much to Helen's annoyance. She thought I should push ahead and press the advantage Kyle's flyers might give me. Melissa got it, though, and she'd kept silent while I told everyone around me that they should vote for Cady, and to disregard the various photocopies of me that had appeared in the halls. Mrs. Turner pursed her lips every time she saw me, but otherwise, she left me alone.

Now, since it looked like we *might* pull this off without getting expelled, Melissa and Helen were playing dress-up-the-nerd with me. With my catalog of potential dresses selected, Melissa had stayed in the homecoming gown section of the department store, theoretically looking for a dress of her own. I suspected she was waiting outside as a guard in case I escaped my dressing room prison cell. I sat on the mauve velvet chair that was wedged into a corner of the dressing room and watched Helen arrange the dresses in an order that mystified me.

"I don't see why I have to buy a dress *now*." I crossed my arms. "We don't find out the results until Monday. Plus, hello, I'm campaigning for Cady. I don't *need* a dress."

Helen slouched against the louvered door of the dressing room, put her hand to her forehead, and closed her eyes, a dramatic indication that she was done with me.

"You are *so* going to win," she said. "If only because the universe knows it'll drive you crazy. And even if you don't, you're still going to the dance with Sean, remember? If the two of you look halfway decent, you can remind that scumbag Kyle and that bi—that *brat* Leah that you are both forces to be reckoned with. Now, *please* try on something reasonable before Melissa comes back with another of these hideous monstrosities. She *has* to be joking with this one."

She had paused to look at the repulsive leopard-and-lace dress. She was right on both counts. Sean and I had agreed we would go to the dance together, so I was going. Also, that dress was a joke.

Helen yanked the ugly dress out of the pile, held it at arm's length, and wrinkled her nose. Then she looked at the label, and her eyebrows rose.

"Hmm. Betsey Johnson. Ugly *and* expensive. Didn't know

they carried her stuff here. Maybe we can find you a floral one by her instead. Those are nice."

She tossed the Betsey Johnson dress over the back of my chair.

"What's first?" I asked, reluctantly rising to my feet. I might as well get through this torture.

"This." Helen held up a long satin dress so dark blue it seemed almost black. Its slinky fabric pooled on the floor in an elegant puddle. "It's perfect. It's the one."

"Are you serious?" I asked. "That's going to make me look two feet tall. I can't wear long dresses."

Helen snorted and mumbled something like "As if you know anything about fashion." I let it slide. Moving to the second pile, she handed me a short purple taffeta dress and crossed her arms in front of her chest as she watched me put it on.

I slid the dress over my head, and Helen zipped it up for me. It fit perfectly, but I looked like a grape. Or maybe an eggplant, with very little up top and a giant, belled-out bottom. Either way, I looked like I could go to the dance with the guy dressed as a bunch of grapes in a Fruit of the Loom commercial.

"That's awful." Helen scanned me up and down. "You need to try on the blue one."

I looked at the blue dress again. It slinked against the wall, a streak of midnight in a sea of poufiness. I couldn't wear something like that.

"Maybe at the end. I'm too short for it."

Helen muttered something about "tailors" and "it's their job to shorten hems." She pulled another short dress off the rack, black this time. Like most short dresses in the juniors department, it looked like it had been in the store since 1987. They all took the same shape, with an off-the-shoulder neckline, tight bodice, and poufy skirt, in different fabrics and colors.

"You're ruining my order," she grumbled. "While you put that on, I'm going to get Melissa. And I'm taking your jeans with me, so don't get any ideas about leaving."

She snatched my jeans from the bench and whipped them across her arm. The louvered door slammed behind her, shaking the dressing room stall.

Helen was trying to help me. I should listen to her. I took a deep breath and resolved to be nicer. This was for the Gang of Five—it wasn't about me.

I dropped the dress I was holding and grabbed the midnight blue dress instead. I slipped it over my head, sending up a silent thanks that it had a side zipper I could manage on my own. Smoothing down the sides, I turned to gaze at myself in the mirror.

Wow. Helen was right. This *was* the one. The dress hugged close to my rib cage and then glided down over my legs. On my back, the straps crisscrossed in a diamond pattern. I looked like a 1930s film star, my pale skin contrasting with the inky color of the dress, and my red hair looking supersaturated against the satin.

I could hear Helen and Melissa debating the selection of homecoming dresses as they walked into the dressing room area.

"I might have to wear the Prom Dress of Doom that I never got to wear," Melissa said. She'd been all set to go to prom with Mike Thibodeaux, who was a senior last year, but he'd gotten suspended for punching a guy during a basketball game. Melissa was only a sophomore, so she couldn't go on her own. She'd said it was okay, but I don't know what bothered her more—that her date would have been a hotheaded jerk, or that she'd spent money on a dress she never got to wear. "But it's not a fall dress, so—"

Helen pushed the door open without knocking. I'm sure she expected me to be wearing the short black dress and a look of baby-faced petulance. Melissa and Helen angled into the narrow doorway, each trying to push the other out of the way. No way all three of us could fit in the room at the same time, but they tried.

"See?" Helen gloated.

A smile widened across Melissa's face. "I see you came to your senses. That jerk Kyle will be dying of regret and unactionable horniness."

A few weeks ago, I would have blushed, but Kyle's horniness was a topic I had now shoved to the far recesses of my brain. I wanted to forget that anything had ever happened between us—that I had kissed him, or that anything else near second base had happened. I knew Melissa meant to make me feel better, but she didn't. Instead, I felt a little like throwing up, and a little like crying.

I pushed Kyle out of my head and concentrated on the fact that I looked good in my dress. Though I didn't want to seem vain, I couldn't stop looking at my reflection in the mirror.

"Out. To the three-way mirror." Helen shoved me into the hallway. I pulled up the skirt of my dress so that it didn't drag the ground, like a Victorian lady walking over a puddle.

In the large area in front of the dressing room's three-way mirror, Helen looked me up and down, pulled at the fabric, and turned me around several times, all while squinting and frowning. I held my breath, waiting for her to say something critical or mean. Finally, she stopped and turned to me with her face beaming.

"Oh, who am I kidding? I can't torture you anymore with

suspense," Helen said, throwing her hands up. "This is the perfect dress for you."

She danced a little bouncy jig around me, and then gave Melissa a high five. They both looked at me with giant grins. I couldn't stop smiling, either, though some small part of me felt ridiculous for being this happy over a *dress*. I told that part of me to shut up, because this dress *was awesome*.

"In case you're worried, I have an excellent tailor," Melissa said. "Otherwise known as my mom. She can hem it for you."

I didn't want to change out of the dress, but it covered my feet and I couldn't really walk in it. It felt so perfect against my skin, though, the satin shiny but not too shiny, and I kept touching it to see if it was real. I jumped excitedly, but carefully—a little hop in place so I wouldn't hurt it.

"I love it," I said. "Can I wear it home?"

Helen's eyebrows knotted together, like she was worried about something.

"I'm joking!" At least I thought I was joking. I really, really didn't want to take it off.

"I know, but I have to figure out where I left your jeans," Helen said. "I'll be right back."

She darted out of the dressing room area, leaving me with Melissa, who continued to nod approvingly. She almost never looked like that when surveying my clothes. The only time she came close was when I borrowed hers.

"Even if she can't find your jeans, you've won for the day," she said. "That's the best dress ever."

At the cash register, I nearly threw up when I saw the price tag.

One hundred and ten dollars. More money than I had with me. More money than I had, period. Dad had given fifty dollars each to Helen and me, and I had thirty more of my own. My heart broke. I could borrow money from Melissa, but that would be embarrassing—and, no matter how perfect the dress was, I couldn't justify spending that much.

Then Helen handed me her fifty-dollar bill. Or, rather, shoved it into my hand and closed hers over it with a firm grip.

"I don't need it," she whispered. "But don't tell Dad you went over budget."

"What?" I asked, startled. "Why don't you need it?"

Helen smiled slyly. She leaned casually against the counter at the cash register while we waited for the clerk to return from the back room, where she was getting Melissa a different color of the hideous leopard-and-lace dress.

"Oh, I have my ways." Great. The old, immature, annoying Helen had been replaced by a new, annoyingly adult version who offered me money. I wasn't sure I trusted this new Helen, with her world-wise face, and her generosity surprised me. A few months ago, she would have pocketed the extra fifty dollars for herself.

"Just tell me." Otherwise, I wouldn't be able to take the money. I'd be too worried about what she had done to get it.

Her back slid farther down the counter, and she looked straight at me, her hair shaking in a blond wave.

"You. Are. Zero. Fun." She emphasized each word. She stood up and shrugged. "I'm wearing the green velvet dress from the fashion show. Something happened with the returns, and Mrs. Brouillette got the clothes donated to the modeling school. I persuaded her I should get the dress, since it was too long for everyone else."

Machiavellian, my sister was. I was impressed with her initiative and her maneuvering skills. She looked great in that dress, and if mine was expensive, I couldn't imagine the scaling up of economy I'd have to do in babysitting in order to pay for Helen's.

"You don't mind wearing it again?"

"Why would I care?" she said. "That dress was, like, five hundred dollars! And it's not like anyone but you and Sean and Sara and Jennifer saw me in it."

I clutched the blue dress to my chest. I wouldn't have to put it back on the rack or beg Dad for extra money. I didn't have to scramble to find a babysitting job in the next three days or put it on layaway. I wouldn't have to try on thirty-seven more dresses in order to find one half as good as the one in my arms.

"I'll pay you back." I would find that babysitting job, just not this week.

Helen's eyes dropped to her shoes. I couldn't see her face through her thick hair.

"This is totally dorky to say," she said, "but you already have. You believed me. And you figured out how to make other people think so, too. Fifty bucks is a way cheap price to pay."

I had the sudden urge to hug my sister. And so I did. But carefully, so I wouldn't mess up my dress.

I carried my dress out of the store delicately, careful not to let it touch the ground, even though it was wrapped in a plastic garment bag. I didn't want to leave *anything* to chance. It was perfect, and I wouldn't allow a single speck of dust to get anywhere near it. Helen and Melissa beamed at each other, proud that they had finally taught their fashion student something valuable. If I hadn't been so happy about the dress, I might have been annoyed with them, but I didn't think that *anything* could possibly bring me down from the high of buying the most beautiful, most perfect dress in the history of homecoming dresses.

I was wrong.

As we walked back through the mall to the car, Melissa stopped next to me.

"Column left, girls," she hissed. "Now!"

It was too late. I saw what she saw, and I could feel my smile fading.

Leah. Of course.

"Ooh, Athena, let me look at your dress," she cooed, as if we weren't mortal enemies by this point. "I'm *really* looking forward to seeing what's on the sale rack at Mervyn's."

Helen growled and lunged forward. I'm pretty sure she was thinking of the fifty bucks she'd loaned me, that she'd never be caught dead in Mervyn's—the least fashionable department store in the mall—and that any insult to me was also an insult to her fashion expertise. Adding this to her already well-deserved hatred for Leah, and I was sure Helen was about to punch Leah in the face.

I grabbed one of Helen's arms while Melissa gripped the other. I nodded toward her in thanks. Between us, Helen squirmed, kicked, and fumed.

"Look, I don't care what you think about my dress." I clutched the garment bag closer with my left arm while tightening my hold on Helen with my right. "I'm sure you'll see it the night of homecoming, like everyone else."

Leah smiled, evidence that I had zero ability to burn anyone.

"Oh, I wouldn't be so sure of that," she said, punctuating the sentence with a slight giggle. "I'm not sure *any* of you are going to be at that dance." She leaned toward a struggling but silent Helen. "But I'm sure you'll *love* what's going to happen after the announcement on Monday."

She crossed her arms smugly, turned, and walked away. About fifteen feet from us, she turned back. "Oh, I forgot! Since you won't be seeing us, I wanted to remind you that I *will* be going to the dance with Kyle. And you'll be stuck at home, probably grounded, with only your imagination to keep you company. And, believe me, what we'll be doing will be far more interesting than anything you ever did with him."

32

On Monday, we all waited in our usual lunch circle with jittery nerves—except Jennifer, who was off with the rest of the student council counting homecoming court votes in a corner of the lunchroom. Everyone voted in homeroom, and then the student reps from each class went around to each homeroom to pick up the ballots. From second period on through lunch, they sorted and counted them, and then we'd all have a quick end-of-day assembly to hear the winners announced.

Suddenly, I felt someone standing behind me, blocking the sun. Next to me, Melissa sucked in a tense breath, but Helen beamed up and waved. I couldn't think of many people who'd cause that reaction. Or any, actually.

"Oh, hey, Angelle!" Helen patted the step next to her, indicating that Angelle should sit down with us.

Angelle gingerly crammed herself into the space between

Sara and Helen. It *might* have been my imagination, but it looked to me like Sara intentionally didn't move to make room for Angelle.

I was really starting to like that girl.

"I, um, don't want to interrupt y'all," Angelle said, which would have been a more appropriate statement if she'd said it before squeezing herself into our circle. "But there're two things I wanted to tell y'all." She balanced her lunch tray delicately on her lap, looking either unsure of how to eat outside, or nervous to be around us, or a combination of both. Either way, her pause left a space so large that I could feel Melissa leaning toward her with curiosity.

"The first is…" Angelle took a bite of today's cafeteria lunch, a rubbery-looking hamburger, and chewed, leaving us all in suspense. It didn't feel like she was intentionally keeping us on edge—she was likely either nervous or just plain hungry—but the effect was the same. Melissa tensed up, likely with the same fear that I had, that Angelle was about to ruin the delicate balance of our group.

Helen gestured for her to go on. "The first is?"

Angelle nodded, then swallowed. "The first is that Miss Laurel Anne confirmed that Melissa and Athena didn't take any posters."

Helen sank back, collapsing against the step like relief infused her whole body. "I knew it, but I'm so happy to hear her say it!"

Melissa gave me a silent look that said, *Are you kidding me?* And believe me, I *got* it. It felt incredibly unfair that Helen would need reassurance after all we'd done for her, after all this time. Helen *had* basically decided that we—or at least I—had nothing to do with the posters in her locker, so her relief was a little outsize in comparison to whatever doubt she might have had left.

I shrugged a silent response to Melissa. I could get mad at Helen for underestimating us, but what would be the point? I'd been the one to ask—actually, sort of bully—Angelle into making the call. Besides, having everything cleared up would let us move forward, and there wouldn't be another fight three weeks from now that brought up the possibility that we'd done something unspeakably cruel to her.

The rest of what Angelle might say was the real dirt. I had no idea what the second thing was, but the way she was acting made me scooch to the edge of the step I was sitting on.

"And what's that second thing?" Melissa asked coolly, almost covering the fact that she was insulted that Helen required backup proof of her innocence.

Angelle swallowed her bite of burger, hard, a gulp of fear as much as anything. Her lunch tray shook a little on her lap as her knee bounced up and down. She definitely hadn't mastered the eating-outside business.

"I, um… Well, I don't know if I should tell you this," she said, looking at her burger instead of us. "Because I don't know if I agree with your campaign, totally. But I…I also know I didn't do the right thing by Helen. And I don't think it's pro-life, what Mrs. Turner is doing to her. It's not fair for her to be punished for someone else's abortion."

Next to me, Melissa was a coiled cobra, waiting for the right moment to strike, to shout out that no one deserved to be punished for an abortion. I grabbed her arm in warning. I wanted to hear what Angelle had to say, and she wasn't going to say it if we yelled at her self-righteously for being a self-righteous jerk. She might not have apologized to Helen enough for that whole business with the pro-life club, and she might be half insulting us with ambiguous intentions, but the girl was sitting on something *big*. Our self-righteousness could wait until after we got the information we needed.

"Umm, well, so…" Angelle hesitated. She moved the tray from her lap, unable to control her nervous leg bouncing. "There's something going on with Mrs. Turner and Mrs. Bonnecaze. I'm… I don't know, exactly, but it seems like… Well, Mrs. Turner is taking over advising the pro-life club, basically, but Mrs. Bonnecaze is kind of going along with it? They're coadvisors now, which was never a thing before, and something feels off about it."

She paused for a moment and glanced toward Helen. "And, well…after that gross stuff was found in your locker, we—me and Chad, the vice president—called a meeting of all the officers to see if we could reinstate you as a member, with an apology. And we voted unanimously that we should." Helen's face flooded with gratitude, but Angelle's expression remained uneasy. "Mrs. Bonnecaze said she agreed, too, and she said she'd talk to Mrs. Turner, because apparently *she's* the one who asked Principal Richard to bar Helen from all clubs, not Sister Catherine, and Mrs. Bonnecaze thought that she could explain everything that had happened. But I guess it didn't work."

Helen's jaw clenched. It wasn't news to us that Mrs. Turner had been the one to intervene against her, but it was infuriating that Mrs. Bonnecaze's appeal failed. And that fury made me hate myself all the more for falling into her blackmail trap. I almost regretted not campaigning for myself—there was nothing I wanted less than to be on the homecoming court, but it burned to give Mrs. Turner any kind of victory.

"What did you do then?" Helen asked, sounding frustrated. I was frustrated with Angelle, too. Angelle was supposed to be her friend, but had sucked at basic human decency until about five minutes ago. Or maybe that was just my judgy perspective.

"Nothing," Angelle said, and Helen's whole body sagged with defeat. Angelle must have picked up on it, because she rushed to elaborate. "I mean, I *tried*. Really. But whatever conversation Mrs. Turner had with Mrs. Bonnecaze wasn't good, at least not for Helen. Mrs. Bonnecaze came back from it saying that she'd changed her mind. Not about Helen's guilt—" Melissa cringed at the word *guilt*, and so did Helen. Melissa because she didn't believe anyone should be guilty for having an abortion, Helen because she didn't believe that guilt applied to her "—but that because of the So What? thing, she couldn't support having Helen back in the club, because it would mean that she wasn't sufficiently pro-life."

Helen let out a strangled yowl, not unlike the one that a cat lets out when you accidentally step on its tail.

"Are. You. Fucking. Kidding. Me?" Helen never swore. Maybe being around Melissa was starting to rub off on her. The weariness was gone, replaced by a fury that was barely contained and entirely understandable. "First I get punished for something I didn't do, and *now* I'm getting the *same* punishment for *pointing out* that I *didn't* do it?"

I worried for a second that Helen would turn her anger on me and Melissa because we'd been the ones who'd come up with the slogans in the first place. And one of them was definitely more pro-choice than the other, which was why Mrs. Bonnecaze had sent me to Sister Catherine's office.

Angelle shrank back from the anger radiating from Helen. "I know, it's awful, and that's not even the worst of it. Mrs. Turner is planning...something. I'm not sure what, exactly, but I know she's gone around Mrs. Bonnecaze *and* Sister

Catherine *and* Principal Richard for whatever it is. I overheard her saying she was going to the diocese, and maybe someone even bigger."

Everyone in our circle had various states of worry on our faces, including Angelle. It was bad enough for Mrs. Turner to go to the diocese, which ruled the Catholic high schools in town like a vague, shadowy force that nobody really understood, but "someone even bigger" could mean anything. It didn't seem logical to me that anyone outside our school would be swayed by a few rumors, but, unlike Sister Catherine, Mrs. Bonnecaze had folded when she talked to Mrs. Turner. Our fate would likely be determined by whether that "someone even bigger" was more like Sister Catherine or more like Mrs. Bonnecaze.

"What are we going to do?" Sara asked nervously. It was a question we all must have been thinking. And the problem was, there wasn't any easy answer. "If we stick to our homecoming plans, she's *really* going to hate us."

"And if we don't, we're back to where we started," Helen said. The certainty in her voice surprised me. "I know it's not fair to ask everyone to keep going with everything when you could end up with the same punishment as me—or worse—but what's the point if Mrs. Turner wins? We can't give up now."

Melissa, Sara, and I nodded and murmured our agreement, but Angelle just sat there as uncomfortable as ever. She'd never been my first choice for the homecoming court scheme, and I was glad that she had decided to warn us about Mrs. Turner, but something about her—eyes downcast, that leg vibrating with the frequency of a jackhammer—told me that she wasn't all-in. Now that she'd warned us, and we'd decided to keep going, she could just as easily flip on us.

"How about you, Angelle?" Melissa had picked up on her hesitation, too.

Angelle glanced to the left, avoiding Melissa's gaze.

"I don't know," she said. "This is so *easy* for y'all. I want to help Helen, but… I don't know."

"Are you *serious*, Angelle?" My words punched the air. "None—NONE—of this is 'easy' for any of us. Do you know how hard it was to find slogans that we all agreed on? Or that wouldn't get us kicked out of school? Or how hard it was to get people to care? And Helen's right—in the end, if we give up now, we're basically saying, 'Oh, sucks to be you! Enjoy being ostracized!'"

It was possibly the angriest motivational speech anyone had ever given in the history of motivational speeches. Angelle looked like she might cry, and I felt the tiniest bit of guilt at the tone—but not the content—of what I'd said. I didn't want to bully her into joining us, but I did want her to see how hard it had been to get to where we were.

"You're right," Angelle said, looking at her lap. "But I'm not you. Look, I promise I'm not going to tell on you to Mrs. Bonnecaze or Mrs. Turner or anyone else. But I can't do it. I can't disrupt homecoming. I don't see how it will help anything."

So we'd lost one. She'd been the weakest link all along, for sure. But a worry crept into my mind. If Angelle was feeling this way, who was to say that her nerves wouldn't spread through the rest of our recruits? I knew Sara and Melissa would stick it out, but what about Cady Jenson, or all those seniors we didn't know?

As the freshmen and sophomores filed into the gym, I tried to imitate Sara's perfect posture. Maybe that would help me focus on the results. I was suddenly nervous about the outcome in a way that pushed away all my worries about Mrs. Turner and replaced them with more trivial ones. I felt like I was in a lose-lose situation here—either I'd win, and I'd have to parade around in front of everyone at two events, or I'd lose, and Leah would smirk at me for the rest of the week while reminding me she'd be at the dance with Kyle.

I looked out over the crowd of freshmen and sophomores already on the bleachers. From here, they made up a faceless sea, with a few signs held up here and there. I spotted one for Sara and noticed that Wisteria was holding one of the flyers Kyle had made with my face on it, mounted on a fluorescent orange posterboard. A surprising feeling of thankfulness ran through me—Wisteria barely knew me, but she'd been genuinely supportive from the beginning. Even if I didn't want to win a spot on the court, it was nice to have her in the audience cheering me on.

Below the underclassmen, the juniors and seniors crawled over the lower seats. They were clearly more invested in the whole process. Some of them carried posterboard signs supporting one of the four juniors—Leah, Melissa, Angelle, and Missy Bordelon. The seniors took extra time to spread out across the space left at the bottom of the bleachers, high-fiving their friends and shouting out the names of the senior girls nominated for the court. There were eight of them, so that meant a lot of shouting. I only knew Jamie Taylor, so I'd voted for her for homecoming queen.

Sister Catherine stood in front of a microphone, a large red envelope in her hands. Her tidy gray veil hid her severe gray hair—which we'd all seen once when she substituted for the gym teacher—and her crisp white shirt shone with starchy saintliness, while her straight blue skirt, all business and modesty, landed right below her knees. She signaled to one of the members of AV club, and the PA system popped to life.

"First, we would like to thank all of these girls for their clean campaigns." She looked across our row. From what I remembered, she hadn't said anything like that last year, but after Mrs. Turner's outburst, it didn't surprise me. The campaigning blitz hadn't featured a single violation of anyone's photo.

"Unfortunately," she continued, "I can't say the same for some of you out there."

A collective sound of protest-ish murmuring spread out from the bleachers. Freshmen turned toward each other, looking panicked. Everybody else looked confused. I could see Trip Wilson smacking Sean's arm to get his attention.

"Someone has violated a large portion of the ballots," Sister Catherine explained. "When the student council convened to count the votes, they discovered that only a small percentage of the usual number of ballots was in the box. After an exhaustive search, the missing ballots were found in a trash can in the lunchroom, with what appeared to be red Kool-Aid poured over them. Needless to say, they were not in any shape to be counted."

In the bleachers, two junior guys I didn't know high-fived each other, then continued with an elaborate secret handshake. It seemed unlikely that they'd done it, though. No one would be obvious enough to give away their participation in whatever had been done to the ballots.

"This act shows a remarkable amount of disrespect to the girls here. It's unclear if the culprits intended to target any particular girls, but that is beside the point. They all deserve better than this." She paused for a moment, then declared, "As a result, we have decided that the entire group of nominees will participate in homecoming court this year."

The mass murmur in the bleachers returned, this time turning into a near roar. I could hear various girls near me exhale. Sara let out a burst of loud, sighing relief, Leah a slow hiss.

Sister Catherine added her own sibilant *shhh* to the mix, a percussive sound that popped in the microphone.

"We do not have time to redo the entire vote, as the student council has already spent enough time outside class today," she said firmly. "However, we will redo the vote for the homecoming queen tomorrow morning, which will then be announced at the game." Her expression turned even more stern. "Please don't take this as a signal to commit further vandalism against the homecoming court. These girls worked very hard on their campaigns and deserve your recognition."

She waited for people to applaud. A lot of people were still confused, though, and only a smattering of claps drifted from the bleachers.

"Finally, we will catch the students who committed this act against these lovely young ladies," Sister Catherine added. "And they will be suitably punished."

Funny how no one had said that about Helen's locker. I guess getting back to normal with the homecoming court was more important to the school than giving any sort of justice to my sister.

33

On Wednesday morning, Mrs. Turner's bright and evil voice crackled over the intercom for a school-wide announcement during first period. "I'm pleased to announce that Principal Richard and I have arranged for some important visitors to address the student body today. We will hold a special assembly during third period for the entire school in order to call special attention to the issues surrounding the homecoming court. We invite all members of the court to sit in the front when you arrive in the gym. I look forward to seeing you all there!"

A mix of rage and fear surged through me at the sound of Mrs. Turner's cheerful "I look forward to seeing you all there!" To be fair, the rage overwhelmed the fear, but I'd been waiting for her to get back at us since she'd threatened me in her office. Sister Catherine's solution to the vote tampering couldn't have pleased her—or perhaps it had, in a perverse way that had spurred her to action. She probably blamed us for destroying the ballots, too.

An hour later, still filled with rage, I joined the rest of the homecoming court in the gym, where we sat in two rows of folding chairs in front of everyone else in the bleachers. Sister Catherine paced back and forth across the gym floor, her hands twisting with worry. When I saw her, I worried, too, because Sister Catherine usually treated Mrs. Turner with a barely masked annoyance. Whomever Mrs. Turner had invited must be someone of real consequence.

Mr. Richard walked into the gym, followed by Mrs. Turner, a nun I didn't know, and a man I did. The nun wore a long white habit that looked much more old-fashioned than Sister Catherine's knee-length A-line skirt and short veil. Her long veil surrounded a moon-round face. It was hard to tell from her clean-scrubbed, ruddy complexion if she was thirty-five or sixty-five, in the way that almost all nuns looked ageless. She had to be some sort of higher authority, though, because old-fashioned, fancy-nun appearances usually only occurred at graduation.

The man who followed behind the nun was Louis Bettencourt. He had no business at our school, at least in my opinion. He wasn't a teacher, or someone from the Catholic diocese that oversaw our school. He was the local representative to our state legislature, and he wasn't a normal politician—not that Louisiana had those anyway. Our current governor, Edwin Edwards, had been elected over a KKK grand wizard based on the slogan "Vote for the crook. It's important." Bettencourt had been the one who invited Operation Rescue to town after his abortion ban was vetoed by the previous governor. His whole reason for existing was to fight abortion.

Two seats down, Melissa had to be seething. But I didn't

know what Helen was thinking, up in her position in the bleachers. She'd met Bettencourt last year, when he came to talk to her middle school's pro-life club. They'd taken a picture together—a crowded jumble of kids and Bettencourt that made the middle school newsletter. In the photo, Representative Bettencourt looked like a gray-haired clone of a younger Ronald Reagan, with a swept-up pompadour and political grin. Helen had flanked him on one side, gazelle-like and taller than he was after her last growth spurt, and her eighth-grade homeroom teacher and sponsor of the pro-life club leaned in on the other. I turned around to try to find Helen in the bleachers, to see if I could read something of her opinion, but it was impossible to find her in the crowd.

Principal Richard shuffled up to the microphone, his face beading with sweat above his mustache. Whether it was from nerves or the early-October heat wave baking them on the walk from his office was hard to say. "Ladies and—" He winced as a squeal of feedback burst from the microphone. He glared at the AV club guy monitoring it, then turned back to us.

"Ladies and gentlemen, today Mrs. Turner and I have arranged to bring in two special guests—Sister Bernadette from the diocesan school board, and State Representative Louis Bettencourt, who, as you may remember, gave our school the generous donation of the land on which it is built."

Oh, I didn't know that *he* was Mr. Swampland. Interesting. At least it explained a little about why he was here, other than his political alignment with our school's pro-life policy.

"As Mrs. Turner was thoughtful enough to arrange for these guests, she will provide a brief introduction," Mr. Richard said. "But first, I want to assure you all that the homecoming game and dance will go on as planned, as long as there are no further indications of protest, either from students or outside organizations."

My ears perked up, and I looked around for Melissa to see if she'd heard this. Next to me, Cady elbowed my arm to get my attention, because *she'd* heard it, too. "Outside organizations"—*that* was something new.

"And, finally, as Sister Catherine noted in a faculty meeting yesterday, much of this controversy emerged from the sense of protecting a student," he continued. "Whether or not that student did anything wrong is irrelevant. We do not support vigilante justice in any form, either pro or con."

Typical Principal Richard doublespeak. He didn't want to get stuck on either side of the issue, but it wasn't out of ambivalence about the issue itself. It was just that he didn't want to be seen as taking a side.

He nodded to Mrs. Turner, who smiled like *she* was on the homecoming court herself as she clacked to the microphone in her signature kitten heels. Today's were leopard print, which stood out against her forest green pantsuit. Aside from the heels, the rest of the outfit was a level of formality above what any teacher normally wore. She was putting in an effort to impress.

"In light of recent activities meant to harm the integrity of the homecoming court as well as a certain...guerilla campaign that violates our pro-life policy, I reached out to the two esteemed individuals who are here with us today." Mrs. Turner stood on her toes to reach the microphone, instead of lowering it to her height. "This school has always prioritized its pro-life policy. Our students have introduced right-to-life bills at the model legislature at the state capitol, raised funds for Operation Rescue's efforts last summer, and participated in vigils for life. But some among you—" She paused dramatically as she scanned the audience, all while still on her tippy-toes. Normally, I wouldn't be able to take her seriously, except for the fact that she was using the school's pro-life policies as a cudgel.

Her gaze settled on me, and then on Melissa. "*Some* among you have violated that policy in ways that illustrate a callous disregard not only for the life of the unborn, but for your fellow students, as well." A disregard for our fellow students? My hands curled into fists. It wasn't like I could punch her, but I really, really wanted to. Her hypocrisy had no bounds. "Recently, with the homecoming vote being spoiled, that disregard has only increased."

Again, she looked pointedly at Melissa and me. I glared back. She clearly thought we had been the ones to sabotage the vote, but I wasn't going to shrink from her dirty looks.

Behind Mrs. Turner, Sister Bernadette coughed pointedly. The nun looked bored at Mrs. Turner's bloviating speech, though she likely wasn't in disagreement with its principles. Mrs. Turner glanced back at the nun apologetically, and then returned her focus to us.

"And that," she said, "is why *Principal Richard* has invited Sister Bernadette today." Mrs. Turner looked at an index card in her hand. "She is our diocese's vice superintendent and has served as a Catholic liaison for the Louisiana Right to Life committee as well as…" Mrs. Turner squinted at the card in front of her. "As well as the Committee to Abolish the Death Penalty. Hmm. Please give her a warm welcome!"

Sister Bernadette moved toward the microphone with the great purpose of a visiting foreign dignitary, her long habit sweeping gracefully across the floor. As she passed them, she nodded slowly at Principal Richard and Representative Bettencourt.

"Young ladies and young gentlemen, I am very sad to be here under such difficult circumstances," she said in the rounded, imperious tones of an upper-crust Southern drawl. "I do not wish to take more of your time than necessary, as your studies are important. I have spoken with Sister Catherine and Principal Richard about the situation, and I would like you to know that they have my full support. I have personally examined the homecoming court's campaign materials and found nothing troubling, so I do not wish to paint these innocent girls as culprits. *However,* as representatives of the school, they must be held to a higher standard, and rest assured, there will be consequences if these protests continue to violate diocesan school policy."

On that ominous note, Sister Bernadette made the sign of the cross and stepped away from the microphone. What did any of this mean? We were considered innocent for now, but if we stepped out of line, we'd face consequences? I was confused, and judging by the hum of the people behind me, so was everyone else. I saw Sister Bernadette exchange the tiniest of bowing nods with Sister Catherine, but that only confused me more because I couldn't tell if it was a good look or a bad look. Mostly, it was an obscure nun look, with slightly raised eyebrows that clearly had some meaning between them, but not to me.

Mrs. Turner rushed back to the microphone, like she was afraid someone else might take her place.

"And now we have the st-state representative, Louis Bettencourt!" It sounded like she had been going to say, "star of our show," but recovered with "state representative." I tried looking back to the bleachers again to see if I could spot Helen, but I couldn't really identify anyone I knew that far back in the sea of faces. "Representative Bettencourt is a longtime advocate for life in our state. He helped secure the votes to override Governor Roemer's veto of our state's strong pro-life law, and, in order to show our city's support for that law, he brought in Operation Rescue to protest. Although the federal courts have unfairly decided that the law is unconstitutional, defying *all principles of state's rights*—" she sounded incensed, but quickly regained her composure "—Representative Bettencourt has persevered, organizing locally and nationally on behalf of the unborn." Mrs. Turner clasped her hands together with joy, unintentionally crunching the index card in her hand. "And we are just *so* honored to have him here today!"

Her unabashed admiration for Representative Bettencourt was miles away from her measured introduction of Sister Bernadette. Bettencourt stood up from the folding chair where he'd been sitting at the far end of the basketball court, watching everyone else speak. From the way he smiled at Sister Catherine on his way to the microphone, I knew she didn't want to hear what he was going to say. The smile was a bit fishlike, a little smug, and utterly devastating. My stomach lurched with the sense that *everything* would be going down the toilet in the next five minutes.

Bettencourt walked to the center of the front row of the homecoming court. He wasn't but eight feet away from me. Arms crossed, he paused dramatically in front of each girl, searching her face for any sign of wrongdoing. It was as if he was silently questioning, *Is* she *the one?* I felt lucky that, unlike the eight seniors, I was in the second row. We only got a diluted version of his stare. But even in our row, he paused a bit longer once or twice, like when his eyes fell on Melissa, and when he nodded sympathetically toward Leah and Angelle.

"We all try to do good," he said, arms outstretched, more like a preacher than a politician. Though, to be fair, in Louisiana it was sometimes hard to tell the difference. "But sometimes what we think of as good is the *wrong* thing. When we're very small, we're told not to be tattletales or crybabies. We're told not to get others in trouble for minor offenses. But when we grow up, we learn that there are more important things, and we must listen to our hearts."

He paused for effect, and I wondered uneasily where he was going with this. "Over the summer," Bettencourt continued, "I received a call from the sheriff's department, when a man of uniform followed his conscience instead of an unjust law. He let me know what preparations the sheriff's department was making to hamper our protests—Operation Rescue's protests. He wasn't 'telling' on his boss. He was working for the *greater good*. At that time, I knew what had to be done. We had to be prepared for what came. To be prepared to *sacrifice* for the unborn." He stopped in front of Jamie... Or was it Melissa he was looking at? She sat behind Jamie, and the indignant scowl on her face was a magnet for his attention.

"Yes, we often think we are doing good when we protect others. But sometimes, for the greater good, we need to make sacrifices. It is hard, indeed, to turn in a friend, but we must remember that we are *helping* them embrace the pro-life cause."

He stopped his pacing again, this time in front of me. His pale blue eyes peered into mine. This time, there was no doubt his scrutiny was intentional. "Sometimes, we must help those closest to us. Even if it means being called a tattletale. Because you are not children anymore."

With the end of that sentence, he paused and locked eyes with me again for a few seconds—deliberate enough that everyone could see—and then looked up at the bleachers, as if to reinforce to them that *I* was the one who needed to rat on Helen. I could feel my skin turning red, but not from the embarrassment of being singled out. No, I was *angry.* Angrier than when Mrs. Turner made the same veiled accusation. I wondered if Helen had seen how he'd looked at me—of course, she knew I'd never turn her in for something she hadn't done, but this guy was someone she had once admired, and he was singling her out *through me.* It was way worse than finding out that Bill Clinton had cheated on Hillary Clinton with Gennifer Flowers, in terms of political disappointments.

"It is *truly* unfortunate that you young people are forced to make such hard decisions." He scanned the crowd, his eyes occasionally landing on someone. "What has happened at this school is a tragedy. If it is in fact the case that a girl has committed such an unspeakable act, it is up to her to ask forgiveness. But those who support her are doubly at fault, for they undermine her faith in that forgiveness." He paused meaningfully. "We must all be on guard for such misguided actions. And that is why I have invited some of my friends from Operation Rescue and Louisiana Right to Life to attend your football game on Friday. I wish to show my support for your pro-life policy and let those who would violate it know that justice *will* be served."

I stared, horrified, as Representative Bettencourt backed away from the microphone, holding his hands outward in a gesture that seemed entirely overblown. This whole thing was a joke, an unfair way for Mrs. Turner to get what she wanted. I looked at the others behind her and Bettencourt. Principal Richard looked shell-shocked and uncertain about what had happened, and confused as to how rumors about a freshman had solidified into a certain violation of the pro-life policy in the mind of a politician—and school donor. Meanwhile, Sister Bernadette and Sister Catherine exchanged another look in their obscure silent nun language.

"Thank you, Representative Bettencourt, for that *interesting* speech," Sister Catherine said after she took the microphone back. Her face was unreadable, a solid wall of nun obfuscation as she clapped for him, an indication that we were all supposed to do the same. I might have been imagining it, but it seemed quieter than for usual speakers, even the boring ones. Everyone had to be wondering who would turn them in for wearing buttons and patches and voting for a sympathetic homecoming queen.

"I believe it's time for everyone to get to class," Sister Catherine continued after the applause ended. The other nun and the politician and the principal all glad-handed students as they exited, seemingly unaware of, or possibly ignoring, the weird vibe from the student body. I moved to follow my row of the homecoming court out, but Sister Catherine signaled for me to walk with her.

I braced myself for another lecture on how I should turn Helen in as we walked in silence toward her office, where she signaled for me to sit down.

"I know that this has been a difficult time for you and your sister," she said. "But I want to praise you for how much courage you've both shown."

I wasn't courageous. I always dragged my feet on everything—it was just what I did, and I'd made things worse by ignoring Helen's problems while cavorting with Kyle. So much so that I could only think of the word *cavort*, which sounded like something my grandma would say. I waited for Sister Catherine's compliment to turn into an insult or a threat, like the rest of the adults.

"I know that you're protecting your sister," she began. *Aha.*

Here we go. I braced myself for her to tell me I needed to turn her in. "As you should, since there's every indication that she's done nothing wrong. She's a sweet girl."

While my feelings toward Helen might have improved over the past few months, I wouldn't quite go *that* far. But I felt a little less on edge hearing it from someone else.

Then Sister Catherine surprised me further by adding, "And you should *keep* helping her, because you have a good sense of what's right and wrong." Her eyebrows were slightly raised in a knowing look. "Unlike some people. But we're entering dangerous times, and further acts of protest will be..." She paused, searching for the right words. "Further acts might be *read* with different intentions. So while I don't ask that you stop protecting Helen, I do suggest that you tread carefully. And I implore you to watch out for your friend with the purple hair. That one has the potential to get herself in a lot of trouble."

I nodded, unsure of what to say. Sister Catherine was *on our side*, at least as much as any authority figure was at our school. But she was giving us a warning, too—which meant that our homecoming protest was going to be viewed in a whole different light if we went forward.

34

Our homecoming plans were on hold, for real, and the homecoming game was on, also for real. After Representative Bettencourt's speech, he held true to his word about bringing in Operation Rescue to "observe." The local representative from Operation Rescue—our old friend Miss Laurel Anne from the fake abortion clinic, it turned out—was eager to turn our school's "controversy" into a means to get more attention for Operation Rescue now that the national organization had left town.

She told a reporter for the Baton Rouge *Advocate* that they would recruit a "small group" of "experienced pro-life protesters" to show up at the game, but simply as observers. Louis Bettencourt's appearance, she said, meant the school was *serious* about supporting pro-life endeavors—but they were going to check on us anyway, probably with some fetus posters in hand.

And so Thursday morning, the Baton Rouge *Advocate*

printed an article in its religion section, complete with a sidebar interview with Bettencourt himself, all about how he was *so sure* he could turn this "controversy" into "a means to provide the children with much-needed guidance." The only person from our school quoted in the article was Mrs. Turner, and the first thing I saw on Thursday morning at school was an apoplectic Principal Richard rushing into the main administrative office with the newspaper in his hand.

Then the So What? buttons and patches began to disappear. In first period—English—I saw Rochelle Dugas cramming her "So what if she didn't?" patch into the front pouch of her JanSport backpack. I looked around to see what everyone else was doing. It wasn't like *everyone* in my class had been an avid supporter of our campaign, but a sinking feeling came over me when I saw that I was the only one with anything still on my bag. And as the day progressed, more patches and buttons disappeared from people I thought were solid. If the rest of the student body folded this easily, this quickly, would the other girls on the homecoming court stick with us?

Friday arrived, and with it, the homecoming game. Sister Catherine had sent the homecoming court home with instructions for how we were to dress at the game, specifying that "khakis or knee-length skirts and polos or button-down shirts are highly encouraged." The dress code was meant to make us look as uniformly bland and noncontroversial as possible, to the point that we all looked like we had after-school jobs at Blockbuster. On the list of forbidden items were jeans, tight-fitting bodysuits, tank tops, and camisoles, and skirts that exposed more than an inch above the knee.

I ended up wearing a boring but tasteful black skirt and floral button-down blouse from Helen's closet. At least it wasn't a polo shirt—or, for that matter, a pair of accursed khakis. I wanted to be subversive and wear my Docs, but Melissa vetoed me. She said it would waste our potential to do something truly radical at the dance if I violated the dress code at the game. I told her it was unlikely that Sister Catherine or Mrs. Turner or Principal Richard or even the protesters would care if I wore sixteen-hole boots and not a pair of sensible flats or pumps. Actually, they probably wouldn't even *notice*, since we were being paraded around the field on the backs of very slow-moving convertible cars on loan from a local car dealership, our feet barely visible. But I acquiesced anyway and wore some boring black flats.

Finally, it was time to head out to the football field and get into the cars that would present us to our adoring crowds. I took my place in line next to Cady, who had pulled her slick, auburn hair back into a thick French braid. She'd nailed the age-appropriate business casual look, with her tidy corduroy skirt and boatneck top, and sensible but visible enough makeup that made her look stunning. She should have been the only sophomore representative on the court, and I felt like I was intruding on her moment to shine. It wasn't my fault—*at all*—but the Catholic guilt crept in anyway.

"Hey, Cady," I said. "I, uh…just wanted to let you know that I voted for you. Not that it matters now, of course."

Cady turned to me and rolled her eyes, a reaction I didn't expect.

"Oh, please," she said. "Athena, I voted for *you.* I *hate* this crap. And I loved your campaign pictures. You looked gorgeous. And this whole thing with Helen is so unfair. *She's* the one who gets punished for the crap that *Leah* says about her?"

I wanted to say something nice in return, but I felt a shove from Melissa behind me. Our march from under the bleachers to the football field began, and as we entered the stadium, my stomach lurched with nerves. There were *so* many people out there. The "small group of observing protesters" was about fifty strong, crowded in a group on the visiting team's side of the stadium. They held up signs ranging from the fairly reasonable "protect the sanctity of life" to the "now familiar to the point of desensitizing" fetus posters that had lined Helen's locker. There was a gap between them and the rest of the visiting crowd, as though the upper crusts of St. Christopher's and St. Ursula's couldn't bear the tacky proximity to abortion politics. Or maybe the visiting fans just wanted to be closer to the fifty-yard line.

The ride around the football stadium passed in a blur. Cady and I shared a car—all the girls were doubled up because of the vote scandal—and we probably would have talked if I hadn't had to concentrate so hard on maintaining my princess wave. Helen had drilled me on it last night: wave from the wrist, no jazz hands. Plaster smile on face. Try not to squint under the bright field lights. Try not to look too much in the direction of the protesters. Try not to think about how they were judging our every movement.

Instead, I looked out to the bleachers, trying to find Helen and Jennifer in the sea of red and black. They said they would sit close to the football team and Sean so that I could see them. Mrs. Estelle and Dad were here, too, somewhere, but the glare of the field lights made it hard to recognize faces. I wondered how Sean could stand this every week without sunglasses.

"Is that your sister sitting with Sean Mitchell? Man, Leah's gonna be *pissed*," Cady said, subtly shaking her head, but still managing to maintain her delicate beauty-pageant wave.

"I'm pretty sure Leah's already pissed at Helen," I said, forgetting all about my wave. "And probably Sean, too."

"True enough," Cady said, through smiling teeth. "But now Miss Psychotic America has a reason."

She motioned toward the bleachers with raised, wiggled eyebrows. I followed her gaze to the suited-up football players. Sean was sitting with the rest of the offense. Helen sat next to him, a delicate, reedy creature in a sea of sweaty, beefy boys. After a few seconds, one of the linebackers lumbered off the bench, leaving a gap right in front of Helen and Sean.

And then I saw it—they were holding hands.

Leah was *definitely* going to be pissed.

Suddenly, I didn't need to force a pageant-worthy smile onto my face anymore. I doubted Leah would see the same sort of irony in the situation that I did. We'd all suspected that her reason for sabotaging Helen was because she was afraid this would happen, and now, thanks to her malfunctioning, perpetual-motion gossip machine, it had.

But more important, it looked like my suspicions about them had been right on the money all along. The way Sean had acted at Helen's fashion show, their new, almost-flirting dynamic—Melissa and I had both known that *something* had changed between the two of them, and their holding hands out here, in plain sight of the entire school, was the proof.

I shivered with glee. Helen liked Sean, Sean liked Helen. I was going to tease them mercilessly.

Or maybe not. They'd both taken enough crap lately.

I couldn't focus much during the first half of the game. I alternated between dying to tell Melissa what Cady and I saw and worrying that the protesters would do something to ruin everything. Sean and Helen holding hands was major, major news. But Melissa was busy talking conspiratorially with the senior girls sitting in front of her, and I was currently sandwiched between Cady and Missy Bordelon. Plus, if I tried to tell Melissa about Sean and Helen now, Leah would definitely hear, since she sat on Melissa's right. She deserved every element of hurt that a loud comment from me would undoubtedly deliver, but I knew it wouldn't help Helen and Sean one bit.

At halftime, we filed back onto the field, freshmen first, then sophomores, then juniors, and finally the seniors. Because such a massive number of girls were on the homecoming court, everything seemed to take forever. Sister Catherine, directing our traffic, shook her head several times, like her decision to expand the court was giving her a headache. It genuinely might have been, since every second we were on the field gave the protesters another possibility to spot our imperfections.

We fanned out in a giant semicircle. Cady stood to my left, Missy to my right. By now, we were superfluous, a backdrop for the big announcement of the homecoming queen. In a way, the revote idea was really terrible. With four girls from the senior class nominated, someone would inevitably come out on top. But with eight? Talk about a fractured vote.

Principal Richard made the announcement from the booth at the top of the bleachers, an invisible voice of authority booming down from above.

"The 1992 St. Ann's homecoming queen is Jamie Taylor! Miss Taylor, please come forward and receive your crown!"

Jamie, laughing and crying, ran to the podium like she'd won the Miss America Pageant and not our probably rigged homecoming contest. The other senior girls were crying, too, running up to the podium also and hugging Jamie in a tight circle. They *all* seemed happy for her, in a uniform way that seemed impossible from my perspective as a sophomore. Maybe by the time girls reached their senior year, the nice gene switched on, since there was no point in carrying out sadistic plots to ruin each other when everyone was graduating. Or maybe Jamie was a special breed of awesome girl who everyone loved. Either way, the outpouring reached monumental proportions.

Before Jamie's many fans could run onto the field, Sister Catherine returned the senior girls to the lineup. Our school's cheesy alma mater, composed and recorded in 1985, played in synthesized tones over the stadium loudspeakers, and we all filed back toward the bleachers.

Melissa poked me in the back, a painful, unnecessary jab.

"I've finally figured out what we're going to do tomorrow," she whispered. "Meet me at my car after the game. Bring Helen."

Melissa's blue Subaru was parked entirely too close to Leah's purple Miata for my tastes, so we waited even longer than usual before I would consider it a gossip safety bubble, even though Melissa told me I was being paranoid. From the backseat of the car—Helen had called shotgun, of course, and Melissa was in the driver's seat—I watched as everyone filed past, flush with excitement over our victory.

A cluster of protesters was among the last to leave. A few chucked their signs in the dumpster in the parking lot as they left, but most of them tucked the posters under their arms to save for another day. Half looked disappointed that nothing protest-worthy had happened, and the other half looked pretty stoked that they'd seen a football game that went back and forth until the last two minutes of the fourth quarter. Melissa said it was a messy game, but to me it was exciting that both teams scored a lot of touchdowns.

Helen stared out the car window. I wanted to ask her a

dozen questions about what she was doing holding hands with Sean, but I held back. After what felt like an eternity, she finally turned to me and leaned over the seat back, biting her lip in the way that meant she was nervous to ask for something. She usually had that look in front of Dad, not me.

"So, uh, do you want to swap dates with me?" I asked, hoping I could put her out of her misery without saying something like "Oh, hey, I saw you holding hands with Sean, and it was adorable." She might interpret it as teasing or sarcastic, when I didn't mean it that way at all.

Helen's head bobbed with relief and agreement. "Oh, man! That would be amazing, Athena. Thanks so much," she said, her face lighting up. "I was really nervous that you'd be weird about it, because you and Sean just started being friends again. And, well, I mean… Do you mind going with Trip Wilson?"

Huh. So that was who she was supposed to go with—Trip Wilson. With everything going on, she hadn't told me. It made sense, though. He was popular enough, since he was on the football team, and he was super nice. Plus, he'd told me early on that he didn't believe Leah's lies, and he'd supported our So What? campaign. Still, Helen deserved to be going with the guy she actually *liked*, especially after all she'd been through lately.

"Trip's fine," I said, not liking how it sounded once I said it. Trip honestly deserved much better than *fine*, but I couldn't muster up much enthusiasm for *anyone* after what Kyle had done. "I mean, he's nice. It'll be fun. And then you and Sean can have a real date."

A huge smile broke across her face. "Athena, you're the *best* sister ever!"

Well, that was a first. But I'd take it.

"I hate to interrupt this lovefest," Melissa said. I had almost forgotten she was in the car. She'd been eyeing the crowd silently for the past few minutes. "But it looks like Leah is finally leaving."

I let out a snarl when I saw Leah. She'd managed to disregard the age-appropriate business casual directive entirely, but of course she hadn't gotten into trouble. Instead of a knee-length skirt, she'd worn a teeny-tiny skater skirt that flared out and barely covered her butt. Instead of a modest top, she'd worn a deep, too-tight, scoop-neck bodysuit. Mrs. Turner, and even Sister Catherine, would have given a strong warning or worse to anyone else who'd worn that outfit, but yet again, Leah had somehow wiggled around the rules.

But her clothes weren't what made me snarl. No, what made me snarl was that while Aimee flanked her left as usual, walking on Leah's right side was *Kyle*.

I suddenly feared that they'd think we were stalking them, not just waiting for the crowds to clear out before we left. That would be worse than anything, because so far I'd managed to publicly demonstrate a whole lot of not-caring.

Fortunately, Leah didn't seem to notice us. She marched toward her car with a scowl marring her perfectly Revlon Rum Raisin–lipsticked mouth. It was the same color that Melissa normally wore, more alternagirl than Leah's usual style. I wondered for a second—almost gleefully—if she was trying to look more like the kind of girl that Kyle would go out with. More like me.

Kyle said something, shrugging his annoyingly chiseled shoulders. Leah shoved her bag at him, then searched for something inside it. Aimee looked on, squinting viciously at Kyle like a tiny dog with an underbite. After a few moments of rummaging, Leah finally pulled out her keys and yanked the bag back. She said something angrily, and Kyle shrugged again.

Then Leah leaned in for a kiss, and he *slouched away.* The kiss landed near his ear, leaving a red-brown streak visible even from where we were sitting in Melissa's car, and I let out an involuntary, loud "Ha!" I shouldn't have cared enough to be so gleeful, but schadenfreude is a powerful force.

Leah shook her head, likely in disbelief that Kyle would dare to reject her affection. With a final glare at Kyle, she opened her car door and got in. On the other side, Aimee did the same, but her eyes were trained on us. Whether she'd tell Leah that we'd been watching was anybody's guess.

When Leah and Aimee had finally driven away, and Kyle left for his car, Melissa launched into her plan like she was exploding a dam.

"Okay, so we've been doing the whole So What? thing for forever, and it worked. And I liked it because it was ambiguous and rebellious and cool. And you liked it—" she nodded toward Helen "—because it lent you the possibility of innocence. But I think that, unfortunately, leaving that door open to ambiguity kind of screwed you over."

"You think?" Helen said sarcastically.

"I know! And I've apologized, like, a hundred times for that," Melissa exclaimed, though that wasn't exactly the truth. "But I want to make sure it's clear now that you *are* innocent. So what I'm going to propose is that we revisit the sashes idea, and instead of alternating with 'So what if she did?' and 'So what if she didn't?', we only do She Didn't. Because you didn't."

Helen nodded. "That seems fine. It's not super exciting, but it works."

I eyed Melissa suspiciously. This seemed way too tame for

her—she *had* to have something else up her sleeve. She always did. And if she wasn't saying something, it was because she thought Helen wouldn't like it.

"What else did you have in mind?" I asked her.

Melissa shook her head. "Nothing, as far as the dance goes. But..." She paused dramatically, a gleam in her hazel eyes. "I think I know how to get back at Aimee and Leah. And it won't get us into trouble."

I sighed. "Look, it's *never* going to end if we do that. I want this to stop. Please?"

Melissa's smile evaporated. "I thought you'd gotten over that." When I didn't respond, she added, "I swear, I won't be doing anything that they haven't done. Bettencourt's talk reminded me of something." Helen winced at the politician's name. "It's that this whole thing started because Mrs. Turner believed Aimee and Leah's fake-ass story about Helen. And Bettencourt seems to approve of that method. So what if someone told on them that they were guilty of the homecoming vote violations?"

I knew a bad idea when I heard one, and it was clear that bad ideas were all Melissa had had for the past few days.

"Absolutely not," I said, shaking my head. "We are *not* going to tell Sister Catherine some made-up story about Aimee and Leah being behind the votes situation. The whole point of everything we did was to show that we aren't like them."

Melissa frowned. "Well, we're not. But I think you're misunderstanding me. Aimee *did* do it. Josh Davis and Cody Landry did it *with* her, and I think they might be willing to confess. I overheard them talking about it this afternoon and convinced them they'd get a better deal right now if they confessed, using Bettencourt's speech as bait. If they actually listened to my advice, then they probably went straight to Sister Catherine's office right after school. Since they weren't at the game, they're either avoiding me or they did what I suggested."

Josh and Cody were the type of awkward, gangly boys who'd do practically anything to get close to a girl like Leah, even if it meant being Aimee's lackeys. But as Helen crowed with triumphant glee and Melissa smiled smugly in return, I felt my stomach go sour with dread because there was no way that getting Aimee into trouble was the only thing Melissa had up her sleeve.

What wasn't she telling us?

35

My new haircut was perfect. Helen's hairstylist, Serge, toned down the bright red into a more even and natural color, and the short finger waves made me look like a vintage goddess.

My dress was perfect, too. Melissa's mom had hemmed it so it skimmed the top of my shoes, a pair of patent leather T-strap shoes that Melissa had found in an antiques shop in New Orleans on her last visit to her aunt a few weeks ago. I don't know how she'd managed it, but they fit me perfectly.

Even my makeup was perfect. Helen had pulled out her makeup bible and picked out my colors and an evening look that wasn't ridiculous. My lips assumed a perfect cupid's bow. My cheeks looked like I had real cheekbones, and my eyes blazed a dazzling blue green, offset by Helen's complementary color palette. I looked like some new, improved version of myself—a picture-perfect doll.

I did not, however, *feel* perfect.

As the hours until the dance grew fewer and fewer, my fear of seeing Kyle and Leah together loomed greater and greater. I'd been shoving him into a corner of my mind for weeks now. I didn't think about him when I was doing Gang of Five stuff. I didn't think about him while I was picking out age-appropriate business-casual clothes. I didn't think about him at the game last night. I didn't even think about him all that much after we saw him and Leah in the parking lot.

But now, when Helen and I were waiting for Sean and Trip to arrive, I couldn't think of anything else. My skin prickled with heat, and I hoped I didn't lose my dinner on my pretty blue dress.

"Just so you know," Helen said, "I told Trip to get you a wrist corsage. That way it won't poke a hole in your dress." She looked me over and added, "Don't touch your hair. I know that Serge put a lot of hair spray in it, but it looks great. You don't need to fix it. And don't touch your face. Here, I'm giving you the lipstick..."

She said some other things, but mostly they were about makeup and the pocketbook I would be using and tips for keeping my sash straight when all the girls from the homecoming court had to go to the front of the gym. While she talked, I stared out the window and thought about Kyle.

"Are you even listening to me?" Helen asked.

"Mmm-hmm," I said. "Check for lipstick on my teeth. Don't cry if overcome with emotion. Don't cry if Leah insults me. In case I do cry, go to the bathroom and grab you on the way so you can redo my eye makeup."

"Athena, that's *not* anything I just said," Helen said. "Are you thinking about Kyle again?"

"Yes, I'm thinking about Kyle. I'm wondering where he

could be, who he is with, what he is thinking, is he thinking of me, and whether he'll ever return someday," I said. Better to dismiss it with a joke than get into a real discussion about my feelings right before Sean and Trip were going to show up.

"Do *not* half-ass quote *Kids in the Hall* at me," she snapped. "I'm serious. You never talk about him, but you get this distant, hurt look in your eyes at least twice a day, and I'm not oblivious."

Since the start of school, Helen had matured a lot. But not so much that I wanted to talk about Kyle with her. I didn't want to talk about him with anyone, really, but especially her. I didn't think she would understand. She'd always been pretty and perfect and popular and blah, blah, blah. Until the abortion rumors, nothing shook her. And even those were *because* she was pretty, instead of in spite of it.

"You know, I've liked Sean for *years*," she said, applying another layer of blush to my cheeks. "Do you think he even noticed me? No. He thought of me as a little sister. And he went for *her.* And she was always hanging on him, sitting in his lap, making out with him on our couch. Do you know how that felt?"

I honestly didn't. When I thought about Kyle and Leah, my mind supplied the images, but at least I didn't have to see it in real life. But I did know how pissed I was when I walked in on Leah and Sean making out on our couch. Our couch. Not his. It was vastly inappropriate. And gross. And generally upsetting.

"And now she's manipulating Kyle," Helen continued. "And you are so much prettier, and so much more *real* than that spray-tanned, plastic, stripy-highlighted, fake-personality girl."

Helen's inability to say Leah's name struck me for a moment.

So did the fact that she'd said almost verbatim the inverse of what Aimee had said to Kyle about me.

"But you know what?" Helen asked, grabbing my shoulders and looking into my eyes. "You're the one who has to decide if he's worth it."

I didn't know. I didn't think so, but somehow that made it all worse. Tears came to my eyes, and my lip quivered.

"No, no, no, no, no," Helen said. "Eyes to the ceiling. I'll grab a tissue. Do *not* ruin the work of art that is your face."

After Helen fixed my makeup, we went downstairs and sat eagerly in our living room, trying not to mess up our dresses or our hair or anything. Dad walked in, camera in hand. He looked at Helen's dress and shook his head. She had carefully applied safety pins to the back of the fabric to create a higher neckline until we got to the dance, but Dad didn't look very happy.

"That dress..." He shook his head.

Helen froze in a way that reminded me of when she got home after skipping town to her modeling audition. I didn't know what she'd do if Dad made her change, because she didn't have anything to change into. She'd given me her fifty dollars at Maison Blanche.

"You look *so* grown-up," he finished. "I remember when you were so scared to start kindergarten. And now..." He trailed off before he got too embarrassing. Dad wasn't the type to get so mushy over us growing up, but Helen really did look so much older in that dress. Like, older than me, which was maybe why he didn't get as misty about my outfit.

Helen let out an audible sigh of relief, and so did I. It was one thing for Dad to be nostalgic, and another for him to think her dress was too mature and make her change. Neither of us seemed to be able to find words, though, because there was not much you could do when your dad was being sentimental.

"Anyway, before you two go out tonight—and you both look so beautiful—I want to say how proud I am of you both." Oh, *no.* Dad was getting misty, which meant that I might start to get misty, which meant that Helen might have to redo my makeup for a second time. "I talked with Sister Catherine and Principal Richard yesterday afternoon, and they said you've been dealing admirably with the bullies."

Helen and I exchanged a very dubious "what the hell?" look.

"Um, Dad, I'm sure they said that," I said, hesitating. "But Mrs. Turner—"

"Mr. Richard said she wasn't going to be an issue anymore," he told us. "He said that he wasn't aware of the 'ban' that Mrs. Turner had enforced for Helen's extracurriculars." His eyes widened with skepticism at that, and Helen and I traded an even more emphatic "what the hell!" look, because we couldn't exactly interrupt Dad. We just didn't do that.

"I'm going to have to be *on top of* that school the rest of the year," Dad said vehemently. "You'd think they'd have it together for how much it's costing me for you two to go there." He sighed. "But anyway, they're paying attention now."

Helen looked at me again, and this time I knew she was thinking something else. Reinstating Helen's extracurriculars felt like a concession to put out the fires that Mrs. Turner had started. *No one* wanted Operation Rescue lurking around our football games and dances. While it might have been fine for them to protest outside an abortion clinic, it sent another message entirely to have them protesting outside our Catholic school.

"So...are they going to...apologize to me?" Helen asked, anger simmering in her question.

"Sister Catherine said they were working on that, yes," Dad said. "But she and Mr. Richard are going to speak with us further on Monday. I thought I'd ask you what you wanted before I told them to publicly apologize to you. I wasn't sure if you wanted any more attention than you've already had."

A month ago, I would have thought Helen would want a public hanging of Leah and Aimee, along with an apology. But now I wasn't sure what she'd want—or how tonight's plans figured into all this. If we went ahead with our sashes plan, she'd definitely get some attention. But it could also backfire on us, now that some sort of apology was in the works.

"Okay," Helen said, not giving a whole lot of indication for me to figure out where she was going with this. "I guess I'll think about it. I have until tomorrow, right?"

"Sounds good, kiddo," Dad said, patting her on her knee. "I'm just glad that Mrs. Turner's been handled." He paused, looking like he was trying to be polite and not say anything terrible about an authority figure at our school—which, before this year, he'd liked specifically for its discipline and academic rigor. "I did *not* like the influence that woman seemed to have at your school."

"What do you mean, 'handled'?" I asked, glancing at Helen. She shifted nervously, so that she was sitting on her hands on the edge of the couch. *Handled* could mean anything, from a lip-service "we handled her" to being fired. I had almost no faith that it would be the latter.

Dad shook his head. "Athena, I don't know. It wasn't a particularly long conversation because I had to head back to court. Your principal said we'd discuss it more on Monday."

It was an awkward way to leave things, and that applied to Dad's conversation with Principal Richard as much as it applied to right now. Helen and I exchanged our umpteenth glance of the past few minutes. *A lot* could happen between now and Monday.

"Oh, and that's not the only good news I have for you," Dad said, like he suddenly remembered something he should have told us last week. He was also ignoring the fact that neither Helen nor I looked super happy at his previous news, which wasn't bad, but couldn't exactly be described as "good," either. "It's been a real pain to coordinate with the Ford Agency, but..." He let out a heavy sigh, and Helen straightened up at the mention of Ford. "Your mother and I have managed to figure out a week when we can go up there for Helen's callback."

Helen jumped up from the couch and threw her arms around Dad. After being grounded—or put under my guardianship, basically—she hadn't asked Dad about the progress of the Ford callback for weeks, because she didn't want to irritate him. But this was her dream, finally coming true, and I was so thrilled for her.

When Helen eventually backed out of her hug, I saw that she was crying. Not sobs like at the mall, but enough to make her eyes wet.

"Um, Helen?" I looked at Dad's shirt, where there was a giant smudge of her mascara. "I think you need to fix the work of art that is your face," I said, echoing her earlier words.

Trip and Sean arrived promptly at seven, wrist corsages in hand. Sean gave me a thumbs-up before swooping over to Helen, leaving me standing awkwardly in front of Trip Wilson. He towered over me, a solid mass of muscle and bulk, topped by a shock of blond hair. Despite all the time the football players spent in the sun, Trip's skin was pale and covered with freckles. When he took off his helmet at games, his face was always flushed the same deep red as when he was having trouble with his algebra homework. Or, for that matter, the same red it was now.

"Hi, Athena," he said. "Helen told me you were wearing a blue dress, so I got you a light blue flower. I don't think it matches, but…"

Trip's voice trailed off, and he looked down at the corsage in its plastic box, so tiny in his large hands.

"Oh, no, it's beautiful." It was the first time a boy had ever given me a flower. My sister might have told him to do it, but in my book, it still counted.

"You look…" His face flushed deeper, like a badly painted Santa Claus whose cheery red cheeks approached the level of satire. For a menacing football player, Trip seemed awfully scared of me. He'd never been afraid of me before.

"He means to say that you clean up real nice," Sean said, leaning between us.

I punched his arm. Some things did not—and never would—change.

"You-look-really-pretty," Trip said, like it was a German compound word. Then he looked at the corsage again.

"Thanks, Trip," I said, smiling up at him genuinely. "You look very nice, too."

He blushed again, and I took the corsage box from his hands. I was afraid he would fuss with it until he finally decided that the flower didn't match my dress closely enough and then collapse in the hallway under the weight of going on a date with me.

As I slipped the corsage onto my wrist, Dad stepped into

the hallway, camera in hand—just in time to save me from the awkward situation of awkwardly dealing with someone as awkward as I was. He smiled at me and immediately got to work lining us up against the staircase.

We must have looked like the most unbalanced set of people ever: giant Trip and tiny me, standing next to the most well-proportioned couple ever, Helen and Sean. But I didn't care. Trip had saved me from the embarrassment of having to go to the dance by myself. And who knew—maybe he would get over being afraid of me in time for us to have a real conversation.

36

The student council had done its best to turn the gym into a romantic destination, complete with mood lighting and strings of white Christmas lights that crisscrossed the gym floor in a suspended arbor. They might not have been seasonally appropriate, but they softened the gym's similarity to a very large aluminum can with a shiny wooden floor. That floor, too, was covered tonight, with a layer of taped-down brown paper to spare it from sharp heels and dress shoes. The brown paper was the only thing that detracted from the overall ambiance, but it was a condition that allowed us to have our dances in the gym instead of the cafeteria, which reeked permanently of grease.

Trip held my hand with a gentle clamminess that surprised me. It made me feel like an ass, too, because I was hardly paying attention to him at all, almost like he was my giant pet hamster. It wasn't fair, and I probably should have talked with him about it.

I didn't have a chance to do much, though, because the moment I had been dreading finally arrived.

Kyle.

Walked.

In.

With.

Leah.

My breath caught. How could he still affect me so much?

He didn't look happy—he wasn't wearing that goofy grin I liked so much—but he didn't look miserable, either. I didn't know what I'd expected. I'd imagined him striding up to me and apologizing, or walking in looking abashed, silently suffering on Leah's arm. Or, in the worst of all imaginary scenarios, Leah would have somehow turned him into her undead spawn, and he would laugh and point at me with Leah and Aimee at his side.

He didn't do any of those things. He was just there with her, like it was the thing to do. Like a regular date with a normal person.

Leah, however, looked exactly as I expected. Her fake blond hair was in a bridal updo, with the characteristic crunchy spiral curls descending on either side of her face. She smiled a fake triumphant smile with her fake white teeth as she held Kyle's arm in a fake embrace. Her baby-pink dress offset her fake tan and her fake boobs and pulled in her waist to Barbie-like proportions. Fake, fake, fake, fake, fake.

I hated her, really and truly, for the first time, with a sour feeling that bubbled up from my stomach into my throat.

And she looked so airbrushed pretty, *magazine* pretty, which made me hate her even more. So what if her parents' marriage was falling apart? She was an evil monster who'd tried to ruin the lives of everyone I cared about. Except Kyle, but she'd get him, too, in the end. But, unlike everyone else, he would deserve it.

I clasped Trip's hand tighter, willing myself not to give any sign that I cared. I shouldn't, *wouldn't* care anymore. I was at the dance with a much better human being than either of them.

"Ow, Athena," Trip said. "Breaking my hand isn't going to make Kyle and Leah disappear."

"Oh, sorry." I felt myself blushing as I dropped Trip's hand.

"It's okay," he said. "Um, maybe I shouldn't talk with you about this, but—"

Trip sat down on one of the folding chairs that lined the dance floor and motioned for me to sit next to him.

"There are a lot of things I'd like to say," he said. "I'm much better on paper than in person, though."

Even in the gym's cheesy mood lighting, I could see that Trip's face had flushed red again. He took a deep breath.

"I know you liked him," Trip said. "And he seemed to like you a lot, too. I don't know what happened, but I can tell you, no one thinks this thing with Leah will last. But I also think you should know that if you don't want to wait for him…lots of guys have been waiting for a chance with someone like you."

Was Trip talking about himself, or was there a secret cabal of guys at our school who somehow all found me attractive? I couldn't tell, but something about the way he said it made me think it was about him.

"I don't think it's that I'm waiting for him," I said with a sigh. "It's more like I need resolution. Or maybe a funeral. Followed by a mourning period of an undetermined length."

Trip's face returned to its normal pale-and-freckled color.

"I understand," he said. "Would you like to dance at the funeral? We can pretend it's a jazz funeral, New Orleans–style."

I smiled for the first time. He reached out for my arm. "I think that would be great."

"By the way, geometry is so much easier than algebra," he said as we stood up to dance. "I wish you would've told me that last year."

"Really? I thought it was a lot harder," I said. "Goes to show what I know."

And suddenly, Trip and I were on the dance floor, dancing to the worst song I could imagine, Extreme's "More Than Words." I didn't want to creepy dance to a song where a guy was trying to coerce his girlfriend to have sex with him. But I ignored the song's subject matter, since Trip hadn't confessed his love for me, and I hadn't had to let him down gently, and he hadn't told me to go after Kyle. Instead, I reminded myself that I was there with a friend. And the more we danced and talked about school, the truer that became.

After four songs, Melissa pulled me out of my dancing with Trip with a quick "Sorry, gotta borrow her for a minute." He looked confused and a little disappointed, but he didn't have much of a choice when Melissa was gripping my arm with such urgent force. She wore the Betsey Johnson dress from the mall—the one Helen had hated so much. Its animal-print-and-lace glory flounced around her as she marched me toward the girls' bathroom.

"What's going on?"

"Emergency meeting," she said. "Our plans have changed a little."

In the girls' bathroom, Helen, Sara, Cady, Melissa, Missy, and all of the eight seniors, including, most important, our homecoming queen, Jamie Taylor, crammed into the space between the bathroom stalls and the row of sinks. Cady and a few of the seniors were checking their makeup in the mirrors. Unlike the others, Cady seemed to be toning hers down—her mom had gone full-on pageant glitz, and Cady was carefully using a Q-tip with makeup remover to take off some of the excessive eyeliner and shadow.

Before taking charge, Melissa pounded each stall open to make sure that no spies had entered the bathroom while she was retrieving me.

"Okay, I first want to thank everyone for helping out with this," she said. "You've all been amazing. When Athena and Sara started this plan, I didn't think it would be as popular as it has been. And I didn't think we'd get this far. I thought we would end up suspended for sure."

For the first time since we started the So What? campaign, Melissa looked nervous and tired. Her dark mascara and smoky eye shadow only partially covered up the fact that she looked like something had kept her awake last night—and not in a good way, like a hot college guy spending the night with her. Next to her, Helen was the picture of perfection. Despite her earlier tears, she looked poised, not a speck of makeup where it shouldn't be.

"I got word this afternoon that Aimee Blanchard, Josh Davis, and Cody Landry have been suspended for the vote violation." Melissa pumped her fist, and everyone applauded. "Sister Catherine got Josh to confess, and he blabbed on Aimee and Cody. It seems Aimee didn't inform on Leah, though, since she's still out there in the gym."

The girls in the bathroom all booed at hearing Leah's name, and I smiled wryly. Melissa would make a great hype man.

Then she turned to Helen, whom everything had been for,

but who hadn't really been around the homecoming court very much, since she wasn't allowed to be on it.

"You're up," Melissa said.

Helen took a deep breath. She looked like she had during her fashion show—fierce.

"Today my dad told me and Athena that I'm being reinstated to whatever clubs I want to be in, that whatever Mrs. Turner did would be overruled," she said. "But it feels like it's a joke. Like they want to make things go away, so that no one talks about me anymore. But I don't think it's going to work, and I know if everything goes on as planned, and you all make a big scene where you say I *didn't* do it, they're going to be really mad."

Helen didn't say who "they" were, but I suspected she meant Principal Richard or Sister Catherine, who were trying to calm things down just as we were going for our final display of solidarity. "But now that Aimee and those guys have been suspended, I think they'd view anything else as an interruption. That means anything we do might get us suspended, too. Or worse. I just…wanted to let everybody know that."

Jamie shook her head, jiggling the stiff hair-sprayed cascade of brown hot-roller curls framing her face. She took a deep breath, held it for a few seconds, and exhaled slowly.

"No, we're going to do this," she said. "I want to. If I get suspended, it's okay. Besides, I'm a senior."

Helen looked somewhat taken aback at Jamie's stern reply. She hadn't been addressing Jamie, specifically, but it was clear that Jamie was taking all this pretty personally. She looked as fierce as Helen.

"Oooh-kaay," Helen said, looking like Jamie's response confused her, and I suddenly had a sinking feeling.

Could I be right about Jamie? Was *she* the girl who had been Aimee and Leah's inspiration for the rumors about Helen?

Helen looked around at everyone in the bathroom. "Anyway, I just want to thank everyone for being so supportive this semester. I don't know most of you very well, but it's made something that was really hard a lot easier."

Everyone cheered, and Melissa pulled Helen in for a hug. Suddenly, the bathroom was a giant circle of hugging and support. I hugged Helen. Helen hugged Sara. I hugged Cady. I even hugged some random seniors that I didn't know.

After all the hugging, we filed out of the bathroom at random intervals, so it wouldn't look suspicious. Of course, since most of us in the bathroom were on the homecoming court, it made sense for us to be in there, but Melissa was being overly cautious.

As each girl left, Melissa handed out the She Didn't sashes. Sara and I were the last to leave, along with Jamie. We both stiffened when Melissa pulled a different sash—not the ones she'd handed out to everyone else—out of her bag for Jamie.

Sara looked at me, her look of worry all the more visible on her face because her hairdresser had pulled back her errant overgrown bangs into a smooth French knot.

"Do you think Melissa's up to something?" she whispered, tugging on my arm. "She didn't give Jamie a She Didn't sash, which is weird, right? If she's planning something, we could be in detention until we die."

Sara didn't have the same reasons for suspicion that I did, but she was nothing if not observant.

"I don't know, but—"

The sound of music blaring through the bathroom door stopped suddenly, and a microphone popped and squealed. Sara and I ran, as fast as we could in our heels, to the dance floor.

"Ladies and gentlemen, please welcome your 1992 homecoming court one last time!" Sister Catherine said.

I jumped into my place in line between Cady and Missy, my heels nearly slipping on the floor. The reverse side of my sash said She Didn't, just like it was supposed to, and my stomach flipped with anticipation of what was going to happen. I couldn't stop it now.

Sister Catherine stood at the microphone, ready to announce our names, starting with the freshmen. She gave us one last once-over and a short sigh. I think she regretted having to announce sixteen names instead of eight, but, as far as I knew, that had been her decision.

We were supposed to step forward and curtsy—yes, curtsy—when she called our names. Those of us in on the plan were supposed to flip our sashes when we stepped back, creating a wall of solidarity for Helen. I didn't want to think about what was going to be on the news tomorrow if this didn't work out.

"Darcy Kendall, freshman."

Darcy stepped forward, the light blue froth of her dress swirling around her, and curtsied. Then she stood back and flipped her sash: She Didn't.

Huh. I didn't even know she was in on it.

"Sara Lewis."

Sara stepped forward, curtsied, flipped her sash, and went back to standing in line.

"Cady Jenson."

Ditto.

"Athena Graves."

I stepped forward, curtsied, and flipped my sash. And so it went on: Missy, Melissa, no flipped sash for Leah, none for Angelle, and on to the seniors.

I looked straight ahead into the dark gym. My eyes scanned

the crowd for a reassuring face, but due to the mood lighting, I couldn't see Helen or Sean or Trip. Or Kyle, not that I was looking for him.

I heard a rustling to my left, along the line of girls. A heaving sigh soon followed. Then an angry, muttered "I can*not* believe this."

"And now, your 1992 homecoming queen, Jamie Taylor!" Sister Catherine announced robustly, clapping her hands triumphantly.

Jamie took a few quick steps toward the microphone. She took in a deep breath, like it might be her last.

"Sister Catherine, can't you see what they're doing?" Leah said suddenly. "Can't you see?"

She stepped out of line, not curtsying this time. The hair spray–stiff, curled tendrils on either side of her face jiggled like giant springs as she moved forward. She waved toward Sister Catherine, first a small gesture, then larger and larger, alternating with moments of crossed arms and loud exhalations.

"Can't you *see* what they're all doing?" Her voice was loud enough this time that the entire gym could hear her without the microphone.

Sister Catherine looked us up and down. Thirteen of us had turned our sashes to the outside, all declaring, "She Didn't."

"It seems they're protesting unfair rumors about their friend," she said, stepping away from the microphone so that her voice didn't carry out to the audience. "And trying to make people think a little bit about judging others. I suggest you consider doing just that, Miss Sullivan."

Sister Catherine's mouth returned to a tight line. Helen's punishment coming through the guidance office rather than the dean of discipline made a lot more sense now. So did us not getting into trouble for uniform violations. Sister Catherine *wanted* us to get away with it. She probably would have liked the original Forgiveness slogan.

"But what about *my* friend? She's being punished for no good reason," Leah said insistently, moving closer to Jamie and to Sister Catherine's microphone. "What if I protested *that*?"

I didn't know what Leah was trying to do here. She operated in an underground world of secrets and lies, but this was serious flipping-out territory, in public, in front of the entire school. It was totally out of character for her.

Sister Catherine turned off the microphone and walked over to Leah, who now stood in front of our semicircle.

"Your friend confessed to destroying the ballots," she said. "So I suggest you let Miss Taylor finish her speech."

"Miss Taylor," Leah sneered, "is about to tell you all about her abortion last summer. Isn't that right, *Miss Taylor*?"

Sister Catherine backed away from Leah. She had to—Leah didn't so much say the words as boom them in her hyper-projecting cheerleader voice, and no one wanted to be in front of her when that happened.

"Leah Sullivan! Do you think that anytime you have a problem with another student, you can accuse her of having an abortion?"

Sister Catherine rarely lost her temper, and Leah never showed her hand. This was better drama than *90210.* From the corner of my eye, I saw Wisteria, her mouth open and gaping and her hands clutched with tension. She wasn't alone—by now, the entire school encircled the members of the homecoming court.

"But I *did*," Jamie said, her voice a tiny counterpoint to Leah's booming projection and Sister Catherine's angry bellow.

A dramatic shushing murmured in a wave across the homecoming court and fanned out across the gym.

Sister Catherine looked startled for a moment. "Jamie, we can talk about this later," she said quietly. "Don't go any furth—"

"I *did*," Jamie said, louder this time. "And I'm not going to apologize for it."

Even though I'd had my suspicions for some time now, I still sucked in a shocked gasp when I heard her come out and say it.

I had been *right*.

Jamie, our homecoming queen, was the one who'd had an abortion.

Jamie, who had aced the US History AP test *her junior year*.

Who led *at least* three clubs.

Who had dated the same boy for three years.

Jamie, the only person from our school who was being recruited by an Ivy League college, and it was *Yale*.

She was risking *everything* by revealing this. And yet here she was, not apologizing for her abortion, to a nun, in our school gym, while a news crew and twenty or so protesters were outside, waiting for something like this to happen.

Jamie grabbed the microphone from the stand and turned it back on. Sister Catherine stood in front of Leah, seemingly too stunned to move.

Jamie stepped forward, turning her sash. I leaned forward to get a look. Unlike all of ours, hers read I Did.

"This past summer, I had an abortion," Jamie said. A wave of gasps fanned across the gym. "And this fall, someone else got blamed for it." She paused to take another breath. "But I don't think either of us should be 'blamed' for it. I made my choice for a lot of reasons. I didn't want to be a 'teen mom.' I didn't want to miss out on my senior year of high school. I wanted to go to Yale. Some of you might think that all of those reasons are selfish, and that's okay. That's you. But I also knew I wasn't ready to be anybody's mom, and adoption wasn't the right choice for me, either. Abortion was the right choice for me. And I'm not ashamed of it."

She stopped again, but the room remained silent. I would have thought someone would yell something, scream like a protester, but instead, everyone was transfixed. Even Leah. Even *Helen*, who stood near the front of the crowd, staring at Jamie with her mouth open.

"What I am ashamed of, though," Jamie continued, "is that I didn't speak up earlier. I watched as gossip spread about someone else because I didn't want to be found out. I told myself people would eventually figure out that Helen hadn't had an abortion, and everything would blow over. But really, I was afraid that, because I really *had* had an abortion, I would be kicked out of school. I didn't want to lose all the things—all the possibilities—that were still open to me *because* I had the abortion. And I want to apologize to Helen Graves for that."

Jamie looked at Helen, who returned a face of shock. "Helen, you got so much garbage thrown at you, and none of that should have happened. I'm sorry that I didn't speak up sooner, but I'm glad I could do it here, in front of everyone, so all of you can hear me." She broke eye contact with Helen to sweep her eyes across the crowd. "I wouldn't change having my abortion, but I would change what I did after. And I am willing to face the consequences, whatever they might be. Because I'd rather face the consequences than feel ashamed."

Jamie's speech echoed throughout the gym, followed by dead silence where there should have been applause for her bravery. I couldn't believe she'd done it. But she sounded so genuine, so powerful, and so clear in her beliefs. Everyone should at least have empathy for her, I thought.

I looked around, trying to figure out people's reactions. But everything was so still. Finally, after what felt like an eternity of silence, one of the other senior girls pulled Jamie into a protective hug. Another girl joined her. And then Melissa. And me. And Cady. And Sara. All of us protecting Jamie in a big, awkward, but honest and true hug. The only ones not participating were Angelle, who bit her lip nervously and hovered like she wanted to join, but couldn't bring herself to, and Leah, who looked shocked that she hadn't gotten her way—again.

People in the audience around us whispered to each other, a steady murmur that sounded like cicadas in the summer.

Sister Catherine's shoulders sagged. The homecoming dance had turned into the biggest disaster anyone at my school had ever seen, and she had to deal with it. I didn't envy her at all.

"Miss Taylor, we'll talk about this more later, with your parents," Sister Catherine said at last, letting out a heavy sigh. "You'll have to come with me. I'll call your parents, and they'll come pick you up. I'm sorry."

Jamie shrank back into our group, the implications of her words hitting her full force. Leah looked on, her familiar smirk returning to her face. Maybe she *had* won after all.

Then Sister Catherine turned back to Leah, and her eyebrows went up when she saw Leah's triumphant expression.

"Miss Sullivan, what *you* did was quite possibly the least Christian thing I have ever witnessed at this school," Sister Catherine said, loud enough for the crowd to hear. "In my office. *Now.* We're calling your parents."

Leah's smirk slid off her face, replaced with a fierce defiance. She didn't move from her spot adjacent to the homecoming group hug.

"How is it un-Christian to be *honest*?" Leah tilted her head so that the stiff curls jerked as one, and placed her hands on her hips. "My dad won't punish me for this."

Sister Catherine put her hand to the rosary she wore near her waist, worrying one of the Hail Mary beads between her thumb and forefinger.

"Christianity is also about forgiveness," Sister Catherine said after a significant pause. "And kindness. And, above all, loving your neighbor as yourself. Now, if you don't follow me out of this gym right now, you can count on *never* coming back in."

Leah crossed her arms, stomping out behind Sister Catherine. Jamie, her head hanging low, followed, as well.

Right before she reached the door, Sister Catherine signaled to the DJ. He started the music again, a pumping dance remix of EMF's crappy "Unbelievable."

It was a weird way for Sister Catherine to leave things, but I'm not sure what else she could have done.

37

People clustered in twos and threes and fours, trying to figure out what had just happened.

"Did you *hear* what Leah said to Sister Catherine?"

"Oh, my gawd! I cannot believe that Jamie Taylor had an abortion! Do you think she was raped?"

"I don't know! How could she do that, though?"

Lies, whispers, and speculation flew across the gym. A moment of triumph where Helen was finally vindicated had turned into a moment of terror about what might happen to Jamie. There was no awesome moment of special enlightenment about treating people nicely or talking about politics or helping people out. All the gossip just switched from Helen to Jamie, with an extra side dish of speculation as to what would happen to Leah.

The homecoming court gradually drifted apart, as confused as anybody else. We'd watched, powerless, as Sister

Catherine pulled Jamie and Leah from the gym. For all we knew, Sister Catherine was drawing up the expulsion papers right now, calling the diocese for guidance, and apologizing to Louis Bettencourt in order to save her job.

Jamie had sacrificed herself for Helen, and I'd wanted everyone in the room to cheer her on, but she'd been met with silence. Though I hadn't clapped, either—I'd been too stunned. So maybe I was being a little uncharitable to everyone in thinking Jamie hadn't changed *anyone's* mind. I couldn't hear what everyone was saying, and I certainly couldn't tell what everyone was thinking. But even if she got through to one person, it meant something.

But still, it bothered me. She was going to face all the punishment—and more—that Helen had. And we'd all just stayed behind in the gym, like it was nothing. Everything returned to a forced, *fake* normal, and I was beginning to feel like I shouldn't be any different from anyone else, and I should act like nothing had happened. Sean and Helen had their heads together, deep in discussion, at one of the tables that lined the far side of the gym. Sara and Jennifer were off with their dates in the freshman corner. Across the room, Melissa was making out with her date, some college guy I'd never seen before and would probably never see again.

It felt like Trip and I were the only platonically oriented couple at the dance, and apparently I was the only one who was bothered by the fact that we'd let Jamie hang—even Melissa seemed indifferent to everything, and it seemed clear to me that she had helped Jamie plan for this moment. After all the rumors and preparation and plans and dramatic gestures, were we really going to let Jamie fall to the same thing that had almost gotten Helen?

I sat on the bleachers and looked down at the corsage on my

wrist. It was starting to wilt in the humidity of the gym. Sure, we had air-conditioning, but five hundred sweaty teenagers—half of them boys, and half of those boys with questionable hygiene—had started to steam up the place with a gross gym-sock funk. I looked for Trip, thinking maybe I could ignore the nagging feeling about abandoning Jamie if he wanted to dance. But he was doing his own thing, a wild and goofy dance with some of the other football players to Run-DMC's "Walk This Way," which I'm pretty sure they'd been perfecting since they were ten.

I didn't blame him for abandoning me. I was miserable company.

I felt the familiar weight of someone sitting down next to me. Even without looking up, I knew it was Sean.

"Hey, grumpy," he said, patting me on the head. "What're you doing over here by yourself? Don't you have a date?"

I shrugged. "Did Helen send you over here?"

"No," he said. "You're my friend, and I noticed you were staring at the floor like an ad for one of those bullshit teen angst bands you like. What's the name for them? Shoe-face?"

"Shoegaze. And you know that." I smacked him hard on his arm reflexively, like I'd have done when we were twelve, crushing the wilting corsage in the process.

He smiled, raising his hands in a faux defense. "Ah, there you are. You know, with everything that's happened, you haven't punched me in weeks. Well, at least not until earlier tonight anyway."

I let out a cynical laugh. "Well, that's the price you pay for growing up. A lot fewer punches from someone with no upper-body strength."

Suddenly, I noticed that his knee was bouncing up and down like a jittery jackhammer.

"Hey." He cleared his throat. "I, uh, was wondering if you're okay with me dating your sister." He looked at me, and then looked away a second later, as if afraid of my answer.

It was funny. It felt like he should have asked me by now, but then I realized it was only last night that I'd seen them holding hands at the game. Between the hair salon, and the dressing up, and the presentation of the homecoming court, and the grand implosion of our plan, I hadn't talked to him *at all.* Helen had done all the arranging of the great date switch of 1992.

"Of course I don't mind!"

He let out a huge sigh. "Good. I was worried that was why you were over here by yourself—that you were mad at me for setting you up with Trip. I mean, not really 'setting you up.'" He used air quotes on *setting you up*, and then dropped his hands. "But...you know what I mean."

I was at least halfway sure that it *had* been a setup with Trip, but I wasn't going to say anything.

"Ha, no. That's not it," I said, shaking my head. "I'm totally happy for you. I did think this would happen, but like, when she was a grown-up, and not now."

Open mouth, insert foot. I didn't mean to sound like I thought Helen was a kid. I only meant that I thought this would happen in the future, like after college.

Sean smiled. "When she grows up? Helen better not grow up any more, because then she'd be taller than me, and I don't know if I could handle that." He nudged me with his shoulder. "So what's wrong? Are you upset about Jamie?"

I shrugged. "I mean, yeah," I told him. "I'm a little depressed that we probably didn't change anyone's mind, and that Jamie is probably going to get kicked out of school. And we're sitting here like nothing happened, because it's easier to do that than face the fact that if we really did something, we'd wind up in the same boat as her. And it's full circle to what she said about how she was scared to stand up for Helen when she heard the rumors. Only this time, it's not gossip—she actually did it, so it's a whole lot worse."

Sean put his arm around me and squeezed. "Oh, it's not so bad," he said. "You *tried* to change people's minds, and that's what counts. And I'm sure that some people *did* change their minds. And I hate to say this, but it's kind of like what that politician—"

"Louis Bettencourt," I hissed.

"Yeah, that guy," he continued. "He said that everyone thinks they're doing the right thing, even when they're wrong. And even though he and I would disagree about what's the right thing, he's right about that much. I think you guys—I mean, girls—" He corrected himself, probably due to the annoying way that I'd consistently told him not to call me and Helen "guys" for the past year. "You tried to help Helen, and I know she appreciated it. You did the right thing for her."

It didn't make me feel any better.

"But we didn't do the right thing for Jamie," I protested. "Or at least, we didn't stick with her."

Sean pointed toward the opposite side of the gym.

"Well, I think Helen might be talking with Melissa about that right now."

Across the darkened gym, Helen was walking away from Melissa and her anonymous college dude toward Sara and Jennifer, who stood petrified against the wall. Helen was frowning, but from a distance, it was hard to tell if she was angry, or confused, or just thinking about something really hard.

Once she passed them, Sara and Jennifer fell in line behind her as Helen continued her march across the gym. Sara held her dress up so that she wouldn't trip at the quick pace that

Helen was setting. Jennifer's face was blank, like it was anytime she wasn't sure of something, but her hand clutched her tiny purse like she might lose it.

As they got closer, I could see that Helen's face wasn't white with fury. No, her look was somewhere between profoundly confused and despondent, and she barely acknowledged Sara and Jennifer trailing behind her. She threw herself onto the bleachers next to Sean and grabbed his hand in a swift motion, her fingers snaking into his and clutching with distracted force. I saw Sean wince, but I knew he would never say anything.

"Athena, you *have* to talk to Melissa," she said. "I give up. She won't listen to me. She thinks that I'm upset that this is all about abortion now. And I kind of am, but that's not it." She shook her head. "It's all my fault that Jamie's going to get kicked out. This went too far."

"It's not your fault," Sara said over Helen's shoulder.

I looked up at them. "None of this is anyone's fault but Leah and Aimee's. As ever."

I thought of what Sean said to me about Bettencourt, and suddenly, everything made sense. We all thought we were doing the right thing, and for a while, the right thing had been easy. It had been the same thing for all of us—to make sure that no one believed the lies about Helen.

But then it became something else, and the right thing wasn't so clear, and it was different for different people. And now we were stuck.

Helen slumped next to Sean, one hand gripping his ever tighter, the other propping up her chin. Jennifer and Sara stared at me with varying degrees of hope on their faces, expecting me to fix everything.

I wasn't sure I could, but it was definitely, absolutely wrong to leave Jamie alone with Leah in Sister Catherine's office. If we couldn't fix this, she shouldn't go down by herself. The Gang of Five had to stand for something.

"You don't have to come with me for this," I said, getting up from the bleachers. "But I'm going to Sister Catherine's office."

Helen lifted her head. "To do what?"

I shifted my feet nervously. "To be honest, I'm not sure. But I'm not leaving the gym without Melissa."

Sean sighed as Helen untwined her fingers from his. "Go get 'em, tiger…s?"

The gym felt like it was a million miles long as I walked over to Melissa. The other three trailed me, like I had suddenly become their scout leader. I could feel a few people at the tables around the perimeter of the gym looking at us as we pushed our way through the dancing crowd, but most people ignored us. It was pretty easy to be ignored when so many people were literally jumping around to House of Pain's "Jump Around."

Melissa put up her hands defensively as soon as she saw me.

"If you're going to yell at me about how Jamie shouldn't have said anything, I don't want to hear it," she said. "This was her choice, not mine. And I don't get how you're suddenly not pro-choice anymore."

I shook my head. "Oh, my God, I *am* still pro-choice. That's not what this is about." My tone sounded super defensive, matching hers word for word. I lowered my voice. "I just think if we—you and I—really believe in being pro-choice, then we need to stand up for Jamie now, too. So if you want to help, come with me."

38

The thud of the DJ's bass speakers echoed through the hallway from the gym. As we got closer to the main offices, I had a flashback to my urban exploration with Kyle. The terror of being caught was similar, but this time I didn't have any anticipation of being alone with a boy I liked. Instead, I was with four girls, a misfit Nancy Drew and her sidekicks.

Pretty soon, the only thing we could hear was the sound of our heels clacking against the polished linoleum floors of the hallway. I signaled for everyone to slow down—the lights were on in the glass-enclosed entry to the guidance office, which was between us and Sister Catherine. We tiptoed past it, trying to avoid being noticed.

I couldn't help myself from slowing down and looking in. The light was coming from Mrs. Turner's office, and she was in there—*packing.* Her shelf of adolescent psychiatry books was half-empty, and a stack of boxes was taped up and ready to go near the door. She skittered from the bookshelf to the boxes, back and forth as quickly as she could, fully devoted to her task.

Had she been fired? Was that what Mr. Richard had meant by "handled"? Had she quit? Why was she doing this *now*? It was a mystery, sure, but one that I thought could wait. I waved for everyone to keep following me toward Sister Catherine's office.

When we'd nearly gotten past the door, Jennifer stumbled in her heels and slammed into the glass window with a giant *whump*. She wasn't hurt—it wasn't like the glass broke or anything—but tears welled in her eyes. I thought for a moment that she'd sprained her ankle, but then I realized they were tears of sheer terror.

The guidance counselor looked up at the sound. She smiled, seeming satisfied that she'd finally—finally!—caught us red-handed. She scurried over to the door.

"Let me do the talking," Helen growled, pushing her way in front of me. "I got this."

Mrs. Turner hastily unlocked the glass door and pushed it open toward us.

"My, my, look who it is! Aren't you young ladies supposed to be at the dance? Or is there something you might have to tell me?" She smiled again, and I felt a shiver of anger.

Helen looked down at Mrs. Turner with her "I've got intimidating height" thing. She was close enough that she was absolutely, *definitely* within Mrs. Turner's personal space.

"No, we're just on our way to see Sister Catherine." Helen mixed the intimidation with a sweet tone of voice that was somehow both frightening and obsequious.

It worked. Mrs. Turner's smug smile dwindled into a confused frown. "I'm sure you'll find *success* at whatever you want to see her for," she said, snappier than usual. Then she recovered and shook her head in mock sadness. "It's such a shame.

She won't have my help much longer, and I fear for you young people. You young ladies most of all."

She nodded at us, a look of counterfeit understanding settling onto her face. It was a favorite tactic of hers, most often deployed when trying to lure students into a trap. At this point in our lives, it didn't impress any of us—but it did prompt a question.

"Oh, where are you going?" Helen asked, much more calmly and sweetly than I would have thought humanly possible. "I'm sure the school will miss you terribly."

I was amazed at my sister's ability to lie in an absolutely convincing fashion. Or maybe it would be more accurately described as acting—it was too bad they didn't give out Oscars for getting horrible guidance counselors to tell you everything you need to hear, because she totally deserved one.

Mrs. Turner fussed with her voluminous shoulder-padded blazer, smoothing it with pride, and puffed up her chest. "I'm going to be the new volunteer youth coordinator for Representative Bettencourt."

I was 100 percent sure that Melissa was rolling her eyes behind me, because Helen shot her a warning look that would have stunned a grown man or perhaps a large bear.

"Oh, how nice." Rather miraculously, Helen didn't give away the reason that she thought it was nice—namely, that her packing meant Mrs. Turner would be out of our lives forever. "A *volunteer* position?"

Mrs. Turner's smile faded a bit, then brightened again to a superhuman wattage. "Yes, but it's an *amazing* opportunity. I'll get to work with young people in such a *connected* way. It's really *such* a wonderful thing."

Such a wonderful thing...to work with kids, for free, for a politician. Yeah, right. My money was on *handled* translating to *fired*, but I knew she would never admit that to us.

Mrs. Turner reached out to squeeze Helen's arm affectionately. Helen didn't even flinch. She just stood there, a beatific, saccharine-sweet smile fixed to her face, without saying a word.

"Helen, I was so glad to hear that the…issue…surrounding you has been cleared up." Mrs. Turner's eyes were suddenly full of ersatz concern and welling with dewy tears. "Of course, I always had faith in you."

If I were Helen, I would have had a hard time keeping myself from punching Mrs. Turner—or, at the very least, from jerking my arm away from hers. But Helen hid any fury she might have felt, the only telltale sign a small clenching and unclenching of her left fist.

"Thank you, Mrs. Turner," she said, looking down at the guidance counselor. "But we have to go see Sister Catherine now. Good luck to you with your new position."

"Of course, of course," Mrs. Turner said, nodding. "Thank you."

She gave Helen another squeeze and rushed back into her office, as though the packing absolutely *had* to be done on the night of the school homecoming dance, which only cemented my thought that she'd been fired. Mrs. Turner waved—a little too enthusiastically—at us through the window, and then returned to pulling books from the shelf.

Harsh fluorescent lights flooded the glass cage of the disciplinary office. Even during regular hours, they turned the skin of anyone sitting underneath them a shade of pale, sickly green. Maybe it was by design, so that anyone who crossed its threshold felt some level of guilt by coloration.

The door to Sister Catherine's office was closed, and Jamie sat by herself on one of the chairs that lined the glass box on three sides. Her mascara had bled into gothy circles around her eyes, and her eyes and nose were bright red from crying and nose wiping. She held a wet, crumpled tissue in one hand. Every once in a while, she'd bring it up to her nose distractedly and blow. She didn't seem to notice us at all through the glass, though, to be fair, none of us had slammed against the window this time.

"What are we *doing*?" Melissa whispered. "We can't wait out here and watch her like a bunch of creeps."

My shoulders tensed with annoyance. "Of course not. We're going in to support her."

I pushed open the glass door into the waiting room. The sounds of loud, but muffled arguing came from behind the closed frosted-glass door to Sister Catherine's office. From the extreme Southern accent and high pitch, one of the voices likely belonged to Leah's mother. I couldn't quite make out what she was saying, but I did catch snippets. "In-school suspension, young lady! You should be lucky you aren't *expelled*!" and "What is going through your *mind*, young lady? What made you disrupt *homecoming* like this? Do you have *any* respect for the crown?" and even "I raised you better than this! Three months alone with your father, and you're nearly kicked out of school?"

It was enough to know Leah hadn't found the unwavering parental support she'd expected, because she'd bet on the wrong horse showing up.

I would have taken a moment for smug satisfaction, and I'm sure Helen would have, too, but we couldn't. Jamie needed us. She looked up, her eyes passing over each of us in turn. It didn't quite feel like she really *saw* us, though. It was more like she was looking at us through a fog, or maybe through a veil into another world.

"What are you guys doing here?" Jamie asked slowly.

"We thought you might like some support." I sat down next to her. I looked her in the eyes, but her eyes darted back to her lap and the crumpled tissue.

"I don't need it," she mumbled. "I knew this could happen."

Helen crouched down near Jamie while simultaneously grabbing Melissa and pulling her down to Jamie's level. Melissa seemed to get what Helen was doing and didn't argue.

"Yeah, but it's our choice to help you," Helen said. "Like you helped me, even though you didn't have to. I appreciate that more than I can ever tell you. And I know that whatever punishment you get is as much because of something that happened to me as it is anything you said."

Suddenly, the room fell quiet. At first, I thought it was because we were all letting Helen's words sink in, but then I realized that the sound of arguing coming from Sister Catherine's office had stopped.

The door creaked open, and Helen and Melissa jerked up from the floor, spinning around at the sound.

Leah's mother was the first to walk out, her mouth a tiny frown of pearly pink lipstick. She was dressed in pink sweats with a pink bandanna over rollers in her hair, an outfit that clearly indicated she'd rushed from her new apartment, wherever that was, to come get her daughter. But she hadn't rushed so much that she forgot the lipstick.

She pulled Leah behind her, hand gripped tight on her daughter's reluctant wrist. Leah's glower was almost exactly like her mother's, but with an extra splash of defiance. Unlike Jamie, Leah still looked perfectly made-up, her curls crisp enough that they might be able to survive a nuclear holocaust, along with all of Louisiana's roaches.

She sneered at us as she went past. "This isn't over," she gloated. "You'll see!"

Leah's mom jerked to a stop and faced her daughter. "Young lady, if this isn't over *right now*, you'll be the one who sees nothing but the inside walls of my apartment for the next six months!"

She banged open the office door and dragged Leah through it. Leah didn't say anything else, but I didn't believe for a second that she wouldn't be back at her old torture games as soon as her suspension ended.

After a few moments of the tensest silence I'd ever felt, Sister Catherine emerged from her office, her face grim. When she saw all of us surrounding Jamie, her expression softened.

"Girls, I understand that you want to keep Jamie company," she said, nun-calm. "But her parents are on their way, and our discussion should be private."

Melissa opened her mouth to protest, but I shushed her. "We know, Sister Catherine. But we'd like to stay. If it weren't for us, she wouldn't be here."

Sister Catherine raised her eyebrows. "I'm pretty sure that none of you are responsible for her choosing an abortion, even if Melissa was at the protests this summer."

Melissa looked genuinely surprised that anyone at the school knew of her summer exploits, even though she'd been clearly visible on the national news and had never, ever been shy about her politics. Once again, she opened her mouth to protest.

This time, Helen stepped forward. "No, we didn't have anything to do with that. But if it hadn't been for the rumors about me, then she wouldn't have told everyone about it, and she wouldn't be in trouble now. It's not fair that she should be kicked out of school for that."

Sister Catherine's shoulders drooped ever so slightly. She grabbed one of the chairs that lined the glass wall and motioned for us to sit down in the chairs near Jamie.

"Girls, I understand you want to help." She glanced at Melissa and Helen, but then her eyes finally came to rest on mine. "It is very compassionate of you. And I want to reassure you Jamie isn't going to get kicked out."

"I'm not?" Jamie asked in a small voice.

Sister Catherine shook her head. "No, of course not."

"But the student handbook says—" Helen said, puzzled.

Sister Catherine raised her eyebrows. "Am I hearing you protest?"

"Of course not!" Helen said, a little too loudly. "But I remember that the school's policy is to be pro-life in any case, and—"

"And is it pro-life to make an example out of Jamie?"

"No, but Representative Bettencourt—"

Sister Catherine smiled kindly at Helen. "Is a politician, not an educator," she said, leaning forward. "We have school policies about all sorts of things, but we also have to approach students with compassion in our hearts."

Except not everyone at our school had compassion. Mrs. Turner certainly didn't. And Sister Catherine herself had told me we were close to landing ourselves in trouble.

"But what about everyone else?" I asked. "The protesters are still out there, and if they hear that Jamie had an abortion, they'll call for your head, and this'll never end."

Something in Sister Catherine's eyes told me she knew that, too. But nuns are calmer than normal people—or at least the ones working in high schools are.

"You're right," she said. "But Jamie can't be punished for whether or not she had an abortion. That would be in violation of many medical privacy laws, and her parents would have to give permission for us to theoretically even know about it." She nodded meaningfully at all of us, though Jamie still stared at the crumpled tissue in her hand and Sara and Jennifer had shrunk into their chairs. "She's going to face the same possible punishment that Leah did, which was for interrupting the homecoming court."

My eyes darted from Sister Catherine to Jamie. My heart sank at the thought of her being punished when we were the organizers. "But that's not fair. We interrupted it, too."

Sister Catherine smiled wanly, like she was almost amused that I was continually one step away from talking myself into punishment. "Am I to take it you want an in-school suspension, Miss Graves?"

"Well, no, but—"

"Then I suggest that you and your friends go back to the dance and enjoy your freedom," she said. "Miss Taylor's parents will be here soon."

It felt rotten to leave Jamie by herself, even knowing she wasn't going to be kicked out of school. I looked at Melissa and Helen, who seemed to get what I was thinking.

"Sister Catherine, can't we hang out with Jamie until her parents get here?" Helen asked, positioning herself protectively between Sister Catherine and Jamie. "I mean, if you want us to." She looked at Jamie for approval.

Jamie nodded, looking tired and drained, but not nearly as terrified as a few minutes ago. She hadn't said anything the whole time. If I were her, I'd be playing the events of the past hour on repeat in my brain, paralyzed and unable to think of anything else.

So we sat, all of us, in the quiet glass box until Jamie's parents arrived, dour-faced and disappointed, and shut the door on us.

39

While we walked back to the gym, I felt like the world had changed, and yet it hadn't. Leah was going to have an in-school suspension, and so was Jamie, and we weren't able to stop it. And I wasn't so certain that Sister Catherine wouldn't be in trouble if Bettencourt got wind of things, but it did seem that with Mrs. Turner out of the way, that avenue of communication might be a lot narrower.

Still, I felt a little relief—no, a *lot* of relief—that it wasn't worse. Mrs. Turner hadn't made good on any of her promises and was leaving, and Leah was suspended.

"Athena, I wanted to say I'm sorry I didn't tell you," Melissa said, right before we got close enough that the music blasting from the gym would drown her out.

"It's okay," I said. "I get why you had to keep it a secret." And I did. Melissa thought she'd change people's minds, but I wondered if we had.

She hugged me and then peeled off. "I gotta go find my date. Catch you later?"

"Of course."

"Ciao!" She waved at the four of us and darted off onto the dance floor to find College Boy, whose name I still didn't know. Somehow, I suspected it wasn't important information.

"Hey, Graves!" Trip bounded up to me, his face red and his blond hair sticking up. His shirt was hanging halfway out of his pants from the exertion of his "dancing" with the football team. "Where've you been? You missed the football team's salute to the homecoming court."

I mustered a half smile. I was a *terrible* date—I'd missed out on the only chance my date would have to impress me. Every year, the football team sang a dumb love song to the girls on the court, à la "You've Lost That Lovin' Feeling" in *Top Gun*. I suspected it was usually a terrible ensemble of howling boys, but I couldn't say for sure. I'd missed it last year, too, because I didn't have a date for the dance.

"We were offering Jamie some support."

Trip's smile morphed into a knowing look. "Is everything going to be okay?"

Helen nodded at me to indicate that she was going to leave us alone—and suddenly I got that this was definitely a setup on *her* part, if not Trip's or Sean's. She pulled Jennifer and Sara behind her, but let go and waved when she was about fifteen feet away. I tried to ignore her and looked up into Trip's face.

"Yeah, I think so. Maybe not now, but eventually."

"That's great! Hey, do you want to dance some more?" He looked down at me with excitement. "They're going to be playing some *reeediculous* stuff, and I bet you'd feel better if you could let loose a little after all that. Like, I think 'I'm

Too Sexy' is coming up, and Andre and Matt have a thing planned."

After seeing their "dances" to "Jump Around" and "Walk This Way," I could only imagine what they had planned—it probably involved lots of flailing and inaccurately synchronized moves. Suddenly, I was smiling.

"I don't think I could match their energy. But it's pretty entertaining," I shouted. "I—"

The DJ suddenly cut the music in the middle of my sentence, and I swallowed my words.

"Ladies and gentlemen, we have a special request from one of your young gentlemen," the DJ said in his cheesy voice. He sounded less than enthusiastic, though. He probably wanted to return to normalcy, like post–World War I Warren G. Harding, after the near world war that had erupted around the homecoming court.

Whatever. One of Trip's buddies probably requested "Strokin'," like they tried at every dance, only to have a chaperone cut it off once they realized how smutty it was. Or maybe it was "Me So Horny," the *other* song that guys liked to get the DJs to play. I raised my eyebrows at Trip, who shook his head. He and the football players didn't have anything to do with it.

"I need to apologize to someone tonight—"

I froze. Kyle. It was Kyle's voice. I didn't want to turn around to look at him, but somehow my feet moved for me.

"Athena, I know you're mad at me." He looked super charming and adorable to a slightly hateful extent in his black button-down and black jeans. "But I wanted to let everyone know how awesome you are. Not because you're smart and pretty and a good musician, which you are, but because you stood up for your sister and for what you believe in. You may never want to speak to me again, but I wanted to let you know I'm sorry."

He turned to give the microphone back to the DJ, then pivoted once more.

"Oh, and this was the only song that the DJ had that I know you like, so I'm sorry if it's not really an apology song."

The opening chords of Nirvana's "Smells Like Teen Spirit" blasted through the PA system, to the sound of applause from everyone but me.

"Take him back!" someone shouted. It was Wisteria, of course.

I didn't know what to do. I should talk to him. No, I *shouldn't* talk to him. It would be rude to talk to him, when I was there on a date with Trip, who was probably vaguely embarrassed by the spectacle of the whole thing. But it would be rude *not* to talk with him after that speech.

I had wanted this. I'd wanted Kyle to say something other than a litany of excuses for why he liked the most loathsome human I'd ever met. And he hadn't—not really. He'd apologized *after* Leah disappeared, which didn't show a tremendous amount of intestinal fortitude, as my dad would say.

I didn't feel the way I'd thought I would—though, honestly, I wasn't exactly sure *what* I'd thought I would feel.

I looked at Trip, not sure what to do next, except pretend the last fifteen minutes hadn't happened.

"You know that scene at the end of *Pretty in Pink*, where Duckie tells Andie to go after Blane?" I asked Trip, looking up at his still-nervous face.

Trip nodded enthusiastically and then blushed again, a deeper scarlet than the red he already had from running around like a maniac all night. Boys, especially linebackers, weren't supposed to have an extensive, play-by-play knowledge of Molly Ringwald movies.

"That's my sister's favorite movie," he mumbled.

"Don't be Duckie," I told him. "Be the anti-Duckie. And don't let me go talk to him, so I don't have to hear his bullshit variation on how he always believed in me and didn't believe in himself."

"I can't do that." He shook his head so hard that little droplets of sweat spattered out. "I think you *should* talk with him. Not that you should get back together with him—we can still have that jazz funeral we were talking about—but I think you need to kick around the dead body a little first."

That I thought Trip had carried the jazz funeral imagery a little too far must have shown on my face.

"Sorry. That was gross."

"It's okay," I said, laughing. "I started it."

"Anyway, go get your closure," he said. "I'll be here when you get back, trying to get the DJ to play 'Strokin'.'"

I walked toward the corner of the gym where Kyle stood. I hated the fact that I still found him super hot, that my feet still moved toward him. Part of me couldn't tell if I was being unfair toward him. I'd forgiven Sean, but that was different. Sean was my oldest friend, and we had a longer track record of awesomeness and support that predated any meddling from Leah.

"Hey." I didn't have other words.

"I'm just going to say it," he said, grabbing my hand and looking at me with those frustratingly gorgeous eyes. "I'm lame and a coward, and I've wanted to apologize a hundred times. I thought maybe you'd talk with me again after I put up all of those posters, but you never even looked at me."

He took a deep breath. I let him talk, to see if what he said could possibly make up for all those times when I had waited for him to call and say something, anything that indicated I'd been more than his after-school make-out girl.

"You never looked at me, but I looked at you. I saw someone who took the high road, who supported her friends, and who did things that were challenging," Kyle said. "I saw the kind of girl I'd be proud to date, if she'd let me."

He was good with words. I'd give him that. He hadn't said anything about Leah, though, or that he was sorry he'd believed Aimee about me.

"Leah," I said. "You came with *her* tonight. Would you be saying this if she hadn't gotten pulled out of here by Sister Catherine?"

The question would bother me forever if I never asked it.

Oh, those amber eyes. Such confusion. Such woundedness.

"I've planned this speech in my head for weeks," he said, looking at his feet. "I'd hoped we wouldn't have to talk about her, but I knew we would." He cleared his throat. "Anyway, here it is. Athena Graves, you were right. Completely right. Always, truly, totally right about her spreading gossip with Aimee. But despite what you think, I didn't cheat on you with her. Nothing happened until after you stopped talking with me, and it was a mistake. I knew she had a lot of problems, especially with her parents, and I thought she needed someone to talk to. But I've also learned that I don't want to be that person."

I hadn't expected that answer, and I didn't know if it made anything right. But I didn't know what to say, either.

"I'm sorry, Kyle," I said finally. "But you can't make things better in five minutes. I don't know how I can trust you again."

"What would make you trust me?"

"I have no idea." Suddenly, I was exhausted. I couldn't think, and I didn't want to talk with him. I didn't want to forgive him, or be his girlfriend, or ask him why he'd done that stealth campaign for me for the homecoming court. "But for tonight, I have a date, and I've got to get back to him."

I walked back toward Trip, who was just leaving the DJ's table, laughing loudly now that "Strokin'" was finally blasting from the speakers.

He spotted me and shimmied over, singing the song's lyrics in time with his shuffling dance. Then he stopped, eyes widening as though he suddenly realized he was singing a very dirty song directly to me. "Uh, how did it go?"

I shrugged. "Good, I guess."

"I guess the body is alive?" Trip looked a little disappointed.

Was it? I didn't think so. I wasn't sure I knew who Kyle was, not really. "Mostly dead, I think."

"Well, mostly dead means a little bit alive, right? Do you need Miracle Max?"

I shook my head. "This isn't *The Princess Bride*, and he's *definitely* not Cary Elwes."

Trip held out his arm. "Well, if you're not going back over to him, do you want to dance?"

"To *this*?"

His face lit up with glee. "I can't believe I actually got them to play it!" He sounded as excited as a five-year-old, until he realized that I was never, ever going to dance with him to that song. "But maybe we can wait until the next song."

I looked up at his eager face. I couldn't figure out if he had a crush on me, or if he just liked dancing—and, from what I'd seen already on the dance floor, the possibility of the latter was as strong as the former. But it didn't matter. As long as it wasn't a terrible song, I was in.

"Let's dance," I said, taking his hand.

"'Let's Dance'! That's a great song! Maybe I should ask for some Bowie! My older sister *loves* him!" Trip said, his face lighting up. "You're a genius, Graves! Thanks for the suggestion! This party could use Bowie's kind of weird!"

He grabbed me for a spontaneous twirl, during which my feet actually left the ground. I had to grab on tight and felt a jolt of something I wasn't expecting—actual attraction. Extreme heat, and not because he'd been sweating. Like I wanted him to kiss me after he got done swinging me around. Like Kyle didn't exist.

I gulped hard as he set me down and took a deep breath to figure things out. I didn't want to ping-pong from one boy to another, but I didn't want to push Trip away, either.

"I'm sorry, I'm sorry. I got carried away." He looked down at me, face flushed with embarrassment instead of his dance-induced exertion. He backed away by about three feet.

I pulled him back toward me. Not into an embrace or anything, but close enough that it felt *right* looking up into his blue eyes, which were pretty amazing looking. How had I never noticed them before while I was tutoring him?

"No," I said, smiling up at him. "That was good. Just warn me next time."

"So you're saying there'll be a next time?" Trip grinned. "All right!"

Trip and I danced to all the fast songs, all the weird songs, all the old songs, and even all the slow songs for the last hour of the dance. By the time the bright lights went up at midnight, blinding all of us and destroying the atmosphere the student council had tried so hard to create, I'd almost forgotten about the earlier drama. Almost.

"Hey, Athena!" Melissa waved to me from across the gym. She was practically dragging her date behind her, gripping his hand like she might lose him. He was a willowy, black-haired guy who, if I squinted, vaguely approximated the picture of Suede's Brett Anderson she'd taped in her locker. He also looked about as happy as I imagined an up-and-coming English indie rock singer would be at a high school dance—which is to say, not very, and very impatient to leave the gym.

Melissa's olive skin was flush with the fresh experience of dancing—or, if I was reading the situation correctly, making out with her date. Strands of her purple-tinted hair had fallen out of her elegant updo into a sloppy mess around her ears, and her eggplant-colored lipstick was nonexistent, except for a lingering smear near the corner of her mouth.

"Are you in for Denny's?" she asked breathlessly. "Adam and I were thinking of going."

Adam nodded at me disinterestedly. He didn't seem like Denny's material, and certainly not one for ordering Moons Over My Hammy, ironically or not.

"Yeah, I don't think so." Adam's dramatic sulk distracted me from Melissa's eager invitation. "I think I'm just going to find Helen and head home. Try to figure out what to do next now that all this—" I waved my hands in a big circle, not sure what I was even gesturing toward "—is over."

Melissa dropped Adam's hand and turned to me with hands on her hips. "What do you mean? We won! We should be celebrating. With milkshakes and greasy food."

Jamie getting a suspension didn't deserve to be in the win column, even if it was satisfying to see Leah get the same.

"I guess I don't see it that way," I said. "I don't know if we actually changed anyone's minds. We didn't even change *Helen's*."

"Of course you did." I turned to see my sister standing behind me.

"Wait, what?" Melissa's eyes widened in shock, followed by a fist pump of victory.

She rolled her eyes. "Not about being pro-life. Duh," she said, sounding more like she would have before her recent transformation into a human being. "But about how we can work together. Just because I'm not going to be having an abortion anytime soon doesn't mean I need to be a jerk about it. Jamie didn't deserve any of that."

Melissa threw up her hands. "You've basically just described being pro-choice. It's not the choice that *you* would make. But it's still a *choice*."

"Yeah, you can keep saying it like that," Helen said, somewhere between defiant and joking. "And I'll be over here, still cherishing my values."

Melissa rolled her eyes, then linked one of her arms with mine and the other with Helen's. "Sure you two don't want to go to Denny's?"

"Moons Over My Hammy!" Helen exclaimed. "I'm in!"

"Athena?"

It might turn into a totally awkward triple date, or Adam might abandon us after the first five minutes of realizing he was with high school girls, or Trip and Sean might end up talking the whole time about football. But it was a moment I could never have imagined a few months ago, and it was so worth it.

"Yeah, I'm in." And chances were, I always would be.

★ ★ ★ ★ ★

Historical Note

While Athena's narrative is fiction, the history behind *Rebel Girls* is not. When writing this book, I chose the aftermath of Baton Rouge's early-1990s protests for a few reasons, none of which is '90s nostalgia. The first and most important reason was that I wanted a setting parallel to today's politics—something close, but not identical, to today—where I could open up discussion about abortion without tying it to today's laws or politicians. This choice was both philosophical and practical. I didn't want readers to view Athena or Helen or Melissa or Jamie in terms of today's rhetoric, which, if anything, has become a heightened version of the early 1990s.

More practically, I was afraid that *Roe v. Wade* might be overturned, or made obsolete, before this book was published. The number of legislative attempts to regulate reproductive rights at the state level have significantly increased since 1992 (mostly due to that year's Supreme Court ruling in *Planned Parenthood v. Casey*), even though the country has remained divided in their opinions about abortion at approximately the same percentages over the past forty years.[1] But in 2016, the Guttmacher Institute, which tracks abortion policies, noted that the previous five years (2010–2015) featured more attempts to restrict abortion at the state level than any other five-year period since *Roe v. Wade*.[2] In light of that, I felt genuinely concerned that unless I wrote *Rebel Girls* as a dystopian set "five minutes in the future," where abortion was outlawed, it wouldn't properly reflect reality.

And so I went back to my hometown, and the events of 1992.

Since the Supreme Court decision of *Roe v. Wade* in 1973, Louisiana has been one of the most active states in the fight over reproductive rights.[3] It's understandable that the state would continue to pass laws against abortion—its population is largely conservative, with a mix of Catholics and evangelical Christians. When I was growing up in Baton Rouge in the 1980s and 1990s, it wasn't unusual to see protesters outside the Delta Women's Clinic, which I frequently passed as my mom drove me to the orthodontist. Before I even got my braces off, the protests at the clinic had started to heat up.

In 1989, 186 people were arrested for blocking access to the Delta Women's Clinic in protests over potential federal

1 https://news.gallup.com/poll/1576/abortion.aspx

2 https://www.guttmacher.org/article/2016/01/last-five-years-account-more-one-quarter-all-abortion-restrictions-enacted-roe

3 For more on Louisiana's history of anti-abortion laws, consult historian Caroline Hymel's article "Louisiana's Abortion Wars: Periodizing the Anti-Abortion Movement's Assault on Women's Reproductive Rights, 1973–2016" in *Louisiana History: The Journal of the Louisiana Historical Association*, vol. 59, no. 1 (Winter 2018), pp. 67–105.

funding for abortion in the case of rape and incest. In 1990, the Louisiana legislature passed what would have been the strictest anti-abortion law in the nation; Governor Buddy Roemer vetoed it. In June 1991, the legislature passed another similar law, which would have banned all abortions except those where the woman's life was at risk, or in the case of rape or incest, either of which had to be reported to the police within seven days, and the abortion had to be performed during the first trimester. Governor Roemer again vetoed the bill. This time, the legislature overrode his veto with a two-thirds majority.

The state's legal situation led to the protests the summer before *Rebel Girls* takes place. Operation Rescue, a national anti-abortion group, chose Baton Rouge as a sequel to its "Summer of Mercy" in Wichita, Kansas. That protest focused on three clinics, including the one operated by Dr. George Tiller. The one in Baton Rouge was supposed to be even bigger, with the leaders of Operation Rescue expecting hundreds of arrests. But thanks to a hastily built fence that kept both protesters and clinic defenders apart, there were fewer arrests—only fifty-eight—though there was still plenty of verbal harassment toward patients.

Despite the relatively small number of arrests in comparison to Wichita (and other Operation Rescue protests in Buffalo, New York, that spring), the national protests *did* change the atmosphere in the city. Like Athena, I went to a Catholic high school, and was pretty much the only pro-choice student in the school other than my older sister (who was off to college by 1992). My cousin was one of the clinic defenders at the Delta Women's Clinic, and my sister drove her to the protests. But most of my friends were pro-life, and it definitely made me feel much more isolated than Athena. I got into my fair share of arguments with teachers who didn't understand how I could be such a good student and still be pro-choice. From my perspective, I didn't understand how they had such little empathy for rape victims, or victims of incest, or women with ectopic pregnancies (which one of my teachers said did not exist), or anyone who chose to make a decision that wasn't identical to theirs. I also didn't understand how my school could kick out pregnant girls, but not their male partners—a policy that made abortion a much more appealing route for many girls, as well as their parents.

All of this became a lot more difficult to articulate after the protests of 1992. School masses started to emphasize pro-life causes, and I got a *lot* of questions about being pro-choice. I basically clammed up about my own beliefs on the matter, though I did *not* succumb to all the peer pressure to join the pro-life club. I found other outlets for my politics, such as arguing with my teachers about social justice issues like poverty and racism. (Which explains why I went to a Jesuit college for undergrad, and also why I will never be voted alumni of the year at St. Michael the Archangel—formerly Bishop Sullivan High School—even without considering the publication of *Rebel Girls*.)

Though I remember the palpable tension around that time, there were many other things that I *didn't* remember. It took a whole lot of research to flesh out the details of the setting in this story, from the timeline of the protests, to where various cool shops were located around LSU, to what music Athena would be listening to (and when), and where to drop subtle Ross Perot references, because…the 1992 election was super weird, y'all.

I tried to bring in other issues that were important in Baton Rouge in 1992, as well. Although this story largely focuses on girl friendships, bullying, and abortion stigma, anyone going to school at the time was doing so in a mostly segregated school system. Baton Rouge had one of the longest continuously running school desegregation cases in the United States (1956–2003), which would have covered all the years Athena was in school. As desegregation plans were put into place in the 1980s, white parents took their kids out of public schools and placed them into the private system, and the public schools were starved of funding. No new public schools were built between 1974 and 2002, as the white student population dwindled, and by 2000, 74 percent of white students attended private schools. This simultaneous defunding of public schools and growth of private schools has gotten worse with each generation, and it illustrates how structural racism is enforced. Even white parents who didn't identify with the goal of segregation wouldn't send their kids to public school, because the schools were so poorly funded. This created a cycle where school segregation was largely preserved, though ostensibly none of the private schools were themselves whites only. And while Sean's story doesn't take center stage in *Rebel Girls*, I hope enough of it is there for readers to understand that structural racism is never absent.

In the process of preserving as much historical accuracy as possible, I relied on numerous sources, both present-day and archival. Baton Rouge's most prominent newspaper, the *Advocate*, covered the protests, as did the *New York Times*. Celia Farber's coverage of the Wichita protests in the December 1991 issue of *Spin* magazine gave insight into how Athena, as someone heavily invested in popular culture, might have read about the debate. NYU's Riot Grrrl Collection, as well as interviews I did back in my days as a researcher, provided valuable context of how girls at the time shared their ideas through letters and zines. References to *Sassy* and even Sean's issues of *Spider-Man* were double-checked against releases at the time, and the one time I tried to get away with something (letting Athena go see *A League of Their Own* in September, over two months after it was released in theaters), my editor caught me red-handed.

That being said, there were times (okay, *one* time) that I did intentionally bend history to my will. Alas, Eddie Vedder's essay about taking his girlfriend for an abortion when they were teenagers appeared in the *November* 1992 issue of *Spin*, not October, as shown here in *Rebel Girls*. But it is a real essay, which you can read in the *Spin* archive on Google Books for free, and it's something that Athena would definitely toss at Helen. Beyond that one exception, there were other times that I wanted to "break" history to include a particular album or movie within the framework of the novel, but I had to resist, because *Rebel Girls* isn't a nostalgic remix like *The Goldbergs*, and I'm committed to accuracy.

Despite that commitment, there are some additional things I have changed, such as the names of neighborhoods and schools, in order to protect the innocent. More important, no one at St. Ann's is a "real" person, and none of the events that take place at the school in this book ever happened in real life. So if you attended Bishop Sullivan or taught there in the 1990s, and you think something in this story is based on you…then I'm very sorry to tell you that you're wrong, and that all these people live only in my head. Except Mrs. Linda Snyder, who was my English teacher junior year, and who gets a very brief nod in this book for having assigned *The Scarlet Letter.* Mrs. Snyder was not at all boring (even if teenage me thought Hawthorne was). She was a wonderful, generous woman, and the first person to encourage me to write fiction. I'm sorry she's not alive to see the publication of *Rebel Girls.*

Finally, a bit about the *other* inspiration for *Rebel Girls*—the feminist music of the 1990s, including everything riot grrrl. The research I was already doing for my academic book (never to be published, alas!) became super useful, and also inspiring—especially the letters from fans and friends of various more famous riot grrrls found in the Riot Grrrl Collection at NYU. Curvy script and bouncy, typewritten and serious, cut-up and put in zines in ways that created new meaning...all the writing had one thing in common—it grappled with what it was like to be a teen girl, and to feel all the contradictions of knowing you have something to say, but being stuck in a culture that often disregards you. Those voices would *never* come across in a book written for an academic audience, and yet they were the most important, treasured thing I found in the archive. None of their stories were at all like what I've written in *Rebel Girls*, but I hope I've channeled some of the enthusiasm and engagement in that archive through Athena's voice.

To be very clear, Athena is a very early adopter of riot grrrl. She's basically listening to one obscure demo cassette and a few compilation albums and reading a bunch of zines. Even the song from which this book takes its title—Bikini Kill's "Rebel Girl"—hadn't yet been released. She's already in love with the feminism of riot grrrl, even before she has all the music in her hands. And that's generally how riot grrrl made its way into pop culture, through ideas as much as the music itself. Riot grrrl itself wasn't a large movement, but it had a slow burn that continues to influence feminist pop culture. Like this book.

If you want to learn more about riot grrrl, I highly recommend Sara Marcus's *Girls to the Front* (2010). It is a wonderfully written introduction to riot grrrl as a movement, with lots of info about Bikini Kill, Bratmobile, Excuse 17, Heavens to Betsy, and a bunch of other folks who were involved in creating zines and organizing riot grrrl chapters. But because this was a big point in my academic research, I'll make it again here: while riot grrrl is part of the punk rock/alternative rock feminism of the 1990s, it's by no means the majority of it. Despite the slogan, not every girl was a riot grrrl, and there's a huge swath of awesome women in '90s music who aren't riot grrrls. In no particular order: L7, Hole, PJ Harvey, Belly, Throwing Muses, Seven Year Bitch, Babes in Toyland, Liz Phair, Björk, Juliana Hatfield, Gwen Stefani/No Doubt, Shirley Manson/Garbage, the Breeders, Luscious Jackson, Elastica, Sleater-Kinney, and many more women were part of either the alternative or indie rock music scene. Beyond that, the decade was pretty amazing for singer-songwriters like Tori Amos, Sarah McLachlan, Jewel, Fiona Apple, Alanis Morissette, Tracy Chapman, and Melissa Etheridge; for R & B and hip-hop artists like Salt-n-Pepa, Queen Latifah, TLC, En Vogue, and Missy Elliott; and, at the tail end of the decade, all the pop you could ever want with the Spice Girls, Britney Spears, Christina Aguilera, and Destiny's Child.

So, if you read this book, then run to Spotify to listen to riot grrrl bands, and find they're not for you, remember: there's more than one way to be a girl, and there's more than one kind of music to power you to your goals. What you listen to will never be as important as what you *do*.

Acknowledgments

A book is never a solo project, even if it's just one name on the cover. So many people have helped to shape *Rebel Girls* over the years, providing valuable feedback, access to research materials, or just the kind of general support and enthusiasm that every author needs to keep the spark of their book going during the long road to publication.

First of all, a huge thanks to my editor, Lauren Smulski, for taking a risk on a book featuring a hot-button topic that a lot of people wouldn't touch. You've helped transform this book into the best version of itself, even if that meant adding more boys. And second, to Eric Smith, the agent who refused to give up on *Rebel Girls*. We might have parted ways, but I will always appreciate the work you did for my debut.

Rebel Girls would not have been possible without access to the materials in the Riot Grrrl Collection at the Fales Library at New York University. As mentioned in the historical note, letters and zines from the archive served as inspiration for Athena's "voice" and informed the politics of the story. Lisa Darms, the archivist who built the collection and provided access to me as a researcher, has become a friend and colleague (we even wrote an academic article together, which is a level of commitment above and beyond ordinary friendship), but I'm forever grateful to her for giving me access to the archive back when she didn't know me at all. Her archive is not at all dusty, by the way.

So many people have read this book and given feedback at various stages of its existence. I owe my sister, Juli Keenan, and my BFF, Meghann Wilhoite, a mountain of thanks for reading this book *so* many times. Like, a *lot* of times. More times than anyone probably should. Both of you are extraordinarily generous, and I appreciate it more than you could ever know.

Thanks also to Alex Segura and Eva Stein Segura for valuable feedback and friendship, as well as for Alex's super helpful advice on all things publishing-related. Many thanks to Andrea Baroco Lam and Sarah Dockery Sparks, who suffered through my early efforts to write fiction back in college, and who encouraged me to get back to it after an embarrassingly long absence. To my early critique partners, aka The Club, I owe you a huge debt for pointing out to me where this story really started, and why I should cut a bunch of stuff: Laura Lee Anderson, Desiree Roosa, Patricia Miller, and Erin Brady Pike. Thanks to Stephanie Kuehnert for all the advice and encouragement—it definitely helped me along the way—and to Tara Kelly for suggesting a restructuring that greatly helped the pacing. Thanks to Sangu Mandanna, Lizzie Cooke, and Mike Chen for reading drafts of Rebel

Girls, and to Kati Gardner and Samira Ahmed for being good sounding boards.

To my cousin Anita Yesho, for being the first feminist activist I knew, for being the first clinic escort I knew, and for making me mixtapes of obscure bands when I was young and impressionable. And to my cousin Donna Yesho Anglemyer, for showing me around Pittsburgh (Warhol Museum! Randyland! Mattress Factory!) as I took a break from my Amtrak writing retreat during the final push of my revisions for publication.

Many, many thanks to my parents, Michael and Monica Keenan. Dad taught me to write logical sentences, and Mom taught me creativity (and also how to do good voices when reading aloud to children). Both of you ignited a love for reading in me. I wouldn't be a well-rounded writer (or the same person) without both of you.

The biggest thanks of all go to my husband, Ryan Penagos, without whom this book would not have existed. You have encouraged me at every step of the way, from when I said that maybe I wanted to write fiction again? (Read that in Wisteria's voice), to when I wanted to go to my first writers' conference, to when I started thinking about maybe getting an agent, to when I shelved two novels before doing a complete rewrite of *Rebel Girls*. You've been by my side for every mile of the journey, and I can't imagine how I would have gotten here without you. Thank you for being the best person in my world. I love you.

And finally, my readers. You didn't think I was going to forget you, did you? You make this all worthwhile. So, thank you for reading!